HER FATHER THOUGHT HE'D CHOSEN HER A HUSBAND, BUT SHE WANTED NOTHING OF IT . . .

"What do you want?" Shona asked, leaning out of her tower window to see Dugald standing below.

"I want to hear my name whispered on your lips, to feel your petal-soft hand in mine, to—"

She uttered a faint expletive.

"You know, lass, its difficult to be romantic when you keep interrupting my soliloquy."

"Dugald," she demanded, "why are you here?"

"You do not believe I've come to worship you from afar?"

"Not far enough."

"But I am trying to save myself for you, and I've been told that any woman who could resist me must surely be made of—"

Suddenly, the shutters to the tower were closed tight.

"Stone," he finished, and scowled at the intricate rock work of the tower. Without trying, he remembered the feel of her satin skin beneath his hand, the wild vibrancy of her beneath his fingertips. Ah, yes, there would be trouble with her, but it would be trouble worth seeking . . .

LOIS GREIMAN

Highland Brides

HIGHLAND SCOUNDREL

AVON BOOKS ◆ NEW YORK

AVON BOOKS, INC.
1350 Avenue of the Americas
New York, New York 10019

Copyright © 1998 by Lois Greiman
Inside cover author photo by Barbara Ridenous
Published by arrangement with the author
Visit our website at **http://www.AvonBooks.com**
Library of Congress Catalog Card Number: 98-92456
ISBN: 0-380-79435-7

First Avon Books Printing: September 1998

AVON TRADEMARK REG. U.S. PAT. OFF. AND IN OTHER COUNTRIES, MARCA REGISTRADA, HECHO EN U.S.A.

Printed in the U.S.A.

WCD   10 9 8 7 6 5 4 3 2 1

Travis, I thank God for every minute, every word,
every silly bit of laughter we've shared.
You're everything I could ask for
in a son and so much more.

FORBES

Ula of Glen Creag

Lady Mary

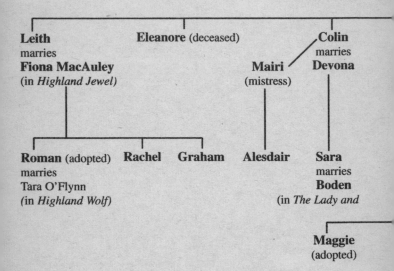

Leith
marries
Fiona MacAuley
(in *Highland Jewel*)

Eleanore (deceased)

Colin
marries
Devona

Mairi
(mistress)

Roman (adopted) **Rachel** **Graham**
marries
Tara O'Flynn
(in *Highland Wolf*)

Alesdair

Sara
marries
Boden
(in *The Lady and*

Maggie
(adopted)

FAMILY TREE

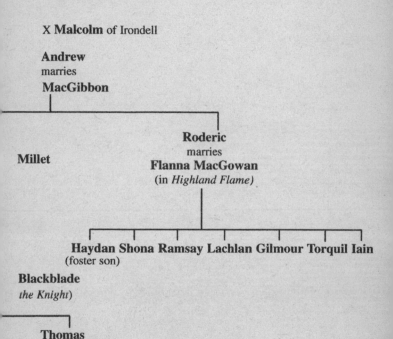

X **Malcolm** of Irondell

Andrew
marries
MacGibbon

Millet

Roderic
marries
Flanna MacGowan
(in *Highland Flame)*

Haydan Shona Ramsay Lachlan Gilmour Torquil Iain
(foster son)

Blackblade
the Knight)

Thomas
(foster son)

Prologue

Burn Creag Castle
Year of our Lord 1509

Lightning forked across the inky-black sky. Ghostly shadows, cast by a single flickering candle, flitted across the curved walls of the tower room, and beneath Shona's bare toes, the rushes felt coarse and cold.

She hunched her shoulders inside her too-large night gown and huddled closer to Sara's side.

Thunder sounded like a witch's cackle. Shona jumped, but suddenly a tiny spot of red fire snagged her attention. Turning toward her eldest cousin, she saw that the glow came from the center of Rachel's palm.

It took Shona a moment to recognize the source, longer still to find her voice, then, "The dragon!" she gasped. Even in the fickle light she could not mistake the silver amulet. "You stole it from—"

Thunder crashed like a giant's wicked fist against the tower, shaking the very stones around them. Shona stifled a scream. The noise rolled slowly away, leaving the air taut in its aftermath.

"You stole it from Liam?" she finished breathlessly. The youngest of the three cousins, she was determined not to let the others know that beneath her voluminous night gown her knees shook like a wet cur.

"Aye," Rachel said. "I took it whilst he slept."

1

"'Tis magic," Shona whispered, transfixed by the blood red stone that gleamed from between the dragon's spread wings.

"It canna be magic," Sara corrected and tightened her hand as though she sensed Shona's fear. "'Tis but stone and metal."

"But Liam said twas," Shona whispered, awestruck by its presence here. Liam was a crafty sort, and not one to part easily with his possessions.

"'Tis the very reason I doubted," Rachel said, her voice barely audible in the hushed silence. "But even Liam must tell the truth sometimes, I suppose. And twas the truth he said when he told me of our great grandmother."

"*Our* great grandmother?" Sara asked. "But how does *he* know about our ancestry?"

"I canna say for certain," Rachel admitted, glancing from Sara to Shona. "But this is the story he spewed. Long ago there lived a lass in this very castle. Her name was Ula. Small she was like me, with Shona's fiery hair and Sara's kindness. Her mother died when she was but a bairn, and she was scared to be left alone at night. Sometimes she would cry out."

"And her father would come and tell her outlandish stories to make her laugh?" Shona guessed. She wished now that she had not been quite so clever in sneaking from her own chambers. Indeed, she almost wished her father would find her gone and come looking for her, for Roderic the Rogue would surely chase away any evil that lurked in this spooky tower room.

"Aye," Rachel said. "Aye, he would tell her stories. But still she was afraid. So he called on the best mason in the land to craft a magical stone dragon near her room to protect her."

"He must have loved her so," Sara whispered.

Shona squeezed her hand.

"They built the dragon out on the roof to overlook the land about," Rachel said. "Now the lass felt safe in the comfort of her quarters. But her father worried that something might happen to him, and Glen Creag would fall into the hands of the evil sorcerer. Then wee Ula would be left alone. He knew if such was the case she would be forced to leave her home, and he wished for her to be bold enough to make the journey. So he had a silver amulet crafted. A magical pendant it was, graced with a gem taken from the enchanted water of Loch Ness.''

''Where Nessie lives?'' Shona hissed.

''Aye. That amulet would protect Ula wherever she went.''

Shona stared at the dragon in breathless wonder. ''And this is that very amulet?''

''Aye.''

''But Rachel,'' Sara said, ''though I dunna understand it, ye never believe a thing Liam says. Why do ye trust him in this?''

Rachel scowled, then, ''Come here,'' she whispered, and stepped toward the window. Sara tugged at Shona's hand until they were peering through the narrow opening. They tilted their heads close together. ''Look out there.''

''Tis dark,'' Shona whispered, but suddenly a fork of lightning slashed across the sky.

''There!''

''A dragon!'' Sara gasped, starting back. ''How did it get there?''

Rachel drew the amulet closer to her chest. ''It must have been there for many years, but ye canna see it from most points, only from here and from that room beside it.''

''Ula's room.'' Shona felt the hairs at the back of her neck rise eerily.

''Tis truly magic, then,'' murmured Sara.

''Aye,'' said Rachel, ''and tonight we will bend its magic to our will.''

''We will?'' Shona's voice sounded squeaky to her own ears.

''Aye. We will. For tomorrow Sara will return to her

home. And shortly after ye will go back ta Dun Ard. Tis impossible to know when we shall be together again.''

The tower room fell silent.

"I will miss ye," Sara whispered.

"And I ye," Rachel said. "Ye are the sisters of my heart."

"We will see ye soon, surely," Shona said. She tightened her grip on Sara's hand. Brothers she had aplenty. But sisters were a rare and precious thing. "When the weather warms . . ."

"One of us will surely be betrothed soon. In fact, the MacMurt has asked for my hand in marriage and—" Rachel stopped abruptly, glancing quickly at the barrels stacked along the curved wall. "What was that noise?"

Shona held her breath and listened, but all she could hear was the frantic pounding of her own heart.

"It must have been a mouse," Sara said, then turned her gaze back to Rachel. "Promise ye'll not move far from us."

"I'm not going to move away," said Shona, yanking her gaze from the barrels. "I will marry Liam and live forever at Dun Ard."

"Liam!" Rachel scoffed. "Not that wild Irish rogue. Ye will marry a great laird as will we all."

A sliver of noise issued from behind the barrels again.

"The mice are certainly restless," Shona murmured, shifting nervously closer to her cousins.

"Please duuna leave us," Sara whispered again.

"That's why I asked ye to come to the tower," Rachel said. "If the dragon is truly magical it can grant us our fondest desires and bind us together. We will each touch the amulet and make a vow to take care of the others."

"But if we're far apart how will we know when we're needed?" Sara asked.

Rachel scowled, drawing her dark brows together over eyes as bright as amethyst. "The dragon will know," she murmured. "He will make certain we are safe or he will send help."

Sara thought a moment, then nodded. Her expression was somber, her blue eyes wide as she reached for Rachel's hand. "We shall all touch it together."

They did so now, piling their hands atop the thing, and squeezing their eyes closed.

"My fondest desire is to be a great healer like my mother," Rachel began.

Thunder boomed again. Shona jumped at the sound.

"I wish to be bold!" she chirped. "Like Father and my mother, the Flame."

The thunder rolled into silence .

"Your turn," Rachel whispered.

"I but wish for my own family to care for," Sara said softly. "My own bairns by my own hearth. Nothing more."

"Now we must make a solemn vow," Rachel said. "Forever and always we shall be friends. Neither time nor distance shall separate us. When one is in need another shall come and assist her, for we that are gathered in this room are bound together for eternity."

"Now we must swear to it," whispered Sara.

"I swear," they chanted.

Thunder crashed like a cannon in their ears. The candle was snuffed out. Blackness exploded around them. Wild energy crackled through the room and shot up Shona's fingers.

She shrieked in terror. The sound mingled with the cries of her cousins, and suddenly they dropped the amulet and raced as one toward the door and down the stairs.

The panicked galloping of their feet gradually faded to silence. The tower room lay in darkness, and nestled deep within the rushes, the dragon smiled.

Chapter 1

Blackburn Castle
Year of our Lord 1519

"**Y**ou must marry me, Lady Shona. You must." James's amber eyes were intense, his expression sincere as he gripped his love's hand firmly between his own and gazed up at her from the time-honored position of one knee. "Say you will."

"Ye know I canna." Shona glanced nervously about at the audience that surrounded them. She would give much to spare James this scene, for someday his pride would prick him for such a public display. Tongues would surely wag. Variations of this moment would be told and retold beside a thousand cook fires, but the unforgettable fact would remain; King James V, sovereign ruler of Scotland, had begged on bended knee for a simple Highland lass to marry him.

The very thought made Shona want nothing more than to forgo this entire spectacle. But she knew she must not, for her plans would be greatly weakened without such a dramatic public parting.

"Ye know I canna marry ye," Shona murmured. "Lord Tremayne would never allow it. He was piqued enough when we sneaked out of Edinburgh Castle for naught but a few hours last Midsummer's Eve. And it did not help matters when ye injured your arm."

"Twas naught but a bruise, and not your fault."

She gave him a smile, both for his quick defense and for the memory of how he'd dressed as a peasant and she'd dressed as a lad. James had walked right past Tremayne's oversized nose without his noticing, but there had been consequences. Indeed, Tremayne had raved about her propensity for "putting dangerous notions into the king's head." He'd even gone so far as to accuse her of plotting against the throne for her own devious reasons. How much more would he do if he knew her present plans? She dared not think about it. "Ye know I would do anything for ye, James. But had it not been for your other advisors, my head might have already been forfeited just for my *ungodly* influence on ye. What would Tremayne do if he thought ye wished to *marry* me?" She grinned. "Some say I have been less than respectful of your lordly title."

"Some wart-faced old men who have disliked you from the first," James said.

"Be that as it may, I dare not cross Tremayne again, or—"

James wrenched to his feet, his brow wrinkled in agitation, his mouth taking on that surly tilt it did when he pouted. "Tremayne does not rule my life. You *can* marry me. Indeed, I *insist* that you do."

"Insist?" She smiled at him. In truth, she was more comfortable with an insistent James than a melancholy one. "Even though ye know tis not in Scotland's best interest?"

He scowled as if considering her words.

"I think not, Your Majesty. For ye are good and wise, and ye will wed with a thought for Scotland's future."

"Never could Scotland do better than to have you for its queen," he vowed earnestly.

"Me?" She laughed and slipped her hand from his. "A humble maid from the north? Not for ye, Your Majesty. Someday ye will marry a rich king's elegant daughter, and the union will greatly aid our cause."

"I do not want someone's elegant daughter. I want *you*!" His voice was growing louder.

Shona stood. "Your Majesty, your new servants watch," she reminded him. "Not to mention Hawk." She glanced at her uncle, the mountainous warrior who, after the last attempt on the king's life, had been chosen as the monarch's personal body guard. "The Hawk watches. Ye would not wish for him to think ye are acting like a child."

"But I *am* a child!" wailed the boy, and bursting into tears, threw his arms about her waist.

It was true, Shona thought, hugging him to her. He might be the crowned king of Scotland, but he was also a seven-year-old boy. A boy who had lost his father in the bloody battle at the Field of Flodden, a boy who had lost his mother to another marriage—a marriage that had forced her to give up guardianship of him. He was treated now not as a child at all, but as either a pawn or an heirloom. Twas little wonder he looked to her for stability and nurturing, though she was hardly the nurturing type.

"There now, James," she soothed, stroking his auburn hair as she glanced helplessly at Kelvin, the young boy she'd brought to entertain the king. "Twill all come out right. Ye'll see. I will return to visit ye now and again."

"You will stay!" he yelled, tightening his grip. "I command you to stay!"

"Hawk will stay," she countered.

"Hawk! You would leave me with a bird that eats its own siblings?"

She couldn't help but laugh, for such a statement was typical of the young king. He was known for his love of histrionics, but it would do little good to take them too seriously. She'd learned that some months ago during her time at court. In truth, it had been her relationship with James, and not with the mythical suitor her parents had hoped she would find, that had made her stay in the lowlands bearable.

"If I promise the Hawk willna eat ye, will ye let me go?" she asked.

"Never! I will never let you go!"

"I canna stay, James. I must return to my home. Ye know that. But Kelvin and I will come back as soon as ever we can to visit ye."

"Kelvin!" the king sobbed. "I don't want Kelvin. He's nothing more than a commoner and a thief."

"A thief?" It was true that she'd found the boy picking pockets on the streets of Edinburgh only a few months before, but she'd hoped she'd put a stop to the lad's thievery. Cupping her palm beneath James's chin, Shona tilted his face up so that their gazes met. "A thief?" For a moment she saw the sharp gleam of mischief in the boy's eyes.

"He stole my favorite brooch," James accused, though he was nearly weighed down by gems as it was.

Shona hurried her gaze to the red-headed lad who stood behind the king. It was impossible to know exactly how old he was, since he'd long ago been orphaned. But he, too, must be approximately seven. He was slim and small, like the king. His eyes could even show the same mischievous gleam, though right now they expressed little more than shocked innocence. An innocence that was apparently not reliable, since on his narrow chest rested a round brooch set with a large bloodstone.

"You know how I love that brooch," said the king, abruptly discontinuing his tears to gaze solemnly up into her face. He sighed. "Twas a gift from my sainted grandmother."

In truth, he had received it from his stepfather, the sixth earl of Angus, a man James didn't even like. But now hardly seemed the time to attempt to improve his honesty. It could well be that Kelvin had been a bad influence on him in that regard.

"Give him the brooch," Shona said softly, staring at Kelvin.

The boy opened his mouth as if to protest his right to

it, but finally, instead of speaking, he unpinned the metal circle from his tunic and stepped forward.

James dropped his arms from about Shona's waist and turned toward the urchin. They stood eye to eye, and for a while they remained unspeaking, as if sharing some private thought. But finally Kelvin handed over the brooch.

"I've left ye all the others," he said, his brogue heavy. "Ye could have spared this one."

"I am king. I've a right to be greedy," James said flippantly, and suddenly the other boy grinned.

Twas a grin that gave Shona grave misgivings. It was very possible she was daft to think she could foster this wayward child alone, while insanity might well describe her thinking he would make a good companion for the king. Still, despite their frequent squabbles over the past four weeks they'd spent together, the boys had become frightfully close. Perhaps too close, considering the waif's dubious past. Mayhap Tremayne was right and it was best that Kelvin would not be staying to influence the king any longer.

"Tis time we left," she said.

"Indeed," Kelvin agreed happily. "To the Highlands."

Though the journey from Blackburn to Dun Ard had been slow and damp, Shona was finally home. She filled her lungs with the crisp spring air and felt her muscles relax. Nowhere in the world did it smell like it did in the Highlands of Scotland. Nowhere was the air filled with this heady mixture of heather and freedom.

Beneath her, Teine Lochan pranced in place. The mare had been left behind when Shona had gone to Blackburn, left behind, too long confined.

"Do ye want to run, then, lassie?" Shona asked, still holding the reins taut.

The mare stopped prancing. Arching her regal neck, she mouthed the bit, her muscles tense and quivering.

"Then run," Shona yelled, and leaning over Teine's withers, she loosened the reins.

Suddenly they were winged, flying like falcon across the verdant moor, swooping like swallows, as if they might catch the very essence of life, if only they flew fast enough. Shona gripped the mare's barrel with leather clad thighs, dropped the reins into the swirling flaxen mane, and lifted her arms to the wind.

The voluminous sleeves of her white tunic flapped like wild sails. Her hair streamed behind her. Caught in the glory of freedom, her fiery tresses crackled against the steed's chestnut hide like a cat o' nine tails, whipping the mare to greater speed.

On and on they ran until finally, tired and sated, they wandered into a quiet dell where a stream rolled along beneath the sinking sun. Perhaps she should return to the castle, Shona thought, but the water called to her, and she answered, letting the mare graze unfettered on the grasses that grew beside the chattering burn.

There was much to think about, much to dwell on. Shona had returned to Dun Ard less than three days before, but even here in her haven she could feel Scotland's turmoil. The Highlands were not immune to the troubles that bedeviled the country. For with the last king's death at Flodden Field some five years before, his son had been crowned, a boy far too young to take the government into his own hands. A French regent was elected, but the regent had returned to his homeland, leaving Scotland rudderless.

It was that state of unrest that caused her father, called Roderic the Rogue by those who knew him, to plan a gathering of the Highland clans. At least, that was what he said, though Shona firmly believed it was just another attempt to find her a suitable husband. Lord William, duke of Atberry, had long been a strong contender for her hand, but no vows had yet been exchanged.

Shona sighed and sat down, her legs curled under her on a rocky ledge. Bending forward, she let the brisk waves wash over her fingers. She was one of a lucky few, she knew, for she was nearly a score of years old and still she had not been promised away. Indeed, her parents would not give her to any man unless she herself approved the union, thus the delay. Whom could she approve when she had basked so long in the love of Roderic the Rogue?

Removing her soft half boots, Shona swung her legs over the stone and dipped her toes into the waves. In all the world, this spot was her favorite. There was a tiny cove here where the warm water was trapped by a bar of sand. It felt like sunshine to her soul just to sit thus, away from the tension of court, the bother of prying eyes. Would she ever feel such freedom again if she married? And how could she decide on a spouse?

Cousin Sara had thought herself well wed, and now she was. But her first husband had proved to be a cruel man.

Perhaps she would not marry at all, Shona thought. Perhaps she would join a cloister. But that was laughable. Shona MacGowan, in a holy order! Twould be rather like housing a badger with goslings.

Shifting her attention, Shona gazed into the new, lacy foliage of the trees around her. Overhead, a tree pipit sang to her, and against her heart her amulet seemed to purr contentedly.

She lifted it from beneath her tunic and examined it. Dragonheart, she called it. Twas in this very spot she had found it some months before, but even then it had not been new to her. No. Many years ago, Liam the Irishman had found it. This was the same amulet Rachel had stolen from him and that the three cousins had made a sacred vow on.

Shona smiled at the memory. She had been young and carefree then and had almost believed in the incantation. Indeed, crafted of silver and set with a single ruby in the center of its chest, Dragonheart looked precious and magical. But she was far too old to believe such nonsense now.

And yet it did seem miraculous that she would find it

here, for it had been three years since Cousin Sara had held it. Three years since the wizard called Warwick had tried to take it from her and had subsequently been killed by Boden Blackblade. His back pierced by Boden's sword, Warwick had fallen into the river and Dragonheart had fallen with him. Neither had been seen again. How odd that Shona would find the bonny amulet miles from that spot, lying clean and sparkling upon the sand.

It would be nice to believe it had some magical mission.

"Mayhap ye have come to find me my true love," she murmured to it. It said nothing. She searched for other possibilities. "To bring peace to Scotland? To give me wisdom? To gain wealth for Dun Ard?" Still nothing. "To hang on your chain like a hunk of pretty metal and stone?"

The dragon seemed to smile up at her. She scowled. What a fool she was to try to imbue this simple bauble with magical powers. The truth was, she had decisions to make and deeds to do, and regardless of Liam's whispered warnings of the dragon's mystical powers, she was on her own. For rarely had the Irishman been caught telling the truth.

Not a hand's breadth from Shona's toes, a fish splashed.

Startled, she jerked her feet up in surprise, then crouched on the edge of the rock to stare into the water. Caught in the tiny harbor were five fat salmon, enough for a large pot of soup and sorrel, Da's favorite.

Glad for this distraction from her thoughts, Shona rolled up her sleeves, lay on her abdomen, and reached into the river. But the first fish slipped through her fingers with ease. Wriggling forward, she tried again. Another glided quickly between her hands, then another and another.

Finally, frustrated but determined, Shona rose to her feet and glanced about at the pastoral setting. It was just as quiet as before. Never, after many years of coming here, had she ever seen another living soul in this place.

The sun had sunk nearly to the horizon, casting a bright pink glow to the world. The water splashed by in silvery hues of blues and greens, and in that water were five fish destined to be her father's dinner.

Without another thought, Shona slipped out of her leather breeches. Hanging them over a branch, she stepped down from the ledge and into the water. It splashed in chilly waves above her knees and against her thighs, lapping at the fabric of her long, belted tunic. She shivered at the feeling but refused to stop. Those fish were teasing her. Anyone could see that.

She knew people sometimes thought her a bit foolhardy, even reckless. True, she had, upon occasion, acted with less than absolute maturity. Such as the time Da had brought that shaggy black bull in from the meadow. She'd taken one look at the bovine and bet Lord Halwart's son she could ride the beast longer than he could.

It had turned out neither could ride the animal. She learned, with the help of a bruised rump and extensive cuts, that black bulls did not care to be ridden. But how was she supposed to know that unless she tried?

Besides, this was nothing like that. She was merely going to catch some supper, and since leather breeches were notably binding when wet, she had removed them.

All logical, all sensible. Bending to peer into the water, she made a grab for the closest fish. It streaked through her fingers and away, circling its small area of confinement. Shona reconnoitered and tried again. This time the salmon shot between her legs, getting caught momentarily in her shirt and flopping frenetically against her inner thighs. She gasped at the tickling sensation and grabbed at the same time. The fish fought its way out of the saturated fabric and dashed for freedom.

Shona splashed about in a wild circle and scowled into the depths again. She should have brought her bow. That would show these foolish fish who was smarter. After all, it would hardly be the first time she had shot her dinner. But she hadn't brought her bow, and though she kept a knife strapped to her waist, it would do her little good here.

Concentrating for a second, she made another wild grab. To her utter amazement, the fish came away in her hands. It was beautiful, streaked in a rainbow of colors that flashed with metallic brilliance in the sun. But it was one long, slick muscle. Loath to leave the water, it wriggled madly. Shona wrestled to hold it, but the fish was slippery and her footing unstable. The mud oozed between her toes, and the sand sifted from beneath her heels, conspiring against her. The salmon jerked, the footing gave way. Shona shrieked as she slapped the water with her backside and slid beneath the surface. Silty water filled her mouth and nose. She scrambled wildly and came up sputtering, breathless from the cold, her hair streaming across her face like scraggly tendrils of doused flame.

It took her a moment to realize something was odd. It took her longer still to understand that a small bream had become trapped in her tunic.

No bigger than her middle finger, the fish was caught between her midriff and shirt and slapped frantically to be free. Shona squawked at the sensations, danced around a circle in an effort to shake it loose, then finally stuck her hand down her neckline to fish it out. But it wriggled along her back and out of her reach. Finally, wiggling herself from the creepy feelings, Shona ducked back into the water, loosed her belt, and flipped up her hem.

A current washed past, pulling the bream away, and suddenly the fish was free and gone. Shona let out a heavy sigh of relief and took a weary step toward shore.

"Might you be keeping any trout in there?"

Shona jumped at the sound of the voice, splashed back a pace, then peered at the rocky shore. Through the mud, seaweed, and hair, she could just barely make out the shape of a man on the craggy ledge.

Her jaw dropped. Good Lord, how long had he been watching her? she wondered, but when her vision cleared she realized the intruder's gaze was caught on her breasts.

Snapping from her trance, Shona clapped her attention to the front of her shirt. Wet as a sponge, it clung to her like a peel on an apple. Her nipples stood out in sharp relief, even showing their darker hue through the fabric.

"Heaven's wrath!" she hissed, and slapped her arms across her torso.

From the rocky shore the intruder grinned crookedly. Even through her mess of hair, she could see that his teeth were ungodly white against his dark skin. "You'd best come out and check for eel," he said. He spoke the Gaelic, but a kind of lilting old world dialect. "They can be decidedly unappreciative of a thing of beauty, but have a taste for tender flesh."

Shona searched wildly for an appropriate response, then finally scraped the hair out of her eyes a scant inch and sputtered, "Who are ye?" The tone was much higher pitched than she would have liked, but the cold had settled into her bones. And if the truth be told, despite her . . . well, fairly extensive mishaps of the past, she wasn't accustomed to being caught in the middle of a frigid burn dressed in nothing but a man's saturated tunic and the meager shreds of her own tattered pride.

"They call me Dugald."

Dark Stranger, she translated roughly, then cleared a bit more hair from her eyes, hoping against hope that this Dugald was merely some traveler she would never have to face again.

To judge by his clothing and his accent, he was not a Highlander, for he did not wear the traditional plaid. Instead he was dressed in snug black hose and a slashed and puffed doublet that was undoubtedly padded at the shoulders. The costume had a decidedly Italian appearance. A *rich* Italian appearance. And he wore it like a prince, with his hair perfectly groomed and arrogance seeping out of every pore. Still, that didn't necessarily mean he was anyone important. Once she had met a man dressed like a jester. He'd turned out to be the duke of

Argyll and hadn't been amused by her assumption.

"Just . . . Dugald?" she asked, hoping against hope that he was no one she would ever meet again.

A bit more grin showed against his dark skin. "In truth, I have many names. Some call me Dugald the Deft," he said. "Lady Fontagne called me Dugald the Dazzling, but most call me Dugald the Dragon."

"The Dragon?" Shona murmured. Against her chest, Dragonheart felt warm.

"Aye. Did you not know that dragons are very clever and wise . . . and powerfully alluring." He grinned. "In fact, twas the queen of Kalmar who first gave me the name after my short acquaintance with—"

"The queen?" she whispered frantically.

"Aye." He peered at her from the ledge as if wondering whether she might be some lunatic newly escaped from an asylum. His eyes were a strange, icy blue that tilted up ever so slightly. "I heard there was a flame-haired vixen ripe for marriage at Dun Ard. I've come to win myself a wealthy bride. And who might you be, lass?"

Dear God, he was a nobleman, an early guest bent on meeting *her*, and here she was up to her knees in mud. He would think her a wild-haired wanton for exchanging niceties as if she were decked out in her Michaelmas finery.

Heaven's wrath, her father was going to kill her. But . . . wait a moment, this Dugald had no way of knowing if she was a milk maid or a marquess, and if she had even the wits of a turnip, she would keep it that way.

"Your name?" he asked again, as if she might have forgotten it.

She paused for a instant, worrying about her speech, which was damnably refined after her months at court. But after a moment, she came up with a suitably rustic accent and said, "Me name be of little account to a man such as yer noble self."

"I've rarely been accused of being noble," he said. "But why not come out anyway? I could assist you in ridding yourself of any more unwanted fishes."

"I assure ye, I dunna need your help."

"Forgive me for saying so, but I beg to differ. I've seen more efficient techniques for fishing. Although none more interesting." His smile slashed across his face again, ungodly white and as roguish as a satyr's. "Come out, damsel. I'll help you warm up."

When fish flew, she thought, assessing her possible means of escape.

"There is no need to be shy, I assure you. I'm quite harmless."

Shy. Now *there* was a characteristic she hadn't been accused of. But neither was she naive, and if this fellow was harmless, she was a brown thrush, complete with beak and pinfeathers.

Her hesitation seemed to amuse him. He chuckled softly. The sound was deep and rippled strangely through her innards. She must be hungry.

"Come on up, lassie," he said, his tone softer now as he looked down at her from his rocky ledge. "I'll give you a ride home."

Turning her attention to her left, she eyed his horses with some misgivings. One carried a large pack, the other, his saddle. Neither would carry her, she vowed.

"There's no need to fret," he said, reaching out his hand. "I assure you, Eagle has no more wish to harm you than I do."

Eagle. Twas a strangely grandiose name for his stallion, Shona thought. For though the steed stood seventeen hands at the withers and had canon bones the size of cabers, he was, without a doubt, the ugliest animal she had ever seen. Half his right ear was missing. He was the color of trampled dust, and his nose, large as a battering ram, bowed dramatically forward in the center. He seemed, in fact, strangely incongruous with his master's careful refinement.

She brought herself back to the conversation with a start. "I know naught of horses, but he looks quite frightening,'' she said, realizing she'd been quiet too long.

"You've no need to worry. Eagle has a weakness for damsels in distress. Come on, then. He'll not even notice your delicate weight on his back.''

"Oh, nay, I couldna. I'll find me own way home.''

"You live close by, then?''

She didn't answer and hoped her reticence made it seem as if she were too overwhelmed by his manly and noble presence to respond.

"Mayhap you are a serving maid at yonder castle?''

She shook her head rapidly, letting her hair fall back over her eyes.

"Where, then?''

"I mustna tell,'' she murmured, trying to sound feeble. "Me da wouldna like it.''

"You're not wed?''

She shook her head and remained silent. Her voice was rather deep for a woman's and quite distinctive; she had no wish to help him identify her later, should they meet again.

"I'm certain your father would be more displeased if you were to catch your death before returning home. Come hither.''

She didn't.

"I've a blanket in my saddle pack. I could wrap you in it.'' That smile again, disarming, yet decadent, somehow, as if he'd made a thousand such offers in similar circumstances. "Twould be no hardship to keep you warm until you reached your father's hearth.''

And give him an opportunity to see her face—and much more. Not likely. "Please, good sir,'' she said, with all due meekness. "Could ye na simply leave me in peace. I have no wish to shame myself further.''

It took him a moment to answer, then, "I've seen nothing as of yet for which you should be ashamed, lass,'' he said. She noticed his voice sounded somewhat husky now. "Come out. I'll not hurt you. You have my word on that.''

The word of a scoundrel. If he were any kind of a gentleman, he would go away and leave her alone. Or better yet, he would have pretended he had never seen her splashing about in the burn like a banshee gone mad.

It was bad enough that she'd taken a dousing. She would not return to Dun Ard perched in front of this scoundrel with her tunic stuck to her chest like fresh butter on a scone and her legs bare as a bairn's bottom. If her father heard of it, he was likely to marry her off to the first hairy lout who could master the pronunciation of his own name.

She glanced rapidly about. Where the devil had Teine wandered off to? The mare would come if she whistled. But it hardly mattered, she realized, for she couldn't allow this man to know she had come here on her own horse. That would certainly give him a clue to her identity.

Neither could she stand here like a dunce, waiting for wrinkles to form in her knees. She cleared her throat and said a quick prayer to Dympna, the patron saint of raving lunatics.

"If I was to come out . . . would ya promise na to . . ." She hunched her shoulders, hoping she looked small and uncertain. "Ta take advantage of me person?"

He tried to look wounded. He managed, rather, to look a bit like the devil on a binge. "Do I seem that sort to you?"

Absolutely, she thought, but didn't say as much.

He laughed nevertheless, as though he could read her mind. "You're a clever lass," he said. "But you have my word, I'll do nothing that you don't beg for with your own lips."

Heaven's wrath, this man was nothing but a running string of indecent innuendos, every one of which suggested a ridiculously elevated opinion of himself. Nevertheless, it would do her little good to set him in his place just now. Instead, she bit her lower lip and blinked innocently.

"Very well, then," she said, and splashed through the

water, still hugging her breasts, painfully aware of every bit of thigh that showed as she drew closer to the stony ledge beneath his feet.

Finally they were only a few inches apart, though he stood a good foot and a half taller. He squatted, offering his hand and a clearer view of his face.

She could refuse his hand and hop up on shore herself, but the effort would take some scrambling and thus give him a view of things better left unseen. Or she could accept his assistance—in which case she would have to remove her arms from her breasts, which would also give him a view of things better left unseen. Damn!

His smile brightened as if he were thinking the very same thoughts, and in that moment she made a decision. Unbending her arms, she offered him her hand.

For a moment he remained as he was, frozen in place with his attention focused on her chest. "No eels," he said quietly, and reached out to grasp her fingers.

Their gazes met.

"But something far better," he added huskily.

She made no attempt to stop her blush, but even as the hot color raced across her cheeks, she braced her feet against the rocky ledge and yanked with all her might.

Not if she lived to be a hundred would she forget the look on his face. For a moment it was all smug satisfaction, and then, as if he'd been struck by lightning, his silvery eyes widened. He teetered momentarily on the edge, tried hopelessly to correct his balance, and finally careened past her to splash head first into the water.

Shona couldn't help but laugh. But in an instant his hand brushed her arm. She shrieked, jumped toward shore, and heaved herself onto the rocks. All but naked, she was quick and light.

Still weighed down as he was with his fashionably ponderous clothing, he was slower. But even so, his fingers scraped her ankle. She jerked her leg away and leapt frantically to dry land. One glance behind told her she would not beat him in a footrace.

She had no options, she assured herself. Leaping forward, she grabbed the stallion's trailing reins, yanked herself into the saddle, and wheeled the steed away.

Shona heard Dugald's sharp expletive only inches behind her but dared not wait around to discuss the sin of blasphemy. Kicking the stallion's sides, she pushed him into the woods and away, whistling as she went.

Trees skimmed past. From her right, Teine sped toward them, racing along with her head bent low and her reins flapping.

A few minutes later Shona pulled the stallion to a halt. Dismounting, she caught the mare and set the stallion free. He refused to go. She scowled at him and tried to shoo him off. He merely rested his oversized head on her shoulder and blew hot air into her ear.

Finally, frustrated and impatient, Shona looped one of his reins loosely over a branch, fed him a few choice stems of fodder, and hurried off.

Dugald the Dolt would find his mount soon enough. Until then he could enjoy the knowledge that she had outsmarted him. She allowed herself a tiny smile.

It was then that she realized she'd forgotten her breeches.

Chapter 2

The hall was filled with revelers. Guests had been arriving for days and now occupied every available seat as they shared trenchers and goblets. Every maiden was dressed in her finest, every lord groomed to perfection.

Upon the dark wood of the wall above the huge stone fireplace, the MacGowan crest was centered between two pair of crossed spears. It was a symbol of power and tradition, but tonight power was forgotten as pleasure was sought.

Roderic the Rogue skimmed the faces of the men present and quickly classified each one—too old, too weak, too callous, too cocky. He ticked off their shortcomings silently in his mind. How would he ever find someone for Shona? Or rather, how would any man ever survive marriage with the Flame's only daughter?

His attention hurried along, then returned to a young man who sat with his back to the wall. Why Roderic's attention was caught, he wasn't sure. The man wasn't particularly impressive in either height or bulk. He was dark of skin and hair, wore a black tunic, and was staring at Shona. A typical Scotsman. Yet there was *something* different about him. Noticing Roderic's attention, the stranger shifted his gaze to the Rogue's, nodded once, then turned his eyes smoothly back to Shona.

"Daughter," Roderic said.

Beside him she jumped at the sound of his voice. "What?"

He raised his brows at her. "Is something amiss?"

"Nay, everything is grand," she said. "Whyever do ye ask?"

He scowled. What the devil was wrong with her? True, twas wise to hold a gathering at Dun Ard at this time of political unrest, but his main objective was painfully obvious, both to the world at large and to Shona, he feared. He had gathered all the most likely suitors here to find her a husband. And that was not going to be a simple task, for despite her bonny figure and her angelic good looks, she was trouble. And the more innocent her expression, the more trouble was sure to follow.

God help him. He took a deep breath and prayed for the safety of his clan and Scotland at large.

"Listen, lass," he said, "in truth, I dunna even want to know what ye have done to make ye so fidgety. I only wish to know who that man is."

Her eyes, he noticed, looked exceptionally large this evening and very green, exactly like her mother's. "What man?"

Expressive to the extreme, her eyes were his weakness, and she well knew it, so he scowled, to make certain she didn't think she was fooling him with her false innocence.

"The man who is staring at ye," he said.

She laughed, but the sound was high-pitched and a bit giggly. Shona was not the giggling type. "Why, Father! I should hope in all this array of folk there would be more than *one* man staring at me. Else I fear your plans have gone awry."

He deepened his scowl, though he already felt himself weakening. Flanna had said more that once that their daughter played him like a brass-stringed harp.

She smiled. The hall lit up. Roderic tried to staunch the bittersweet swell of nostalgia he felt at that smile, for in his heart he knew it would lead to no good. Even when she'd been a gap-toothed child, that smile of hers had boded trouble. He reached beneath the table to grasp his wife's hand. Flanna, known as the Flame, sat to his right, and though she was conversing with the guest to her right, just the touch of her fingers gave him a soft burn of satisfaction.

"Dare I ask to what plans ye might be referring?" Roderic inquired.

"Tis said that Roderic the Rogue dares all," Shona said, dimpling.

Flattery. Twas a clever woman's quickest defense, he thought, but he forced his mind back to the matter at hand. "Just what do ye think our reasons were for calling this gathering?" he asked.

"To marry me off."

He laughed. "Mayhap ye think yourself too important. When all Scotland is in turmoil, might it not be that these festivities have nothing to do with ye?"

She glanced about the assemblage, then quickly brought her gaze back to his. "There seems to be an inordinate number of unwed noblemen here."

"Can I help it if young eligible men arrived among the crush?" he asked. "Mayhap they heard there is a flame-haired maid here who needs a firm hand, and they came to see if they were up to the task."

She opened her mouth as if to disavow his accusation, but glancing up, he spoke again.

"He is still staring at ye, Shona. Ye must know who he is."

"Nay." She shook her head for emphasis, but Roderic couldn't help noticing that she never looked up to see who he meant.

"Isn't he the fellow who lost his horse?" Flanna asked, and leaned against her husband's arm to join in the conversation.

"His horse?" Shona asked, sounding surprised.

Roderic shifted his gaze from his daughter's wide eyes to his wife's. The similarities still shocked him.

"Is he the man Bullock spoke of?" Roderic asked.

"He said someone arrived at the gate yesterday morning asking if anyone had seen a stallion running loose."

"A stallion?" Shona's surprised tone was a bad sign, for in truth, she knew everything that happened at Dun Ard, from the birth of each new lamb to the courtship of every maid.

"Aye." Flanna pressed her breast against Roderic's arm to look into her daughter's eyes. "I saw him just this morningtide. A fine specimen he is."

Roderic turned toward his wife and felt his brows rise toward his hairline. "Are ye referring to the horse or the man, Wife?"

Flanna blinked, showing an expression of perfect innocence. The frightening thing was, he feared she had learned it from their daughter, for the Flame of the McGowans usually had little use for coquettishness. God help him.

"The stallion, of course," she said. But Shona had seen the stallion; he was as ugly as mud. "Though the man's eyes *are* quite arresting. Rather almond shaped. What was his name again, Shona?"

"I dunna believe ye've introduced me to him," Shona said, and forced herself to keep from squirming in her seat. It was a shaded truth at best, for she knew who he was. His name was Dugald, and he was a conceited lout. But hardly could she afford to tell her mother that, for she would surely ask how they had met, and that story put her in a rather poor light. "But if ye dunna even know him, why has he come for the gathering?" Shona asked, then gasped softly and reared back as if struck by some awful thought. "Mayhap he is a spy and he should be thrown out of our midst."

That was the wrong thing to say. Shona could feel her parents' intensified gazes on her now, but dammit, why did that blasted Dugald keep staring at her? In the past two days she'd been introduced to more men than there were fleas in a pillow, and each one had had enough good manners not to stare blatantly at her. True, Stanford had a tendency to glance at her with big moony eyes, and Hadwin would often smile at her, and there were a dozen others who would follow her about when she left the hall. But Dugald the Daft was the only one without even enough courtesy to turn aside when she glanced his way.

What was wrong with him? Was he always so rude, or did he, God forbid, see some resemblance between her and her evil twin who'd given him a dousing at the burn? But no. He couldn't know she was the one he'd found in such disarray. He couldn't. She'd been half dressed, soaking wet, and hidden behind her hair.

"Throw him out of our midst?" Flame asked.

"Well . . ." Shona cleared her throat. "If ye dunna know him . . ."

"I dunna know half the folk here," Flanna said. "'Tis the way with festivals."

"Mayhap he's one of the crush who heard ye needed a firm hand," her father suggested.

"Me?" Shona tried to sound wounded, but she was afraid her innocent act was losing its edge. Without trying, she could remember how her nipples had shown through the saturated fabric of her borrowed tunic, and she feared her dreams of the night before had been less than saintly. Still, if she didn't want her father to marry her off to the first old coot who could croak "I will," she had better improve her act. "I have been naught but the epitome of genteel manners since my return from Blackburn Castle, Father."

"Umm," he replied. It wasn't a good sign. Her father was generally nothing if not loquacious. And she had given him her best smile, too, even added the big-eye thing, but he still didn't seem to be softening.

She hurried on. "After all, tis my duty to look after Kelvin since I found him alone and helpless in the streets of Edinburgh."

"Ahh." Roderic nodded and gazed at the urchin who sat across the table from them. Shona only wished the lad could look a bit more tragic. But her eldest brother Ramsay was regaling young Kelvin with a tale which, if they were lucky, might contain a shred of truth. Kelvin's expression was a wee bit short of what one might call sober dignity. Mischief and mayhem more closely summed it up.

"So ye intend to set a good example for the waif, then, lass?" Roderic asked.

"Oh, aye," Shona said, willing the boy not to pull any pranks at this moment. "I know the lad is a tad high spirited at times, but I am certain with some somber influence he will grow into a fine, responsible man."

Her father was watching her far too closely. And though she couldn't be sure, she thought that despicable Dugald fellow was still staring at her, too.

"Just so I understand ye, Shona, are ye saying that ye intend to be that somber influence?"

She lowered her eyes. Her cheeks felt warm, and though she couldn't quite stop her fingers from fidgeting upon her goblet, she hoped she managed an expression of abject sincerity. "I know I have been less than . . . sensible at times in the past, Da. But I am no longer a child. In fact, I am nearly a score of years in age. Mayhap God sent Kelvin to me for the express purpose of teaching me maturity and self-control."

"Self-control?"

She yanked her gaze to her father's, hoping against hope that she hadn't heard laughter in his voice. But though his eyes gleamed, making him look little older than Kelvin, his mouth remained in a firm line. She held her breath. "Ye must admit I have behaved admirably since my return to Dun Ard, Da."

"Aye." He nodded. "Your mother just commented on how responsible ye've been of late."

She granted him a smile, breathed a silent sigh of relief, and offered him a bone. "'Twas certain I was to mature well, what with two such fine parents as I have."

She thought she saw his chest puff out a bit, then he smiled that smile that still made maids from Copenhagen to London swoon. "Aye, we have done well. Still, I am worried . . ." he said, and paused.

"Worried?" She touched his arm. She was in her element here. Manipulating men was a God-given gift. "Whyever for?"

He leaned closer. "Because I wonder how your breeches came to be hanging on the drawbridge."

"My . . ." She felt her skin go cold and her face pale. "*My* breeches?"

"Aye," he said, and took a sip of wine.

"Whatever makes ye think they were mine? That is, how on earth could my breeches have gotten to the burn?"

"The *burn*?" he asked and snapped his gaze to hers.

"The *bridge*! I meant the bridge."

His eyes were as sharp as a hawk's. "Ye seem strangely befuddled this night, Daughter. Are ye feeling quite well?"

"Aye. Fine. I just . . . I simply dunna know why ye thought the breeches were mine. Why would I leave them there? That would make no sense." She widened her eyes and tried a new ploy. "Has Liam arrived? Do ye suppose one of his magic tricks went awry and my breeches were somehow whisked away?"

Roderic took a sip of wine. Shona noticed with intense gratitude that her mother was busy talking with the man on her right again, but in a moment Roderic turned his attention back to her.

"As a matter of fact, Liam has not yet arrived. Bullock was at the gate when ye returned from your ride the day afore last. He inquired about your well-being."

"My well-being?" she said. Bullock had long delighted in tormenting her.

"Aye, it seems he thought it strange that ye returned to Dun Ard wrapped in a blanket on such a bonny day."

She cleared her throat. She was not a liar by nature, but twisting the truth was another of her God-given abilities. She hoped to use it wisely now. If her breeches had been left by the burn where she'd hung them, instead of being taken to the drawbridge, she wouldn't have to go bending the truth at all. Damn that Dugald.

She'd thought herself lucky, for once she'd realized her state of undress, she had returned to Dugald's stallion and found a nondescript blanket tucked away in a bag amongst a lot of unidentifiable paraphernalia. She would have liked to snoop around in it, but goose bumps had begun to form all over her body, so she'd mounted her mare, wrapped herself carefully in the blanket, and hurried home. No one should have been the wiser. But despite her clever planning, she now had to think of some explanation for this new mess.

"Listen, Father, I can explain," she began. Just then a movement caught her eye and she swiveled quickly to the side. "Laird Halwart," she exclaimed, sincerely thrilled by the pudgy lord's arrival. "'Tis so glad I am to see ye."

The young man who bowed over her hand was not much taller than she. He was a bit red-faced, from either ale or the warmth in the hall, and since his father's death and his own subsequent elevation to lord, he seemed a bit full of himself. But overall, he was a good enough fellow, and one she had known for many years. In fact, black bulls and sore rumps came rapidly to mind.

"Lady Shona." He kissed her knuckles and lingered dotingly over her hand. "Your beauty challenges the glow of the sun."

Oh God, not the sun line, Shona thought. But she beamed at him nonetheless.

"Father," she said, "ye surely remember Laird Halwart."

"Aye. Black bulls come to mind," he murmured.

"Black bulls?" She tried to look befuddled.

"My laird," Gilmour Halwart said, looking embarrassed by the mention of his youthful foolishness. "My apologies again for letting your daughter ride that beast."

"Apology accepted," Roderic said, then raised his goblet and murmured against the rim, "better men than ye have tried to disallow her."

Shona was certain she had heard her father wrong and

stared at him in disbelief. Roderic might be a rogue, but he was a tamed rogue, and usually a flawless host.

Halwart, however, didn't seem to notice Roderic's jibe. "And my thanks for such a splendid feast," he said.

Roderic all but grunted.

"And my Lady," Halwart continued, shifting his attention to The Flame. "Your daughter only personifies your beauty."

Shona didn't know what that meant, but she had no wish to allow her mother to bluntly question his meaning, and she was too desperate not to use his words. "Laird Gilmour, ye flatter me so."

"Nay. Nay, indeed." He squeezed her hand in apparent earnestness, though what he was earnest about she was completely unsure. "The Highlands were not the same with ye gone."

She tried to blush. "I'll wager you've said that to a hundred lasses."

"Nay, tis not so. There is none other with your . . ." For just a moment his gaze dipped to her décolleté. Shona supposed it was her own fault that men's eyeballs kept falling down her bodice. After all, she'd worn it entirely too low. But the dressmaker had assured her that those that don't have much must show it off to the best advantage. She realized now that she hadn't been nearly offended enough. ". . . daring," Halwart finished finally. "There are none other with your daring. Do ye still delight so in a good romp?"

"A romp?" Roderic snarled, raising his lips from his drink.

Halwart jumped at the tone. "I meant a roam, a walk, a constitutional. Nothing more!"

"Oh. Of course," Roderic said, and though he hid his expression, Shona thought she saw him grin into his goblet.

Halwart cleared his throat, drawing Shona's attention back to his florid face.

"Oh, aye," Shona said. "I do enjoy walking."

"Might ye accompany me to the garden, then? The horse chestnuts are in bloom."

He was still holding her hand, and she didn't particularly like how he kept breathing on it. He had been amusing as a boy, but he'd been rather short and skinny then, and she'd always been certain she could knock him down and pin his ears back, if need be. She wasn't so sure now. Still, one glance at her father warned her it was best to discontinue that conversation, and one more glance at the far wall confirmed her suspicions that Dugald the Distracting was still staring at her with those eerie silvery eyes of his.

"A walk in the garden would be lovely." She rose smoothly to her feet.

"Daughter," Roderic said softly, then motioned her to draw nearer. "I've no wish for blood to be spilled at Dun Ard this night."

She drew back just a wee bit as if affronted. "I hope ye dunna mean to say that ye think I might cause some sort of trouble."

The Rogue snorted quietly, but she thought she saw his lips lift into a trace of a smile. "Have a care, lass," he warned, trying to look stern, "and dunna go further than the garden."

"Ye have my word as a gentlewoman and your daughter," she said, and straightening to her regal height, graciously took Halwart's arm.

Her composure lasted no more than a few seconds, for as she passed the end table, she was certain she saw Dugald's lips curl up in the slightest suggestion of a smile.

She turned swiftly away, her hand delicately placed on Gilmour's arm.

Outside, the air felt fresh against her face. The gardens were lit with lanterns set atop long stakes stuck into the soil. The light danced softly, illuminating the fragile beauty of the place. As they toured the twisting trails, the fragrances of spring drifted to Shona, the sweet smell of quince blossoms, the distinctive blend of fennel and rich, ripe earth.

She was home. Shona filled her lungs with the scents.

"I have missed ye, Shona," Lord Halwart said, placing his hand over hers where it rested on his arm. "As I have said, twas not the same with ye gone."

She smiled at him. The truth was, she really liked men. After spending most of her life in her father's care, it would be difficult not to. But experience had taught her that few men were of Roderic's caliber. Still, she was willing to give this one the benefit of the doubt. "But Laird Halwart—"

"Call me Gilmour, please."

"But Gilmour, ye hardly ever saw me when I was here."

"Far too little of ye," he said, pressing closer. For a moment she felt his gaze rest on her bosom. Hummm. "I hope you know I hold you in the highest regard. Indeed, when I heard you had traveled to court all alone, I was quite distraught."

"I was hardly alone. I had a prestigious guard, and Liam met me along the way."

"Ahh, Liam."

If Shona remembered correctly, Liam had once taken Gilmour's sash to practice a magic act, but the trick had somehow gone awry and the sash had gone up in flames.

"Do you think it wise to consort with the Irishman?"

"Wise?" She stopped to glance at him.

"I mean, Liam is . . . well . . . he's an entertainer."

She laughed. "Aye, he is that," she said, and continued on. "And amongst my most faithful friends."

"I didn't mean to offend," Gilmour hurried to say. "In fact . . ." He pulled her to a halt. "Tis the last thing I'd wish to do, for—"

From the darkness, a woman giggled and a man chuckled.

Gilmour glanced at them peevishly as they passed by. "Might we go somewhere more private?" he whispered.

Shona remembered her father's words. But suddenly

she glanced up, and there, only a few feet away, stood the eerie-eyed Dugald. Gone was his Italian garb. In its place was a black silk tunic tucked into a dark plaid. Twas traditional Highland garb, of course, and yet, the way he wore it made it seem different, regal somehow, with every pleat in place and a silver brooch fastened just so. He leaned back against the stone wall, his arms folded across his chest.

"Good eventide," he said, his strange accent lilting, his gaze never wavering from her face.

She nodded and turned quickly away. She was blushing, though she didn't know why. She'd surely done nothing wrong.

Well, true, she shouldn't have removed her breeches. She shouldn't have been caught half naked. And mayhap she shouldn't have tossed a total stranger into the water. But that last one really wasn't her fault. After all, he'd provoked her.

"Shona?" Halwart said, patting her arm. "Somewhere private?"

"Aye," she murmured, dragging her gaze back to Halwart's. "Privacy would be much blessed."

He turned her away, and she gladly went.

"I know how you love to ride," Gilmour whispered, leaning close. "I've purchased a new saddle. It's in the stable. Twould be an honor if you would have a look at it."

She wanted to say no. But that blasted Dugald was right behind her. "I would love to see your saddle," she murmured.

The stables were lit by a pair of flaming sconces. Horses nickered as the door creaked open.

Gilmour ushered her toward a room. It was dimly lit, illumined only by the sconces on the wall outside the stone chamber.

"Here it is," said Gilmour, motioning to a saddle that rested atop a crossbar of wood. "I had it specially made in Italy."

"Italy." Shona raised her brows. It was made of red

leather. Very bright red leather that was adorned with tassels near the pommel. What, she wondered, could the purpose of tassels possibly be?

"Notice the depth of the seat." He stroked it. "It cradles me like a lover's arms."

Now, *there* was a strange picture—a lover precariously cradling his behind atop his steed. She knew from past experience that he was not a great rider. So the lover had better be quite strong. "It's very . . . red," she said.

"Aye." He stepped to the side, apparently granting her a better view of the masterpiece. "Ye may sit in it if ye like."

She wouldn't, but she stepped closer and bent slightly to notice that his name had been tooled into the leather.

"I wasn't certain ye would come," he whispered in her ear.

Shona straightened at the strange tone in his voice, but as she did, he gripped her arm and pressed his hips against her backside.

A bad turn of events.

"Of course I came," she said, turning gingerly in the small space between the monkey saddle and him. "Why would I not?"

He chuckled, relinquishing his grip as she tugged gently. "Ye have forever been the wild one, Shona. I've never known what to expect from ye. But twould be like you to welcome a bit of frolic."

"Frolic?" She didn't like the sound of that word, but she smiled sweetly as she sidled sideways.

"Do ye remember the bull?" he asked, watching her.

She smiled with some warmth now, for the memory brought back vague feelings of fondness for him. It had been a summer when she had seen too little of her cousins. Thus he had been a replacement, albeit a poor one, for a short span of time.

"I do," she said. "He was quite unhappy to be mounted."

"Then try me." Suddenly Gilmour was gripping her arms and pressed up hard against her.

She tried to retreat, but he was stronger than he'd been when they were twelve. She blinked at him and stuttered, "W-what?"

"Try me," he growled. His breath was not good. "I've no objection to be mounted by a bonny lass like ye."

Shona quickly considered her options. She could scream, of course. But screaming was so melodramatic, and Gilmour had always been sensible enough. So she smiled, trying to ignore the fact that his pelvis was pressed against hers with appalling intimacy, and hoping he'd see the humor in the situation.

"Tis a bit late for me to ride, I fear, Gilmour."

He chuckled. "There is no reason to act coy, sweet Shona. We've known each other far too long. And waited too long. But now we shall finally be united."

She was truly surprised to hear this. "We will?"

"I do not mind that ye are at times . . ." He pressed harder. "Less than proper."

Shona shifted her gaze sideways. She thought she had heard someone enter the stable. What to do now? Hope they rescued her or hope they didn't notice her?

"It's very generous of ye to overlook my shortcomings, Gilmour," she said, still listening to ascertain if someone had opened the door. But no sounds distracted her, so she must have been mistaken, which meant they were still quite alone. "But I fear ye've misunderstood my intentions."

"I think not," he rasped, and fervently pressed his lips to hers.

It wasn't as if she hadn't been kissed before. After all, she'd bested Liam in a bet when she was all of fifteen, and he'd been obliged to give her a few pointers, but Shona was certain her skin hadn't crawled at his touch.

She pushed against Halwart's chest with all her might, finally breaking the suction on her lips.

"Gilmour," she said.

"God, you're a hot lass!" he growled, stepping forward.

"Aye. I am quite warm." She skipped off sideways, looking for a way out. "I think I'd better step outside for . . ."

But in an instant he caught her by the arm and swung her in for another sloppy caress.

"Gilmour!" She covered his mouth quickly with her hand. "I must apologize, for I fear I've misled ye. Twas not my intent to come out here for a private tryst. Though of course the prospect is quite tempting." About as tempting as sticking her hair in the kitchen fire. Still, Gilmour was really a decent sort when sober, and she saw no reason to hurt his feelings. "Please forgive me if I've given ye the wrong impression."

He twisted his face away. She dropped her hand.

"I dunna have the wrong impression. I have a need. A sharp need in my nether parts that will not be quieted until I have you," he said, and crushed her against his chest, but she had found his hair and gave it a good hard yank, so that his head was canted slightly toward the rear and he was forced to turn his eyeballs downward to look into her face.

"Gilmour!" she warned, holding her temper in careful check. It wasn't ladylike to lose her temper and she tried to act the lady whenever possible. "I must not be making myself clear. I am saying that I wish to return to the hall now."

"Soon," he said, and jerked his head forward. Though a good deal of hair remained in her fingers, his lips landed dead center between her breasts.

She gasped on impact and managed to yank out of his grasp. She stumbled, righted herself, then backed carefully away, watching his every move.

"I dunna think I need tell ye how angry my father would be if he knew about this," she said, breathing hard and wondering what to do next. She didn't like to cause trouble, especially after her breeches had been found on the drawbridge.

"Twill be doing him a favor by showing ye your lot in life," Gilmour said, pursuing her.

Her temper slipped a notch. "My lot?"

"Aye." He chuckled, still following. "Ye've been needing someone who can handle ye for a long while. It seems the Rogue isn't up to the job. But I'm just the man to pull in the reins."

She stopped. "Indeed?"

He grinned, seeming to think the game to have come to an end. "Indeed."

"Listen, Gilmour," she said in her most serious tone. "In the past I've considered us friends. I've no wish to change that now by seeing anyone hurt."

"I will not hurt ye, lass," he said, and lunged for her.

"I wasn't talking about me," she snarled, and twisting about, slammed her elbow into his head. He staggered back, holding his ear.

When he looked at his hand there was blood on his fingers. His gaze lifted. It no longer held the warmth of friendship, but of anger and tottering intoxication.

"Damn ye!" he swore, and reached for her.

She jumped out of his way, but not fast enough. His fingers snagged in her bodice. It ripped down the middle. His gaze locked on the sight of her partially bared breasts, then he sprang at her again.

For the briefest of moments, Shona remained paralyzed. He grabbed her arms, and she his. Then, at the precise instant, she jerked her knee upward, connecting it just so with his groin.

Gilmour slammed to a halt. His body went rigid. His eyes widened and he managed one raspy inhalation before he toppled to the floor with his hands cradling his nether parts.

Shona scowled at her torn bodice, then at Gilmour. His face looked waxy and twitched spasmodically while his breath rattled in and out like wind in a raspy bellows.

He didn't sound very good, but she found she was far past caring. He croaked something unintelligible, so she leaned closer, trying to hear.

He croaked again. She straightened.

"Ye are not dying! And more's the pity." She glanced toward her torn bodice, wishing this had never happened. It always upset her parents when she wounded men. "How am I going to explain this?"

Gilmour drew another rasping breath, carefully shifted his gaze to her face as if even his eyeballs hurt, and managed, "I'm still willing to wed you, if the dowry is sufficient."

Her temper let loose. "Wed me? Wed me!" she said, stepping toward him. He cringed away. She thought it quite proper of her that she refrained from kicking him. Twas more than he deserved. "And I'm still willing to let ye live," she snapped. "If ye promise to leave to-night. Do I have your word?"

He said nothing. She stepped closer, and he nodded convulsively. "Aye! Aye, ye've got my word."

Chapter 3

The stable door creaked open beneath Shona's hand. Outside it had begun to sprinkle, but the soft mist did little to cool her temper. Gilmour Halwart was a wart. How dare he ruin her gown! How dared he ruin her *evening*? she wondered, as she stormed toward the keep.

In her silent diatribe, it took several moments for her to notice she was less than presentable. Glancing down at her torn bodice, she realized she couldn't allow herself to be seen like this. Holding the tattered linen to her chest, she scowled through the darkness toward the keep's sheltered sconces.

The rain had driven most of the crowds inside, so she was fairly safe as long as she avoided the main hall. Therefore, she had no choice but to climb the tower wall to the second floor. It should be a simple enough task, for she wouldn't have to sneak through the tower, up the stairs, across the parapet, and back down on the other side to reach her own chambers, as she normally did. Instead, once she reached the shuttered windows, she would be home free, for she had given up her usual chambers to accommodate Dun Ard's many guests. She now occupied a small alcove that contained little more than a narrow cot and a trunk. But that tiny room would be much appreciated this night, for with that spartan existence came a modicum of much needed privacy.

The mill and the herb garden were quiet and dark when she passed them. The free-standing kitchens, however, were another story entirely. Still, she managed to slip by them without anyone noticing her. She slowed her steps as she neared the hall. Laughter and voices issued out on a wave of sound. Two men, both unidentifiable in the uncertain light, exited through the huge double doors. Shona hunkered down behind the well until they were past, then rose to a crouch and sprinted across the open area to the north wall of the keep.

Behind her she heard the men greet someone, but she was out of sight now and fairly secure. Lifting her face, she squinted up through the raindrops. The window to her small chamber was only about thirty feet above her head, but the rain was going to make her task a bit more difficult. Still, she had little choice but to shimmy up the wall or be caught in rather unladylike disarray. So she reached between her calves and grasped the back hem of her gown. Pulling it tightly against her legs, she tucked it securely into her garter, then wiped her hands on her skirt. Midway between her window and the first tower gargoyle, she found her well-accustomed chinks in the stone wall and began her ascent.

The stone, Shona discovered, was slippery when wet. A good thing she had never wasted much time on embroidery. Instead, she had spent her days in more active pursuits. Hunting, for instance.

Shona found another footfall, grunted in effort, and hauled herself up another half a foot. Archery had made her arms strong. It had also, she realized, gripping another stone with tenacious impatience, made it possible for her to climb this wall.

The rain that had begun so sweetly picked up a notch. It soaked her gown, which soon dragged at her shoulders. Some ten feet above the ground, she flattened herself against the wall and waited for the weather to pass. But instead, the downpour increased. From up above she heard a gurgling noise, and she glanced quickly up. The gargoyle grinned lasciviously down at her, and suddenly, like a spoiled child, spat out a rapid stream of water. The torrent hit her directly in the face. Forced off balance, she gasped at the onslaught and clawed at the stone, desperately trying to keep her hold. But all the elements were against her. Her feet slipped, her sodden hem pulled at her, and her fingers, numb with the weight they supported, let loose.

With a soft cry of dismay, she bumped down the stone to fall on her behind with a thud and a muffled grunt. The rain, fickle at best, let up just as suddenly as it had accelerated. Shona glared at the inky sky, grimaced at the pain in her scraped fingers, and swore with verve. But her situation had not improved; thus she still had the climbing to do, and the sooner the better, before the rain began in earnest again.

Rising to her feet, Shona gritted her teeth and resolutely tucked her hem more firmly into her garter. But when she reached for the stone a second time, a small snicker of sound disturbed her.

She swiveled quickly about. There, standing not fifteen feet from the wall, was a man. Grasping her torn bodice, she hugged it to her chest and peered through the darkness at the intruder.

The lightning that illuminated the man's face did nothing to improve her mood. It was Dugald the Dolt.

Shona swore again, but silently this time. Damn this man for being a pest and a regular pain in the arse.

"What are ye doing here?" she asked. It wasn't a very ladylike thing to say, but she wasn't feeling particularly ladylike just now, what with her gown rucked up in her belt and her body bruised like a fallen apple.

"I was just enjoying the weather," he said.

Even in the dark, she could tell he was smiling, because his teeth shone in the feeble light. She hated him more for that knowing smile and for the fact that her legs were half bare and her gown indecent—again.

"Tis raining," she said. She tried to remain civil. After all, she was supposed to decide on a husband during this little soiree, and if she kept maiming men, her options would be sorely depleted. "Why don't ye go enjoy the weather in the hall?"

"In truth, I prefer the view out here."

In half a second she thought of a dozen retorts to his statement, but she bit them all back and donned her sweetest smile, making certain her dimples showed and her voice was dulcet. "I dunna believe I know ye," she lied, "but I hope I can impose on your chivalrous nature. Ye see, I've had a wee bit of an accident and I dunna wish for my guests to see me in such disarray. I would greatly appreciate it if ye would leave me in peace and not tell another soul about this."

"You've had an accident?" His tone soundly sincerely concerned as he stepped toward her. Mayhap she had misjudged him. Mayhap he was constantly watching her because he was hopelessly infatuated with her. In truth, he would not be the first. She could not blame him for that or for the fact that he was probably from a foreign country where they would not consider his overt attentions rude.

"Aye. I am such a goose sometimes. I fell and . . ." She supposed it would be worthless to try to conjure up a blush, since he wouldn't be able to appreciate it in the darkness. "I tore my gown."

"And such a lovely gown it is, lass."

"Well, it *was*."

"Anything would look lovely on such a bonny damsel as yourself."

"Damsel"—the word held an old fashioned kind of appeal. And the flattery didn't hurt either. The night had taken a decided turn for the better.

"I fear ye overrate me." He didn't, of course, but it was the right thing to say.

"Nay. I've been watching you from afar. In truth, you are unsurpassed in both beauty and elegance."

Elegance! She breathed a sigh of relief. That was proof positive that he hadn't recognized her as the woman in the burn. For no one who had witnessed such a scene would call her elegant.

"I fear we haven't been properly introduced," she said.

"Tis true. My name is Dugald, of the Clan Kinnaird." He stepped forward, bowed smoothly, and reached for her hand.

She was in a rather compromising position, and if she were wise, she would probably retreat, but she didn't. Continuing to hold her bodice in place, she offered her opposite hand.

"Ye may call me—"

He kissed her knuckles. A shiver, fine as gossamer, tickled up her arm and onto her neck, seeming to burn beneath Dragonheart's chain.

"I know who you are," Dugald murmured.

"Oh?" The word sounded a bit more breathless than she had intended.

"Aye." Turning her hand over, he gently kissed her scathed palm. The burn branched out, turning into a blaze that ended beneath Dragonheart's warm weight. "You're the damsel who likes to climb towers in the rain."

She smiled a little, but forced herself to pull her hand away and step back a pace. "In truth, that is not my favored activity," she explained. "But as I said, twould be quite embarrassing for me to traipse through the hall in this condition. I was merely attempting to reach my chamber unnoticed."

He glanced quickly upward as if determining the distance to the window. "Mayhap I could give you a leg up the wall." He said the words very evenly, as if he were deadly serious. So Shona considered his proposition for a moment. But the mental image that came to mind made her quickly discard such a suggestion, for if he gave her a leg up, he would be looking directly up her skirts.

"I fear I'll have to conjure up another plan," she said.

"There is only one alternative: I must lend you my plaid," he countered, and suddenly he was loosening his belt. She backed up a pace, but in an instant he'd partially unwound the woolen from his waist and stepped toward her.

''That is quite unnecessary,'' she said, but he slipped the end of the woolen behind her back and to his opposite hand, drawing her closer. She could feel the warmth of his body. The light mist that fell only seemed to intensify his heat. She should draw back and flee, but something kept her where she was, though she found it difficult to breathe.

''This is truly beyond the demands of chivalry,'' she murmured.

''On the contrary. Tis naught but the gentlemanly thing to do,'' he countered.

Their lips were inches apart. He smelled of fine wine and leather, and his voice, when he spoke, seemed to rasp against her nerve endings, like the lick of a tongue against her earlobe. What would it be like to kiss this man? Of course, she shouldn't, Shona thought. Her father wouldn't approve. But then, the Rogue had gone through a great deal of planning and expense to find her a suitable husband. And a suitable husband was one she could be happy with. And surely she couldn't be happy with someone she didn't enjoy kissing. So what better way to decide on a spouse than by kissing him? After all, this was the sixteenth century, a new era. It was practically her duty to kiss him.

Father would probably thank her.

Shona parted her lips, ready for the caress. One harmless kiss, stolen in the dark. He moved nearer, pulling her closer with his plaid.

His lips grazed her cheek. A shiver ran through her; against her breast, Dragonheart felt inordinately heavy. Dugald's breath was warm on her skin, and when his gaze slipped to the high, exposed portion of her breasts, she could feel his heat with tangible intensity.

She waited for their lips to meet, but instead, he lifted one hand and trailed his finger, feather soft, along her collarbone to the hollow at the base of her throat. Once there, he pressed two fingers to her pulse and caught her gaze. The blood beat slowly against his fingertips, and her lungs felt strangely heavy as every nerve waited for their kiss.

He leaned closer still. His arm brushed her breast, and she held her breath in silent anticipation.

"Lass," he murmured, his lips mere inches from hers. "You should be more careful who you accompany to the stable. Such beauty as yours might turn any man to lunacy."

For a moment Shona was caught in the sensual rasp of his voice, the lingering caress of his fingers, but suddenly his words penetrated her fuzzy thinking. Her stomach pitched, and her toes curled in her velvet slippers. She jerked sharply back, stretching the woolen between them. "Ye were there!" she gasped. "Ye saw the whole thing."

The left corner of his lips lifted the slightest fraction of an inch. "Tis not true," he countered. "Twas dark and I did not have a very favorable position hidden as I was between the stalls. Though I must admit, your dialogue kept me quite well apprised as to your goings on."

"Ye were spying on me!" Righteous anger steamed up in her like an onerous volcano. Yanking the plaid from his hands, she scrunched it up in front of her. "Ye heard it all and ye didna come to my rescue!"

"*Your* rescue?" He sounded genuinely surprised. "And why would I be doing that, lass? As I see it, twas poor Halwart who needed the rescuing. After all, twas he who ended up with his pride bruised and his jewels jammed up between his shoulder blades."

"Ye are a knave!" she exclaimed.

"And a moment ago I was beyond chivalrous. Tis the thanks I get for baring my own nether parts—offering you my own plaid to cover—"

She ground her teeth and tossed the woolen at him. "I wouldn't wear your plaid if it was the last scrap of cloth in all of—"

Footfalls from behind startled her. She hesitated a

fraction of a second, then leapt forward, snatched the plaid from Dugald's hands, and whipped it about her shoulders.

"Lady Shona?" A man stepped out of the darkness.

"Stanford!" she said. She'd only met this man yesterday, but he was young, wealthy, and from a good family. Not the sort she wanted to alienate, not when the alternative was someone like this Dugald knave. "What are ye doing here?"

"I saw you leave the hall and I worried for your safety. What with the lightning and the rain, I thought I'd best see to your well-being."

Shona tried to smooth her tone into something akin to normalcy. But her heart was still pounding with anger, and her hands were shaking. "'Tis very thoughtful of ye. What a gentle man ye are," she said, and glared momentarily at Dugald.

"May I see you safely inside?" Stanford asked, beaming as he offered his arm.

Shona reached for it, then remembered she had to keep her blanket in place and pulled her arm back. Stepping forward, she hoped against hope that Dugald would stay hidden in the shadows. But hope and Dugald were not of one mind. He stepped forward. Even so, she saw that his identity was not discernible.

"Will you be needing my services any further this evening, Lady?" he asked.

She felt a blush burn her cheeks. Once again he had somehow managed to make his words sound distinctly suggestive. But she refused to acknowledge that fact, and fervently hoped Stanford couldn't tell that the cad was standing there in nothing more than a dark tunic and a maddening grin.

"Nay. That will be all . . . Farley," she said. "Thank ye for reporting that loose stone to me." She turned haughtily away.

From the darkness she could hear his chuckle. "'Twas my pleasure," he said.

Stanford turned back for an instant before leaning solicitously closer to Shona. "He was not giving you any trouble, I hope?"

Yes. As a matter of fact, he was giving her nothing but trouble. Why didn't the brave Stanford go back and box his ears? Shona thought, but she was not such a fool as to give Dugald the opportunity to tell what he knew of her evening activities. So she smiled brightly and said, "Nay, of course not. Twas but a defective stone in the wall. Our manservant felt it was something that should be seen to immediately. I fear I became chilled in the rain. Farley was kind enough to fetch me a blanket."

"I would have been honored to perform that service for you," Stanford said.

"Ye are too kind," Shona demurred. Behind her, Dugald chuckled again. Damn him!

"What became of Laird Halwart?" Stanford asked. His brown eyes looked wide and kind even in the darkness.

"Laird Halwart?" Shona stalled as she thought frantically. The hall seemed unearthly bright as they stepped through the doorway. "I, uhh . . . fear he had to return home rather suddenly."

"At this hour?"

"He felt a sharp need to do so immediately."

The noise from the hall seemed offensively loud now, for she wanted nothing more than to escape to the solitude of her room. But first she must safely maneuver the boisterous crowds.

Skirting a group of young men, Shona glided past her mother, ignored a fat lord who was motioning toward her, and carefully refrained from galloping toward the stairs.

She was almost there. Nearly. . . .

"Daughter," her father called, turning from a pair of men dressed in hose and brightly colored doublets. "Come hither. There is someone here I'd like ye to see."

Shona ground her teeth in silent frustration. She'd had

quite enough of men for one evening. She felt about as glamorous as a treed ferret, and if Father noticed her torn gown, there'd be hell to pay. But he was intent on parading her before every eligible man in Scotland. And if she didn't answer his summons, he would certainly know something was amiss.

"I am really quite fatigued, Father," she began, still holding the tartan against her bosom as she approached him. But he reached out his arm, wrapped it about her shoulders, and steered her away from his companions. Stanford followed along behind as Shona raised a bemused expression to her father. But just then a golden-haired woman turned toward her.

"Sara!" Shona cried, and launching from her father's embrace, threw herself into her cousin's arms. "When did ye arrive? Why wasn't I told immediately? Did Rachel come with ye? And what of Boden and Maggie? How is sweet Thomas? Have ye heard from Liam?" she rambled.

"She is really quite fatigued just now. Nearly beyond speech, as ye can see," Roderic said. But Lord Stanford did not comment, for he was now the one momentarily beyond speech.

With an effort he found his voice. "Is she . . . is she another of your daughter's, my Laird?"

"Sara?" Roderic sighed. "Nay. I was blessed with only one wee lass," he said, putting his arm about the younger man's shoulders. "'Tis said the good Lord willna give ye more trouble than ye can handle."

"Not a sister?" Stanford said, refusing for a moment to be drawn away. "But—"

"Aye, they look much alike. My own twin's daughter is Sara, but there's no point in gangling about now, lad, for ye'll get no attention from either of them until they've talked things through."

"But I . . . couldn't I just . . . watch them?"

Roderic laughed out loud at the wistful tone, then tightened his grip and steered the younger man away. "'Twould serve ye well to try not to act too pathetic, lad,'' he advised. ''I know tis difficult, but . . .''

His voice trailed away.

''Sara,'' Shona crooned, pushing her to arm's length. ''Ye look glorious. Shining . . .'' She shook her head, trying to ascertain what had changed. ''But . . . ye look different somehow.''

Sara laughed, then lowered her gaze to where Shona's plaid parted. ''And ye look somewhat . . . changed, too,'' she said. Reaching out, she tugged the ends of the woolen back together. ''So I think we'd best get ye to the privacy of your chambers before the Rogue decides to geld one of your suitors.''

''Oh!'' Shona said, remembering her dishevelment and glancing nervously about to make certain no one had noticed her shameful state. ''Aye, let us retire to my quarters.''

They hurried up the winding stone stairs, chattering about everything and nothing until they had entered Shona's narrow chamber.

''Your quarters have shrunk,'' Sara said, closing the arched iron-bound door behind them.

Shona laughed. ''Better that than to room with a bevy of giggly women who snore and swoon at unpredictable intervals.''

She removed the plaid from her shoulders. Sara raised her fair brows as she was granted a better view of the gown's long-suffering state.

''So tell me, lass, is the perpetrator still alive?''

Shona dropped to her knees to lift the lid of a large, nearby trunk. ''I suspect it would do little good to tell ye I have no idea what you're talking about.''

Sara laughed. ''No good atall. Who was it this time?''

Grasping a white nightgown from the pile of clothing in the trunk, Shona rose to face her. ''It was not my fault.''

''I didna say it—Shona!'' Sara said, reaching for the amulet that dangled into sight as her cousin leaned forward in an attempt to untie her laces. ''Ye have Dragonheart.''

"Aye." Shona beamed as she straightened. "I found him in the waters of Burn Gael some months ago."

"But . . ." Reaching out, Sara smoothed her fingers over the ruby that gleamed from the center of the dragon's broad chest. "That canna be, for it was lost in the Burn Creag when Warwick snatched it from my neck three years ago."

Even through the tattered cloth of her gown, the dragon felt warmer suddenly, as if Sara's presence moved it somehow. Shona shrugged. "I canna explain it. It seems our Dragonheart survived though the evil wizard perished. Twas a thrill to find the amulet unscathed. But if ye want it back . . ."

"Nay," Sara said, then smiled nostalgically. "I'm glad ye have it, what with your ties to the king and the turmoil there."

"What do ye mean?"

Sara shrugged. "I worry for ye, and the amulet made me feel safe somehow when I wore it. Even when Warwick was near." She said the words softly, as if the name itself might conjure up evil. "Even when he tried to cast his wicked spells on our minds, we were safe." She ran her thumb gently over the ruby, and gave a fleeting smile. Beneath her caress, it seemed almost to vibrate. "So our dragon is a male," she murmured.

"What?"

"Dragonheart," she explained with a laugh. "It seems he, like all the males in Scotland, couldna bear to be away from his red-headed lassie." Dropping the amulet, she stroked Shona's hair.

"Oh, aye!" Shona snorted. "I called the dragon to me like the mythical sirens of yore. It could not resist." She turned, presenting her back and glancing over her shoulder at Sara. "But I fear I've cured Laird Halwart of *his* infatuation with me."

"Ahh," Sara said, stepping forward to undo her cousin's wet laces. "So *he* was the one I saw fleeing Dun Ard when I arrived."

"Umm."

"I thought his posture in the saddle seemed a bit awkward. What gallant offered ye his plaid?"

Shona scowled as she remembered the infuriating episode by the tower wall. "There was no gallant. I can assure ye of that."

Sara smiled knowingly as she reached for the plaid. It was a fine weave, deep rich blues crisscrossed with shades of dark crimson. "So ye say ye found this likely looking woolen lying about in the . . ." She paused for a moment, thinking. "Let me venture a guess. The stables, I think."

"Remind me to swear ye to silence if Da ever questions ye about my activities," Shona said wryly.

"Your secrets are safe with me, Shona. Always they have been, but tell me who owns this plaid."

"He is of no consequence," Shona assured her, though even now her stomach felt a bit queasy at the thought of him. She ignored the sensation and slipped the wet gown over her hips and onto the floor.

"Ahh. A man without a name."

"I'll not be speaking to him again," Shona assured her, but just then a stone rattled against her latched shutters. "What was that?" she asked, jumping at the sound.

Sara grinned. "It sounded like a stone against your shutters. Were ye expecting company?"

Shona granted her a peeved glare as if to say she was being foolish, but in her mind, an unbidden image of a dark-haired scoundrel plagued her. "I fear your Boden has ruined your sense of humor."

"Tis the truth," Sara said, then, "I'll see who it is."

"Nay!" Shona exclaimed. "Tis no one."

But at just that instant another stone pinged against the blinds.

Shona yanked her attention to the window. Sara raised her brows, then, with perfect aplomb, skirted her cousin to lift the latch from its mooring.

The shutters creaked open beneath her fingers.

"Why, look," she said, peering out and trying to sound surprised. "How charming! There's a man dressed in naught but a tunic. And he's throwing stones at your window."

Chapter 4

Dugald glanced up at the small rectangle of light that opened in the wall above him. He had left his sanctuary on Isle Fois with strict orders, and none of those orders included throwing stones at Shona MacGowan's shutters. But nothing about this mission had turned out as it was intended to.

"Damsel Shona?" he called, canting his head slightly and trying to make out the person framed in the window. It might be her, but he didn't think so, for when light struck Shona's hair it sparkled like rubies. This lady's shone like sunlight.

The woman turned away for a moment, and he thought he heard a hissing noise from the background. The fair lady turned back, and when she spoke, he heard a hint of laughter in her voice.

"I fear Shona is a wee bit preoccupied at the time. Might I give her your name?"

He wondered wryly how many men tossed stones at her window in a single night's course. "Tell her it's the gallant who came to her rescue this eventide."

The lady turned away. There was a distant murmur of voices, then, "She asked which of the mob ye might be."

He laughed out loud. Lord Tremayne was certainly right about one thing—she was vain. "Tell her I'm the one who went naked so that she could be clothed."

But before the lady repeated the words, Shona was at the window.

"Ye were not naked!" she hissed, glancing sideways as if worried that she might be overheard.

"Ahh, so there ye are."

"Of course I am here. What is it ye want?"

"Besides your everlasting devotion? The feel of your sweetness in my arms? The brush of your—"

He thought he heard her swear, and had to exert a good deal of self control to keep from laughing. "What did you say?" he asked.

"What do ye want?" she rasped.

"I want to hear my name whispered on your lips, to feel your petal-soft hand in mine, to—"

A faint expletive again.

"You know, lass, tis quite difficult to be romantic when you keep interrupting my soliloquy."

"And it would be even more difficult if I dumped the slop bucket on your head, so have your say and be done with it."

"I thought, now that you are dry, that you might come down and walk with me for a spell."

"Or I might just let Da know ye are bothering me and see how long your head remains above your neck."

"He was not upset that you accompanied that foolish Halwart to the stables then?"

He could imagine her scowl, even though the light was too poor to allow him to see it. Damn the darkness, for though he was a man who sought peace, he found now that her impetuous nature drew him somehow. Twas not a discovery that made him happy.

"Why are ye here?"

"You do not believe I've come to worship you from afar?"

"Not afar enough."

He held his chuckle. "I am deeply wounded."

Voices rose from the darkness to his left.

"Go away," she hissed.

"Naked?"

"Ye are not naked!"

He shrugged. "But I am trying to save myself for you, and surely if other women see me thus they will be unable to resist. The Duchess of Avery said that any woman who could resist me must surely be made of—"

His heavy plaid hit him squarely in the face. By the time he'd removed it, the shutters were closed, the rectangle of light gone.

"Stone," he finished, and scowled at the intricate rock work of the tower.

So that was where she spent her nights. Twould be a simple enough task to reach her room. He should not delay, of course. The sooner the job was finished, the sooner he could report back to Lord Tremayne and return to his own home.

But he wasn't ready to perform his mission. Dugald scowled at his own thoughts. Something didn't feel right. Something wasn't as it should be.

He glanced at her window again. It was just framed by a glimmer of light.

One thing he knew—if he delayed, there would be trouble.

But without trying, he remembered the feel of her satin skin beneath his hand, the wild vibrancy of her beneath his fingertips.

Ah yes, there would be trouble, he thought, and turned away.

The following morning dawned bright and clear. Shona awoke early and opened her shutters with hardly a thought for the bothersome knave who had been beneath her window the night before. Still, she had to glance down once to make certain he hadn't camped at the tower's base. Her father always took umbrage when some swain slept beneath her window. But the spot was empty now. She firmly told herself she was not disappointed and glanced up at the sky.

It was a rain-washed blue, dotted with lamb's wool

clouds and worshipped by a vast array of greenery below.

Shona ducked back inside.

Muriel would be assisting their many guests, Shona knew. Thus she dressed unaided, donning a bright blue gown. It was embroidered at the neck with twining ivy and accented with slashed white sleeves that laced at the shoulder. She tied her favorite golden girdle about her waist and let the tassels trail nearly to the floor. With a few quick strokes of her wooden comb, she tried to subdue her hair. But after several moments, she decided it was a useless endeavor and twisted it up to the back of her head, where she secured it with brass pins. A few opinionated tendrils escaped her efforts and floated down around the right side of her face like bothersome flies. Scowling into the tiny gilt mirror she held in one hand, she tried to trap them again, but it was no use. In the end, she pulled a few wisps out of the left side of her chignon to match the right and called it good enough.

After rubbing a few rose petals against her neck, she hurried down the narrow hall to the next door, but with one glance she saw that the room was empty. Kelvin and his sleeping companions had already begun the day, she knew, so she continued down the stairs to the hall.

Even at this early hour it was crowded. In the far corner, near the doors, an old man gave an impromptu puppet show for the mob of children that huddled at his feet. Kelvin was amongst them, sitting between Sara's foster son and a large gray dog that looked suspiciously like a wolf. Next to the beast sat a small flaxen-haired girl with her fingers curled tight in the animal's fur. Nearby, Stanford strummed a lute and sang in a melodious tone.

His gaze lifted to Shona's and for a moment he seemed to forget the words to the ballad. She smiled at him and he blushed before finding his voice and singing on.

A score of faces turned toward her as she made her way down the stairs to the table at the center of the hall.

Sara sat near her husband, her gaze on his face as she talked to him. Boden leaned closer to whisper back, and they both laughed.

For a moment something ached in Shona's breast, ached for that indefinable element that made Sara glow and Boden beam. That something had kept him close by her side since the day they married. But whatever they shared seemed only more intense now, almost as if they were one soul, bound for eternity by their fierce devotion to one another.

Would Shona ever have that? Indeed, would she even be able to understand it? She was not like Sara—the ultimate lady, the shining, perfect jewel any man would covet.

Oh, it wasn't as if men didn't covet her, Shona thought, as she watched the couple. But they did so for entirely different reasons. While Sara was a jewel to be treasured, Shona was a prize—a prize that consisted of a bonny face and a vast dowry.

Since her parents had married, Dun Ard had thrived. Because of his loyalty to the Crown, the Rogue had gained a baronage. All this could not help but draw suitors. But who amongst them pursued her because of herself—what she was inside?

"Ye dunna wish for them to starve to death, do ye?" Sara asked.

"What?" Shona drew herself from her reverie.

Sara smiled. "Your suitors," she explained quietly. "If ye dunna sit down, they're apt to stare until they waste away with hunger."

"At least Da would know then that this gathering has not been for nothing." It was not like Shona to be irritable, but the last few days and one Dugald Kinnaird had taken their toll on her natural exuberance.

Sara laughed, then scooted even closer to her spouse, patting the bench beside her as she did so. "Are ye saying that the Rogue has to pay to get men to stare at ye?"

"He seems to think so."

"Then his coin is paying high dividends," Sara said. "I dunna think there is a male amongst the crush who is not agog."

Shona scraped a few recalcitrant tendrils of hair back behind her ear. She'd never been good with hair. "Mayhap they think some vermin has taken residence upon my head," she muttered.

"Ye are most probably right, Shona." Sara chuckled. "They only stare because they are astounded at your ugliness. Dunna ye think so, Boden?"

Her husband, large and quiet, turned his wry grin on Shona. His eyes crinkled becomingly at the corners. Now, *there* was a bonny man, Shona thought, but he was also one who had, long ago, been captivated by Sara.

"Tis an ongoing difficulty with you cousins," he said. "Certainly the Rogue must spend half his day browbeating his men, lest they do nothing but stare at you aghast." Lowering his gaze, he lifted a hand and touched Sara's cheek. "Tis always my most basic problem." His eyes were filled with such incredible tenderness that Shona felt her mood drop a notch lower.

"I dunna think my flagging spirits can endure much more of your adoration for your wife just now, Boden," she said. "Could ye not at least pretend that you notice I am in the same room?"

He laughed as he looked up. "I think there are enough men about to fawn over you, Shona. Hardly do you need my poor attempts."

"Ye could at least make an effort," Shona muttered.

"Never fear," Sara said, looking past Shona. "I believe I see a bit of a spirit-lifter approaching even now."

Glancing up, Sara saw Stanford approaching. A bit tall and gangly, he moved with a sort of birdlike stride. But even as she watched, his movement changed radically. His legs flew off in opposite directions and his arms windmilled wildly. Trying to right himself, he grabbed hold of the nearest thing—which happened to be Effie, a broad-hipped woman who had served at Dun Ard for more years than Stanford had lived. They collapsed in a wild tangle of skirts and limbs.

The hall went absolutely quiet, and then, into the silence, the aging widow squealed as if pinched. "Och, lad, do I make ye so lusty that ye canna even wait for some privacy?"

The hall erupted with laughter. Amidst the uproar another man rose from his seat. Stepping over Stanford, he approached Shona, bowed, and offered a boyish grin.

"Laird Hadwin of the clan Nairn," he said, reaching for her hand. "I dunna know if ye remember me."

Shona drew her attention from poor Stanford, who was bumbling to his feet, his face red. "Of course I do," she said, and remembered to flirt prettily as she offered her hand. After all, her father had invested a great deal here. "How could I forget?"

His smile increased. Kissing her knuckles, he drew himself to his full height, which, if he were lucky, was just above Shona's own. "I know tis a great deal to ask, but I wondered if ye might walk with me down by the burn. Tis a bonny morn."

"The lass hasn't even broken the fast yet," Boden said, but just then another man skirted Hadwin and bowed.

"Tis just the reason I had this basket prepared. Tis good to see ye again, Lady Shona," said the newcomer, and nudged the smaller man aside as he lifted a large wicker in one hand. Not much younger than her father, Laird William had hair that was sprinkled with silver.

"I didna know ye had already arrived, William," Shona said. A niggle of nervousness twisted in her gut. It wasn't that she didn't like William, for he was always perfectly polite and thoughtful. It was simply that she knew, as did most of Scotland, that he hoped to marry her. And since he was extremely wealthy and well placed, twas generally thought she would agree. That idea made her somewhat tense, since in actuality she had no idea what she would do. "Word was that ye might be delayed until after the games begin."

"His arthritis is improved," Hadwin said. "But ye know how this type of weather bothers such old joints. Best for him to stay inside. Why don't I take that basket off your hands, William?"

"Please forgive my young cousin here," William said, ignoring the other's grip on the wicker handle. "He does not mean to be a pest. He simply cannot help himself."

"You're in my way, William," said Hadwin, still smiling.

"Then move," William suggested.

"My lady," Hadwin said, stepping forward again. "I would be the last person to say anything bad about my cousin, but I fear the rumors ye have heard about him are true."

"Rumors?" Shona asked.

"Aye." Hadwin leaned forward to whisper loudly. "He is already wed—to three women." He lifted the proper amount of fingers. "And all of them quite large and jealous."

"Indeed?" Shona said, laughing.

"Indeed. Tis an ugly thing when—"

"And it will get uglier if you don't get out of my way," William said, and reaching out, pushed the other man aside. "Lady, I entreat ye, have mercy on me, I was forced to spend the entire night in my cousin's wearing company and I am in great need of the healing balm of your beauty. Might ye accompany me on an outing?"

She considered refusing, but one glance at her father reminded her that he was still peeved at her, and since it had been two years since Roderic had asked her to consider William as a possible husband, now seemed a good time to act the dutiful daughter. "I *am* quite hungry," she said.

"Tis settled, then," William said, and turning slightly, offered his arm.

Shona rested her fingers near William's wrist.

"Never fear, my lady," Hadwin said softly. "I know tis your duty to entertain even the old gaffers this day. But dunna be too selfless. When ye can no longer bear the boredom, you've but to signal, and I will come to your rescue."

Shona laughed. "I thank ye for your concern and will keep your words in mind."

"I am forever in your service. In truth—"

"Shut up, Hadwin!" ordered William, and steered Shona toward the door.

In actuality, William turned out to be quite interesting. The morning was indeed lovely, with only enough breeze to ruffle the dark, spiny leaves of the mistletoe that grew at the south end of the garden.

"Your cook makes a fine Brie tart," William said, pouring Shona a bit more wine.

"Aye. Bethia has been with us as long as I can recall. There are few who can organize kitchens as well as she, I think."

"A woman? In charge?"

Shona laughed at his surprise. "I never thought it strange. I suppose we at Dun Ard are a wee bit odd."

He smiled. A nice smile on a comfortable, slightly round face. "I suspect all the great houses could be considered strange. In truth, when my young cousin was crowned king, the servers all wore—"

"Your cousin?" She did not try to contain her own surprise. "Your cousin is King James?"

He laughed out loud. "Surely ye knew."

"I must have forgotten," she admitted, and chastised herself for her lack of memory. That seemed like the sort of thing a true lady would remember, especially if she were seriously considering a man as a husband. But somehow, William of Atberry always managed to slip her mind.

He laughed. "Tis like ye to forget such a thing, Lady Shona. But in truth, my sire kept his title rather quiet. After his brother was banned to France for his attempt to gain the crown, Father thought it wise not to call too much attention to himself. It has seemed best to carry on that tradition. In this time of unrest, the powers that be are often looking for someone to blame for political atrocities. Those closest to the king usually are bequeathed that dubious honor.''

She had heard that sort of thing a number of times. It never failed to make her nervous. ''Ye know James?'' she asked.

''Aye, I have met him,'' William said. ''And I heard ye are one of his favorites.''

Shona forced a smile for the compliment and willed herself to be calm. ''I spent a good deal of time with him at Stirling.''

''I, too, have spent some time at court. When were ye there?''

''Father sent me some months back. I believe he hoped to teach me some manners, but I fear his efforts failed.''

''Nay. Never that,'' William countered. ''For ye are all fine elegance. All softness and light.'' He reached for her hand, but suddenly noticed the scathed palms and scraped knuckles. ''Lady, ye are wounded.''

She laughed, grateful for the change of subject but nervous as she remembered the night just past. All elegance, indeed! ''Tis naught but a scratch,'' she said, and tried to pull her hand away.

He bore it solicitously higher into better light.

''But such a fair maid as you should never bear even so mild a wound,'' he murmured. ''How did it happen?''

''When I was returning from the stables last night it began to rain. In my haste I tripped, and—''

From the corner of her eye she saw a movement and turned distractedly toward it. Dugald Kinnaird stood not a score of feet away. He was dressed all in black. Her gaze skimmed his high leather boots, his clinging hose, his slashed doublet worn over a silken tunic. Twas simple enough garb, really, but there was something about the way he wore it that drew the eye. His gaze was as steady as a hawk's and his lips were lifted in the vaguest semblance of a knowing grin.

"Ye fell?" William asked, still holding her hand.

"Aye!" Shona snapped her attention back to him. "Aye. I, uhh . . . fell."

"Poor, sweet little hand," William crooned, bearing it to his lips. He was going to kiss it, to fawn over her, she knew, and though she didn't harbor any particular attraction to this man, she could not help but feel some satisfaction that the irritating Kinnaird was watching.

But suddenly a pain sparked her neck. She grimaced and drew her hand back to massage away the ache.

"Is something amiss?" William asked, leaning closer in his concern.

"Nay. Nay. I simply had a twinge of pain," she said, and rubbed her neck beneath Dragonheart's chain.

"Let me relieve it," William said, but when he leaned closer, the pain smote her again.

She pulled away with a grimace, then noticed a group of young boys running beside the gardens. Kelvin was amongst them. Her gut wrenched nervously at the sight of him, but surely twas better to ride out the storm than hide in the shadows.

"Kelvin," she called, marshalling her courage. "Come hither." She glanced at William, but if he were irritated by the interruption it didn't show on his face. "Kelvin spent a good deal of time with the king also," she said.

"Truly?" William studied the boy's haphazard clothing and raised his brows as the lad drew nearer. "Is he a relation of yours?"

"Nay, not by blood," Shona said, as the boy came to a halt before them. "But mayhap by spirit. Tell Laird William what ye think of our king, Kelvin."

The mischief that seemed a perpetual gleam in the boy's eyes sharpened a mite. "Shall I tell him the truth or what ye ordered me to say when questioned?" he asked.

She gave him a grin for his irreverent attitude. Though

she supposed she should reprimand him for both his words and demeanor, she couldn't help but commune with the imp in him.

"William is James's cousin," she said.

"Ahhh, then I liked the king very well indeed," Kelvin said solemnly.

From her left, Shona heard someone laugh. The sound was deep and husky. Shona felt the hair prickle on the back of her neck, and though she didn't turn toward the noise immediately, she knew in her gut it was Dugald Kinnaird.

"You are a poor liar, lad," he said, approaching.

Able to ignore him no longer, Shona turned slowly. When she glanced up, she felt a glow of heat that seemed to begin at Dragonheart and diffuse through her body.

"I dunna lie poorly," Kelvin argued staunchly. "I lie quite well."

Dugald laughed again. "Then mayhap tis the subject matter that makes your statement unbelievable. For you see, I, too, have met the king."

A frown marred the boy's gamin face, but in a fraction of an instant it was gone, replaced by a devilish smile. "And ye didna find him all brilliance and goodness?" he asked.

"Rather I found him vain and aloof," Dugald said.

"Tis our king ye speak of!" William said, affronted.

"Indeed," Dugald agreed, turning his attention to the older man. "Our king, who will be lucky to live to see his tenth birthday."

"Ye speak treason," William said, showing the first spark of emotion Shona had ever seen in him.

"Treason? Hardly that. I speak only the truth. I thought surely all of Scotland had heard of the attempts on the lad's life."

"Nay. Not everyone," William said, rising to his feet, "mayhap only those who had a hand in those attempts."

"Are you suggesting I might be plotting some heinous crime, Lord William?" Dugald almost smiled, but he had no wish to goad this man too far. Indeed, he didn't plan to fight him, only to bait him a little. For there was nothing like a bit of badgering to bring out a fellow's most elemental characteristics. And in this game of cat-and-mouse, knowing a man's true nature might mean the difference between life and death. "If you're accusing me of something more dastardly than stealing a lady's virtue, I fear you're sadly mistaken, for I am far too busy trying to win a wealthy bride to bother with politics."

"Ye are a—" William began, but Kelvin interrupted after one glance at Shona's shocked expression.

"I know the king quite well," he said. "In fact, it may be that I cherish him as much as any. Still, I must confess that at times he can indeed act vain. But mayhap the king of the Scots has a right to be."

Dugald turned to the lad, intrigued not only by his point of view, but by the unexpected maturity found in one so young and ragged. "Aye, mayhap if we were all abandoned by our mothers and raised by a passel of old men with wrinkled hands and shriveled hearts, we would be the same," Dugald suggested. In fact, he himself had been called vain by more than a few.

"His sire died when he was but a babe," Kelvin said.

Dugald watched him for a moment. He would be a fool to be drawn into this lad's life, for the boy had close ties to the lady Shona, ties Dugald could ill afford to become tangled in. There were excellent reasons why one might remain aloof. But sometimes he found that attribute disintegrating, crumbling beneath the weight of too close a contact. Better to stay back, stay apart, and do his job at the first possible opportunity. He knew that from long experience. Though sometimes it was more difficult than others. He had a tattered eared horse with a bad attitude to prove it. "And where is *your* sire, lad?" he asked quietly.

Kelvin raised his chin slightly. "He had more important things to tend to."

So they had more in common than their opinion of

the king. "Come. Let us discuss the hardships of abandonment," he said, keeping his tone light and bending to add, "and mayhap you can expound on the difficulties of being fostered by a woman who makes the king's vanity pale in comparison."

"What say ye?" Shona asked.

Dugald turned to her, careful to hone an expression of overt innocence. "I but said, 'I'm certain his difficulties pale, now that he is fostered by a woman who is the king's companion.' "

Not for a moment did she look like she believed him. "Mayhap I should come with ye," she said, her brow slightly wrinkled.

Dugald bowed to her. "I am flattered by your offer, Damsel. But you'd best finish your meal, for surely such a delicate maid as yourself might easily swoon dead away if you miss your breakfast."

"Truly," Kelvin said, the gleam back in his eye, "she is not as fragile as she appears. Indeed, I asked to ride with her on the upcoming hunt, for she is the best archer in all of Dun Ard."

"Indeed?" Dugald asked, and placing an arm over the boy's shoulder, turned him away. "You pique my interest." That much, at least, was the truth. In fact, this Shona MacGowan became more intriguing with each passing moment. Too intriguing, for although Lord Tremayne might be a high-handed, arrogant bastard, his sources were impeccable and his loyalty to Scotland beyond question. If he said Shona MacGowan posed a threat to the crown, it was so.

Still, her murder would not rest well on Dugald's soul.

Chapter 5

For the tenth time, Shona glanced across the long trestle tables toward the pair near the door. She was just checking on Kelvin, she assured herself, but when his red head leaned toward Dugald's, she felt the breath lock in her throat.

She frowned at the odd rush of feelings, then told herself that she was merely concerned for Kelvin's welfare. After all, she had hardly seen him all day. Although the weather had been idyllic and William properly fawning, Shona hadn't enjoyed herself, for her mind constantly returned to the dark stranger.

What were Dugald and Kelvin talking about? Now and then when the crowd hushed she could hear snippets of their conversation, but it was like trying to lick Berthia's mixing bowl when the batter had already been scraped out—very unsatisfying. She had thought it terrible when Kinnaird had stared at her as if he knew every asinine prank she had ever pulled. But now he was ignoring her completely—even after she'd offered to spend some time with him. True, she had done so only because she was afraid of what Kelvin would tell him and vice versa, but still, he could at least have had the good manners to be thrilled by her offer.

God's wrath, she'd charmed everyone from peasants to kings. Who was he to act as if he were suddenly disinterested? And how dared he do so after yowling at

68

her window like a prowling cat the previous night? What kind of game was he playing?

The question stuck in her mind. Abruptly it took on a new and sinister meaning. Why would a man like him, a man who admitted he wanted nothing more than to find himself a rich bride, be content to spend the day with a young beggared waif? Who was this man? She knew next to nothing about him. Surely she could not trust him, especially where Kelvin was concerned. He'd as much as said that his own father did not want him. Was he a bastard, then? And what did he have against the king that would make him risk saying things that could brand him a traitor?

The thought struck her like a blow, taking away her breath. William had been angry, thus prompting his accusations of treason, but mayhap his words were true. Mayhap Dugald of Kinnaird *was* somehow involved in the schemes to assassinate the king.

She would insist that Kelvin spend no more time with the man, she decided, but just then she heard the lad laugh. It was a musical sound—lovely, and too scarcely heard. Glancing their way, she saw that the boy's eyes were round with wonder as he stared at Dugald's palm. In its center lay a simple hazel nut. Shona scowled. Twas nothing spectacular there, she thought, but at the boy's pleading, Dugald closed up his palm, then opened it a moment later. The nut was gone.

Kelvin promptly searched the stranger's sleeves only to come up with a puzzled frown. Even from across the room, she could hear Dugald laugh. Huh, twas just like his sort to make fun of a child's perplexity, she thought, but in an instant Dugald leaned sideways to speak to the boy.

She watched Kelvin's face light up and knew Kinnaird had promised to teach him the trick. Shona stared, eager to see how the deed had been done, but just then Dugald shifted his gaze to hers. A glimmer of amusement shone in his eyes.

Shona snapped her gaze away. Damn him, damn him,

damn him! What did she care if he taught Kelvin silly parlor tricks? The man had probably never done a worthwhile thing in his life, having plenty of time to play ridiculous games. Most likely they were harmless, but one thing was certain, she could not risk the boy. And thence . . . she almost smiled . . . she would have to learn more about this man. For instance, what were the strange implements she'd seen in his saddle bags? Some kind of tools for seduction? His features had a slightly foreign cast to them, and cousin Mavis, who gloried in shocking Shona whenever possible, said such men did ungodly things to their women—things that made them beg for more. Shona never did ask Mavis where she got this information, but knowing Mavis, that question was best left in silence. Mother's French relations were a scandalous lot. When Mavis arrived she would probably be drooling all over Dugald, begging him to do ungodly things to *her*.

The idea was disgusting. But what kind of ungodly things could make a woman beg for more—and more of what?

Shona scowled. For someone who had spied on nearly every person at Dun Ard, she knew pathetically little of what went on between men and women. Once, however, when she was no more than thirteen, she had heard an odd noise coming from the stable loft. She had climbed the ladder and found the miller's son lying between the milk maid's spread legs. They were both gasping, and his buttocks were bare and pumping up and down.

After some deliberation Shona had decided that that must be fornication, but she sincerely doubted that any woman would want more of *that*. Still, the couple had been wed soon after, so apparently the milk maid had had no objections.

She'd watched animals mate, of course. Even though it wasn't proper, it was very interesting. Stallions' members were very large; dogs, strangely enough, locked together; and chickens made a great deal of noise. None of it looked particularly appealing. Still, what would it be like if this Dugald fellow—

"Lady Shona?"

"What?" She jumped at the sound of her name.

"Ye agreed to sing a ballad with me," said Stanford.

"Oh, aye. Aye." Her cheeks felt hot, and though she knew she was a fool, she rushed one quick glance toward Dugald just to make sure he couldn't read her thoughts. He was looking directly at her.

She stumbled nervously to her feet, tripped on her hem, and tipped over her wine goblet.

"Lady Shona, are ye quite all right?" Stanford asked, grabbing her arm to steady her.

"Aye, aye," she said, feeling like a jester gone mad. "I am so clumsy at times. Tis a good thing ye were here to save me."

Stanford's moony eyes widened and his face turned pink, starting at his ears and spreading up to his receding blond hairline. "Twas my pleasure, Lady."

"Thank ye," she said and was quite sincere, for just now her self-confidence was flagging. But he was still holding her arm, and a sharp pain was bedeviling her neck, so she pulled gently from his grasp. Before she could massage the ache, however, the pain was gone.

Stanford stared at her, then drew himself together with a start. "I . . . I am told ye are adept at the psaltery," he said, tentatively raising the stringed instrument toward her.

"Adept? Nay." She would not look at that damned Dugald again. She would not. "I fear Cousin Sara is the musician. Truly, she has the voice of an angel."

"It could be no more melodious than yours," he murmured fervently.

Flattery. How nice, and much needed since Kinnaird's arrival. If that black-haired devil was thinking of marrying *her*, he could think again.

"Lady Shona?" Stanford called her back to the matter at hand.

"What?"

"I said, your voice is sweeter than the sweetest honey."

"Oh." Kinnaird was laughing again. She knew without looking up and ground her teeth to keep her eyes averted. "Ye are too kind, good Sir."

"Not atall. I would be honored if ye would sing with me."

She smiled at his earnestness and accompanied him to the corner where a gittern rested against the wall.

Once there, she resolutely determined to ignore Kinnaird. They tuned their instruments and sang a ballad about the bold lads of Glen Garney, then one regarding the horrible battle of Flodden Field. The last haunting notes dwindled in the hall. The hushed assemblage came to life slowly, returning to their talk and food as if they'd been temporarily transported somewhere else.

Shona smiled at Stanford. "Thank ye. Ye have great talent as a minstrel," she said, and prepared to return to her table.

"I have written a song."

She turned back toward him. "Your pardon?"

"I have written a song . . . about ye."

"About me?" He was such a cute thing, all deer hound eyes and blushing sincerity. If that blasted Kinnaird would only leave her and hers alone, she could do some serious flirting. Maybe she'd even *marry* . . . someone.

He cleared his throat. "I call it 'The Fairest Flower of Scotland.' "

She dimpled. "Me? The fairest flower?"

He nodded solemnly.

Maybe she *should* marry Stanford. "Please. By all means, sing on."

He drew his gaze from her with an effort, then strummed a few times on his gittern. Finally he began to sing. In truth, he had a fine voice. And Shona could hardly complain about the words. In fact, had she been a more modest maid she might have been embarrassed by his gushing praise. As it was, she merely sat with her hands clasped together in glee.

The notes rose a bit higher as Stanford began comparing her skin to that of a unicorn's hide. Her grace was like that of a gliding swan. Her . . .

But suddenly there was a great crash as a spice cellar careened from a table, bounced off the nearby wall, and landed spinning on the floor. Shona leapt to her feet, but Stanford, determined to finish his testimonial to her beauty, continued on.

Pepper billowed into the air like a burgeoning storm cloud, stinging her nose and tearing her eyes.

Stanford, however, was as tenacious as a dog with a bone and pitched his volume up a notch to reach the high notes. But as he tried to draw in enough air to finish his song with a flourish, his nostrils filled with the potent powder.

For a moment he stood as if frozen, with his mouth open wide and his hand outstretched in supplication to her charms. The first sneeze came like a cannon blast, the second like a volcanic explosion, until he was bent over double and stumbling backward to escape the horrible stuff.

"Lady," Hadwin said, rushing to her side with a lace handkerchief and an expression of deepest concern. "Let me assist ye."

"Nay!" croaked Stanford. He stumbled along the wall toward her like a drunken goat herder and nabbed her sleeve. But just then another sneeze gripped him. Straightening by jerky degrees, he arched backward and expelled his air in a great bellow of wind that fanned Shona's face like a wicked northwesterly.

"Please! Lord Stanford!" Hadwin said, drawing Shona back a pace. "Have ye no manners atall?"

"This is. . . ." Stanford drew back again, then bellowed out another gargantuan sneeze. "This is *your* doing!"

"My . . ." Hadwin began.

But suddenly Stanford grasped the shorter man's shirt

front in a bony grip and leaned into his face like a snarling hound. "Ye are trying to ruin my chances with Lady Shona."

"I am doing no such thing."

"Ye lying cur. Ye'll—"

"My lords." Roderic's voice was soothing as he stepped up to the snarling men, but when Shona turned desperate eyes to him, she saw that his gaze was sharp and none too happy when he glanced her way.

"It wasn't my fault," she hissed.

He lifted his brows dubiously, then turned back toward the pair who were locked in immobility. "Gentlemen, let us discuss this rationally. I've no wish for bad feelings between our guests at Dun Ard."

"I'll not be made a fool of by this undersized barbarian," Stanford snarled, tightening his grip.

"Truly, Laird Stanford," Roderic said, his tone less friendly. "I canna allow this kind of behavior. Ye are making my Lady Flanna quite upset. She may swoon . . . or something."

Panicked by her father's words, Shona glanced toward the Flame and saw that the tender mother she knew was gone, replaced by the red-haired warrioress who stood at the helm of the clan MacGowan. Apparently she had seen no need to bow to propriety this noon, and had not changed from her riding clothing. Dressed in dark leather breeches, her legs looked long and powerful. But it was her hands that worried Shona, for one of them was wrapped hard and fast around the hilt of her dinner knife. Fire sparked in her eyes and trouble in her stance.

Shona swallowed. She could generally handle her father, but her mother was quite another story, fiercely protective of her clan and home.

"Truly, Laird Stanford," Shona said. Her tone sounded a bit desperate, but she'd witnessed her mother's temper before. It wasn't something she wanted a possible husband to see. "I am certain Hadwin meant no harm."

"I do hate to disagree," Stanford snarled. "But I saw

him overturn the pepper cellar with my own eyes. And twas he who tripped me up this morn.''

Turning from where he fairly hung in Stanford's fist, Hadwin smiled at her. ''Indeed, I fear our Lord Stanford is sadly deluded. I can hardly be to blame if he is a clumsy clod who canna—''

''A clumsy . . .'' Stanford sputtered, and drew his left fist back.

But the blow was never delivered, for suddenly Dugald Kinnaird joined the menagerie, distracting them all as he positioned himself close behind Stanford. He raised his hand behind Stanford as if to pat his back.

Stanford's eyes widened, and then he became very still.

Dugald turned his sardonic gaze to Shona. ''Trouble, Damsel?'' he asked.

Her brows lowered and her temper rose. It wasn't really what he'd said, but the way he'd said it that provoked her. As if this incident was hilariously funny and entirely her fault. His mouth quirked up in the oddest manner, and his lashes were ungodly thick.

''No trouble atall,'' she assured him.

He smiled. ''Isn't there some rule against this sort of thing?''

She had to force herself not to grit her teeth. Although he had removed his hand from behind Stanford, the gangly laird still hadn't moved his arm, as if it were somehow locked in place since Dugald's arrival.

''What sort of thing?'' she asked, jerking her gaze back to Dugald's face.

''Causing your swains to squabble over you like teased cockerels? Shouldn't you put some sort of limitations on it?''

In an instant she had come up with an appropriately scathing rejoinder that all but quivered on her tongue. But her father was standing close by and there were still the aforementioned swains to impress with her genteel demeanor, so she conjured her most syrupy smile.

"I fear ye misunderstand, Dugald the . . ." She paused.

He remained silent for a moment, but mischief sparkled in his silvery eyes. "Dugald the Dragon," he supplied.

"This has nothing whatsoever to do with me, Dugald the Dragger."

The sparkle deepened. "Indeed?" His left eyebrow could move without influencing any other part of his face. It was very annoying.

"Indeed," she said.

"Then mayhap they were simply arguing over the price of pepper?"

"Maybe so."

"Is there a problem afoot?" Flanna asked, approaching from behind.

Shona jumped as she rushed her gaze to her mother's face. But the older woman's expression was benign. It was really amazing how softly feminine the Flame could seem when she put her mind to it. Still, it was best not to play with fire, for the Flame guarded Dun Ard's peace with notorious ferocity.

Nervous, Shona exchanged a knowing glance with her father.

"Nay. None atall," Roderic said, then, reaching forward, yanked the clutch of Hadwin's shirt from Stanford's fist. "None atall. Ye can put down the knives, my love."

Heaven's wrath! Shona hadn't noticed that her mother had not only carried *her* knife, but had somehow acquired *another* along the way. True, they were only dinner knives, neither particularly sharp nor long. Still, Flanna MacGowan wasn't called the Flame because she lit the sconces in the evening.

Now she merely smiled sweetly, first at Stanford, then at Hadwin, but it was not difficult to notice that she kept her fingers wrapped about her impromptu weapons. "Dun Ard is my home, good sirs," she said softly. "It may seem little more than a garrison to such esteemed lairds as yourselves, but indeed . . .'' She motioned toward the castle at large. "I have birthed my bairns here. Tis where I was born, and tis where I shall die. I have no wish to see discord within these walls," she said, and with those words, stabbed her knife into the nearest table. Sinking deep into the wood, the handle reverberated like a leaf in the wind. "Do ye understand me?''

Stanford paled. Hadwin blinked. Dugald's left brow rose just a notch.

"There is no trouble, is there, my lads?" Roderic asked, his tone suggesting prudence.

"Nay," Stanford said. He still looked stiff, but he was wriggling his fingers now, as if mobility was just returning to them.

Stanford glanced at Dugald and shook out his pale fingers. Kinnaird smiled in return.

"Is there trouble, Laird Hadwin?" Flanna asked.

"Nay," Hadwin said. "No trouble atall, my lady. And might I say . . .'' He cleared his throat and straightened to his meager height. "Never have I seen a woman look more becoming in a pair of breeches?''

Flanna smiled. "Ye mean ye have never *seen* a woman in a pair of breeches," she said, and to Shona's relief, relinquished her knife to Roderic's insistent tug.

Father and daughter exchanged a relieved glance, then Roderic motioned to the two trouble-makers. "Mayhap ye should take your seats, lads."

They remained motionless for a moment, still glaring at each other.

"Before the Flame finds more cutlery," he suggested.

The two glanced toward the lady, then sidled sheepishly away.

"Well, my love," Roderic said, the shadow of humor just playing at the corners of his mouth as he looked at his wife. "Ye were as subtle as ever."

Flanna smiled. Her demeanor would have gained nothing if she had batted her lashes. "I can but try," she said. Mayhem sparkled in her eyes as she turned them on her spouse. They shared a silent moment, then,

"I dunna believe I've been properly introduced to our guest here."

Dugald bowed at the waist. The movement was ultimate elegance. Not a single dark hair dared stray from where it was bound at the back of his neck, and though she could feel a hundred gazes staring at them, Shona feared most of them were women looking at *him*.

"I am called Dugald, of the Kinnairds," he said.

"I have heard of a man called Dugald the Dragon," Flanna said. "Might ye be him?"

He smiled. But it was not that irritating smile Shona hated. It was a gentle, almost self-deprecating grin that probably made girls from Holland to Africa swoon. Personally, it made Shona want to smack him. True, he was a full hand taller than she and outweighed her by a good five stone, but his ridiculously elevated opinion of himself was bound to be his downfall. In hand-to-hand combat, he would probably be too worried about his hair to land a decent punch. And surely he would not want to dirty the pretty jeweled knife that always hung at his side.

"I believe the person who first called me a dragon was being facetious," he said.

"Look, Roderic, modesty," Flanna said, turning toward her spouse.

Shona couldn't stop the snort that escaped her. She tried, but it was hopeless.

Dugald turned slowly toward her, his quicksilver eyes steady, his expression just hinting at the humor that boiled below the surface.

"Your pardon, Damsel. Did you say something?" he asked.

For a fraction of an instant, she was tempted almost beyond control to speak her mind, but in the end, she offered her best honeyed smile.

"The pepper," she said, dabbing daintily at her nose with the handkerchief Hadwin had given her, "I fear tis irritating me."

He tsked his sympathy and canted his head at her.

"With such a delicate thing as yourself, I am hardly surprised."

She opened her mouth to speak, but when she shifted her glance momentarily to her parents, she saw they were watching her as hawks might eye a fat hare.

"I suppose I canna expect to be so hardy as Dugald the Dreadful."

"Dragon," he corrected.

"My mistake," she murmured.

"Daughter!" Roderic said, and though his tone was fairly even, there was a definite edge to it. Somehow, just the sound of it conjured up images of pasty-faced lords with multiple chins and fat fingers, each of them reaching for her. "Mayhap ye could sing a bit of a ditty to settle the crowd." He leaned somewhat closer. "If ye are quite finished with your theatricals."

She opened her mouth to argue with him. After all, none of this was her fault. It reminded her of the time she'd been blamed for setting the draperies on fire. How was she to know that pork fat would burn? she thought, but one glance at Roderic's face convinced her not to bring up that particular incident. She conjured a suitable smile. "What would ye like to hear, Father dearest?"

His brows rose a shadow of an inch. "Something sweet," he suggested.

In truth, subtlety did not run in her family. She didn't know where she had acquired the trait. "As ye wish," she said demurely.

Roderic nodded.

Dugald smiled.

For a moment she was painfully tempted to give him just one small kick to his shins, but never had it been said that Shona MacGowan lacked control. Well, rarely had it been said. Well, it hadn't been said *today*—at least, not to her face.

Turning, she saw that Kelvin was seated beside her younger brother Torquil. As a companion, Torquil was only marginally more suitable than this irritating Dugald fellow. She'd have to look into that relationship before

someone found a mouse in her pallet or a frog in his
soup. After all, Torquil had not yet gained her outstand-
ing maturity.

Faces turned toward her as she picked up the psaltery.
Twas a pretty instrument, crafted from etched rosewood
and oiled sinew, and it would look so fine with Dugald's
head sticking out of the middle, with splinters bursting
away from his ears and strings twanged cozily around
his neck. She nearly sighed at the images. But suddenly
her father cleared his throat.

No subtlety whatsoever.

She hummed a few notes, plucked a string or two,
and began to sing.

The hall fell silent. The ballad rolled away from her
in undulating hills and valleys of sound. In truth, her
voice was nothing special, but she had a gift for emotion,
and she used it now, hoping her father would forget
about wayward breeches and billowing clouds of pepper.
The notes rose higher, brimming with feeling, the
strength of hope, the desperation of love, the . . .

But suddenly the whisper of a noise rattled Shona's
concentration. She stopped, letting the climactic finish
hold on her breath, then, "Rachel!" she whispered, and
abandoning her instrument, flew across the hall and
through the arched doors. She paused on the stone steps
and stared toward the drawbridge. Hoofbeats echoed for
a moment, then a horse emerged past the entrance.

"Rachel," she said again, and ran across the courtyard.

The person who appeared was not her ebon-haired
cousin, but a large dark man accompanied by a petite
flame-haired lady. Not for a moment did Shona delay.
Instead, she hiked up her skirts and sped toward them
all the faster. By the time she reached the first horse,
Rachel had emerged.

"Cousin!" They were in each other's arms in an instant.

Dugald reached the doorway of the great hall just in
time to see Lady Sara join the pair. They stood huddled

together in bright shades of beauty, their arms wrapped about each other with sweet intimacy.

But Shona was not sweet, Dugald reminded himself. She was manipulative. She was cunning. And she had access to the king. He must delay no longer. And yet . . .

Her laughter lifted on a soft breeze and found his ears with unerring accuracy. Emotion speared through him, but he steeled himself to it. Shona MacGowan was not a victim of any sort, and neither her guileless laughter nor her soft beauty would convince him otherwise. She was no oversized lop-eared horse he could save from an infuriated master who had felt the sting of the beast's teeth too often. In fact, she needed his protection no more than a wolf needed a dagger and sheath. So she held no allure for him.

Still, if the truth be told, he had never seen such beauty gathered in one spot. Three lassies as lovely as spring with hair of seemingly every hue, red as flame, black as ebon, gold as sunshine.

But he was no fool for a bonny face. He would do what he must. He just needed a bit more time to figure things out . . . learn more about her. Tremayne had said she was vain and self-centered, and that it was far more than coincidental that she had been present during the first attempt on the young king's life.

But if she was a cold hearted murderess as Tremayne said, why would she go thrashing about in icy water just to catch fish for her father's supper? And what about Kelvin? Why would she foster such a ragamuffin boy, who obviously had no earthly possessions and reminded him disturbingly of himself?

Twas questions such as those that plagued him. Twas questions such as those that he would learn the answers to, but just now he had better concentrate on the matter at hand.

With some regret, Dugald turned his gaze from the trio of women to the man who had arrived first. Leith, the Forbes of the Forbes. His reputation proceeded him. But why was he here now?

"Brother." Roderic moved past Dugald and trotted down the steps to the courtyard, his boots ringing on the stones. "So ye have decided to grace us with your company?"

For a moment the courtyard remained silent. The Forbes dismounted. Though the movement was a bit stiff, there was great power in his large frame as he turned toward Roderic.

"I debated long and hard before setting out," he said, his expression somber. "After all, ye have long coveted my boots."

Roderic threw back his fair head and laughed, then, opening his arms, he slapped Leith into his embrace. "So ye still fear ye canna keep your footwear safe from me, Brother."

"Long ago I learned that nothing is safe from ye. Twas my idea to stay home and warm my brittle old bones by the fire. But my wife wished to come," he said, glancing at the woman on the dappled palfrey.

Roderic turned and drew his arms away from his brother. There was a smile on his lips.

"Lady Fiona." He said the name reverently. "Ye could have left your husband at home. In truth, he is wont to whine over a pair of boots long rotted away, and does little to brighten the mood of this gathering. But ye . . ." He lifted his hands to help her dismount. "Your beauty brightens the darkest of days."

Fiona laughed. By all accounts she was nearing fifty years of age, but neither her face, nor the melodious tone of her voice, showed it. "Still the Rogue, I see," she said.

"Until I die." Roderic chuckled and reached for her hand, but before she could dismount, Leith had pushed him aside.

"Do I disremember, or dunna ye have a wife of your own to pester?" he asked, swinging Fiona to her feet.

Her skirts swooped around her ankles, and when she landed, she looked as fragile and supple as a willow in the wind.

"Ye two stop, now," she chastised. "Or do ye want the Flame to hear ye argue?"

"Nay."

"Nay."

"Too late," said Flanna, stepping silently between the two. "So ye were arguing with your brother?" she asked her spouse.

"Not atall."

"Am I going to have to fetch my dinner knife?" she asked.

Roderic chuckled, and leaning close, whispered something in her ear.

It almost seemed like the Flame blushed. But Dugald was certain he was mistaken, for the stories that surrounded her exploits were brash enough to set one's hair on end. Indeed, it was said that some twenty years past she had abducted Roderic of the great Forbes clan and held him for ransom under threat of death. And yet as Dugald watched the foursome, he could not help thinking they looked like nothing more than two content, well-matched couples.

But long ago, by his grandfather's fire, he had learned not to believe illusions. Ninja *created* illusions. They did not believe them. Even a bastard child must learn that.

Dugald pressed the thoughts from his mind and refocused.

The Rogue, the Flame, Fiona the healer, and Laird Forbes were all now present. Rarely had a foursome held more power . . . or more loyalty. And that was not counting Boden Blackblade or his wife Sara, who fostered the child, and therefore owned the allegiance, of the duke of Rosenhurst.

Aye, the powers of the Highlands were gathering like a summer storm. If Dugald had the wits of a hare, he would do his job and retreat before the tempest overtook him.

But . . . his glance skimmed to Shona where she laughed with her cousins.

True, she caused an inordinate amount of trouble.

Maybe he should have let Hadwin and Stanford fight over her, but Hadwin had a perpetually misplaced pleat at the back of his plaid that spoke of a hidden knife. It was a strange thing for such a good-natured practical joker, and there was something about gushing blood at a meal that disturbed Dugald. It had seemed like nothing more than practical good sense to numb Stanford's arm with an herbed needle and curtail any more trouble. Dugald hadn't done it for Shona. Nay, she was spoiled and vain.

Still . . .

She had doused herself in a cold river in a wild attempt to do her father one small favor. She dared besmirch her reputation by fostering a bedraggled waif, and she had been ridiculously patient with the annoying Lord Halwart.

Would a murderess do any of those things?

Chapter 6

6 6 I feared ye might not be coming, Rachel,"
Shona said.

The solar was lit with a trio of candles set high on a
three-pronged iron stand which cast sleepy shadows over
the upholstered couch where two of the three women
sat.

"The games begin tomorrow," Rachel commented,
"and I did not wish to miss seeing the men make fools
of themselves over ye. By the by, who was that likely
looking fellow near the door of the great hall when I
arrived?"

"He is called Dugald the Dragon," Sara said, turning
her gaze to where Shona sat on the floor.

"The dragon, aye?" Rachel laughed. "And is he so
clever and alluring as the name suggests?"

"Aye," Shona agreed sarcastically. Even her cousin's
much missed presence could not keep her from feeling
grumpy when that dark-haired cur was mentioned. "He
is as alluring as a boil on my a . . ." Shona glanced at
the three children who had long ago fallen asleep on the
floor, Kelvin with his red hair tousled, Maggie beside
her hound, and wee Thomas, no more than three years
of age. "As a boil on my ankle," she finished poorly.

"Oh? And why is that? He looked to be quite dashing," Rachel said.

"Aye, I'd like to dash him on the head," Shona muttered.

Rachel's brows rose questioningly. "What was that?"

"I believe she said she'd like to dash him on the head," Sara replied.

"Our Shona? Surely not. Never have I met a lass who gloried in men's attention more than she. Can ye shed some light on this, Sunshine?"

Sara laughed, at both the use of her old nickname and Rachel's shocked demeanor. "All I know is that on the night of my arrival I found Shona in some disarray . . ."

"Disarray? With our Shona, that might mean anything from a missing button to unleashed Bedlam."

"In actuality, it was a torn bodice and a pale-faced suitor slumped over his saddle and fleeing for his life."

"Ahh. I can only assume Pale Face was *not* one Dugald the Dragon."

"Nay, indeed. In fact—"

"In truth," Shona interrupted irritably, "this tale is not all that entertaining."

"I beg to differ," said Rachel. "In fact what, Sara?"

"In fact, Dugald was the one without a plaid and calling at her window well after dark."

"Without a plaid?"

"It seems he lent his to Shona."

"Truly?"

There was an evil twinkle in Sara's eye. It really wasn't fair that everyone thought her so sweet, for in truth she had a nasty side which was evidenced even now by her glee over Shona's misfortune. After all, things just happened to Shona. She couldn't help it. And it was hardly just that her cousins, who were supposed to care for her, would feel such joy over her misadventures.

"I would not lie about something so serious," Sara said.

"I must say I rather wish I had arrived earlier," Rachel commented. "To be here to see Dragon Dugald at the window."

Shona bristled. "If ye find him so appealing, Cousin, mayhap ye should pursue him yourself. He is quite a catch. Or so he seems to think."

The room was utterly quiet, and then her cousins laughed out loud.

"It is not like her to get so prickly," Rachel said.

"Indeed not. Could it be there is something about this Dugald that our dear cousin has failed to mention."

"Mayhap."

"And mayhap ye should quit talking about me as if I'm not in the room," Shona snapped.

They laughed again. Why in the world had she been so anxious to see them? Shona wondered. They were an irritating duo and always had been.

"Perhaps we should change the subject," Sara said. "We might provoke her to violence. I hear she's been continuing her swordsmanship lessons."

"And dunna ye forget it," Shona grumbled.

"Aye, should we vex her too greatly, we may find a half score of smitten swains threatening our existence."

"I fear my Boden might be amongst the first," Sara said, but Shona snorted.

"If I had to exist on your Boden's paltry attention, my poor pride would wither to dust in less than a day's span."

"In truth, I think *this* noble young fellow would be the first to her rescue," Rachel said, glancing at Kelvin's slumbering figure. He had fallen asleep wrapped in a blanket on the floor some hours before. "Never have I seen such devotion in one so young. So ye are fostering a lad, Cousin?"

Shona glanced at Kelvin. His hair, bright as her own flame-torched tresses, had fallen over his brow, making him look even younger than usual. Fondness and unfamiliar maternal feelings flooded her. He had gained weight since she had taken him under her wing, but still he looked too thin, all half bare legs and gangly arms. His lips were slightly parted, exposing the gap left by the loss of both front teeth.

The castle was quiet. At this late hour, only the three cousins remained awake.

"Fostering would seem the wrong word." Shona smiled at the lad and easily forgot her cousins' baiting. "For it implies I have some control over him."

"I think ye underestimate yourself there," Sara said. "The lad would jump through fire for ye."

"Whose child is he?"

"In truth, I have no idea. I found him in Edinburgh."

"In an orphan's house?"

"Nay, in my pocket. He was trying to filch some coin."

"Another Liam," Rachel said wryly.

Sara laughed, and reaching over the edge of the couch, gently stroked the golden hair of her adopted daughter who slept some inches away. Her hound, a gift from their cousin, Roman, opened his eyes. They gleamed an eerie yellow in the candlelight, but he did not move, as if he were snared by the tiny fingers wrapped in his fur.

"Sleep, Dog," Sara murmured. "There is naught amiss."

"Dog?" Shona said. "It seems ye could think of a better name for such a handsome creature."

"They are trying to convince us that he *is* a dog and not the wolf he appears to be," Rachel said. "Just as Liam tries to act like a gentleman instead of like the scoundrel he is."

"Ye are forever too hard on him, Rachel," Sara said, drawing her hand away from the reed-slim girl she had called her own for the past three years. "Liam has much good in him."

"Truly? And where might I find it?"

Sara shook her head and Shona sighed as she gazed at Kelvin.

"Does Liam know the lad has taken his place in your heart?" Rachel asked. "Or is he still searching for some way to gain from the boy's misfortune?"

"You're being ridiculous," Shona said. "Liam barely

met the boy. They spoke for only a few minutes on our
way to Stirling.''

"I'm certain that will pose no problem whatsoever for
Liam,'' Rachel said. "Mayhap he'll proclaim the child
his very own. I dunna think he has ever completely forsaken the idea of wedding one of ye. Or mayhap he
hopes to marry ye both.''

Sara laughed. "Ye forget that I am already wed.''

Rachel flipped a narrow hand impatiently. "Tis no
more than a small inconvenience for a man of Liam's
. . . scruples. Besides, it could be he plans to make your
Sir Blackblade disappear in a puff of blue smoke and a
bit of mumbo jumbo.''

"I believe he already tried that,'' Sara said. "Boden
was not amused.''

"Tis not Liam's way to give up, though,'' Rachel
countered. "It could well be that he still hopes to whisk
the two of his 'wee lasses' away to his castle.''

"He has a castle now?'' Shona asked, warming to the
conversation. Rachel's annoyance over Liam was always
amusing, and it was especially so after their talk of Dugald. What a treat it was to torment Cousin Rachel after
they had done the same to her. "And here I thought he
was just a wandering magician and an occasional acro-
bat.''

"Most probably he has several castles,'' Rachel said,
rising to her feet to pace the room. Talk of the Irishman
always made her agitated. "I fully expect him someday
to proclaim himself the firstborn son of the king.''

"Which king might ye be referring to?'' Sara asked.
"Since our own is only seven years old, that parentage
seems a bit suspect.''

"The truth rarely stands in his way,'' Rachel said,
then turned toward the children, took a deep breath, and
seemed to relax. "What bonny babes.'' But after a moment she scowled as if seized by some strange thought.
She turned her bright amethyst eyes slowly toward
Shona. Their gazes met. "Tis strange, isn't it, that the

base born are no less lovely than those who think themselves quite noble?''

The hair prickled eerily on the back of Shona's neck. She loved Rachel dearly, but she could be spooky sometimes. Twas oft said, and sometimes by herself, that Rachel had inherited the sight from her mother.

''Aye,'' Shona said, careful to keep her tone casual. ''Aye, tis strange indeed.'' She turned toward the night-blackened window, but still she could feel Rachel's gaze on her.

''So ye saw our young king safely to Blackburn Castle,'' Rachel said.

''Aye.'' Shona cleared her throat. ''Tis true. I left him in the care of the Hawk.''

''But still ye worry for him,'' Sara said softly.

Shona turned toward her. ''I grew quite fond of him during my time at Stirling.''

''Tis said he is somewhat spoiled and wayward,'' Sara declared.

''Mayhap our Shona feels a kinship with him, then,'' Rachel quipped.

Shona made an evil face. ''He may be little more than an orphan, and therefore desires our sympathy, but at least he does not have to endure his cousins' barbed tongues.'' She sobered. ''He is hardly more than a babe and cares little for affairs of the state.''

''A babe, mayhap,'' Sara said. ''But our king nonetheless.''

''Aye,'' Shona sighed. ''But it should not be so. His shoulders are not broad enough for the burden placed upon them. Have ye heard of the attempts on his life?''

''I hoped they were but rumors.''

''They are far more than rumors,'' Shona said, her voice low. ''I was there during the first attempt. The poison that killed his guard was meant for him. Since then there have been two other attempts, and there will be more, of that I am certain. In fact—'' A whisper of a noise disturbed her concentration. ''What was that?''

''What?'' Rachel asked.

"That noise."

"I heard nothing," Sara said, but Shona gripped Dragonheart and stared silently at the door. It stood open, and though no sound now disturbed her peace, the noise had come from just outside the solar.

Quiet as nightfall, she slipped across the room and out into the hall.

Something moved in the darkness, something no more defined than a shadow. But she could feel its life. Heart pounding, Shona flew down the passageway, but already the shadow was gone, had disappeared into nothing.

She returned more slowly and closed the door behind her.

"What was amiss?" Rachel asked.

"There was someone listening to our conversation," Shona said.

"To us? Why?"

Shona stared at the door, still listening, still alert. Why indeed?

Morning came quickly. Surprisingly, breakfast passed without mishap, and finally the assemblage roamed from the hall and outside to a broad open field where the first of the Highland games would take place.

Shona spread a woolen on the ground and watched as Sara urged her children onto it. Thomas, the foster son of a distant duke, waddled quickly onto the plaid and plopped down. But Margaret delayed. Even now, after being in Sara's care for some years, she rarely talked. Perhaps her past experiences with people made her more comfortable with her animals—her silver gray hound, her weasel, which was forever close at hand, and any of a dozen other creatures that she nurtured in the folds of her gown.

"Come hither, Maggie mine," Sara said.

The small girl approached finally, her dark eyes wide. "Did ye need something, Mum?" she asked in her quiet voice.

"Aye. I missed . . . Dog," Sara said, smiling into Margaret's eyes.

The girl's expression couldn't quite be described as a smile. It was something more subtle. "He misses ye, too," she murmured, and sat down close by her mother's side.

"Will Boden be running in the footraces?" Rachel asked as she sat down beside Shona.

"I dunna think so," Sara said.

"Whyever not?"

"It seems he believes the competition might be quite fierce."

"'Tis only a footrace," Shona said.

"Aye, but there is talk that the winner will share a trencher with ye this eventide."

"I've heard nothing about this."

Rachel laughed. "Do ye think the prize gets a choice whom it is rewarded to?"

"And what of ye?" Sara asked, irritated despite herself. A lass liked to be sought after, but if the truth be known, this was becoming somewhat tiresome. "Why are ye not on the marriage block? Ye are, after all, older than I."

"Me?" Rachel motioned to herself. "The truth is, Cousin, I give Father no reason to want to be rid of me."

"Da is not trying to—"

"Shh," Rachel said, watching as Roderic and Flanna, resplendent in their ceremonial garb, stepped forward to address the assemblage. "I think your parents are about to give ye away to the highest bidder."

"Really, Rachel, ye are too cruel," Sara said, but in a moment she laughed.

"I dunna know why I missed either of ye," Shona mumbled.

"My Lady Flanna and I welcome ye all to Dun Ard," Roderic began, shushing the crowd with his raised voice. "In these days of unrest, tis good to know our friends and kinsmen can band together in times of merriment as well as in times of need. But today let us not dwell on the troubles of our Scotland. Today is for pleasures of every sort, for feasting, and—"

"Get on with the races," someone shouted, sloshing ale over the brim of his mug, "so we can get back to the drinking."

Roderic laughed. "Spoken like a true MacGregor," he quipped. Folks chuckled. "But I canna argue. Let us begin the races without delay. It has been decided that there will be nine different courses."

He went on to explain the distance and path of each. The prospective runners paced, some shaking their legs and setting their plaids to waggling as they warmed up.

"What prize for the winner?" someone yelled. The voice sounded quite gleeful and suspiciously like Sara's husband's, Shona thought.

"I say the winner shares a meal with the fair Shona," Hadwin suggested, his voice loud. He was a muscular fellow and quite cocky, despite his short stature.

"Very well, then," Roderic said. "The winner shall share a trencher with the maid of his choice, unless there are objections."

A refusal would surely be unseemly, Shona thought, and remained mute with the rest of the crowd.

"Tis agreed, then, Hadwin," her father said. "If ye win the most heats, ye may share a trencher with my daughter." He paused. A spark of mischief gleamed in his eyes. "And if ye survive the evening, ye will be allowed to compete in the games tomorrow."

There was general laughter.

Roderic joined her a moment later, still grinning as he and Flanna settled on the blanket behind her.

Shona turned to scowl at him.

"Ye would not wish me to send a braw young man into battle without warning him of the consequences, would ye?" he asked.

"I have not killed a single one yet," she muttered.

Roderic threw back his head and laughed.

"Mayhap that dubious good news would warn them better," said Flanna. "But tell me, Husband, why is the

Rogue not competing? Long ago I heard a rumor that he could outrun a horse for a hundred paces.''

Roderic leaned close to his wife's ear. ''Since my marriage I save my energies for more important duties.''

''Hush,'' she said, glancing toward Shona, then, ''Whom do ye favor amongst our bonny visitors?''

Shona scanned the gathering of runners. William glanced her way and nodded gallantly. She smiled in return, then hurried her gaze away. Hadwin of Nairn was strutting around in circles, Stanford was standing, hands on his hips, glaring at the shorter fellow. A couple dozen other men did the same sorts of things, but amongst the lot, Dugald Kinnaird could not be seen.

The realization that she was looking for him irked her to no end.

''Surely there must be one of our guests who interests ye,'' Flanna said.

''Can Kelvin be considered a guest?'' Shona asked, finding the lad amongst a group of boys.

A drum roll sounded loud and clear in the morning air. The crowd hushed again. Bullock, a broad man and one of Flanna's most faithful warriors, stepped forward with a banner in one hand.

''Line up, lads,'' he ordered.

The men did so, jostling each other as they found their places.

''At the ready . . .'' Bullock called, then, lowering the banner with a sharp sweep of his hand, he yelled, ''Run!''

The pack lunged away as a unit. Plaids swirled, bagpipes skirled, tassels twirled. People shouted for their favorites, their sons, their fathers. Twas a fairly short distance, no more than thirty rods, but the group broke up early. The sprinters burst ahead, their legs galloping, their arms pumping. And suddenly, as quickly as it had begun, the race was ended as Hadwin burst across the finish line. Grinning, he raised his fists high in gleeful triumph. The others scowled and paced and puffed.

''Well done! Well done, lads!'' folks shouted. Ale and

other intoxicating refreshments were poured and guzzled with parched relish.

A trio of musicians took the field and entertained them with a gusto that revved the crowd to further enthusiasm.

But soon the next heat was about to begin. Again the runners lined up, eyeing the finish line marked with stones, setting their heels, some bare, some booted, firmly into the dirt. The distance was farther this time, nearly a quarter of a mile and most of it uphill.

The drums rolled. The competitors grew still, their faces taut, their bodies tense.

"Run!" Bullock shouted. Again the runners launched themselves across the green, scrambling for distance. Hadwin pistoned ahead early on, but the course was longer and steep, making his bulk a detriment. Stanford and a handful of others galloped up, running level. In desperation, Hadwin glanced sideways and pressed himself to greater effort. The two fervent rivals ran side by side. Turning his head to glare at his competitor, Hadwin veered slightly, pushing Stanford into a patch of mud.

Stanford slipped, nearly falling to his knees, but Hadwin, too, had ventured too close to the mire, and though he did not fall, he was left behind as the others galloped toward the finish line.

The winner's triumph was somewhat lost in the boisterous moment as Stanford screeched accusations at Hadwin. The smaller man puffed out his chest and declared his innocence.

Seeing trouble afoot, Flanna motioned to a number of her men and Roderic rushed forward to keep the peace.

In a matter of moments, the quarrelsome fellows were dragged apart, and the music began anew, accelerating in tempo and growing in volume in an attempt to hush the noise of the combative competitors.

Drawing a deep breath, Shona all but rolled her eyes to the heavens.

"How exciting," Rachel said. Shona refrained from giving her an elbow in the ribs as Magnus, the ancient toy maker, was hustled into view.

He was old beyond even an estimate of age. His face was shadowed by a battered broad-brimmed hat, and his bent body covered by a nondescript tunic, doublet, and trews. Although his left arm seemed paralyzed, marionettes came to life in his hands, and soon he had the crowd entranced.

Finally, when the competitors had been given time to cool off, another heat was run. Though Shona's most ardent suitors strove valiantly, the race was won by a young man named Marcus, newly married and beaming in humble pride as he accepted the congratulations of the crowd.

The nooning meal followed, but soon the crowd wandered back out to the green for more games. The next race was won by Fiona's son Graham; the second, by a jubilant Stanford.

Refreshments followed again. Shona and her cousins watched as ale was swilled and voices rose. The day was wearing on, and most of the revelers had spent it drinking.

Finally it was time for the determining race to begin. Again the competitors lined up. The banner was dropped, the runners bolted. The distance was approximately four furlongs set in a rough circle that ended where it had begun.

Women cheered, men shouted. The runners raced on, tightly gathered, led by Hadwin and Stanford and a half dozen others. But Stanford seemed to be pulling ahead. Red faced and desperate, Hadwin put on a burst of speed as they rounded the final bend, but suddenly he faltered and bumped into Stanford. They wobbled unevenly. For a breathless heartbeat it seemed as if they would find their footing. The crowd rose to its feet, straining to see, and suddenly the pair went down in tangle of plaid and flailing limbs. Behind them the rest fell like sheaves beneath a scythe, tripping and careening in a pile of cursing, groaning chaos.

Onlookers roared in dismay or laughter, officials

shouted, and Stanford, apparently beyond control, threw himself at Hadwin.

Before anyone could stop them, they were tearing at each other like game cocks while the rest of the fallen field rose to the spirit and began throwing punches at whoever might be in the way.

Mud flew, women shrieked, babies cried, and from the sidelines, Shona stared in open-mouthed horror.

"However do you manage it, Damsel Shona?" someone asked.

The voice was almost lost in the ribald chaos, but even without turning, Shona knew it was Dugald Kinnaird's.

Chapter 7

The games had turned into a battle, with fists flying and mud splattering. Shona watched it in open-mouthed fascination. "Tis not my fault," she murmured.

"Of course not," Dugald agreed. "In fact, I am quite impressed. You made it nearly to the end of the day without causing a fight."

"Tis not my fault," she repeated, her temper rising as she turned to glare at him, but when she did, his mocking blue gaze struck her with lethal force. His crooked smile stole her breath and his nearness seemed somehow overwhelming.

Beside her, Rachel and Sara were suspiciously silent as they looked on, but somehow it seemed beyond Shona's ability to turn away from her tormentor.

"Might ye introduce me to your friend?" Rachel asked.

"Friend?" Shona questioned.

Rachel laughed as she turned to Dugald. "Ye must be the one they call the Dragon."

His attention turned away to rest on Rachel's petite features. "Tis a title I have oft regretted, I assure you," he said, his posture perfect, his costume the same, without a drop of sweat or a smudge of dirt.

Off to Shona's right, grunts and curses and wails rose skyward.

"Where did ye come by such a name?" Rachel asked.

"I fear the story is not all that interesting," Dugald demurred.

"I have found the tale a man is most loath to tell is oft the one most worth the hearing," Rachel countered.

He grinned. His teeth were exceptionally white against his dark skin, Shona noticed, and though she tried to stop herself, she couldn't quite help but wonder why it was that when he looked at her dark-haired cousin, not a tad of his cocky condescension showed in his expression.

"If you are truly interested I would be happy to tell you the yarn while we sup."

"'Tis impossible to separate Sara from her husband," Rachel said. "And it appears that Shona will be sharing a trencher with . . ." She glanced toward the track, searching the mob for an unscathed body. "My brother Graham, I believe, since he is one of the few still standing."

Dugald laughed. Then, offering his arm to Rachel, he led her across the drawbridge to the great hall.

Shona wasn't sure what woke her, but she lay immobile in the darkness, her heart pounding with fear. Why? Had she experienced a frightful dream? Had a noise startled her? But she remembered no dream, and just now the night seemed as silent as stone.

She lay still, calming herself with logic. She was safe here at Dun Ard. All was well.

But just then a noise whispered in the darkness, so quiet it seemed to be no more than a thought. Yet she was certain she hadn't imagined it.

She forced herself to sit up while her mind foolishly told her to lie still, that if she didn't move, she would be invisible.

But invisible from what?

She glanced stiffly about, her heart beating hard against her ribs, and her lungs forgetting to breathe. The room was tiny, containing no more than a single trunk and her bed. There was nothing frightening there, nothing at all. Swinging her legs carefully over the edge of the pallet, Shona rose to her feet.

It was not like her to be afraid, not here in Dun Ard, where she had always been safe. And yet the night seemed filled with a thousand evil things. Evil things that snarled at her from the darkness, that threatened her very soul. She stood paralyzed with an unknown fear.

A miniscule scrape came from the hallway. With a soft pant of fear, Shona grasped Dragonheart in her fist. The amulet felt cold in her palm, but the feel of it in her hand brought back a thousand memories—vows made in a high tower on a stormy night, bonds forged long ago, promises to be bold and brave like the Flame and the Rogue.

Without another thought Shona slipped to the door and wrenched it open.

The narrow hallway was empty. But there was something, a terror so frightfully sharp it seemed difficult to draw a breath.

Her fingers tightened on the dragon. Twas not the way of the MacGowans to hide, she reminded herself, and very silently, very carefully, she slipped along the wall to follow something or someone she could neither see nor understand.

The night was as silent and stifling as death, but Shona forced herself to move on down the hall until she had reached Kelvin's door. Pressing the portal carefully open, she peeked inside. He lay in happy exhaustion, his limbs tangled with those of the other boys who shared his bed. All was well there.

Shona moved on, skimming down the darkened hallway. Her feet were bare and made no noise against the wooden floor. But her gown was white and utterly visible in the darkness. Still, she could not turn back, could not return to her room. Someone had been at her door, someone had planned to enter her room. She was certain of it, though she had no idea how.

Stairs spiraled downward. She stepped onto them. The stone was cool against her feet. It was impossible to see to the bottom, to make certain no one lay in wait for her, yet she had little choice but to continue, for something drove her on.

The stairs opened onto the great hall. Shona let out a single breath and glanced about. Sleeping bodies were sprawled everywhere, but not a soul moved. Whoever had been at her door was not there. But he was somewhere, somewhere close.

She must know who it was, and therefore she must be absolutely silent. Without making a sound, she skirted the bodies and slipped along the wall toward the door.

A passageway opened on her right and from there she heard an indefinable whisper of sound. She turned with a start. A shadow flickered at the edge of her consciousness, but in a moment it was gone. She squinted into the darkness, and there, far away, she thought she saw a faint line of light.

Quiet as nightfall, her hands damp as she pressed against the wall, Shona slipped down the darkened hall. It seemed like an eternity before she realized that the glow she saw was nothing more terrifying than light shining from beneath a closed door.

She moved closer still. Whoever had been at her door must have come this way, but the numbing terror was gone now, replaced by the rush of excitement such clandestine adventures always caused.

She tiptoed closer still.

Voices murmured from the far side of the door.

"The king is little more than a babe," someone said. She did not know the voice but remained perfectly still, holding her breath and listening. "Do ye not see the trouble in this?"

"Aye." Uncle Leith's voice was distinctive. "The trouble is clear, Archibald. What is not so clear is what steps to take to assure Scotland's success."

Archibald! Archibald, the earl of Angus—the husband of their exiled queen, and King James's stepfather? Shona wondered. When had he arrived? She should have known. She should have kept better track. After all, she had responsibilities now. What did he want here? And where was the queen?

"'Tis certainly clear that our success does not lie in the hands of a French regent who does not even remain on Scottish soil," said Archibald.

"In all honesty, ye must admit that the regent has used all good wisdom to rule our land." Her father's voice was solemn and thoughtful.

"All good wisdom!" said Archibald. "Good God, man, the regent does not even speak lowland Scottish, much less the Gaelic. What can he know of our needs? I would think ye would be the first to be offended by his lack of interest."

"And what is your interest in this?" Leith asked.

"My interests lie with the interests of Scotland," Archibald said.

"Do they? In truth, it seems that your interests sometimes lie with those of England."

A movement jerked Shona's attention away. A shadow off to her right! Or was she imagining it? No, it was there. Fear prickled up her spine, but she could not entertain it.

A noise scraped along the edges of her consciousness, calling her on, down the narrow passageway, across the great hall. Not a soul moved there, but when she focused on the door, it seemed she could see it shift ever so slightly. Had someone just exited there?

She glided swiftly across the open area, skirting the sleeping bodies of men and hounds. In an instant the latch of the huge, arched door was beneath her hand. It creaked in quiet protest, but she did not delay. Outside the air was still and damp, eerily silent. Nothing moved. She hurried out into the bailey, but still nothing caught her eye.

But someone had been at her door, and someone had been near the room where the men talked. Who had it been?

Gathered at Dun Ard were her kin, her friends, her . . . Kinnaird! His face appeared suddenly in her mind—

his knowing smile, his eerie eyes. Where had he been during the games? Maybe her wild idea hadn't been so far-fetched; maybe he truly *was* a spy.

And if that was the case, twas her job to find out. Through careful questioning, she had learned, amongst other things, that he slept in a private barracks above the stable, for she had fully intended to search his belongings. But the time had never seemed right. Surely, she had thought, she couldn't do so at night, for then he would be in the very room she meant to search. But what if he had been the one at her door? Then his room would be empty and she would know that he had been prowling about.

Shona glanced back at the great hall. It would be wise to change her clothing, at least, but there was no time. If she was going to learn the truth, she must go now.

Dragonheart lay warm and approving against her breast, and somehow its reassuring presence pushed her on. It was no more than a piece of metal and stone, of course, but it reminded her who she was—a MacGowan, a Forbes: invincible.

Hence, she hurried forward through the darkness, past the herb garden and the mill. Inside the barn it was darker still. A horse nickered from its stall, but no one questioned her purpose for being there, so she crept, quiet as thought, up the ladder.

Above the stables the loft had been divided into individual barracks. She hurried past the closed doors, counting them as she went, then stopped at the fourth.

What to do now? She could hardly just barge in and demand to know where Dugald had been, for perhaps he had been there the whole while—or perhaps he wasn't there at all.

The hair prickled on the back of her neck. If she were wise, if she were prudent, if she were a lady, she would hustle back to her own chambers.

She lifted the latch to the room. It moved as silently as if it had just been oiled. She held her breath. Her heart pounded. She pushed the door quietly open.

But suddenly something smacked against her back. She was thrown inside. The door swung shut behind her, pitching her into absolute blackness. She tried to scream, but something struck her head and she was flung sideways. She landed diagonally across a bed and tried to scramble away. But a blanket was yanked over her head and wrapped tight about her throat, muffling her screams, cutting off her breath. She clawed to escape, to breathe, but darkness as black as hell filled her head. Terror found her. Reality escaped, fleeing beneath the oncoming unconsciousness.

She was going to die. She knew it. There was no use fighting, and yet she did, scraping frantically at the cloth. Her fingernails met flesh. Skin curled beneath her nails, but it gave her no satisfaction. She was dying, fading, going limp. Of course—limp.

It took every whit of discipline Shona had to force her muscles to loosen. But she did so, stifling the desperate terror of dying, and forcing herself to drift flaccidly toward oblivion.

An eternity of screaming silence passed before she heard a scratchy hiss of satisfaction. The blanket let up a tad. She felt the rush of air against her face. Sweet, so sweet, but she did not take it into her lungs. She did not move. Instead, she waited, one second, two, three, a lifetime. And then, like a striking snake, she jerked up her knee.

It slammed against something solid. Her attacker stumbled backward, but she had no air, no strength left, and already he was returning, lunging at her, something raised in his hands.

She felt it descend, heard the hiss of air as it rushed toward her head. She rolled across the pallet, but not soon enough. It grazed her skull and struck the mattress, spinning her toward oblivion.

Malevolence drew nearer, and she was powerless to escape. There was nothing she could do. She had failed.

But suddenly the door was yanked open.

Someone leapt into the room on a pale shaft of light.

A hiss of noise cut through the night air, and then all was silent.

She tried to see who had arrived, tried to clear her vision, to speak, to warn him as he stepped toward her. She felt the newcomer's presence more than saw it, imagined him leaning over her, imagined her assailant slipping behind him.

"Careful!" she croaked.

He jerked back at the sound of her voice.

"Behind ye!" she rasped.

She saw the pale shadow of his face turn away. But in a moment he was staring at her again.

Heaven's wrath! Couldn't he see the attacker? Couldn't he feel the evil?

She tried to struggle up, to save them both from the man who had attacked her, but a hand on her shoulder held her down.

"Stay!" he ordered, and turned away to disappear through the door.

Strength seeped weakly back to Shona. She dragged herself to a sitting position with her back against the wall and tried to still her spinning world.

Footsteps echoed on the floor and stopped. There was a sound like a knife slipping into its sheath. A spark flashed in the darkness, hurting her eyes. Instinctively, she covered her face and flinched away, but the spear of brightness only settled into a small flame, lighting a candle nearby.

It illuminated dark features and set silvery eyes ablaze.

"What the devil are ye doing in my room?" asked Dugald Kinnaird.

Shona tried to find her equilibrium, or at least think up a good lie. But there was little hope of that, for her head pounded and her eyes throbbed in sockets that were suddenly too small.

"Where is he?" she croaked. The words sounded fuzzy to her own ears.

"Who?"

Who indeed. "The man," she mumbled. Every inch of her battered body ached, while her jaw felt as if it had been attacked by a battering ram.

"You came here to be with a man?"

His voice sounded oddly sharp, unlike his usual seductive timbre. She tried to focus on him and found that she was marginally successful. Her hands were still shaking, but her lungs no longer felt as if they were being squeezed by a wine press, and her head felt as if it might, despite her first impressions, still be attached to her neck.

"And what man did you hope to see?" he asked, drawing nearer. "What man could you *wish* to see dressed in naught but a nightrail, Damsel Shona?"

All right, so she had been about to snoop through his private things. But that was hardly the issue here. She had been attacked! Could he be so dense that he didn't realize that? What had happened to her assailant? How had he slipped away so quickly, so silently that this Dugald did not even realize he had been there? "Where is he?" she croaked again.

"Who? Who did ye plan to meet here?"

The truth seeped slowly into her battered mind. He thought she had planned a tryst here. Dear God, he was dumber than a rock!

"Who?" he repeated, stepping forward.

He seemed different somehow tonight, sharper, harder, not the handsome scoundrel sniffing out a rich bride, but something entirely different. Who was this man? she wondered, and realized suddenly that he was dressed in loose fitting breeches and a simple belted tunic, all of it the same shade as the night.

"Tell me who you planned to meet here, lass, or I'll have to tell your father you've been sleep walking where you shouldn't."

The threat cleared her head better than Fiona's bitter tonics.

"Who did I plan to meet? Oh, I dunna know." She tried to shrug and felt strangely disembodied. "Any man that would have me I suspect, Dugald the Daft.''

"That's Dugald the Deft," he corrected through his teeth.

"Oh!" She was really not in a mood for conversation. "And what makes ye think so?"

"I did not take the name myself."

"Of course. I believe ye claimed it was the queen of Kalmar.''

"Actually, I believe it was the Queen of Spain who mentioned it first.''

"Was it after your 'short acquaintance' with her also?" She dared a fuzzy glance about the narrow room. It was empty but for the two of them. Why was she here? she wondered foggily.

"Mayhap I saved her from a fate worse than death,'' Dugald said.

"Ye mean ye ceased bombarding her with inane questions?'' she asked, settling her gaze on him.

Dugald gritted a smile at her. "I . . ." he began, but stopped himself and pushed out a heavy breath. "Who slept here before I arrived?" he asked, settling himself on the pallet beside her. "Who were ye hoping to meet?''

"Oh, I dunna know," she said, and remembered suddenly that she had come to search his room. Hadn't she? Lying carefully back, she twisted about to peak under the bed.

"Your lover must be quite small," Dugald said.

She gave him a look.

"To fit under the bed. He's not there is he?"

"Nay," she said. "Just your saddle packs and a mouse. Might he be a friend of yours? Rodents are quite gregarious, ye know.''

"Who did you come here to meet?"

"It hardly matters I suppose." She tried to leer at him, but she feared it came off rather like the twisted grin of a rabid wolf. "Now that I know tis your room, I'd best be leaving." To her absolute amazement, she gained her feet.

"Sit!" he ordered, and nabbing her sleeve, yanked her easily back down.

Her head swam with the sudden movement. She fought back oblivion.

"So I am not good enough for you?" he asked. "When another man would have been?"

Shona considered his words for a moment. "Aye. That seems to sum it up well enough," she said, and lurched to her feet.

He snatched her sleeve again, but this time his fingers became tangled in her hair. It yanked against her wounded scalp. She whimpered at the stab of pain and toppled to the mattress.

The room went absolutely silent.

"You're hurt?" His tone was cautious, as if he couldn't quite believe his own words.

There were any number of acceptable actions she might take with a dunce like him, Shona thought. At the very least she could give him a ladylike slap for his rude, and, she might add, lunatic assumptions. But it felt very good suddenly to just lie there.

"You're hurt," he said again, but as a statement this time.

"Truly?" she said. "I thought something seemed amiss. The walls dunna usually swim about like this."

"What happened?" His tone was stony.

She drew a deep breath. "Well, ye see, I was lonely. So I thought to myself, I must find a companion to share the dark hours with. Thus I wandered down the passageways, across the hall, through the bailey, into the stable, and voilà! Here I am. How was I to know it would be your room?"

Silence again, then, "Tis little wonder your father is so desperate to see ye married off."

"He is *not*—" She sat up too suddenly. Her head spun. Her body screamed. She put her fingers to her head, making certain it was still there. "He is not desperate to marry me off," she said, her tone peeved. "He is merely endeavoring to find me a suitable match."

"And the devil was unwilling?"

"Indeed, Dugald the Dumbfounded, with your charm I canna imagine why ye yourself have not convinced some lovely heiress to be your bride."

He grinned at her, showing a bit of the silky charm she had come to expect from him. "Mayhap I have so many offers I cannot decide amongst them."

"And mayhap I am really an onion dressed in a night-rail, but I rather have my doubts."

He laughed. "Does your father know about your nocturnal wanderings?" he asked.

"By that do ye mean to ask if your head would be forfeited if he found me here?"

"Just so," he commented wryly.

It was her turn to smile, though the expression did her head little good. "Not to worry. Roderic the Rogue always encourages immorality in his children."

Dugald rested one hand on the pallet and raised a brow at her. "Does he, now?"

"Ye think I would lie?"

"I know you would lie. You've done little else since our first meeting." Reaching up with his free hand, he touched the burgeoning bump on her skull.

She jerked away. It was a bad idea, for her brains threatened to spill out of her ears.

Dugald drew his hand back with a scowl. He let out a slow, deliberate breath. "How did you get that knot?"

"What knot?" she asked sweetly.

"The turnip-sized lump on the side of your pate."

"'Tis a family inheritance. Indeed, they used to call my grandsire, Auld Turnip Head."

"Tell me, Damsel, are you always so ornery in the wee hours of the morn?"

She thought about it for a moment. "'Tis an odd thing about me," she said. "But whenever I'm ..." The night's events seemed to be getting more foggy by the moment. She scowled at the realization. "Whenever I'm klonked on the head, then accused of ... what shall I say, loose morals, I tend to become a bit peevish. Might I leave now?''

The hint of a grin lifted his lips again. ''What shall I think when I return to my room only to find you sprawled across my bed?''

''Just what ye thought, of course. That I could no longer bear to be without ye. That I could not resist your allure. That regardless of everything I—''

''You've a knack for dramatics,'' he muttered, and rose irritably to his feet. In a moment he had fetched a wooden bowl from the top of a stool. Snatching a cloth from a leather bag beneath the bed, he dunked it into the water in the dish, then settled back onto the mattress. ''Would it be such an onerous task to tell the truth?'' he asked, and wringing out the rag, touched it to her head.

Pain jolted through her cranium. She jerked away. ''Are ye calling me a liar again?''

He snorted and settled the cloth back against her skull. ''Nay. Not atall. You were lonely so you wandered aimlessly across a hall full of half-dressed men you do not know, ventured through the bailey into the stable, and just happened to land in my room.'' Quiet settled in. ''What really happened?''

She scowled. ''Someone attacked me . . . I think.''

His dark brows lowered over quicksilver eyes. Twas strange, in the full light of day, those eyes looked alluring, true. And sometimes there was an element of mystery to them. But this night they looked altogether different. It was almost as if the veneer of civilization had been stripped away, showing the primitive edges underneath. But hardly did that description fit with what she knew of him. He was a preening coxcomb, a womanizer.

''You think? You think someone attacked you? In *my* room?'' he asked. ''Which, by the by, was empty but for ye when I arrived here.''

''You're thinking mayhap I banged myself in the head just for sport?'' They stared at each other. The cool rag felt soothing somehow against her scalp. Too soothing.

"I must leave," she said, and lurched to her feet.

But suddenly he loomed over her. He was not a huge man, she knew. But now he seemed to be so much larger than herself with a strength far beyond hers.

"I dunna think so," he murmured, his hand gripping her arm. "Not yet."

Chapter 8

Shona narrowed her eyes at him. Except for a few vague details, her mind was beginning to clear and questions of her own were beginning to echo in her head.

"Where were ye?" she asked.

"Your pardon?"

"When I arrived here. Where were ye?"

"'Tis a bit unseemly for a lass in your position to be asking about my whereabouts," Dugald said. His hand felt inordinately warm through the sheer fabric of her nightrail's sleeve. "When in truth, you've given me no good answer to why you came here atall."

Why indeed? Her every move now seemed foolish. Shona tried to steady her thoughts, but Dugald stood so close she could smell the heat of his skin, strangely erotic, trickling through her system like fine wine.

He stepped closer still. She leaned back. The world shifted shakily, and he slipped his hand about her waist as if to steady her.

Instead, it did the opposite. His fingers, long and firm against her back, set up an odd tingling that coursed through her every nerve.

"Tell me the truth," he crooned. "Why did you come here?"

"Why?" If she remembered that, mayhap she could chastise herself properly. But as it was, she was having difficulty thinking at all, for the bump to her head seemed only exacerbated by Dugald's nearness. "Do ye want the truth," she asked, "or a twisted but oh-so-interesting fabrication?"

He moved his hand slowly up her side. "The truth would be interesting enough, I'm thinking."

She swallowed as his hand crossed her spine, drawing her closer. "I was sleeping," she began.

"Ahh, sleeping." His left hand moved up her arm and skimmed beneath the weight of her hair. His fingers were feather soft as they caressed her flesh there. "And?"

"And I heard something."

"Such as?" He slipped his splayed fingers carefully onto her scalp, massaging gently, and making her knees go weak with the gentle movement. "A bang, a crash, what?"

"Twas more like a . . ." The tiny circles made by his fingers seemed to be drawing the pain right out of her skull like primitive magic. "More like a scratch."

"A scratch? Did it wake Kelvin and the other lads just down the hall?"

She scowled. "How do ye know where Kelvin sleeps?"

He delayed his answer for only a fraction of a moment. "Tis only logical that you would not allow the boy far from your side. You are well attached to the child," Dugald said. "You would not wish him far away. He was not awakened by the noise?"

She closed her eyes against the feelings his touch evoked. There was a strange, disconcerting sorcery to his touch. A sorcery she would flee from right now, if she had the good sense of a goose.

"Nay." No one else was. Indeed, now, in a lighted room, with Dugald's magical fingers on her skin, she wasn't at all sure there had been a noise at all. Perhaps it was only her oddly heightened senses playing tricks on her again.

But something evil had happened in this room. She

thought someone had attacked her. But Dugald had seen no one. No one but herself sprawled across his bed like a wanton doxy.

"Where were ye?" she asked again.

"I was but answering the call of nature. And what of you?" he asked.

Shona scowled. Everything seemed bleary and uncertain now. "It just so happens I . . . followed someone here." It was almost the truth.

"Who?"

"I dunna know."

He paused for a moment, then, "You followed an unknown someone here in the dark, without the meanest weapon of any sort, and not a soul to protect you from the multitude of strangers that fill your home?"

"When ye say it like that ye make it seem like less than sound reasoning."

He laughed as he settled his shoulder against the wall near the door. "Would you like to hear what I think?"

"Nay," she said, not pausing for a moment. "Not in the least."

"I think you cannot bear to have one man amongst the crush that is not wrapped around your delicate finger."

"Tis difficult to say, since that has never happened," she countered haughtily.

"It has happened now, for as tempting as it is to be wrapped around any part of you, I fear I cannot afford the cost of the trouble you would cause me."

"Is that so?"

"Aye."

"And here I thought ye were merely looking for a wealthy bride and would not concern yourself with how much trouble your money source caused ye. After all, Baroness de la Mire does not sound like a lambkin."

He was silent for a moment, his eyes absolutely steady on hers. But where she thought she might see anger, there was only the spark of humor. "I have not mentioned the baroness. You've been prying into my past,

Damsel.'' He leaned forward slightly. "Dare I hope it is because you care?''

Shona silently berated herself. She had not meant to allow him to know that she had been asking questions about him. For surely that showed an interest she did not harbor. "Nay,'' she said quickly. "Ye may not.''

"Then why are you here?''

"Tell me, Dugald the Deaf, do ye always have such trouble hearing? I swear I told ye my reasoning before.''

"Tis a strange thing about me,'' he said. "When a person is attacked, I always expect there to be an attacker. Someone who is actually visible.''

She gritted her teeth at him, angry with herself for feeling so vague and uncertain of the events just past. "Could it be that ye have as much trouble seeing as ye do hearing?''

"I assure you, I have no trouble with any of my facilities.''

"I am quite impressed. Shall I inform the heralds?''

He ignored her sarcasm. "If someone attacked you, who was it and why would anyone wish to harm you? Did he . . .'' Dugald paused for a moment, his gaze sharp. "Did he perchance, have other thoughts in his head?''

"Truly, I have no idea.''

"Did he mean to rape you?''

The words came out harsh. She drew in her breath. "I had better go,'' she said and turned away.

He caught her arm. "Tis good to know that you learn from your mistakes.''

"Which means?''

"Are ye hoping to be attacked again on your way back? Or shall I escort you?''

She smiled, then jabbed him sharply in the ribs with her free elbow. "I prefer to be attacked,'' she said.

"That was my suspicion.'' He rubbed his ribs, looking irritable.

She drew herself up. "So ye still think I came here for a midnight tryst?'' she asked.

He scowled. "In truth, I dunna know—"

She jerked her arm out of his grasp and twisted about.

"Nay," he said, his tone harsh. "I do not believe you came here for a tryst. Instead, I think you are a spoiled little princess who has never had to learn the hard lesson of humility."

They were standing very close, nose to nose.

"And ye think to teach me?" she asked.

His grin was slow, his dark lashes thick as sable over his half closed eyes. "There are many things I'd gladly teach you, lass. Humility is not amongst them."

She leaned closer so that her nipples were pressed ever so lightly against his chest. "Do ye know what I think?" she asked, making certain her tone was husky, her eyes half-lidded.

"Nay."

She hoped she didn't imagine the sudden huskiness in his tone.

"I think . . ." She leaned closer still, so that his breath brushed against her cheek. "I think ye could not teach a rock to sink!" she said and jerking away, shot for the door.

He let her go.

"Perhaps not, Damsel," he said. "But I could teach you to fish, if you've a wish to learn."

His words snapped her to a halt. She spun toward him, her heart pounding and her fists clenched.

He stood wholly still, his expression bland.

Still breathing hard, she tried with all her might to believe that he wasn't implying what she thought he was implying. In fact, she had almost convinced herself when she realized that his expression was far too innocuous.

"Ye knew," she said simply.

"Whatever are you speaking of?" He blinked at her with such marvelous sincerity, such childlike innocence, that for a moment she was tempted nearly beyond control to slap him silly.

"Ye knew all along it was I?"

"It was you what?"

Her teeth ground of their own accord. "How old are ye, Dugald?" she asked sweetly.

He raised his brows. "In truth, I am not entirely certain. A score and three years, I think."

"Do ye wish to reach a score and four?"

"I had rather hoped."

"Then I suggest ye tell me the truth. Did ye recognize me when ye first saw me in my father's castle?"

"Think on it, lass," he said, settling his shoulder against the wall. "If you do, I am certain you will know the truth. After all, who else but the Rogue's daughter would have the gall not only to pull me in the water, but to add the effrontery of stealing my horse?"

Shona shifted her gaze nervously away. That entire episode was not something she was proud of. But it hadn't been her fault. After all, she hadn't asked this lout to come along when she was in a state of dishabille. "I didn't actually steal your horse," she said.

"Ahh."

"I just borrowed him for a short span of time. He just didna wish to leave me."

"He has always had poor judgment. He did not wish to leave his former master either, though the fellow was intent on beating him to death. In truth, I think the trouncing addled his brain."

"Why not be rid of him then?"

"'Tis not always as simple as one might think. For instance, I've been trying to get rid of you," Dugald said wryly. "But you've been bedeviling me from the start."

She should hate him. She wanted to hate him. She did hate him. But his eyes were as haunting as moonlight, his hair as black and sleek as sable, his every feature as perfect as a marble work of art. And when he smiled, her insides went all sloppy. She resented that. But perhaps she shouldn't have pulled him in the water.

"Would it help if I apologized?" she asked, knowing her voice sounded a bit petulant.

"Apologize?" He stepped forward like a hunting cat.

Their gazes locked. "'Tis no need for that lass, for truly . . ." His gaze slipped away from hers, skimming her bosom before returning to her face. "The view was quite worth the drenching."

Suddenly she couldn't breathe. Dragonheart was burning a hole in her chest, and her hands felt damp. Not to mention her head, which had every right to be spinning even without his sudden proximity.

"I'm quite certain I should slap ye for that," she said breathlessly.

"Aye." His tone was breathy. "I'm certain you should. But why don't you kiss me instead?"

In all honesty, she never meant to do it. In fact, kissing him was the furthest thing from her mind. But suddenly her mind seemed to have little to say about the matter and her lips had taken over.

The kiss was neither rough nor demanding, but so light it seemed that if she but breathed, the spell would be broken and he would disappear. She felt her body go limp and her mind follow suit.

Slowly, ever so gently, he slipped his hand behind her back and pulled her closer. His tongue touched her lips, stroking along the lower ridge.

She shivered beneath his touch, melting like a snowflake in the sun. The kiss grew deeper, taking her breath, her will. His arm slipped about the circumference of her waist, drawing her closer, pulling her under the magic of his spell.

Her body throbbed like the strum of a lute, singing for his touch, for his caress. Her breasts, taut-tipped and eager, pressed against his chest, joining the duo beat of their hearts. Somehow, her thighs were straddling one of his.

And she did not care, for she couldn't possibly get close enough, could not kiss him fast enough, could not feel enough of his skin . . .

Skin! She needed skin, she thought. And suddenly she was ripping open his belt. His tunic fell open. Her hands skimmed his chest. It was as hard as a stallion's, and he was hot . . . everywhere. His back, his shoulders, and when she skimmed her fingers along his abdomen, his muscles danced. His kisses, hot and ravenous, moved rapidly away from her lips, down the arch of her neck, over her shoulder, the hollow of her throat.

Need burned like summer lightning through her breasts, zinging like cannon fire through her belly and down to her loins.

"Bed." She never knew who actually said the word. It was just there, in the room with them. "There's a bed, just yonder!"

"Bed! Aye, bed!" The word was repeated like a sacred litany, and suddenly she was lifted into his arms, her side pressed against his hard, naked flesh.

Her nightrail slipped past her knees, baring her thighs, and somehow the ties on her bodice had become loose. But they were just a nuisance, a barrier between her and euphoria.

Down below, a horse kicked the wall of the stable. The noise broke through their combined trance.

Reality twanged between them like a loosed arrow.

Shona struggled in his arms, and he nearly dropped her, so hot was his desire to set her free.

She stumbled to her feet and scurried backward, pulling her bodice together with fingers that had suddenly gone cold and shaky.

"What are ye doing?" she sputtered.

"Me?" He looked shocked and somewhat befuddled. "What were *you* doing?"

She gasped at him like a prudish maid, which she was not, but neither was she the hussy she had seemed to be.

"Tell me, Damsel, what kind of spell do you weave?" he asked, then dropped his gaze to her chest. "What is that?"

"What?"

"An amulet?" He took it into his hand. "A dragon!" His gaze smote hers. "A dragon to draw a dragon. Is that it? Is that how you've bewitched me? How you've drawn me into your web?"

"Draw ye . . ." she spat, and yanked the pendant from his hand to stuff it quickly under her nightrail. "I dunna even like ye!"

"Apparently that makes little difference. For it seems you are not happy until you have every man drooling in your wake," he said, and lunged.

She tried to duck away, but he caught her about the waist. She twisted like a wildcat in his arms, swinging her elbow at the same time. It connected solid and sure against his left ear, knocking him off balance, but not so far gone that he lost his grip on her.

They went down together in a swirl of white linen. And suddenly they were on the floor, face to face, breathing hard and staring into each other's eyes.

"Shona." Her name was but a whisper on his lips.

She froze, breathing in the sound like sweet summer air. Her hands cupped his face of their own accord, memorizing his every feature. She tried to draw away, but the magic held her there, and suddenly she was drawing him hopelessly in for a kiss.

A whisper distracted her. She glanced up.

"Da!" She all but screamed the word and jerked like a mad marionette, for standing in the doorway, big as life and mad as hell, was Roderic the Rogue.

Dugald's gaze flew to her father. Then he slipped off her and rose lithely to his feet.

Shona tried to rise with him, but her legs became entangled in her nightrail and she tripped. Dugald reached out without a word, steadied her, then drew his hands back to clench and unclench them at his sides.

"Laird Roderic." He said the words with deep timbre, nodding shallowly.

"Dugald of Kinnaird," Roderic said.

"Father, what are ye doing here?" It really wasn't what she had meant to say, but all her good sense had been sucked out through her lips, and the sight of the sword strapped to her father's waist rather undid her.

"Twas the strangest thing," Roderic said. His voice was low. Too low. Too deep. Oh, God! "I was talking with my brother and a few others when I thought I heard something in the hall. I told myself it could have been anyone. In fact . . .'' His gaze was hawkish on her face. ''I told your mother twas nothing. But something bothered me, niggled at me, and I had to make certain my daughter was safe.''

He took a step into the room. ''My sweet daughter, the apple of my eye. My bonny wee lass that I have nurtured through her tender years to bring her with pride into chaste womanhood.''

She stumbled back. Her father had never struck her, but never had she been found nearly naked in the arms of a virtual stranger, either.

''But alas? Her bed was empty. Where could she have gone? I asked meself. Mayhap to the stable.'' He took another step toward her, his fists clenched. ''So I come here and what do I hear from up above?'' He growled the words, taking two angry steps closer, but suddenly Dugald stood between them.

''Harm her and you'll not see the light of day,'' Dugald said.

The room went absolutely silent. Past Dugald's ebony head, Shona could see her father's brows shoot into his hairline.

''Your pardon?'' he said.

Dugald didn't answer, but stood steady yet relaxed, his legs slightly spread, his bare feet unmoving.

''Are ye threatening my life, lad?''

There was a moment of silence, then, ''Nay, hardly that. I am merely suggesting that you do not touch the lass until your ire has cooled.''

''I have no intention of harming my daughter,'' Roderic said and stepped forward, his hand on his sword. ''I canna say the same about ye, however.''

Dugald moved neither right nor left, but crouched ever so slightly. ''Is this incident worth a death?''

''It may well be,'' Roderic assured him.

''She would miss you.''

''She would miss *me*?''

"If you die," Dugald explained, his tone absolutely steady.

"Ye've got balls, lad, I'll say that for ye. Though that may not be the case for long," Roderic said, and loosened his sword.

Dugald crossed his arms at the wrists in front of him. But even though he was unarmed, he suddenly looked anything but helpless.

Panic spurred through Shona. Without thought, she lunged at Dugald and shoved him aside. "Cease! Both of ye," she demanded, breathing hard. "There's no reason for any of this."

"No reason?" Roderic said. "On the contrary, Daughter, tis my right and my duty to defend your honor."

"My honor doesn't need defending."

"Ye are in your nightrail!" Roderic stormed.

"He's seen me in less!" The room went absolutely silent. She winced, then licked her lips. Where did those words come from? "I mean, he's already seen me, so unless ye can work magic, ye cannot change that." Dear God, she was usually much better at this game of words. She softened her voice and hoped she hadn't completely lost her feminine wiles. "I didn't intend to come here," she said quietly. "We were sleeping—"

"*We*?" Roderic roared the word.

"I! I meant *I* was sleeping. But I heard someone at my door—"

"He was at your door!"

She opened her mouth in a futile effort to explain, but in that instant Dugald stepped forward. "Please cease trying to defend me, Lady Shona."

She snapped her mouth shut with a scowl first for Dugald, then for her father. "It's not his fault," she gritted. "It's quite simple—"

"I do not care whose . . ." Roderic began, but suddenly he became silent and eyed her askance. "What did ye say?" The anger drained from his face to be replaced by . . . shock?

"I said, tis quite a simple explanation, really, if ye'll just—"

"Before that."

She drew a careful breath. "I said, it's not his fault."

Never had she seen her father look more astonished, though for the life of her she couldn't say why. After all, it wasn't as if she'd never admitted guilt before.

"Are ye saying this be *your* fault, Daughter?"

"Nay," she began cautiously, but Roderic was already slashing his hand through the air, cutting off any further discussion.

"Then it is his!" he said, stepping toward Dugald.

"Nay!" Lunging forward, she caught Roderic's arm in both her hands.

He stopped to stare at her from close proximity. "This is not like all your other foolish exploits. When the garden wall collapsed ye said twas not your fault, that the muskrats must have been digging down below. I gave ye the benefit of a doubt. When Blind William's favored ram suddenly turned an odd shade of blue, ye said twas not your fault. Possibly the beast had eaten too many bluebells, ye said, so I let it go, lass. But this . . . someone will take the blame for this."

She shifted her gaze quickly to Dugald and back. He looked absolutely calm. So she was right. He was as dense as a rock. Hadn't he ever heard that the Highlanders were a barbarous lot? Hadn't he ever heard of the rack? And that would be lenient if her mother found out.

Roderic moved to pull his arm from her grasp, but she snapped her mind back to the issue at hand and tightened her grip.

"Then tis my fault," she said.

The room went absolutely quiet.

"Then tis ye who shall suffer the consequences," Roderic proclaimed, and yanking his arm from her grasp, ushered her from the room.

Chapter 9

"**I**'ll lock her in at night."

Roderic's statement made no sense at all, Flanna thought as she lumbered out of a sound sleep. She was quite accustomed to these nocturnal discussions that seemed to start from nowhere, but that did not make her any more amenable to the idea of being awakened in the wee hours of the morning.

"What time is it?" she asked, managing to sit up in the middle of their huge bed.

"I'll tie her to her trunk!" he said, his tone no less agitated.

She watched as he paced the floor like a nervous cat. Or rather, she watched the dark shape that must be him. In his agitation, he had failed to light a single candle. Twas like him. "And might I ask whose trunk we are speaking of?"

"Twould do no good, of course. She'd only toss the trunk out the window and fall down after it. Tis not as if she would worry about a few broken bones."

"Indeed not. But whose bones are we talking about?" she asked. She was trying to be patient, but Roderic had begun to pace again, and apparently had forgotten that he didn't share a room with a deaf mute.

"Sneaking out in the midst of the night. What possesses her? Where would she get such an idea?" he asked.

"Indeed. Who would do such a thing?"

He sighed. The tone sounded heavy in the darkness. "Mayhap I should be happy to know she has taken an interest in someone. But . . ." He paused. "Am I so petty that I need her adoration more than I need her happiness?" he asked. "But she is so bonny, so lovely and fresh," he whispered. "Who could blame me for wanting to hold on to my youth through hers?"

The Flame sat very still in the center of the bed she had shared with her husband for more than a score of years. At times she had been certain no one could hold the Rogue's heart forever. For he was everything that was right about a man, all good strength and fine intention, all bonny muscles and intriguing smiles, and slow, warm hands. Women fell for him at every turn like ripened fruit in autumn. But the years had proved her wrong. Roderic had been true to her—until now, at least. Could it be that after all these years another woman had stolen his heart, had caught his interest? she wondered, still fighting the fog of sleep.

"Roderic," she said softly. "Ye know I am rather fond of ye. But if ye dunna tell me who you're talking of, I'll have to oil the rack."

For a moment there was absolute silence, then a snort of laughter as Roderic crossed the room to sit on the bed.

"I speak of Shona, of course!" he said.

Ahh, so her heart was still safe, and he was still loyal—twas mayhap the greatest miracle of her life, but now she must concentrate before he irritated the hell out of her.

"Shona! Our daughter," he said, as if her reticence must prove her confusion. Twas true, she was not the most astute of women when awakened from a sound sleep, but hardly was she likely to forget her own first borne.

She gave him her patient smile, knowing Roderic would be glad he didn't have to see it. "I know she is our daughter."

"Aye, well, she is all yours this night."

Flanna remained silent for a moment and smiled into the darkness. "Ye are giving up your share of her?"

"Aye." He sounded grumpy at best. "Aye. She is a MacGowan through and through."

"Truly?"

"Aye. Do ye know that when I threatened to kill him she had the nerve to take umbrage and—"

The sleep evaporated from Flanna's brain. "Ye threatened to kill someone?"

"Aye, and *he* threatened to kill me if I harmed her. Me! Harm my own daughter."

"Might I ask whom?"

"That Dugald lad," Roderic snarled.

"Dugald?" Her mind was spinning now, trying to catch up to her husband's leaping logic. "He protected her from the Rogue? Dugald the Dragon did that?"

Even in the darkness, she could tell he scowled at her. "I truly dunna think he deserves such a grandiose title, wife. What has he done to gain it? I wonder. He did not even compete in the footraces, and I've heard of no great feats he has performed. And if tis just for his looks. Well . . ." He scoffed. "He is handsome enough in a bonny sort of way, I suppose, but not all that tall when ye—"

She could not help but laugh. "Mayhap we could debate his attributes at another time," she said. "For now, ye might just tell me why ye decided to kill him."

"I found them together in his room," Roderic said, his tone dark.

Flanna stiffened immediately. "Who?"

"Dugald and Shona! They were . . ." He paused, as if he had trouble saying the words aloud. "She was dressed in naught but her nightrail, Flanna, and they were lying on the floor."

There was absolute silence as a wild host of emotions raged through Flanna. But finally reality settled in. They were talking about Shona. Shona! Therefore, nothing was ever as it seemed to be. "Why?" she asked.

"Why what?"

"Why was she lying on the floor with the lad?"

"Why!" He rose to pace irritably, like a great, leonine beast, treading the boundaries of his domain. "I like to think that after a score of years as my wife ye are not so naive as to be uncertain of the purpose."

"In our daughter's veins races the hot blood of the Forbeses, and my own ... more noble blood." She waited for him to laugh. It wasn't a good sign that he failed. She sighed to herself. In truth, their roles were usually reversed. Twas Roderic who was quick to see the humor in things, but not if his daughter's safety was compromised. "Think on it, Roderic," she said. "Long Shona has been old enough to want what only a man can give her. But long she has resisted. Why would she cease to do so now?"

"She would not be the first sweet innocent lass to be seduced by some evil fellow with a heart of stone and a brain of mush. I meant to kill him immediately, but she ..."

He paused.

"She what?"

"She said it was her fault." He said the words most reluctantly, but she heard them nevertheless.

"Our Shona? Our Shona took the blame?"

He nodded as he plopped down on the bed once more.

"Husband," she said, cupping his cheek in her palm. "I fear ye have been dreaming again. Our daughter is the one who causes trouble, not the one who admits to causing trouble."

"Well, she admitted this time."

"Our Shona?" Flanna sat up straighter, her mind spinning. "Are ye certain? The lass with the red hair and the mischievous eyes? The one who drags a gaggle of smitten lads about in her wake?"

"This is not a laughing matter, Wife," Roderic said.

"Nay," she admitted, but she could not quite keep the glee from her voice. For some years she had known she would have to be the one to find a mate for their daughter, for even though Roderic professed his intentions of doing so, it was unlikely he ever would. In truth, he cherished his only daughter too much to let her go to anyone who was less than perfect, and since perfection was a difficult commodity to come by, he probably wouldn't be marrying her off any time soon. "Nay." She returned to their conversation with a start. "Nay, tis surely no laughing matter," she said, but there was laughter in her voice.

He snorted in anger. "Ye women!" he said and jerked away. She caught him by the hand.

"Where are ye going?" she asked.

"It just so happens I've an execution to plan."

"I thought ye had changed your mind."

"Hardly that," he grumbled. "I am but considering how best to see the job done."

She could not help but laugh. "But it's the middle of the night, love. Canna this weighty matter wait until morn?"

"She was in the man's room! Dunna ye realize the significance of this?"

"Did they have sexual intercourse?"

"Flanna!" he snarled. "How dare ye use those words when referring to our daughter?"

"Did they?" she asked.

Roderic paused. "She *said* they had not."

"And ye think she lied?"

He snorted. "She lied about the garden fence. We do not have muskrats here."

It took Flanna a moment to realize he was referring to an episode from years past. "Shona did not actually say muskrats had dug below the fence. She merely said that they *might* have."

"She lied about Blind William's ram."

Flanna felt a soft wave of nostalgia as she remembered their daughter as a small, energetic lass with too big a heart and too wide a reach. "She didna say the foolish ram *had* eaten too many bluebells. Just that twas a possibility. In truth, she was just trying to save poor

William some effort. If the wool was dyed aforehand, twould save a step in the cloth-making process.''

"Heaven's wrath, wife!'' Roderic swore. "Tis not your place to defend her. Tis mine.''

"I'm rather enjoying the chance,'' she said. "Mayhap ye are making too much of this.''

"Too much of this! We are not speaking of a stinky ram or Bethia's long-suffering kitchen garden. We are speaking of our daughter's virtue.''

"And ye think she would compromise that?'' Flanna asked softly. "Ye think she would when there was a chance of hurting ye?'' She drew him gently nearer. "The man she has adored since the very day of her birth. The man who took one look at her wee face, all squashed and purple, and proclaimed her the fairest flower in all the world.''

"Twas not squashed and purple,'' he murmured. "Twas lovely beyond words. Her mother's daughter.''

"The man who would say things like that,'' she said. Turning his hand over, Flanna kissed his fingertips, his palm, his wrist. Roderic drew a slow breath.

"The man whom she loves above all others,'' she added.

"Our wee lass is growing up. Growing away from us,'' he said.

"Nay, never away from her sire,'' she argued, and tugged at his belt until it came loose. His plaid fell away in heavy, woolen folds, exposing the hard evidence of her effect on him. She kissed his neck as she loosened his cat-face brooch. "Never away from the Rogue. She would not do that, and hence she would not chance hurting ye by fornicating right under our noses.''

He sighed.

"Unless . . .'' She smiled mischievously with her grin hidden against his neck. "Unless this Dugald the Dragon is as spectacular as his name implies.''

"Gawd's wrath!'' Roderic snarled. "I've decided. I'm going to have him skewered and—''

"Now?'' She could not help chuckling as she slipped

her hand down his body to his obvious arousal.

Roderic cleared his throat as her fingers settled gently over him. "Right now," he said, but his tone was softer.

She stroked him gently. "But couldn't it await the morn? After all, I've done nothing wrong, husband. Tis no reason I should suffer a dearth of your company because of this night's foul events."

She watched his head fall back slightly as she stroked him. His flaxen hair brushed the great strength of his shoulders as his body tensed. "Ye are right, I suppose," he groaned. "Mayhap the punishment will be all the worse if he has to wait to receive it."

"Aye," she whispered. "And mayhap our pleasure shall be all the greater."

Shona sat up with a start. Flanna couldn't help but notice she looked rather pale.

"Mother!" she said, her voice raspy with sleep. "I . . ." She shifted her gaze to the closed door as if wondering if her father would be barging in at any moment. "What might ye be doing here?" she asked.

The sweetness in her voice could have kept her usual gaggle of swains woozy for a month. There was not a soul in all of Christendom that could cause more trouble yet look more innocent than Roderic's headstrong daughter.

"I fear ye well know why I've come," Flanna said, keeping her tone absolutely level, and hoping she herself could play the actress half so well as her daughter. She was taking a huge gamble here, she knew, but two facts stood clearly out in her mind. Shona had accepted blame for the situation, and even more important, Kinnaird had vowed to protect her. True, Flanna knew little of the man with the eerie eyes and the seductive smile. But she knew one thing—only a fool or a hero would stand up against Roderic the Rogue—and Dugald was no man's fool, of that she was certain. "Tis a matter of grave import," she said, warming to her task. "Indeed, a man's very life depends on your answers."

"A man's life?" Shona's emerald eyes opened even wider, seeming to swallow her face.

"I have never seen your father so angry," Flanna said, and fidgeted as she seated herself beside Shona. "So ye must tell me the truth. Did the lad called Dugald disgrace ye?"

"Disgrace me?" Shona fiddled suddenly with her blanket, scrunching it in her hands. "Nay, Mother, he—"

"Shona!" Flanna interrupted sharply. Her daughter— a master at the game of words. "Today ye must tell me the absolute truth. Did ye fornicate with this Dugald Kinnaird?"

Shona's mouth fell open slightly and her cheeks turned pink. Flanna silently congratulated herself. It was not so simple a task to shock her daughter. But she seemed to have succeeded.

"Nay! I did not."

Flanna let out a great gust of air and allowed her body to slump slightly as if she might swoon with relief. "I canna tell ye how happy I am to hear that. That is to say . . ." She rose quickly to pace the narrow room. "'Tis a well known fact that your father adores ye, and true, tis his job to see that your virtue is safe, but emasculation . . ."

"Emasculation!"

Flanna turned toward Shona. She had thought the lass pale before, now her nightrail looked dark by comparison.

"I dunna think he deserves that even if—" Flanna began, but Shona interrupted her.

"*Emasculation*?" she squeaked again.

"Listen daughter," Flanna said, hurrying back to sink onto the girl's bed. "I can understand how ye might find the man desirable. After all, he is quite a spectacular specimen, and your father told me how he was willing to defend ye even knowing Roderic's reputation with a sword. But ye must be a realist."

"A realist?"

Flanna nodded earnestly and reached for Shona's hand with both her own. "Certainly we want ye to be happy, Daughter, to find an agreeable husband. But this Dugald . . ." She paused.

Shona scowled, creasing a single line in her fair brow. "I dunna know what ye are saying."

"Ye are a MacGowan, Daughter. The blood of kings flows through your veins. France's kings, plus our own. Ye canna wed this Dugald."

"Wed him! I have no intention of wedding him. I dunna even *like* him."

"Nay?" Flanna tightened her grasp on her daughter's hand. "Truly? Then why were ye in his room?"

Shona's cheeks turned pink again. "Tis rather a long tale, I fear."

Flanna smiled. "Ye are, after all, the daughter of the Rogue. I would expect nothing less than a lengthy tale."

"I, ahh . . . I was sleeping."

Flanna nodded.

"A noise awakened me. I worried for Kelvin, so I rushed into the hall to see what had caused the stir. I thought I saw a shadow moving, so I followed it. Then I lost it. So I thought . . ." She scowled as if trying to remember. "I thought I would look in the stable."

Flanna forced herself not to rattle some sense into her daughter. Why was it that Roderic's children would never consider *not* following a malevolent shadow? "And then?"

Shona cleared her throat. "I went up the ladder to the barracks. But . . ." She paused.

"But what?"

Shona looked baffled, as if she couldn't remember the night's events, but in a moment she shrugged. "Did ye know Kinnaird is sleeping above the stable?"

"Nay, I didna," Flame said, then waited to the count of fifteen for her daughter to continue. "Might I ask how ye ended up on the floor with him?"

Shona scowled. "He was most rude. Asked me what I was doing there."

"Shocking!"

"I thought so. I told him the truth, but he didna believe me."

"Humph. And so?"

"So I decided to leave, but he grabbed my arm. He said he only wanted to escort me, but I dunna trust him."

"Indeed?"

Shona leaned forward, warming to her story. "Where was he when I arrived, that's what I wish to know. And what about during the footraces? I have my suspicions about him."

"Such as?"

"I believe tis he who tried to assassinate the king."

Flanna sat in dumbfounded disbelief. She knew Shona as well as anyone in the world, and yet even *she* could not guess how her daughter had taken such a giant leap of fancy.

"Tis quite a serious accusation, Shona."

"I know, but—"

"And I thought ye had defended him to your father. In fact, he said ye took the blame for the entire incident."

Shona's face scrunched up, reminding Flanna nostalgically of her daughter's sorry excuses during her childhood. "I had no wish to see the man killed."

"Truly?"

"Of course not. That is to say, not until his treasonous plans are revealed."

"Then ye have no feelings for him. No hopes of marrying him."

"Certainly not!"

Flanna sighed. "I am quite relieved to hear that. For tis time to give some serious thought to marriage. Your father and I still believe the laird of Atberry might be a fine choice."

"William?"

"Ye have no objections to him, do ye? He seems a good man. And surely ye canna complain about his appearance. He's quite attractive, don't ye think?''

"Aye." She said the word slowly.

"And of course . . ." Flanna leaned closer. "He is the King's cousin. If, God forbid, something should happen to His Majesty, tis possible that some day William himself might become King of all Scotland.''

"Nothing will happen to the King,'' Shona said, her face utterly serious.

"I pray ye are right,'' Flanna said. "Still, twould surely be advantageous to be married to his cousin. I shall let ye sleep now. And worry not, daughter, I will speak to Roderic on your behalf.'' She rose to her feet and turned away.

"Mother?''

"Aye?'' Flanna glanced over her shoulder, her hand on the door latch.

"Would ye be happier if ye had married a cousin to the King?''

Flanna laughed. "I married the Rogue, Daughter. The Rogue, who makes jokes at the most inopportune of times, who drives me to distraction, who weaves tales so outlandish that only an imbecile would believe them. Whose smile lights the heaven.'' She sighed. "Aye, I could have married a more noble man, a wealthier man, but Roderic's very voice thrills me, and when he touches me . . .'' She let her voice trail off, then started as if just now remembering her daughter's presence. "But we are not speaking of me, Shona. We are talking of ye. And surely ye are far too fine a lady to be married off to some foreign lad who has nothing more than devilish good looks and more boldness than is good for him.

"Indeed, Daughter, if the truth be known, the Dragon reminds me a bit of the Rogue, and goodness knows ye are too much like your father to marry someone of the same ilk. Nay, lass. Tis a solid man of position ye need, Shona, and ye are wise to know it,'' Flanna said, and lifting the door latch, stepped into the hall with a smile.

Chapter 10

D espite her attempts, Shona couldn't get back to sleep, for worry tormented her. Finally, nervous and confused, she dressed in the simple gown she had worn on the previous day and slipped out of her room.

One glance told her that Kelvin and the other boys were still fast asleep, as was most of the castle. Finding the spiral stone stairs that led to the parapet, she lifted her skirts and hurried up them, her feet still bare and her hair loose.

From the top of the tower, the world seemed brand new and rosy pink. The day was dawning clear and cool with a fresh breeze that trickled through her hair and caressed her cheeks.

Below her the earth rolled away in gray-green hills and dales that were as familiar to her as her own hands. The view should have soothed her, but it did not, for uncertainty tormented her.

Her sleep had been fitful at best. Not only had it been interrupted by the shadowy no one outside her door, but her head hurt as if she had somehow struck it on something hard. She scowled, trying to recall the events of the night, but her first clear memory after leaving the hall was that of Dugald leaning over her.

What had possessed her to allow him to touch her? For indeed, it *had* seemed as if she had been possessed by a force more powerful than herself.

What strange manner of garment had Dugald been wearing? And why, beneath that garment, had his chest felt as solid as tempered steel, instead of soft and flabby, as a wastrel's chest should? She remembered touching his skin, remembered the hot flash of feeling, the sharp loss of control, the desire, so intense it all but overwhelmed her. Indeed, she had remembered those things even in her dreams.

Shona scowled across the Gael Burn, barely noticing the rushing water that cascaded over itself in its flight to the sea.

She had kissed *him*—wildly, foolishly. She had nearly given up her virginity to him. But that didn't mean she liked him. She hadn't lied to her mother. Hardly that. The man irritated her no end. But something had come over her. She had been temporarily hexed, bewitched. She glanced pensively down at the amulet that lay nestled between her breasts. It felt cool this morning, and light. But last night it had seemed the opposite, heavy and hot as if it were urging her into Dugald's arms. Or had her own emotions made it seem so?

"A bonny morn."

Shona jumped nervously and spun toward the speaker.

"Magnus!" she said, spying the ancient toy maker where he sat atop the parapet some fifty feet away.

"I didna mean to startle ye, lass," he said.

But he had. Even now her heart was beating overtime. Twas not like her to be so jumpy. But lack of sleep had never agreed with her.

"Tis not your fault," she said. "I didna see ye sitting there."

The old man chuckled and nodded as his gnarled fingers worked at something she could not immediately identify.

She watched the rhythmic movement of his hands as they wove in and out, and gradually she felt herself relax.

"Ye were deep in your thoughts," he said.

Pulling her gaze from his magical fingers, Shona

sighed and circled the tower wall, watching the panoramic view change as she moved.

"What would such a bonny lass as ye have to worry on so?"

A lump on her head. Her inexplicable attraction to a man she detested. Her father's wrath. A lifetime spent in an uninspired marriage.

"Tis naught," she said. "I couldna sleep."

"Tis the same with me." The old man wore a faded brown hat that drooped over his ears like wilted husks. He tilted his head in an attempt to see past its sagging brim. "But tis pain that keeps me awake."

"If your arm pains ye, my aunt Fiona might help ye."

For a moment she thought she saw his eyes glitter beneath the floppy folds of his hat, but then he waved away her concern. "Tis just old age gnawing at my bones. But tis kind of ye to concern yourself with a worthless old man." His hands never stopped while he talked.

"Hardly worthless," she said, letting her own worries drop away for a moment. "The children cherish ye and the toys ye craft."

"Do they, now?" The old man chuckled and held up his latest creation. With nothing more than a twist of straw, he had crafted a tiny, marvelous bird. "Behold, a brown wren," he said, lifting it high. "If ye try ye can imagine it flying, soaring over the treetops, just as your thoughts soar, aye, Shona of Dun Ard?"

"Aye," she said. It almost seemed as if the bird would fly, as if this old man had somehow imbued it with life.

"And I have not yet even added the feathers," he said, and opened a small pouch. But just then a gust of wind twirled about them.

The tiny feathers lifted like dust in the wind. They swirled momentarily about his grappling fingers. But he was too slow, and before he could fetch them back, the capricious breeze whirled them over the wall.

With a cry of dismay, Shona ran to the parapet to

retrieve them. She grabbed at them, nearly reaching them. But suddenly a new gust lifted them farther out and they flitted away, dancing on the wind as if reveling in their newfound freedom and laughing at her earth-bound ways.

"They are gone," Shona said, still leaning on the parapet to watch the feathers. "I am sorry."

"Not gone," Magnus said philosophically. "Only displaced."

"Beyond our reach," Shona said.

"Nay," Magnus crooned. "Not beyond *your* reach, surely. Nothing is impossible for Shona of Dun Ard, the daughter of the Flame and the Rogue."

Shona didn't turn toward him, but continued to watch the feathers fall. They were mesmerizing somehow, entrancing. It was as if she watched her own future float before her, as if her own life were just as unfettered.

She was the daughter of the unquenchable Flame, the first child borne of the notorious Rogue. Nothing could stop her. The thoughts were as soft as a whisper, slipping through her mind, dancing with the soaring feathers.

Aye. She was her parents' child. Surely she could soar—like the feathers, like the breeze. She filled her lungs with air and let her head fall back slightly. Wind rushed through her hair. It soared about her like cool, licking flames, making her feel as if she had wings. She was invincible, she was unconquerable. The world was hers, and if she wished to fly, surely she could. She stepped onto the parapet. Exhilaration swelled through her. Power filled her.

But Kelvin's image suddenly brought reality. She was no longer a child, able to risk her life and limb for no good reason. She had responsibilities now. What was wrong with her? Shona shook her head, trying to clear it, but the wind would not be quieted and whispered to her again.

"Ye are the keeper of dreams and the thinker of thoughts, the planner of great plans."

She did have plans, great plans, though only a few

knew of them. And none other must find out. But that had nothing to do with this moment, the breeze whispered. A fresh gust of wind caught her hair, twisting it into a cat o' nine tails, but she barely noticed, so exhilarating were her thoughts. She could fly, she could soar.

"Ye are the companion of kings," the wind murmured. "The keeper of the Dragon."

Time halted. The feathers soared. Her thoughts flew with them. The world seemed to stand still, to watch her every move.

"Fly, lass," something whispered.

She pushed off.

"Shona!"

She gasped at the sound of her name and jerked away from the edge.

"Shona!"

She turned like one in a dream.

Dugald rushed forward and grabbed her arms. "What the devil are ye doing?" he rasped.

"Lass!" scolded old Magnus, sounding breathless. "I feared ye would fall. Ye must not stand so close to the edge."

"What kind of foolishness is this?" Dugald scolded.

Shona scowled at him. "Ye act as if ye thought I was about to throw myself from the tower."

"Weren't you?"

"I was but trying to fetch Magnus's feathers."

"They are of little import," said the old man, his hands shaking. "And surely not worth endangering the life of one such as yourself."

"I was not about to endanger my life," Shona insisted. But it was strange. The wind had whispered secret things, and it did not usually speak to her.

"I will fetch my frills," Magnus said, and shuffled from the rooftop.

The world went silent.

"You are certain you are safe?" Dugald asked. He loosened his grip on her arms.

She tried to speak, to laugh at his concern. But instead, her gaze met his and she was frozen for a moment, lost in his thoughts. "Of course I am safe. Why would I not be?"

Quiet again. Twas not like her to be at a loss for words, but somehow now she could find neither the words, nor the ability to say them. For suddenly every instinct in her insisted that she kiss him.

"Shona," he murmured. His tone was taut and his expression absolutely sober. He leaned slightly closer. She knew his longing as well as her own, could feel his very pulse racing in her veins. Why didn't he kiss her, she wondered. But just when he leaned closer still, he stopped. A muscle jumped in his jaw.

"Last night . . ."

Aye. They had kissed. She had liked it. Let's get on with it, her mind said.

"I would ask you some questions."

"Questions?" she whispered, and leaned toward him.

His breathing was harsh, his body tense, as if he were trying his best to restrain himself. "Aye. You said you saw someone. I need to know . . ." He paused and scowled. "I need to know who—" he tried again, but his words disintegrated, and suddenly he was kissing her with all the passion that soared between them.

"God's wrath!" someone growled.

"Da!" Shona gasped the word and tried to jump from Dugald's grip, but he held her arms in his protective grasp. "I can explain."

"Can ye now?" Roderic's voice was uncharacteristically low as he stepped onto the tower

"Aye. Tis not what it seems."

"Truly? It seemed as if ye were kissing him."

She winced. "Very well, then. It is what it seemed. But I have a likely explanation."

Roderic raised his brows. "His lips were on fire? Ye were but attempting to put out the blaze?"

Shona laughed a bit too loudly. "Nay. Of course not." She cleared her throat. "I, uhh . . ." She finally managed to snatch her arms out of Dugald's grasp. What the hell was wrong with her? What had she been thinking? "Dugald saved my life. I was but giving him a chaste kiss to express my thanks."

She was amazed to see how her father's eyebrows could shoot into his hairline, and when she glanced at Dugald, she was surprised to see that his brows, too, could rise to an astounding height.

"Saved ye?" Roderic asked. "Do ye mean to say that ye would have perished had ye not been kissed at that precise moment?"

She laughed again. Still too loud, she reprimanded herself. "Nay, Father, ye tease me," she said, but for the life of her she could not think of another single thing to say.

"Then might I ask, Daughter, what horrible evil threatened ye here on Dun Ard's tower roof?"

"I . . . nearly fell while I was leaning over the parapet."

"Fell?"

"Aye. I was hanging over the edge watching some feathers fall. Twas as if I was entranced, as if the wind was insisting that I leap from the parapet, for suddenly it felt as if I could fly, as if Dragonheart gave me his power. And I was not thinking. I could feel myself soar like a bird on the wing. Already I was falling," she rambled wildly. "But suddenly, like an earthbound angel, Dugald caught my hand and snatched me from the slavering jaws of death." Dear God, that was the weakest statement she had ever heard. What a pity it had come from her own lips.

"Let me get this straight in my mind, Daughter. Are ye saying that though ye have climbed down this tower since your infancy, ye can no longer be trusted to stand near the edge?"

"Ye knew I climbed down—" she began, but she stopped her words abruptly and bit her lip. "Considering the circumstances, I think ye should be thanking Dugald instead of . . ." She paused. "Instead of considering what you're considering."

"And what am I considering, Daughter?"

"I shudder to think," she murmured.

"Surely there is no need to shudder," Roderic said. "So long as Dugald the Dapper agrees with your tale, he will indeed have my thanks and none of the horrid possibilities that worry ye."

The world was quiet. Shona turned her gaze on Dugald, imploring him to corroborate her story.

"Did ye save my daughter's life this morn, lad?" Roderic asked.

"In truth, my lord," Dugald said, "I cannot think of a maid I would sooner save. But I fear I am no hero."

Shona winced. "He must have forgotten," she said weakly.

"Mayhap your kiss has addled his senses, Daughter. Why don't ye go see your mother while I discuss that problem with him?"

"Nay, I—"

Roderic turned his gaze on her. His eyes, blue as river water and sharp as glass, cut clean through to her soul. "Mayhap I mispoke, lass. I didna mean to ask for your agreement."

She swallowed. Rarely did her father get truly angered, but when he did, she would rather not be in the vicinity. Still, she was not a child, to be sent flying hither and yon at the first sign of trouble. "I hardly think he should be reprimanded for saving my life when—"

Roderic lifted his hand. "The lad's chances of surviving this gathering already look grim. Methinks ye should leave before ye dash what wee bit of hope he has left."

She swallowed once, cleared her throat, and fled.

Dugald stood with his back to the parapets. His conscience beat relentlessly on in his brain. What the hell was wrong with him? He knew better than to get involved with this woman. She was a traitor. A vixen Tremayne had called her. She was planning the king's death. Tremayne was certain of it, but he was not so foolish as to call for a public execution and risk the wrath of her family. No. She must die of a seeming accident, quietly, painlessly, as only Dugald could do it. And Dugald had agreed, for if he were loyal to anything it was to Scotland and its boy king. So why now did he feel this overwhelming desire to hold the very woman he had been sent to kill?

"Would ye care to tell me your version of the story?" Roderic asked.

Dugald drew himself back to the matter at hand. "I doubt I could improve on your daughter's tale, my lord. She's quite innovative."

"Try." Roderic's tone brooked no argument.

"From down below I saw her leaning over the parapet. I but came up to make certain she was safe."

The world went silent.

"You're right. Ye would not do well as a storyteller."

Dugald watched the man the world knew as the Rogue. Under different circumstances, he might like this man—might even admire him. But it was always best not to become overly fond of someone you may have to kill before lunch.

"I have done some checking into your history, lad," Roderic said.

A spark of fear speared through Dugald, but he doused it quickly, for he could not afford that luxury. "May I ask why?" he said evenly.

Roderic remained quiet for a moment as he paced the perimeter of the tower. "Despite my daughter's . . ." He scowled as he searched for the proper words. "High-spirited nature, she is a good lass, and I am rather fond of her."

Dugald watched him as he would watch any adversary, from behind hooded eyes that spoke of a spirit jaded by debauchery.

"It seems ye are, too," he finished.

"Fond of her?" Dugald asked, genuinely surprised. He didn't like to be surprised. It was poor planning. And that he couldn't afford either.

"Mayhap fond is not the proper word," Roderic said.

"Perhaps 'attracted' would be more apt in your case."

Dugald offered a wry grin. "I think that if you had these conversations with every man that was 'attracted' to your daughter, you would have little time for anything else."

For a moment, he thought he saw the flicker of a smile on the Rogue's face. But it was quickly put away.

"I dunna worry until she is attracted back," Roderic said.

"In which case you march the swain up here to reprimand him?" Despite his dry tone, Dugald could not help feeling a spark of joy to know that Shona's obvious attraction to him was not a common day occurrence.

"Only if the match is unacceptable."

Anger followed quickly on the heels of joy. For more than a score of years he had been unacceptable, first in Japan, then in France. In truth, Scotland was the homeland of his heart, for in the wild hills of his island haven he had found a fragile peace of sorts.

"You needn't worry," Dugald said. "Your daughter is . . . well, there seems little point in denying her allure, and I do not doubt her good breeding, but if the truth be told, I am looking for something different in a bride."

"Such as?"

"Someone who can give me limitless funds without causing me undue trouble." He flicked an invisible mote of dust from his sleeve. "The tailor does not work for free, and I am a peace-loving man. I much prefer a good bottle of wine to a battle."

The anger was perfectly obvious on Roderic's face. "Then I suggest ye look elsewhere for a bride," he said. "For if ye touch my daughter again, the tailor will be spending his time taking in the inner seems of your breeches." He stepped closer until his face was only inches from Dugald's. "Do ye understand me, lad?"

Dugald shoved down the anger, tamping it carefully away, but he could not quite keep the sharp edge of it from his voice. "Aye," he said evenly. "I understand you very well."

Chapter 11

❧━━━━◦✦◦━━━━❧

Dugald did not compete in the games again that morning. On the previous day, he had taken advantage of the nearly empty castle and searched several rooms for some sort of clue. But clues were difficult to find when he didn't know what he was looking for. All he had learned was that Shona was hard on her clothes, Hadwin kept a pair of bone handled knives hidden under his mattress, and William and the earl of Angus both slept surrounded by a bevy of their own guards.

Today, Dugald watched Shona. He knew he shouldn't. He knew he should do the job he'd been sent to do—trained to do, since birth. Dugald the Dragon had been hired, for there was none who could match him in the art of killing—even when he was retired, settled onto his own estate on the windswept Isle of Fois.

He had refused the mission, but Lord Tremayne knew which strings to pull to make his marionette dance. When the promise of wealth hadn't changed Dugald's mind, there was the boy king to consider. Young James, orphaned by his father, all but abandoned by his mother, and sure to die before ever reaching manhood if the evil plots against him were not foiled.

And Shona MacGowan was at the center of those plots, Tremayne had said. A cold, calculating wench with designs against the crown. Dugald narrowed his eyes as he watched her laugh with her cousins. Mayhap

145

she did have designs against the throne, but as for cold and calculating . . .

A dozen images of her flashed through his mind—Shona with a man's wet tunic clinging to her breasts as she fished hopelessly for trout that were destined to elude her. Shona laughing with Kelvin. Shona, warm and potent as hot rum when she kissed him.

None of these images corresponded with the picture Tremayne had painted of her. True, she was spoiled and conceited, seeming to think herself capable of anything, but why would she wish to kill the king? Tremayne's belief that she planned to marry above herself and see her husband on the throne, seemed ridiculous, now that Dugald had met her. Especially in the light of King James's marriage proposal to her. Strange that Tremayne hadn't told Dugald about *that*. Stranger still to hear it from Kelvin, who had relayed the tale with sober sincerity.

If Shona MacGowan was the grasping wench Tremayne made her out to be, why hadn't she snatched at James's proposal? True, she was at least a decade older than the king, but such marriages had taken place before. Indeed, Eleanor of Aquitaine had made such marriages fashionable four hundred years before. Or if she had no wish to marry the lad, why not at least hold that proposal as a threat over the king's advisors in order to gain what she could? Hardly would Tremayne allow a wild Highlander access to the throne, especially one with the power of the MacGowans and the Forbeses behind her.

Could that be why Dugald had been sent to kill her? Could it be that she was no threat to the king at all, but only a threat to Tremayne's grandiose plans for James's future?

Ridiculous, Dugald told himself. Tremayne was nothing if not loyal to the crown. But . . .

Dugald's gaze skimmed the crowd, then returned to Shona a moment later. There was something about her that attracted the eye, something more than her bonny looks—an allure, a bright boldness.

He watched as she accepted the drinking mug Hadwin had won for the hammer toss. The stocky warrior's left eye was swollen nearly shut from the fisticuffs of the day before. Still he beamed as she smiled at him, looking as if any pain was worth her simplest attention.

Her laughter wafted out on the morning breeze, and her hair glowed like burnished rubies in the sunlight. Surely she was . . .

Was what? Dugald asked himself. Too bonny to be a murderess?

In truth, he didn't know what this woman was capable of, and if he wanted to keep his *own* head attached to his neck, he'd blindly do the job he'd been sent to do or at the least, find out who the real culprit of the assassination attempts were.

And if it was she . . .

Dugald narrowed his eyes. He'd do what he had to do, he told himself. But just at that moment, she lifted her eyes. Their gazes met across the crowd, and suddenly it was as if there were nothing standing between them—not her father, not her multitude of swains, not his own mission. There was only that lightning bright spark that had flared between them before, draining his body, filling his soul. He was draw to her like a lamb to slaughter and felt himself pulled forward.

But in a moment Hadwin offered her his arm. Her gaze shifted rapidly away. Her smile lifted again, but not for him, the son of a heathen beauty and a lowly French knight. Nothing changed that heritage, not training, not secret alliances. Not even in Scotland.

It was not much later that Dugald returned to the hall with the assemblage for the nooning meal. A few times, he allowed himself to be drawn into a conversation by a woman named Mavis, who shared his trencher. As it turned out, she too was part French, a distant cousin of Shona's on her mother's side, and a bonny young woman who had already been widowed once. She was now, it seemed, married to a man more than twice her age. And not happily married, if her hand on Dugald's knee was any indication. He obliged her flirtation. After all, it would surely seem strange if he did not. But she could shed little light on her cousin's true nature. Indeed, it seemed they were not the best of friends. And so, as Dugald flirted, he let his attention flit elsewhere, absorbing the nuances of the crowd around him and filing away information to be considered and analyzed later.

The earl of Angus was here. But his wife, the queen, was not. It was not like the queen's ambitious husband to mingle with the lowly northern clans. What did he hope to accomplish here? Was it he who had planned the king's death?

Before arriving at Dun Ard, Dugald had heard rumors that the Munro was gathering his unruly island clansmen. Was it true? And if so, why? Twas a well-known fact that the Munros always rode with mayhem in their wake.

Why had William of Atberry, the king's cousin, come? Was he here solely to win a wealthy bride, or were there other purposes? It seemed strange that if he had a chance of marrying Shona, as rumor suggested, he didn't show more passion for the possibility. In truth, the only true excitement he had shown was when Dugald had slandered the king. Why was he so quick to defend the young monarch?

And what of Stanford? He was moody and calf-eyed and probably willing to do anything Shona asked of him, including a bit of murder. Hadwin, on the other hand, was gay and amusing while hiding away a small arsenal of knives.

Then there was the person Shona had followed to Dugald's room—unless she had been lying about the entire episode. Indeed, that possibility seemed greater with each passing hour, for she had neglected to tell her father of the incident. In fact, the events of that night seemed fuzzy to Dugald, with only the feel of her skin and the touch of her lips remaining clear as crystal in his memory.

Did the MacGowans plan these festivities merely to celebrate the end of winter, or were there other, more sinister reasons? And if so, what part did Shona play in them?

True, she was bold, but she was also undisciplined. Surely she didn't possess the ability or the strength of mind to murder the king.

But something about that theory disturbed Dugald. He said she lacked ability, but never in all his life had a woman befuddled him as she had. Never had he been drawn against his will, against his better judgment, knowing any mistake might be fatal.

What kind of power did she have that drew him so irresistibly to her? That forced him to take risks that should not be taken, that made him forget what years of training demanded he remember?

Mayhap she was nothing more than the alluring, high-spirited maid she seemed to be, but if such was the truth, he'd damned well better find proof.

The day dragged on, through the sword dancing, the stone throwing, the caber toss. A host of strutting men paraded across Dugald's line of vision. An array of bonny women glanced beneath their lashes at him, and toward evening, Mavis approached, her hand light on her husband's arm, her eyes coquettish.

"Dugald the Dragon," she crooned. "I've come to introduce to you my husband, Lord Bevier."

Dugald bowed slightly. "Tis an honor to meet you, Sir," he said.

The old man turned toward Dugald, his eyes black and shiny as beads in his wrinkled skin. "What's that?" he said.

"I said, tis an honor to meet you," Dugald repeated, louder this time.

The old man nodded as if unable to hear, but unconcerned by that problem.

"My lord is a bit hard of hearing," Mavis said. She smiled at her husband, fussed with his frilly white collar, then turned back to Dugald. "Though not so hard of other things."

Dugald had to struggle to keep his mouth from falling open.

She only smiled.

"Just beyond the drawbridge there's a lovely little spot under some mulberry bushes. I'll meet you there just after the sun sets."

"What?" said old Bevier loudly.

She turned to him and played with his collar again. "I said, I am set for life, since meeting you." Leaning forward, she kissed the old man's parchment cheek. "Let's go to bed, my dear," she murmured, but on the last word she turned her gaze to Dugald.

Mother of God, she was about as subtle as a palm strike to the forehead, Dugald thought, and turning away, hustled off to the sanctity of his room.

Darkness fell slowly. Folks began settling in for the night. Dugald sat cross legged on the floor of his room, his hands open on his knees as he breathed softly in and out. The lonely skirl of bagpipes filled the night. Somewhere far off a woman laughed. Perhaps it was Mavis. Maybe she had found another to keep her company. But he knew it wasn't Shona, for her laughter was like quicksilver in his belly, like sunlight on his skin, like . . .

Dugald rose irritably to his feet, only to find there was nowhere to go but around the narrow boundaries of his borrowed room.

She was not for him. The fact that he had won himself a title would mean nothing to an earl or an earl's daughter. He was, to them, nothing more than a bastard and a foreigner. Never mind that Dugald had been granted two estates and a good deal of coin by grateful nobles. He was still what he was.

Dugald paced again. From the sheath at his side, he drew out his knife and gazed at it. It was ornate, beautiful, obviously for show. But suddenly he swiped it to the side. The blade snapped forward, sliding out of itself to quiver razor sharp nearly four feet in length.

Dugald scowled, retracted the blade, rotated his neck to relax the tension there, and paced again.

Minutes seemed to tick by with the slowness of a dirge. It had been more than a dozen years since he had left Japan. He had accepted much of the western culture, finding it easy enough to adapt—to their clothing, their religion, their language. But had he become so European that he had forgotten how to wait?

Dun Ard slowly settled into silence, and in that silence, Dugald finally opened his door. It made not the slightest noise. The oil he had placed on the hinges was still doing its job.

Perhaps he would be wise to stay put. After all, he'd almost been caught eavesdropping on the previous night. But hardly could he have allowed the Forbes and the Rogue to meet without him. How could he have guessed Shona would be creeping about in the darkness, too?

Off to his right, he saw the soft glow of candlelight and listened for a moment to the sound of two soldiers playing tables. Nothing there. He would have to go to the main keep, for twas there that the men of means met. Twas there he had eavesdropped on their meeting last night. But Shona's passing had disrupted him.

The great hall was quiet. Not a soul stirred there, though there were bodies strewn everywhere. Dark, barefoot, and silent as the night, Dugald crossed the open space and stepped quietly into the passageways and beyond.

But if the troublesome Highland lairds were planning some mischief, they were planning it only in their sleep this night.

But what of the lairds' troublesome daughters? Dugald wondered. And suddenly he realized that he was heading toward the tower as if something were calling him there against his will. He turned about and forced himself back the way he had come. Had he not already found enough trouble? He was supposed to be acting like a man bent on obtaining a rich bride, but not one who would risk his balls for a few minutes with a lord's hot-blooded daughter. Especially when there was a bonny young widow who would gladly numb that pulsing need in him.

The hall was still silent when he stepped into it again. He trekked quietly through it, but when he was nearly to the door, a hound raised his bristly head and grunted a bark. Beside him a soldier stirred. Another sat up and muttered something indistinguishable.

Dugald staggered as if just stumbling out of a sound sleep. "Shut up, ye damned cur," he slurred. "Canna a man even relieve himself without having it announced?"

"Sleep outside if ye canna hold your ale," muttered the sitting man, then squirmed about slightly as he tried to settle back again.

But as he did so, he inadvertently elbowed his neighbor, who woke with a start.

"I didna know she was your wife!" he gasped.

"What the devil are ye talking about?"

"She said she was free. I thought—"

"My Muriel! Ye were with my Muriel?" grunted the first man.

"Murial? Her name was Flora." There was a silence, then, "Who the hell are ye?"

Dugald stepped outside. The air felt fresh and damp against his face. The moon, just escaped from behind an embankment of clouds, shone cool and bright upon the silent bailey.

Twas time for him to get some sleep, Dugald realized, for surely he wasn't thinking clearly. It was not like him to lose focus so. Certainly he had his weaknesses, as did any man, but he did not have most men's foolishness. He knew his lot in life, and his lot did not involve the flame-haired daughter of a Highland laird who would just as soon behead him as talk to him. In fact . . .

What was that?

Dugald froze with his back pressed against the wall. Every trouble-honed instinct prickled. A movement, dark as the night and careful as a whisper, scratched at his conscious. There! By the tower. Nay, *on* the tower. Sheltered in the arched shadow, the shape ascended slowly.

Dugald almost smiled. Twas Shona again, he thought, but suddenly the climber stopped and turned his head. The moonlight shone on pale eyes. Dugald froze, unable to move.

And suddenly, like a gust of wind, the figure was gone, disappeared.

Dugald exhaled, realizing suddenly that he'd been holding his breath.

Where had the figure gone? Dugald stumbled forward. His legs felt stiff, his chest tight, but he forced himself on. Still, he found nothing. Whoever had been on the tower was far gone.

But that could not be. Dugald turned rapidly about, searching. People did not simply disappear. Not even where he came from.

Drawing in a few slow breaths, Dugald forced himself to think. Where would the intruder have gone?

The answer came quickly: Shona's chamber. The man was obviously intent on reaching her room. Dugald turned and rushed toward the hall, then stopped abruptly.

He had no reason to believe the climber was not someone Shona would be overjoyed to see. Perhaps she had invited him herself. Twas none of Dugald's affair whom the woman entertained in her bedchamber.

But what of the fear and evil he had felt when those pale eyes had turned on him? If someone truly had attacked Shona on the previous night, there was no reason to think he would not do so again.

Fear coiled tight in Dugald's stomach. He had no choice but to make sure she was safe.

But he dared not disturb the argument that may still be going on in the hall, so he chose another route and hurried toward the mill. Passing the pond, he swept silently up the stairs that led to the parapet. After reaching the top, he stole along the stone walkway. His bare feet were absolutely silent against the floor, but he knew that two sentries kept watch at this end of the castle. Caution and more would be required.

Thus, he stopped around the corner from the guards. Silent as death, he climbed atop the parapet, grasped the stone edge, and swung over the wall. Dangling some forty feet above the ground, he moved hand over hand along the cool stone. It took him nearly fifteen minutes to reach a point where he was certain he was out of their range of vision. But finally he pulled himself back onto the parapet. Crouching there, he flexed his shoulders and let the tension drain from his muscles.

In a moment he was ready to move on. Rising silently, he slipped across the tower and down the spiral stairs.

The passageways on the next floor were as dark as sin, but Dugald had not been idle since his arrival at Dun Ard. He knew this castle well. Knew a bevy of boys occupied the first room on his right, knew Shona slept in the next.

Finally, seeing her door just ahead, Dugald stepped into a small alcove to wait and listen.

Nothing happened.

Somewhere in the heart of the castle, wood groaned as it settled. Farther down the hall, someone coughed once. Silence again.

Whoever had attempted to scale the wall had apparently felt no need to reach Shona's room by other means—unless she had already allowed him inside.

The thought caused something to clench in Dugald's gut, but he pushed down the rush of emotion. Closing his eyes, he forced himself to concentrate every ounce of his attention on the room next door. Minutes ticked away, but a quarter of an hour later, he had still heard nothing from Shona's chamber.

If she was entertaining someone in her room, the fellow was surely the quietest lover ever known to mankind. And it would be unlikely that any man would be silent with Shona. Nay, she was a woman who would make a man scream.

She was alone, Dugald surmised with a soft sigh. Still, it would do no harm to walk past her door and make certain no one waited in the shadows on the far side of her room.

It was harder than seemed practical for him to pass her chambers without so much as touching the latch, but he did so. His feet were silent against the floor. All the world seemed asleep. He turned away. But suddenly hinges creaked behind him. Something catapulted through the darkness. He swung around, but fingers were already tangled in his hair, and against his neck he felt the sharp prick of a blade.

He stood very still, concentrating, drawing inward, preparing, analyzing. His assailant was behind him to the right. Eight inches back. Dugald had but to twist and strike and all would be silent again.

"Who are ye?"

Dugald's breath stopped in his throat.

The voice was Shona's!

He forced himself to remain very still, forced his muscles to relax, to ignore the survival instincts that had kept him alive so long, to find that other self that he showed the world. "I suppose twould do me little good now to tell you what the czaress named me after I saved her from Genghis Khan."

"Dugald!" She hissed his name. The blade eased a fraction of an inch away from his neck, but in a moment it was back. "Genghis Khan died two hundred years ago."

"Oh. He must have been some other fierce barbarian, then. What was his son's name?"

The point of her blade pricked his throat. "Why are ye here, lurking at my door?"

"Lurking?" How the hell did she know he was lurking? He had been absolutely silent. "I was not lurking."

"Ye have been here for most of an hour, just beyond there, hiding in the alcove. Why are ye here?" she repeated, and tightened her grip in his hair.

"I but wished to relieve myself. Is this not the way to the garderobe?" he asked.

"Ye may think me foolish if ye like. But dunna think me soft." She said the words quietly, but the tip of her knife bit deeper into his neck. "For I must tell ye, I've a bit of a temper when I am awakened from my sleep."

"I suspected as much," he said, his head still tilted backward.

"Then I'd suggest ye tell me why you're here."

"Lady Shona?" a boy called sleepily from the next room. "Is something amiss?"

"Nay." The knife didn't stray a hair's breadth from Dugald's neck, but her tone was immeasurably gentler. "Nay, all is well, Kelvin. Go back to sleep."

Silence settled in again.

"Mayhap we should go elsewhere," Dugald suggested.

"Why?"

"So my screams of agony don't disturb the lad?"

He heard her snort, but whether it was humor or anger, he wasn't sure.

"Where would ye suggest?" she asked after a moment.

"Your chambers." The words came unbidden. Twas the strangest thing, but as soon as she touched him, he forgot all about emasculation, decapitation, and all the other unpleasant things Roderic the Rogue had planned for him. Even now, when her fingers were wrapped in his hair and she held a knife to his throat, he could think of nothing but how her hands felt against his skin. And suddenly it seemed like the most natural thing in the world to be closeted away with her. To feel her fingers soft as lily petals on his skin.

She remained silent, and for a moment he thought he felt her tremble just the slightest bit. But in a second she spoke, her tone sure. "Do ye, mayhap, have a wish to die? Might there be some kind of prestige in being killed by the Rogue of Dun Ard?"

"In truth, I believe your father is beginning to like me."

"Every time I meet ye I think ye are more deluded than the last. I would not have thought it possible."

"I am hardly worth killing," he said. He kept his tone casual, but her nearness was doing strange and unwelcome things to his system, a system so carefully trained that he would have thought it almost beyond such distraction. Yet even now the wild, primitive scent of her filled his lungs like opium, entrancing him.

She paused for a moment, then her fingers loosened in his hair and she stepped toward her door with a nod. "Ye're right, I suppose. I would hate to spill blood in the passageway."

In a moment they were inside her chamber together.

For the second night in a row they were alone in a room with her dressed in naught but a nightrail and his heart racing along like that of a mountain colt's.

She licked her lips. He watched the movement, watched the small, pink tip swipe her sweet lips, and suddenly, against his will, against all good judgment, he took a step toward her.

For an instant she remained as she was, then she stepped rapidly back, as if afraid he might touch her. "Are ye going to tell me why ye're sneaking around my room, or shall we simply wait for my father to come along and stick your head on a pike?"

He grinned. "Considering the options, I believe I shall tell you."

She waited.

Time slipped away, filling his mind with her potent presence.

"Mayhap I simply could not be away from you any longer," he said finally. He had meant to say the words with some sarcasm, to hold to the image he had tried to create of himself. But instead the words came out breathy, earnest.

Her eyes were as wide as forever as she watched him. But in a moment she shook her head.

"And mayhap ye are planning some mischief."

"Such as?"

"I dunna know. But it seems every time ye are near I find myself all aflu . . . in trouble."

She had nearly said he made her all aflutter. That slip of the tongue should have made him smile, but in that moment he noticed that the ties of her nightrail had come loose, and somehow that knowledge made his mouth too dry to muster a grin.

"In truth," he said, doing his best to sound casual. "I dunna think I can be blamed for either Blind William's blue ram or the failing garden wall."

"That was not my fault," she said, looking peeved that her father had told him of her childhood pranks.

"Need I remind you twas not *I* who felt a need to go afishing in naught but my tunic? Twas not *I* who entertained the lusty Lord Halwart in the stable, or indeed, who burst into *your* room in the wee hours of the morning." He wished suddenly that he hadn't reminded her of that, for now he could think of nothing but how she had felt in his arms, how her hair, bright as flame, had twisted about their bodies.

"I was . . ." She scowled, as if trying to remember. "I was following a marauder."

Reality surfaced slowly. He was not here to seduce or be seduced. It must be the Frenchman in him that made him so easily distracted. Or maybe it was just *her* . . . the perfection of her face, the brightness of her . . . he stopped his wayward thoughts. "As was I now," he said.

"What?"

He backed away a pace, carefully putting more space between them. The moon, full and round and fat, cast silvery light through the window. Mayhap twas the moonlight that bewitched him.

"There was someone trying to climb the tower to your window," he said, trying to clear his thoughts.

Her soft lips parted in surprise, but in a moment, she

pressed them closed and lowered her brows. "How do ye know?"

Now there was a likely question. Damn him. He had better get his head on straight before he lost it completely.

"What were ye doing awake?" she asked.

He grinned, careful to make the expression crooked and devilish. "Did you not know? I am a bold and clever spy."

"Are ye, now?"

"Aye," he said. "'Tis my job to sneak about in the darkness."

"And for whom do ye spy?"

"Italy?" he said, making it sound like a question.

"And let me guess, the queen called you . . . incomparable?"

"Actually, she was but a princess." He smiled. "And she called me, marvelous."

"Dugald the marvelous. It has a ring to it."

"I thought so."

"And what did ye do so marvelously?"

He was drawn toward her, against his will, his better judgment, his fading good sense. "Do you truly wish to know, lass?"

They were inches apart suddenly. Her lips begged for a kiss, her skin for a touch, and he was powerless to refuse. He leaned forward. Her breath was warm against his face.

"Nay!" She jerked abruptly back, and he noticed rather suddenly that her fist was still wrapped about the hilt of her knife. "Tell me what ye were really doing at my door."

He settled back, calming his heart, steadying his nerves. She was not for him. "I could elaborate on the spy story."

"And my father could be even less amused than I," she said.

Good point. Roderic had been unimpressed by his

story telling abilities. ''Mayhap I was with your cousin,'' he said.

''Rachel?'' She actually went pale when she said the name, and Dugald could not help but feel a spark of satisfaction at that. But neither would he slander *that* lady's name, for there was something about her that spoke of a soul far purer than his own.

''I believe her name was Mavis,'' Dugald corrected.

Shona's mouth fell open then snapped shut. Her brows scrunched together and lowered. ''She has long been intrigued by the talents of foreign men.''

''Has she, now?'' Dugald asked, loving the flash of jealousy he saw in her eyes.

''I hope ye did not disappoint her,'' she said, turning away.

''Do you?''

''Of course,'' she snapped, pivoting back. ''I could not care less if ye seduced every woman in . . . in . . .'' She paused, breathing hard, her brow furrowed.

''I did not say I *was* with her.''

Her jaw dropped. ''What?''

''I did not say I *was* with her. I said I *might* have been.''

Absolute silence filled the room. He could see the struggle she waged in an effort to keep the words to herself, but finally she spoke.

''Were ye?''

Jealousy was a glorious thing.

''Was I what?''

She gritted her teeth and closed her emerald bright eyes for a moment, but she finally spoke. ''Were ye with Mavis?''

''Nay.''

He hoped to God he did not imagine the relief on her face.

''Then why were ye in the bailey during the wee hours?''

''I could not sleep,'' he said. Sometimes the simplest

lies were the best. "I had but gone for a stroll when I saw a figure on the wall."

"And ye think he was trying to reach my window?"

"He was directly below it."

"There would be no point in climbing the wall," she said. "Even if he could reach the window I would awaken before he could get inside. I have very good hearing."

"Mayhap you were already awake and expecting him."

Her eyes looked as round as an owl's in the darkness. Moonlight gleamed off her wild hair, setting it aglow like uncut jewels.

"Let me tell ye one thing, Dugald the Droll," she said. "If I were to invite a man into my chambers, he would surely be one who *could* scale the wall."

"Any possibilities thus far?"

"I am holding a wall scaling contest for the most likely swains on the morrow," she said.

"Truly?"

"Aye. I have high hopes."

"Am I invited to participate?"

"I wouldna bother if I were ye. I noticed ye took the stairs."

"But had I known the criteria of winning your affection . . ." He shrugged.

She scowled at him. "The participants will only be those who do not taunt me at every turn."

"Ahh. And whom do you favor thus far?"

She was silent for a moment.

"Stymied, are you?"

"William." She said the name quickly.

"William?" He winced. "A bit old, don't you think? And he has a big nose."

"Did ye know he is the king's cousin?"

"His cousin! Truly. Then his nose is not big, but regal. And surely he will be able to climb a wall." He took a step toward her. "And as for his expertise in bed—"

"And Stanford is the laird of a large castle near Edinburgh," she said, cutting him off quickly as she backed away.

"Stanford is going bald. And have you noticed? He walks like a duck?"

She opened her mouth to speak, but he interrupted.

"Were I you, I would not even mention Hadwin. He's rather amusing, but I fear his sense of humor may cause his death before he is able to father a—"

"Shhh!" she hissed.

"I fear tis true," he said.

"Shut up!" she ordered, staring at the door.

"What is it?" Dugald jerked toward the portal, his hand ready on his jeweled knife.

She stared at the door, her eyes wide and her body paralyzed. He was just about to ask again, but suddenly she grabbed his arm and shoved him toward the back wall. "Hide!"

"What?"

"It's my father!" she hissed.

Chapter 12

Shona propelled Dugald toward the window, her mind spinning. She could push him out. But no! Surely her father would hear his screams as he fell.

She spun wildly about, searching for a place to hide him. Behind the door—too risky. In her trunk—too full. In her bed!

Dear God, she must be insane, she thought, but there was no time to delay. With a shove she knocked him onto the mattress and leaped in beside him. Throwing her leg over his waist, she spread herself across the bed and yanked the blankets over them.

Beneath her Dugald lay perfectly still. She couldn't see his face, for the woolen covered it, but she could feel his breath on her arm.

Dear God, help me, she prayed, and closing her eyes, forced herself to breathe normally.

Footsteps echoed down the hall, drawing nearer and nearer until they finally paused. Her door squeaked open. Faded candlelight fell across her floor.

Shona twisted about, then propped herself on one hand, squinting against the light. "Da?" Her voice was raspy and uncertain, as if she'd just awakened. As if she hadn't just tossed a man in her bed and was even now draped over him like a blanket over a stallion's back.

"Aye." Roderic's tone was soft. "'Tis I."

"Did ye . . . did ye want something?" Like a swain beheaded and eviscerated perhaps?

"Nay. Nay, lass, I was just . . . making certain ye were safe." His tone was ultimately gentle tonight, reminding her of all the times he'd told her marvelous, outlandish stories to help her sleep.

Guilt swelled inside her, but truly, she had no wish to torment her father. In truth, she loved him and did not want to cause him any heartache, but things always seemed to happen to her. She didn't know why.

"Aye, Da, I am well."

She heard him sigh. "Go back to sleep, then."

He turned away. The door closed a few inches. She waited. He turned back.

"Shona?"

"Aye?"

"If I had to choose between a sweet daughter and ye . . . I would still have chosen ye."

The portal closed. The night went black. His footsteps, light and steady, strode away.

Silence reigned.

Below her, Dugald pulled the blanket from his head.

"He does not think I am sweet," she said, stunned by this revelation.

"Truly?"

Their faces were inches apart, and her breasts, she noticed, were pressed firmly against his chest with Dragonheart crushed between them.

"Truly. Me!"

"I am shocked."

She turned her head to glare at him. "Think on this, Dugald the Discourteous, which kind of maid would save a man she does not even like from her father's anger? A sweet maid or a sour maid?"

"A sweet maid?" he guessed.

"Aye," she said, and prepared to swing away from him, but suddenly she was caught in his eyes and found she could not move.

Time ceased. Reality faltered. There were only the

two of them, trapped in this strange situation, and she could not resist, could not hold back.

Against every rule she had ever been taught, she leaned forward. Her eyes fell closed. Her lips met his. Lightning forked through her. His arm circled her waist, crushing her to him, and suddenly she was straddling him and yanking his tunic upward. Their lips parted long enough for her to rip his shirt from his body, then they were kissing again, with her hands drinking him in. His chest was hard. His hands were like heaven, caressing, loving, drawing her against him.

Raw need ripped through them, forcing their hands, erasing their morals, their good sense.

She could not feel enough, could not be felt enough. Muscles bunched and strained. Passions ignited and soared.

From the next room, a boy coughed once.

Shona jerked to a halt.

Reality returned with a jolt. She gasped a small mew of dismay and launched herself from the bed to stare at Dugald, but he was already on his feet on the opposite side of the pallet.

They stared at each other like startled cats.

Shona moved her lips. No words came. She tried again.

"I didna mean to. I dunna know what's wrong with me. I'm usually . . . ."

"Sweet?" he guessed.

She scowled. "Ye think I am a brazen hussy," she said.

"I did not say that."

"Ye think I tricked ye into my bed."

"I—"

"Ye think I have no morals atall."

"I think if you do not lower your voice I will not live through the night," he said.

She glanced at the door and scowled, letting her emotions cool and her tone drop. "Was there really someone trying to climb the tower?"

He stared at her for a moment, then nodded.

"Was it ye?" she asked.

Even in the darkness she could see that he smiled. "Rest assured of one thing, Damsel Shona," he said, his tone low. "If I decide to scale the tower, you will see me at the window."

His husky tone called her to him, but she held herself back with careful control, making certain her own voice was haughty. "Indeed? I am very impressed, Dugald the Dizzy."

"If you were the prize I might reconsider. And that's Dugald the *Dragon*," he corrected.

"Such a grandiose name. But how do we know whether ye deserve it when ye refuse to exhibit your incredible prowess?"

"If proof is what ye want, lass, you should not have interrupted our play."

She turned, her breathing escalating a mite. "If that's what ye are so impressive at, I fear ye'll have to try the Lowland games. We are not so decadent this far north."

He watched her in silence, then stepped smoothly forward. "Tell me, Damsel, which do you think is more important, the ability to make a woman happy, or the ability to make a man miserable?"

"Miserable?"

"Aye. Miserable," he said, then touched her face and ever so slowly slid his knuckles down her cheek to her throat. "Or happy?"

She felt his fingers like a thousand sparks of emotion against her skin, burning gently into her soul. She swallowed hard and forced herself to speak. "I fear ye overestimate yourself, Sir."

"Do I?" he whispered. "I come from a place known for its sensual delights." His fingers continued along her collarbone, pressing her gown away so that she shivered at his touch.

Fire was eating slowly at her soul. Her head was filled with the scent of his skin, the feel of his fingers against her shoulder.

"I could give you that delight," he whispered, and cupped his hand gently over her breast.

She jerked away, breathing hard. "There's more to life than . . ." She paused, searching for words, trying to rid her mind of the lurid images he conjured up. "Than . . . that."

"Is there?" She both feared and hoped he would step closer. But he did not. "And what is more important, Damsel?"

For the life of her she could not remember. Couldn't even imagine, and now he did step forward.

"Morality!" She threw the word out like a spear. "Goodness. Strength. The ability to protect those weaker than yourself."

He scowled. "So you think these foolish games prove any of these things?"

She had no idea what she thought. In fact, it may be that her brain had been fried to a wafer by his mere nearness. "Aye," she said.

"Then in order to prove my worth to you, I would have to compete?"

There were several inches between them. Still, she could already feel his unnatural pull on her, as if she were being dragged forth by the chain around her neck. "Nay," she said, desperately trying to drive back his allure. "Ye would have to win."

Absolute silence filled the room, then he nodded once and stepped toward the door. "Then I shall win," he said.

The day dawned cloudy and cool. The hall was filled with the sound of pipes and conversation. A half dozen men flirted with Shona. She graciously flirted back. Hadwin gave her a garland of wildflowers for her hair, and Stanford said she was fairer than any blossom. But though she tried to enjoy the flirtations, her mind turned relentlessly to Dugald.

He sat across the hall near her cousin, Mavis, who giggled and pouted at regular intervals.

They deserved each other, she thought heatedly. For Mavis was nearly as conceited as Dugald. And what did he have to be so vain about? True, his features were as regal as a marble statue's, his eyes unearthly entrancing, and his kiss . . .

She felt her face redden at the memory of his kiss. In truth, he was probably no great talent at kissing; she was just inexperienced. If she were wise, she would test other ponds—just for comparison's sake.

Kelvin scampered up, interrupting her shameful thoughts. "Lady Shona." His smile was gap-toothed, his hair messed, and when he bowed to her he looked like nothing more than a tiny mischievous lord. "Twould be my pleasure to see ye to the game field. They're about to begin the dancing."

She smiled, grateful for the interruption. "And are ye competing, Kelvin?"

"Nay. I'm saving my talents for the swordsmanship."

"Are ye, now?"

"Aye." His eyes lit up even more. "If I win, will ye marry me?"

She laughed, then leaned toward him and murmured. "I believe we've already discussed that."

"Aye," he said, "but—"

"Lady Shona," Stanford interrupted. "Might I escort ye to the green?"

She offered him a smile, but she could not help but notice that his feet did turn out rather like a water fowl's.

God's wrath, she reprimanded herself. She wasn't planning on choosing her husband because of the shape of his feet. Still . . .

"I am sorry," she said, "but I promised Kelvin."

"Beaten out by a lad?" Hadwin asked, stepping up and grinning around his swollen lip.

"If ye care to keep your teeth, I would suggest ye shut your maw," Stanford warned.

"Better to lose my teeth than my hair," Hadwin said, nodding to Stanford's receding hairline.

"Better my hair than—"

"Gentlemen," Shona said, "have I mentioned how I love to watch the Highland Fling?"

"Nay."

"Nay." They turned simultaneously toward her.

"Tis true. They are giving a dagger to the best dancer. Tis a lovely blade."

"I will win it for ye, Lady," Stanford vowed solemnly.

"Consider it a gift from me," Hadwin countered.

She smiled at each of them in turn. "Ye'd best go practice," she said, and laid her hand on Kelvin's bent arm.

The pair bowed and rushed off.

Kelvin laughed. "Promise me ye will not marry either of *those* two."

"Marry them?" She sighed. "I feel rather like spanking them."

He laughed, then sobered. "And what of *him*?" he asked softly.

She followed his gaze. "William of Atberry?" she asked, nodding to the older lord as they passed.

"Aye."

"I dunna know."

The lad was silent. They had crossed the bailey and were heading toward the bridge.

"And what of me when ye wed?" he asked finally.

The bridge echoed a deep resonance beneath their feet.

Shona looked down into the lad's solemn, dirt-streaked face. The crowd tromped on. Laughter wafted back to them, but she had no desire to join in the merriment. Instead, she turned the lad aside, taking a faded trail that led off to the left. Lifting her skirts, she skidded down the bank of the Gael Burn and drew Kelvin to a halt beside the babbling water.

A log lay half immersed. Shona took a seat there, then patted a spot to her right. Kelvin joined her.

"What do ye think will happen when I wed?" she asked.

"I think ye will leave me," he said simply.

Her heart ached for him. He had seen far too much loss in his short life. "Have I not proved my loyalty to ye yet?" she asked.

He glanced away. "There have been others who proclaimed their love for me."

"I tell ye this now," she said. "For as long as I live there will be a place for ye at my side."

"Truly?" He lifted his small face to gaze at her.

"Truly."

His expression was tense, but finally it relaxed a mite and he shrugged. "It does not matter, really," he said, standing up on the log. "I can care for myself."

He wobbled a little, but his bare feet finally took root on the crumbling bark. Spreading his arms wide, he paced along the length of the log.

"It could well be that some day I will have to take care of *ye*," he said.

"Ye think so?" she asked, slipping out of her shoes.

He grinned. "I would bet all I have on it."

She snorted and stepping up on the log, took two shaky steps toward him. "And why is that?"

He shrugged. "Ye are only a maid."

Glancing up at him, Shona sighed. "'Tis too true," she agreed. But suddenly the bark beneath her feet began to give way. She slipped sideways with a shriek of dismay.

Kelvin reached for her. Eyes wide, she caught hold of his hand, but instead of trying to hold herself up, she yanked him off his feet.

He hit the water in a geyser of silvery spray. "Help! Help!"

"Help?" she said, laughing, with her toes curled against the log's smooth truck. "But I am only a maid."

"Shona!" His arms windmilled.

"Say ye need the help of a maid."

He was being swept downstream.

"Aye. I need ye!"

She canted her head in thought, waiting a few seconds. The current took him farther along. "All right, then," she said, "Put your feet down."

"I canna reach the bottom!"

"Trust me," she called.

"Shona!" he gasped, but suddenly his head went under. One hand snaked into the air. But in an instant he rose from the depths like Neptune on dry land.

He was sputtering like a fish, with his hair streaming across his face and his clothes hanging heavy against his shoulders. "Ye pulled me in!" he gasped, affronted. "*Me!*"

She forced a smile, though in truth she had been momentarily worried that the river bottom had somehow changed since the time she had waded there. "A *maid* tossed ye in, lad," she said. "And it could well be that a *maid* will be your undoing, if ye dunna learn to show some respect. Ye'd be wise not to forget it."

Kelvin scowled as he pushed the hair from his eyes. "Couldna ye have taught me a lesson without getting me soaked?" he asked.

"Nay, lad."

Shona turned toward the sound of Dugald's voice. He stood grinning from the bank. He wore rich brown hose, a white tunic, and a russet doublet that was elaborately slashed and puffed. He should have looked ridiculous. She quite resented it that he didn't.

"Damsel Shona most enjoys teaching lessons and giving dousings at the same time."

Shona scowled at him. "And if Damsel Shona is seen with Dugald the Debaucher, her father will have his head."

Dugald laughed, then bowed. "I will leave you, then . . . with my head intact," he said. "It looks as if the two of you will have to return to the keep for dry garments." He sighed. "And I was so hoping you would watch me dance. Now I will be forced to prove my grandness in another way.''

Lifting her skirts, Shona traipsed along the log to step onto the bank. ''Dunna bother,'' she said.

''Oh, but I insist,'' he countered, and leaning closer, he whispered. ''Let us say tonight, in your chambers.''

Chapter 13

B y the time Kelvin had changed clothes and they had reached the green, the Highland fling had been danced, and the dagger was being presented to Hadwin.

Stanford was looking grumpy, and Dugald, when Shona glanced at him, was watching her. She turned quickly away. What was wrong with the man? Surely he had been joking when he mentioned meeting in her chambers.

She glanced toward him again, but he was gone. She scowled, though God knew the farther away he went, the happier she would be.

"Nay," someone murmured.

Shona turned abruptly only to find Dugald standing only inches behind her, his chest all but pressed against her back.

"Nay what?" she asked, finding her breath with some difficulty.

"Nay, I do not think you should accept the dagger from him."

"I didna know I asked your opinion."

"In truth, you did not," he said. "But I assumed you were too shy to trouble me."

"How astute ye are."

"'Tis true. In fact, the Duchess of Windway was going to call me Dugald the astute," he murmured, his gaze still on Hadwin. "But she thought 'the Darling' better suited me."

"Are ye certain it was not 'the Dolt'?"

He smiled into her eyes. "Quite certain."

"Ye would be," she said, then, "be gone before my father sees ye."

"Truly, Shona, I do not think you should accept Hadwin's winnings. Twould not be seemly."

She narrowed her eyes at him. "And may I ask why?"

He chuckled softly. "Tis quite obvious. That is to say, surely twould not be right to encourage another man's hopes, knowing I have stolen your heart."

"Stolen my—"

"After all," he interrupted, leaning closer. "I assume you do not share a bed with every man you meet."

She stared at him in silent shock.

"Do you?" he asked.

"Tis hardly *your* affair who—"

"Oh. Tsk," he said, bowing slightly. "I wish I could stay and chat, but I am told the archery contest is next and I must go win it."

She felt her back stiffen. "Tis that simple, is it?"

"Of course."

"Are ye not afraid ye will muss your hair?"

He grinned at her like an evil satyr. "I've been told I look quite adorable with my hair mussed."

"The queen of France, I suppose."

"Nay, twas the baroness de Lindon."

"Of course."

"The point is, lass, you should not accept a gift from any but your heart's true desire."

"Which would be . . ."

"Me." He smiled again.

"And mayhap tis ye whom I will not take a gift from," she said.

He grinned. "Truly? Then mayhap I should give it to your cousin."

She opened her mouth to berate him, but with a grin and a bow, he turned away.

Shona stared after him.

"Oh," he said, turning back. "I need a scrap of cloth to bind about my arrow. Would you like to give me a piece from your sleeve?"

"I'd like to give ye a punch in the—" she began, but he turned away with a chuckle.

"Do not trouble yourself," he said. "I will ask Mavis for one of her ribbons."

Shona watched him go. She would love to enter the contest herself and show Dugald Kinnaird some humility. Or better yet, perhaps Dugald Kinnaird could be the target. They could tie him to a tree and—

"Lady Shona," Hadwin said, bounding up to her. "Twould be an honor if ye would accept this gift from me."

A disconcerting chuckle drifted toward her. She glanced irritably in Dugald's direction, but he failed to turn around. Still, she knew it was he, and every hair on the back of her neck stood on end.

"Lady," Hadwin said.

"Oh." She brought herself back to the present. "Ye are too kind. Surely ye should keep such a wondrous—"

"Nay," he interrupted. "I would that ye have it."

That chuckle again, as if it were right in her ear. She mentally ground her teeth.

"Tis ever so kind of ye, Hadwin," she said, accepting the knife. "Thank ye."

"And may I escort ye to the archery grounds?"

"Twould be an honor," she said, and hoped Dugald would turn around at that second and die of jealousy. Unfortunately, he did not turn around at all.

Not far away, a pair of narrow carts sat upon a small green knoll. A round target stuffed with hay and covered in cloth hung on each cart, and upon the center of the shields, circles were marked with black paint.

The prospective archers were stringing their bows. Someone played a lute not far away. The whimsical melody filled the space between the grove of rowans and the next verdant hill. Soon a woman's voice was added to the music.

Hadwin bowed and left to join the other competitors. Shona scanned the crowd. There were perhaps two dozen prospective archers, snapping their strings and testing their supple weapons.

Her own fingers itched as she watched them. There was something exhilarating about the smooth feel of a fine oaken bow in her hands, something that she desired now.

"Ye said ye had no wish to shame them, lass."

She turned at the sound of her father's voice. "Whatever do ye mean?"

"Ye know exactly what I mean, so dunna bother to look the innocent."

She tried to look offended instead. "I am innocent," she grumbled. "And I am sweet."

He laughed. "Then rid yourself of the gleam in your eye afore ye frighten someone."

She scowled. "It seems to me, if they are afraid of competition they shouldn't be stringing their bows."

"Shona," he said, his tone warning. "Do ye wish to die unwed?"

She thought about it, but apparently she took too much time, for in a moment he urged her again.

"Shona?"

"Nay I dunna," she said grumpily.

"Then behave yourself. Just because I taught ye the skills of a man does not mean ye dunna need a man."

"Then I would have a man who wouldna be afraid of a woman who can shoot an arrow."

"We men are a tender lot, daughter mine," he said. "Best not to bruise our frail opinions of ourselves. We like to think we are quite superior, in raw strength if naught else. Ye dunna wish to scare them off."

"But ye weren't scared," she said. "And ye were up against a woman who abducted ye at knifepoint and threatened to skewer ye to a tree."

"Aye well." He sighed as he put his arm about her and turned her toward a pleasant spot beneath a bent hazel tree. "If the truth be told, I am a better man than most, Shona."

"Or as Mother would say—"

"Shush, Daughter," Roderic said. "Watch the show and prepare to look impressed."

She all but grunted.

The archers lined up, several per target. The arrows bore tiny scraps of cloth of varying colors. The competitors lifted their weapons shoulder high. Despite everything, Shona found she was holding her breath.

"Be ready," called Bullock, who officiated again.

The archers drew back on their strings. The crowd fell silent.

"Let fly," yelled Bullock.

The arrows hissed like swarming locust toward the targets. There was a barrage of twangs as some struck home, some soared into the distance.

Bullock stepped forward to check the results of the target nearest himself. "The three arrows closest to the mark are the gray." He paused. There was a moment of silence before a young lad, not past his sixteenth year, raised his arm in triumph. "Gilmour of Lairg," Bullock called.

The crowd cheered.

Bullock held up the next arrow. "The red." Bullock grinned. "Me own son, Michael."

Shona smiled and cheered, feeling the joy of the moment, despite herself.

"And the green," Bullock called, lifting the last arrow. Dugald raised his arm.

Shona fell silent, and in that moment Dugald glanced at her, his devilish eyes laughing.

From across the field, another official called the three top archers. But Shona failed to notice their names. The targets were moved back. Only the six best archers shot this time. Again Dugald's arrow soared skyward only to arch like a magical rainbow and land with sickening precision in the bull's eye.

Shona watched as he stepped forward to accept his award. Her fingers curled into fists. She pursed her lips. She had told her father she would not compete, and she would not. She would not.

Dugald lifted the brooch he had won and turned toward Mavis.

And Shona stepped forward, pulled against her will. Her mind demanded she remain silent, but her lips were already moving. "It hardly seems right to let this brooch leave Dun Ard," she called.

Dugald turned toward her, his brows raised. She had no time to notice the rest of the crowd that must be staring at her as if she'd lost her mind, which, in fact, might be the case.

"Are ye thinking of wrestling the lad for it?" Bullock asked, leaning toward her.

Shona didn't bother glaring at him. He would only laugh anyway, for he knew her too well. Instead, she gave him a smile that said she was just a girl, fragile, bonny, harmless. "Of course not. But mayhap there are others who would have liked to enter." Beside her, she felt her father's glower.

"Then they should have been here, lass," Bullock said.

"Aye." She tried the smile again. "But surely Dugald of Kinnaird is not scared of a bit of competition. After all, he canna be called 'the Dragon' for nothing."

She dared not look at her father. But suddenly Dugald stepped forward. He held the brooch in one hand. There was the slightest smile on his face and a quicksilver spark of mischief in his eyes.

"If you are so fond of the brooch, Mistress Shona, I would give it to you. There is no need for you to fret."

"I am not fretting." She returned his smile, upping his brilliance. "But I am certain a man with your . . . vanity . . . would have no wish to win unless he knew he had beaten all comers."

He glanced about him, looking innocent. ''Is there, mayhap, some other man who would challenge me?''

She gritted a smile at him. ''Not a man, but a woman.''

His brows rose again, but in that moment she realized he was not the least bit surprised. He bowed, still smiling and lifted his bow toward her. But suddenly Hadwin rushed forward, his own weapon strung and ready.

''Please, Lady, twould be my pleasure if ye would use mine.''

Out of the corner of her eye she saw Stanford clench his fists, but she was beyond worrying if the two of them beat each other senseless over this new silliness. Instead, she took the bow and beamed at the bearer before turning back toward Dugald.

''Surely ye dunna mind being bested by a woman,'' she said.

''That depends what arena we speak of,'' he returned softly.

''Archery.''

''Ahh.'' He seemed to be attempting to stifle a grin. ''I would not mind, of course. But I do not think it can be done.''

''Really?'' Every instinct in her, female and otherwise, perked up. ''Then ye willna object if I try.''

''But I have already been awarded the brooch,'' he said quietly. ''What would I receive if I win this contest?''

Their gazes clashed. The crowd receded in her mind. ''What would ye like?'' she murmured.

They seemed very close suddenly, and the day very warm. His lips were full, quirked upward in that irritatingly male half smile, and his eyes an unearthly blue that never failed to steal her breath.

''What would ye like?'' she asked again, and against all her better judgment, she was pulled closer.

They almost touched. She could taste his kiss like forbidden wine as she was drawn under his spell.

''Your amulet,'' he said.

She pulled back with a jerk. Her hand flew to the chain from which Dragonheart was suspended. "Ye jest."

He shrugged, grinning again. "It seems a fair wager. Unless ye fear losing."

"I dunna."

"Then you agree?"

She paused. She would have to be a fool to make such a bet. Liam had warned her to keep the amulet safe. Twas special, he had said. Precious.

"Mayhap there is something else you would not mind parting with. Something more personal?" he asked.

His meaning was clear, for in his eyes, the humor had suddenly been replaced by a more intimate emotion.

Shona gripped the chain harder. Dragonheart slipped into her hand. It felt warm, as if it pulsed with life. She should set this Dugald fellow back on his heels, she knew. She should give him a slap sound enough to echo in his empty brain—if not physically, at least verbally. But she could not come up with a single scathing remark. "The amulet against the brooch, then," she said.

The spell was broken. He moved back a step and nodded. "Two shots," he said. "The highest score wins, and you go first."

She nodded as she let the dragon drop between her breasts. Hadwin's bow felt strange in her hand, but she lifted it now, weighing it, assessing its qualities. It was somewhat heavier than her own, perhaps six feet long, and well strung.

She sensed Roderic's approach beside her, but she dared not turn toward him. Later, she would accept his scolding. Now she must concentrate.

Setting the arrow to the bow, she lifted it and tested the tension of the string. It was nicely balanced. She sited along the feathered shaft. The crowd fell quiet, and suddenly it seemed to Shona that all the world had receded. As if she were the arrow itself, as if she could fly sure as the wind to her target.

She drew back the string and loosed the missile. It

arched into the air like a bird in flight, then hung in the clouds for an eternity. But not for an instant did she doubt its destination.

In a heartbeat it had severed the outer rim of the bull's eye.

The crowd erupted with applause.

She turned to accept their accolades, but when she looked at Dugald, he only nodded and gave her the briefest edge of a grin, as if he knew some secret she was not privy to. Her confidence slipped a hair's breadth.

Dugald stepped into place. Standing sideways, he quickly bent his bow and loosed his arrow. It flew like a falling hawk to pierce the target directly adjacent to Shona's hit.

Shona looked from the target at Dugald and found that he was already staring at her, as if he had not even bothered to see where his arrow landed.

Doubt knotted her stomach. But surely she could not turn back now.

She scowled as she fitted another arrow in her bow. She would not lose, she told herself, and carefully forced her thoughts away from Dugald's otherworldly eyes and ungodly confidence.

The daughter of the Flame and the Rogue could not lose. She was born for this.

Her fingers moved of their own accord, setting the arrow to the string, bending the bow. There was a moment of concentrated delay, and then the arrow sped away. Dragonheart pulsed against her chest, seeming to purr as the bull's eye dragged the arrow into its center.

Joy burst in Shona's chest. The crowd cheered. Shona turned toward them with a smile. From the corner of her eye, she saw her father watch her. His expression was less than jovial. She turned quickly away and waved to Kelvin, who was jumping up and down in his glee. Hadwin was grinning, Stanford was staring with an open mouth, William was watching in silence. Not far away, Sara and Rachel raised their arms in unified support.

There was no way now for Dugald to win unless he

were to split her arrow with his own, and that only happened in minstrels' tales.

She turned toward Dugald, more than ready to accept his defeat, but when she saw him her grin froze on her face. Not a shadow of a doubt shone in his expression, not a breath of uncertainty. Their gazes met and fused. Time halted.

But finally he turned away, lifting his bow as he did so.

Heaven's wrath, he was going to do it! He was going to win. Shona was suddenly certain of it. Panic welled up in her. If the truth be known, she was a terrible loser.

She watched him site along the arrow's shaft, watched him draw back his string, and suddenly her fingers went cold.

Hadwin's borrowed arrow fell from her hands. Not thinking, she bent to retrieve it.

Dugald let his arrow fly just as Shona reached for hers. From the corner of his eye, Dugald saw her bend, saw Dragonheart flash in the sunlight, saw her breasts swell more fully into view. And in that moment all was forgotten but the sharp pull of her allure. His arrow could pierce the moon for all he cared.

Shona straightened. So close was she that he could see a pulse beating in her throat, could smell the fragrance of her skin, feel the thrill of her awareness of him.

Regardless of whether she loved him or hated him, she was drawn to him with that same rabid longing he felt.

"Lady Shona wins by an auburn hair!" Bullock called.

Dugald snapped his attention back to the business at hand. Their arrows were touching, coupled like fervent lovers, lying side by side and—

Mother of God! What was wrong with him? It was not a good sign that he was imbuing the arrows with sexual attributes.

Pulling his thoughts together, he realized the crowd

was chattering, extoling Shona's abilities. He turned toward her and extended his hand, ready to concede his loss, but the soft swell of her breasts was still visible and between them, resting like a smug lizard, the dragon winked at him. His breath stopped in his throat.

"Twas a good match," she said and slipped her hand into his. The physical contact nearly knocked him off his feet, so powerful was the attraction that sizzled between them.

He fought her allure, but there was no hope. "I would have another bout," he murmured, stepping closer, pulled near by invisible strings.

Memories flashed between them—a moon-kissed night, smooth skin, hot kisses, pulsing . . .

She ripped her hand from his. Their melded thoughts were torn asunder. She wiped her palms against the skirt of her gown.

"Are ye saying twas not a fair match?" she asked, her tone panicked, fear bright in her eyes.

He found his equilibrium with some difficulty, forced himself to relax a mite, and smiled. God in heaven, she was hypnotic. And if he had the brains of a water beetle he would leave before it was too late. But he couldn't. In fact, everything in him scrambled for some way to keep her close.

"It seems rather strange that you felt the need to bend down just as I loosed my arrow," he said.

She took a deep breath as if trying to steady her own thoughts. "Is Dugald the Dread so easily distracted, then?" she asked, her tone husky.

Every nerve in him thrummed with desire. There was something about her blatant sense of self, her lust for life, that stirred him.

"Damsel Shona," he said, softly caressing her with the words. "You could distract a field stone, and you well know it."

She offered him the corner of a smile, and even with that meager expression the sun was dimmed by comparison. "Mayhap I could," she murmured, then glanced at the crowd that rushed forward to congratulate her. "But I would not have to try," she added, and was swallowed up by a mob of swains.

Chapter 14

⟨ornament⟩

The hall was crowded and noisy at the evening meal. Someone called for a song. Hadwin yelled for Shona to sing, but Lachlan, one of her five brothers, laughed out loud. If they wanted stag for dinner they could call on his sister, he said. But if they wanted a musician, they would be wise to ask a maid who was not born with an arrow clamped between her teeth.

The hall burst into laughter, and Shona did not bother to hide her smile. Far be it from her to be insulted by her own abilities.

Finally Sara was begged forward. Her voice, sweet and melodious as that of a song thrush's, lifted in a Scottish ballad as ancient as time. It filled the space, shushing the noises, soothing the nerves, binding the assemblage in blissful harmony, if only for a short span of time.

So powerful was her song, that it took several moments for the crowd to realize the music was ended. But finally the company shook itself from its trance, cheered, and called for more.

"Still she sings like an angel," Shona murmured.

"Aye. *She* is sweet," Roderic said.

Shona turned to her father who sat to her right. Twas no great difficulty to tell when he was truly angry and when he only thought he should be. When he was angry, she wanted nothing more than to hide behind the tapestries. When he merely felt it was his fatherly duty to be upset she was wont to tease him until he laughed.

Bethia had once said there was a special pit in the hereafter set aside for lasses who tormented their fathers so. Shona sincerely hoped she was wrong, since she doubted it was anywhere she'd care to visit much less spend eternity.

"Father," she said softly, "I hope the archery tournament didna worry ye."

He raised a brow at her. "Worry me? Why should it?"

She smiled with all the brilliance she could muster. Which, she knew, was just short of the sun's.

"Just because I bested the best of the men, does not necessarily mean I could best ye also."

He was silent for a moment, his gaze steady on hers. "So ye think ye have surpassed your sire's skill?"

"Nay. I just said I have not . . . not on your good days."

"My good days?" He reared back.

"Well, there was that contest at Sara's wedding. But ye were not at your best. What was your excuse? Ye were distracted, I think."

"I've a question for ye, Daughter," he said, leaning slightly closer.

"Aye?"

"Might ye think ye be too old for me to take ye over my knee."

She managed to hold back her laughter, though if the truth be told, he had never yet, in more than two score years of mishaps, taken her over his knee. "Why, Father, I was just trying to make ye feel better. I probably could not best ye if ye were at your prime."

He snorted, but his eyes were gleaming with laughter. "Tell me, Daughter mine, is there a reason for your baiting, or have ye merely run out of swains to torment?"

She dabbed daintily at her mouth with a napkin. "I am running a bit low just now."

"No flies whose wings ye could pull off?"

Despite her act, she laughed, then glanced at her trencher and fiddled with her knife. "I wanted to beg your forgiveness, Father."

He stared at her. "In truth, ye've always had a strange way of going about things, lass."

"I did not mean to enter the contest. Twas just—"

"What?"

"That Dugald!"

"The Dragon?"

"The Difficult."

"Your mother seems to think him quite a bonny lad."

"So does he."

"But not ye?"

She remained silent for a moment, then, "I just couldna bear to let him win so easily. Are ye angry with me?"

He sighed. "Aye. I may never forgive ye."

She smiled at his long-suffering tone. "Truly, I am sorry if I embarrassed ye."

He watched her in silence, and for just a moment his eyes seemed unusually bright. "Ye are what we have made ye, lass," he said softly. "Part of your mother and part of myself. Hardly am I embarrassed by that."

"Even though I am a better archer?"

He lowered his brows. "Ye'd best behave, daughter mine, afore I tell your mother ye are baiting an old man."

She laughed aloud, then leaned sideways to respond, but just then her thoughts were interrupted.

"Lady Shona."

She caught her breath and turned toward the speaker, but it was not Dugald who stood at her elbow. "William," she greeted him.

"I have come to ask if ye might walk with me for a short spell."

She glanced toward Roderic on her right. "Father?" she asked sweetly. "What say ye?"

"So now ye act all sweetness?" he said, his tone wry.

She gave him a glance to keep him quiet. It was one thing to embarrass each other in private; in public was quite another.

He laughed, having recouped a bit of his own dignity. "Go with him. Get wed, have a dozen bairns," he murmured. "And may each of them torment ye as ye do me."

She rose quickly to her feet, eager to lead William away, lest her father shed any more light on her true temperament.

Outside, the gloaming was soft and lingering as they walked to the mill. Swans glided on the water just beyond the paddle wheels, their graceful necks delicately arched and reflected in the dark water.

"Tis a bonny spot ye have here at Dun Ard," William said.

"Aye." Shona absently picked a sprig of lavender that grew beside the pond. "I miss it greatly when I am away."

There was silence for a spell. "Is that why ye have waited to marry, because ye would miss this place?"

She smiled as she watched two cygnets fight over an aquatic weed. "Father says I am still here because he is not so cruel as to wish me on another man."

William laughed. Despite the size of his nose, he had a nice smile. "I think, instead, your father cannot bear to let ye go."

She said nothing, but turned away to wander toward the stable. William followed.

"That is how I would feel."

She glanced at him. Silence followed.

"But if I were your husband, I would not keep you from your father's house if ever ye wished to return."

"Are ye saying ye wish to marry me?" she asked.

He laughed again. The sound was pleasant. "I believe I said that long ago. But ye were wild and undisciplined then, so I have been careful not to rush ye."

He probably wouldn't be happy to learn she had left

her breeches at the burn only a few days before, Shona thought.

"But now . . . seeing you thus . . ." He shrugged. "Ye've grown into a bonny young woman. Mayhap I should speak to your sire again, but strangely it seems as if the decision is yours."

"Mayhap we are odd here at Dun Ard," Shona said, still wandering past the stable toward the front gate. "Mayhap too strange for someone of your standing."

"Of my standing." He looked surprised. "I am just a man like any other."

"Nay," she said. "Ye are the king's own cousin."

"A man just the same, with a humble title and modest holdings."

"I have not heard Atberry House called modest before."

"Mayhap ye have not compared it to Stirling Castle." He broke off a twig from the elm they passed under. The noise sounded abrupt in the evening air, but when she glanced up, he smiled at her.

She watched him. This marriage business was a tricky thing. William seemed a good man, but sometimes when she was with him she felt as if he were slightly disapproving of her but too polite to say so.

"Is that what ye want?" she asked. "To call Stirling Castle home?"

He chuckled. "Are ye asking if I wish to become king?"

"Ye are closer to the throne than most," she said. "I suspect a case could be made for your suit, if ye wished to press the issue."

"Me, as king?" he asked, sounding startled. "I think ye have an even wilder imagination than I suspected."

"Ye've never considered it?" she asked.

"I am but the thirdborn son of the brother of James IV. There is a great chasm of difference between myself and the kingship."

They walked on in silence toward the bailey.

"Is that what *you* wish for, Lady Shona?" He stopped

beside the well. In the bailey, some distance away, she heard the sound of steel against steel as two men sparred. "Do ye wish for a man with great ambitions?" he asked.

The light slowly faded as she watched him. "Indeed, I dunna know what I want," she said finally, and sighed as she turned toward the keep.

"And what if I said ye could be queen?"

"What?" she asked, turning back in surprise.

He was silent, but in a moment he chuckled. "I was but dreaming," he said. "Ye would make a bonny queen. Yet even though I cannot give ye a crown, I would have ye for my wife."

His voice was so earnest, and twould make her parents happy, she thought.

"I know I am not the most exciting man in Scotland, but I could help you in your struggle for maturity."

She almost scowled at him. "I . . ." She shrugged, feeling guilty and at a loss. "I am not ready for such a decision," she said.

Some emotion sparked in his eye, and she welcomed it, almost hoping he would rail at her rather than remain so stoic.

But in a moment the light was gone. "Might I carry some hope that you will decide in my favor?" he asked. "Would you consider giving me some small token of your esteem?"

"I—I dunna know . . ."

"We would make a fine pair. My . . ." He shrugged modestly. "My steadiness united with your . . . fire." His gaze dropped to the chain that held Dragonheart. "The dragon amulet reminds me of you. All fierce passion and bright beauty." He paused.

"What?"

"I would cherish it always as a reminder of your beauty," he said.

"Ye wish to have Dragonheart?" she asked, pulling it into her hand.

"It has a name?"

She laughed as she glanced at the amulet. "I fear it does. Tis silly, I'm certain."

"It would not seem silly to me."

She glanced up at him. Surely it would do no harm to give it to him. After all, she would probably be his bride before long if her father had his way. But the dragon suddenly felt cold in her palm, as if it were drawing into itself. And somehow she could not bear to hand it to another.

"I am sorry, William. But this amulet has special significance to me."

He paused a moment. "Some other small token, then?" he asked, touching her hand.

She waited for a spark of something to flash through her, but nothing did. No lightning. No fire, just a faint pain at the back of her neck.

"Shona?"

"Oh. Certainly," she said, and pulling her hand away, lifted the end of her girdle. In a moment, she had undone a tassel and handed it to him.

He took it in his right hand and lifted it to his lips. "I shall cherish it always."

"Ye flatter me," she said, but just then the lad in the bailey laughed, snaring her thoughts.

"Not at all. Tis I who am flattered," William protested.

From across the yard, steel clashed again, drawing Shona's attention away. The combatants in the bailey parried. The man lunged. The boy turned and suddenly she saw the lad's face.

"Kelvin!" she shrieked and bolted toward the pair.

The man turned at the sound of her voice. She recognized him as Dugald at the same instant that Kelvin lunged.

Dugald hissed in pain as the boy's sword sliced his arm.

"Kelvin!" Shona gasped, jolting to a halt. "What have ye done?"

The boy stumbled back, his face pale. "I was . . . I

was but . . .'' He looked as if he might cry.

"Tis my fault," Dugald said. His tone was level, but when he drew his right hand away from his arm, his fingers were red with blood. "He heard my wish to sharpen my skills with a sword before the contest tomorrow and offered to parry with me."

"He is only a lad," Shona said.

"Aye, but I am an exceptionally poor swordsman," Dugald said and grinned.

Shona felt sick to her stomach. She should have told Kelvin to keep away from Dugald, for she knew nothing of the man's true character. What if the boy had been wounded instead of the man?

"Where did ye learn to fence, lad?" Dugald asked.

"My—"

"I will see ye to your bed," Shona interrupted.

Both man and boy turned toward her.

"Truly?" Dugald asked.

She scowled at him. Her stomach settled a little. All was well. Nothing irreparable had happened.

"I was talking to the child," she said.

"Oh."

"You are wounded," William said, just arriving.

Dugald glanced at his arm again. "My pride more than anything, I fear." He scowled, "And my favorite silk tunic."

"The lad is an excellent swordsman for one so young. Where did he learn?" William asked.

"I'm sure I have no idea," Shona said quickly. "Go up to your room, Kelvin."

He looked up at her, his eyes wide. "I am sorry, Lady," he murmured.

She resisted gathering him into her arms. "I think tis not me to whom ye should apologize."

Kelvin turned toward Dugald. "My apologies," he said softly. "I did not mean to wound ye."

Dugald nodded at the lad. "They say there is nothing like a little blood to teach a lesson."

"What happened here?"

"Rachel." Shona turned to her cousin, feeling more relief than seemed practical. "Dugald has been wounded."

Rachel's amethyst gaze flitted from boy to man and back.

"Did I not hear the lad was raised on the streets of Edinburgh? How could he learn swordsmanship?" William persisted.

"Ye'd best put Kelvin to bed," Rachel said.

"Aye." Relief flooded Shona as she turned toward the boy. Rachel had always been good at cleaning up her messes.

"I'll see to Dugald's wound," Rachel added.

Shona stopped in her tracks.

"Tis little more than a scratch," Dugald said.

"Aye, just a scratch," Shona echoed.

All eyes turned to her. What the hell was wrong with her? She remained immobilized with her hand on Kelvin's shoulder.

"Ahh . . . Boden's old leg wound is bedeviling him," Shona lied, knowing she was a fool, but not quite able to leave Dugald to Rachel's tender touch.

"Sara's Boden asked for me?" Rachel questioned.

"Nay." Shona cleared her throat. "Nay. But ye know how he is. Tis like him to suffer in silence." Twas a foolish thing to say, for Boden was wont to be quite vociferous about his injuries.

Rachel stared at her. Her eyes were the eeriest things. They could look right through a person to her soul. And hardly had Shona found a way to prevent the penetration.

"Then I'd best seek him out," Rachel said, and stepped forward. "Would it be too much if I saw Dugald to the infirmary?" Her voice was soft, the words meant for Shona's ears alone.

Shona felt herself blush and nearly squirmed beneath Rachel's rapt attention. "Tis not what ye think, cousin," she murmured.

"Truly?" Rachel asked. Her brows lifted and her lips

twitched. "Then ye will have to tell me what it is."

"Dugald," she said, turning back toward the men, "if ye will follow me, I will show ye to the infirmary."

"Tis not necessary, I assure ye."

"I assure ye it is," she countered, looking back at Shona. "For I canna imagine my cousin with a one-armed lover."

"What?" Dugald said.

Rachel turned back, her expression angelic. "Tis dark out here. I said, I canna see well, like my cousin whom I love so."

Shona's face burned.

"That's not what she said," Kelvin countered.

Shona tightened her grip on the lad's shoulder and leaned near to his ear. "Nay, but if ye dunna want another drenching, ye will pretend it was," she said, and marched him up to his room.

Chapter 15

Dugald glanced up from his spot on the pallet. Shona stood like a scarlet angel in the doorway of the infirmary. Her hair was loose and flowed about her shoulders in gossamer waves. The light from the sconce set it aglow like crimson flames. Her hands, slim and pale, were clasped before her. She wore the same gown as before, and the high portions of her breasts looked no less enticing, no less alluring. But it was her eyes that drew him in. They were typically wide, tremendously green. An unwary man could get lost in those eyes.

Luckily, he was not unwary. He was trained to withstand every temptation, to overcome any impediment that stood in his way. Still, he would feel more secure if he had at least kept his tunic and doublet on. For without them he lost a bit more of his carefully groomed veneer.

He pulled his gaze away from her with a determined effort and focused on his wound. It was slight, perhaps an inch long, and not deep. It seemed a safe thing to concentrate on until she was gone. Of course, it would have been safer still if he hadn't gotten himself wounded. But after his foolishness at archery, he felt a need to reestablish himself as inept, accomplished at nothing but seducing women.

Mother of God, he should never have become involved in this mission. He should have stayed on Isle Fois, where there were no flame-haired vixens to disrupt his peace. But if he were foolish enough to agree with Tremayne's plans, at least he could have done the job without calling attention to himself, without acting the fool. What had come over him? he wondered. But one glance at Shona reminded him. *She* had come over him. And suddenly he could no longer bear for her to think him entirely incompetent—especially in a field where she excelled.

"Your cousin Rachel washed and treated my arm," he said, searching for some conversation to keep his lust at bay.

She seemed to find her voice with some difficulty. "She did?"

"Aye, but she did not have time to bind it. Thus she said I should wait for you here."

"Oh." She cleared her throat. Twas not like her to be at a loss for words, he thought, but she had said she felt guilty for his wound, which also was out of character. Surely she was more the type to wound him than to bind him.

The change in her intrigued him. After all, he would be a fool not to understand his adversary, her moods, her capabilities, he told himself. But somewhere inside him a more honest man laughed.

She did not intrigue him because of the task that had been set before him. She intrigued him because of what she was, the way she laughed, the way her eyes danced with mischief, and her . . .

Dugald gave himself a mental shake. There were a thousand reasons he could not get involved with this woman. A thousand and one, counting the fact that her father had forbidden him from seeing her. In fact, if Roderic knew they were together now, Dugald would probably be nursing far worse than a wounded arm.

He turned his eyes away from her and tried to concentrate on the gathering of information. "A strange place, this," he said.

"The infirmary? Aye." She took a single step into the room. "My aunt Fiona is a renowned healer." She touched the lavender petals of a bundle of dried flowers that hung on the wall. "Glen Creag is her home, but she has done her best to make certain Dun Ard, too, has all the necessary elements for healing."

"Fiona." He thought for a moment. "Laird Leith's wife."

"Aye."

"So your cousin, Rachel, has inherited her mother's skill?"

Shona skirted the walls, as if avoiding him as long as possible. "Aye, Rachel is also a gifted healer."

He watched her. Never had he seen her look so skittish—even while pretending to be a peasant maid in naught but a drenched tunic. "And you, Damsel Shona, have you gained that skill also?"

She glanced over her shoulder at him as if considering her answer. "Not a smidgen," she admitted.

That honesty, like everything about her, fascinated him. "Then why am I here?"

She stared at him for a second, but finally turned abruptly away to fiddle with a leather bottle set upon a nearby shelf. "Have I not told ye that I felt guilty? Twas my fault that ye were wounded. It only seems right I should have a hand in the healing."

He thought about that for a moment. "So you told the lad to strike me down?"

She scowled at him. "Dunna be absurd."

"Then you must have, at least, insisted that he practice his skills on me?"

"Hardly."

He rose restlessly to his feet. Her nearness made him restive, but her distance made him even more so. "Tis as I thought, then. You are a witch, and you somehow caused young Kelvin to wound me. But why? Oh. I remember—twas because I threatened to give my archery award to your cousin."

She glared at him. The fire in her eyes sent a thrill sparking through him.

"Truly, your vanity far exceeds your charms," she said.

"You think so? The duchess of Hanover thought otherwise. In fact, she—"

"Sit down!" she ordered. "I'll bandage your arm."

"Why would you do that?" he asked.

"I told ye, because I feel guilty."

"Why?"

She looked away as she gathered a roll of fabric from a trunk near the pallet. "I should have been supervising Kelvin more carefully."

"Why?"

She looked up from her knees to scowl at him. "He is my responsibility."

"Why?"

"Are ye always this irritating?"

"Not according to the emperor's concubines. Each agreed that I am the most alluring of men. Why is he your responsibility? Is he some relation?"

"Nay."

"Then why must the burden fall on you?"

She rose from her knees to approach the bed, a scowl on her face and a bandage in her hands. "Why this sudden interest in Kelvin?"

Memories fell softly around him in the darkness, memories of a young boy whose eyes were too pale, whose legs were too long.

Dugald shrugged. "In truth, he is not unlike a thousand other orphaned lads. Naught but a burden on those—"

"Is that how ye see him? As a burden?" she interrupted.

"There have been other young maids who have seen it in just that way," he said. "You can take my word on this."

She stared at him for a moment, but he was careful

to keep his emotions hidden. He was here to learn about *her*, not the other way around.

She shrugged as she settled on the mattress next to him. He watched her, but she refused to raise her gaze to his. "Someone has to care for the lad." Lifting the bandage, she placed the end against his upper arm. Her fingers brushed his biceps. Lightning sparked at impact, shocking him.

She jerked her hand away and dropped the bandage. Their gazes fused, their breathing escalated. Mother of God, she was stunning, with skin as fair as frothy milk. He could not fight her allure, he thought, and reached for her. But good sense smote him suddenly. Drawing his hand back, he pulled himself together. She seemed to do the same. Her cheeks were pink as she turned her gaze quickly downward.

"Shona?" He breathed her name.

She refused to answer, refused to look up.

"Shona?" he repeated.

She raised her gaze abruptly. "Could I have my bandage back?"

He scowled at the question. She nodded toward his lap. His gaze followed hers. The bandage rested between his dark-hosed thighs, nestled with comfortable familiarity against his crotch.

He lifted his eyes to look into hers. The room suddenly seemed very hot and still and airless.

She cleared her throat and snapped her gaze away. "May I have my bandage back?"

If he had a modicum of good sense, he'd snatch it off his lap and run like hell. It wouldn't be the first time he refused a mission. Some years ago he'd been hired to return the runaway wife of a young baron. But it turned out the nobleman had a nasty way with horses. In the end, Eagle had been Dugald's only reward. Twas obvious that no one could accuse him of learning from his mistakes.

"The bandage is yours to take," he said, but made no move to fetch it for her.

She reached out, then drew her hand abruptly back.

"You are a strange lass, Shona," he murmured. "Sometimes as bold as a warrior, sometimes as shy as a babe. Which are you, I wonder?"

"I am neither," she said, her cheeks pink.

"Then what are you?"

"I am just what I seem to be."

He shook his head. It was imperative to figure her out, if not for *his* continued survival—certainly for hers. "I do not think so, lass."

"What do ye mean by that?"

Her tone sounded tense. Why? What did she have to hide?

"I think there is more to you than you are telling."

"I am nothing but a humble maid. The daughter of the Rogue and the—"

He laughed aloud. "Already I doubt your words, for no one could call you humble."

"I *am* a humble maid," she said, but her tone was irritable and her brows lowered over her stone sharp eyes.

"A humble maid who can best the men at archery."

"Twas no great feat."

"Who befriends Scotland's king."

"I can only assume that kings need friends, too."

"Who wears breeches when the mood suits her. Who scales towers. Who chooses her own spouse. Who spends months alone at court. Who fosters a boy without the aid of a husband. Why are you so arrogant? What makes you so self-assured?"

She watched him with wide eyes. There was nervousness there, perhaps even fear, though it was well hidden. Why? What did she fear? Here at Dun Ard she was as good as a princess. Nothing could harm her within the safety of these walls. Or at least, that was what she should believe. He rose to his feet, needing to put space between them in order to think. The bandage rolled onto the floor, unraveling as it went, and seeming to open his mind with it.

"What is the lad to you, Shona?" he asked.

She lifted her gaze from the bandage, her eyes as wide as a doe's. "He is but a lad—in need of a home."

"He looks rather like—our king." The resemblance struck him like a bolt of lightning.

She shot to her feet. "What?"

"When were you first at court?" he rasped.

"I . . . what?"

He took a step toward her. The truth was so close, on the tip of his tongue. "Did you know James the Fourth?"

"James? Aye. We . . . met."

"When?"

She stumbled back a pace. "Why do ye wish to know?"

"The child is yours, isn't he? Yours and the old king's," Dugald declared abruptly. "Tis the lad you hope to put on the throne."

Her jaw dropped in amazement, but her shock was no greater than Dugald's. His theory was ingenious. But what the hell was he doing blurting it out to her?

"Ye're accusing me of dallying with the king?" she asked, her tone breathless.

"Is the child yours?" He knew he shouldn't ask, knew he should use subterfuge to learn the truth. But he could not wait, for suddenly the thought of her with another man, *any* man, was beyond bearing.

"You're insane," she whispered.

"Is he yours?"

"Nay!"

Dugald scowled. Her denial sounded more than honest—enraged, even—putting his theory on shaky ground. Still, he was not ready to give it up, for there was something here she was hiding. "I have met the old king," he said slowly. "Your Kelvin bears a striking resemblance."

"As does half the population of Scotland."

"That's because half the population is his get," he

argued, stepping nearer. "He was not a man known for his fidelity to the queen."

She gaped at him. "And thus ye assumed that I, too, had birthed one of his bairns?"

"You are not exactly loathsome to look at, Shona. Twas well known that James had a weakness for a bonny face. Why were you keeping his heritage a secret? Someone was bound to figure out the truth. Tis a logical conclusion. Think on it. Your close ties to the throne, the boy's features, his demeanor, his hair color . . ."

"Logical!" she gasped. "I would have been no more than . . . twelve when the babe was conceived."

The truth hit Dugald like a summer storm. She was right. He was insane. But it was she that was making him so. She and her blatant sensuality, her silvery laughter, her ungodly allure. "I thought—"

"What?" she raged. "That I have no morals? That I am a slut?"

He drew a deep breath, damning himself a hundredfold for losing his perception. Mother of God, what was wrong with him? he wondered. He wasn't the jealous type. She had bewitched him. But this was hardly the time to worry about such things now, for her voice was anything but quiet. Still, she was not the type to get hysterical, he assured himself. She would not call her father down to behead him. Probably. "I did not mean to offend you, Shona."

"Offend me?"

He winced at her volume.

"In truth, *I* was born outside the bonds of wedlock. In a different culture, in a foreign land. Mayhap my humble circumstances make me see the world from a different angle than most. My apologies." He took a few steps along the wall. "I am but trying to figure you out, lass. To find out who you are. To find out . . ." He paused and reached for her, but managed to pull his hand back before he made contact.

"What?" she asked.

"I am trying to find out why you draw me as you do."

She backed away, her eyes still angry. "In truth, I affect all men like that."

Despite everything, he could not help but smile. "Do you now?'

"Aye."

"Then I am even more surprised that you do not yet have a child."

"I did not say I return their attention."

"But you return mine," he said.

She stepped quickly back a pace. "I dunna think I feel guilty enough to mend ye now."

He advanced a step. "And I do not think it is guilt that brought you here from the start."

"What do ye mean?"

"Are you saying you do not feel it?"

She retreated, but the backs of her knees were against the mattress now, preventing further retreat. "Feel what?"

If he had a grain of goodness in him, he would leave while she still had her illusions and he still had his life. But his hand reached out of its own accord, and suddenly it was scooped behind her neck.

Lightning flared through him. Her head fell back slightly, as if the jolt that passed through him also seared her.

"That!"

"I feel nothing," she denied, but her voice trembled.

"Then you will not mind if I kiss you?"

"Kiss me!" The words were squeaky. "Of ... of course I would mind!" she said, but she didn't move away, didn't push against him. Instead, she stayed just as she was, with the heat of her gaze like emerald fire against his face.

He could not resist, regardless of the consequences! So what if he was flogged, disemboweled, decapitated?

Their lips met. The world exploded, and suddenly she was in his arms, pressed tight against his body. For one brief moment she held back, and then she was kissing him in return, her lips warm and soft, her breasts crushed against his bare chest, her arms clasped about his back.

Passion roared between them, torching all lucidity. There was nothing but their need.

From somewhere unknown, footsteps sounded. Dugald yanked himself back to reality and jerked away with an effort.

They stared at each other like crazed inmates. Dear God, they hadn't even closed the door.

The footsteps faded into oblivion. The world went silent except for their breathing.

"How . . . how much?" he murmured.

"What?"

"How much would you mind if I kissed you?" he asked.

She winced and took a guilty step backward. He watched her, and even now it took every bit of his self control to keep from following her.

Sanity seemed a slippery thing when she was near. He held onto it with hard ferocity. "Why does that happen?" he asked.

She blinked. "Why does what happen?"

He couldn't help but laugh. The sound echoed maniacally in the narrow room. "Again, you did not notice?"

She had the good grace to pause before her next inane question. "Notice what?"

"Shall I demonstrate again?" he asked, stepping forward.

She scrambled backward, bumped into a shelf, and scurried away.

The sight would have been funny were it not for the painful pulse of his blood thundering away from his brain.

"Never have I felt this . . . loss of control. This powerlessness to keep myself from a woman."

She licked her lips and glanced at the door as if she were debating fleeing. Apparently she decided to chance staying. Her gaze flitted back, though she was scowling now. "Even with the emperor's concubines?"

He allowed a sliver of a grin. "Would it hurt you so to admit you are attracted to me?" he asked.

"Attracted to *ye*?" She laughed out loud.

Too loud. He winced. He might be acting the fool, but still he had no wish to be killed by someone called the Rogue who was but protecting his daughter's virtue. Hurrying to the passageway, he glanced out, then softly shut the door.

When he turned back, Shona's eyes looked wider than ever. He moved across the floor toward her, because he was a fool, because he could not help himself.

She leaned away a little, but she was trapped by the bed behind her. He was close enough to smell the sweet fragrance of her hair, the more earthy scent that was nothing but woman. That scent alone was nearly enough to sap every ounce of self-control from him.

"Why are you afraid to say the truth?" he asked. "Tis not a shameful thing."

"And the truth being?"

"That you are as drawn to me just as I am to you."

"Drawn to ye? I dunna even *like* ye!"

"Truly?" he asked, stepping closer still.

She swallowed. "Truly," she said.

"And what kind of man do you like, wee Shona?"

"It matters little. Despite what ye think, and what my father says, I am a sweet lass, and I will marry where I am told."

"Then who does your father like?"

She snorted at his ridiculousness and turned away, but he caught her arm. Fire sparked between them again, but he held on, riding it out and wondering if he would be burned asunder.

"Who would your father choose for you, lass?"

Her teeth were pressed tightly together, as if she, too, were fighting to douse the fire that raged between them. "Someone of position," she said.

He moved slightly closer, daring the flames. "Position? Does that mean someone who could be king?''

''King? Nay.''

Her shocked tone was sincere. It had been a foolish question. Still, he could not help the relief that flooded him. ''Then what?''

''Someone who can give me security.''

Against his better judgment he pulled her against him. ''There is security in my arms. That I promise.''

Dugald could feel her breath fan his face.

''A gentleman,'' she whispered.

''Gentle.'' He tried to keep himself in check. But if the truth were known, there was no hope. His hand reached out of its own accord, touching her cheek. She shivered beneath his fingertips and let her eyes fall closed. ''Do you need proof of my gentleness?''

She shook her head feebly, but he was far past good sense and slipped his fingers gently across her cheek to her jaw. There he turned his hand so that the flats of his nails brushed along the ridge of her chin.

''Dugald.'' His name was no more than a whisper. The sound of it on her lips sent a shiver of excitement through him, an excitement too intense to be denied.

''Aye?'' he murmured, and bending, kissed the corner of her mouth.

She sucked air through her parted lips, and her head fell back, exposing her throat. Regal, pale as frothy milk, warm as life itself. He kissed her there, just below her jaw where her pulse raced like a wild steed, then down, lower, along the slim, elegant column of her neck.

''I didna . . .'' Her words broke off. ''I didna say gentle,'' she reminded him. ''I said *gentleman*.''

He kissed the base of her neck, then, because he was a fool, he eased her sleeve down, tugging it off her shoulder.

It was beautiful, bonny, pale, small. Damn him. There was nothing he could do but kiss it.

''Is it my gentleness you doubt? Or my manhood?'' he whispered.

Soft as feather down, her fingers slid around his waist.

For a moment he could neither speak nor think, so intense was the line of fire she scorched against his flesh. Five brands of flame seared his back where her fingers pressed against him.

"I am not for ye," she murmured. "My father has forbidden it."

He kissed her throat, her jaw, the high portion of her breasts. "Because I am not nobly born?" he asked.

"My parents have long labored to empower this clan. My marriage into a noble house could do much to increase their strength."

He kissed her lips, gently, holding back his passion, but easing her back onto the bed behind her. Her other hand slipped about his back, holding him close, and then she kissed him in return. The sweetness was beyond compare, beyond resistance. He trembled at its intensity.

"So they would sacrifice your happiness to build their empire?"

"I—" she began, but he could hold back no longer and kissed her with all the aching emotion she brought him.

Somehow they were no longer sitting up, but lying on the mattress, wrapped in each other's arms, their hearts beating in unison. Their kisses grew hotter.

Her hands skimmed down his back, pressing harder against him, fanning the flames, gripping his buttocks, pulling him closer. He moaned against her touch and reaching for her skirt, pulled it up, eager, nay, needing, to feel her skin against his.

"Father!" Shona hissed the word against his mouth.

Dugald froze in place. Their hearts rapped against each other's. Their gazes froze.

From the hall, laughter could be heard. Then Dugald, too, recognized the sound of footsteps.

"Ye are a good man," Roderic said.

"I can but try, my lord. And with her at my side, I would try my best."

"I dunna doubt that atall."

"Is it a bargain, then?"

The footfalls were just on the other side of the door now.

Dugald held his breath. Beneath him, Shona, too, failed to breathe.

"Aye," Roderic said finally. "It is a bargain, William."

The footsteps echoed away.

Dugald slipped off her and rose soundlessly to his feet. She scrambled off the mattress, then backed away to press her skirt down over her legs.

They stared at each other, silent, suddenly wary.

"You may not think me worthy of you," he said softly. "But you want me nonetheless."

"'Tis not true," she said.

"Aye. It is. But you're scared to admit it."

"I'm scared of nothing."

"Indeed?" he said, and stepping forward, he drew her into his arms and kissed her.

She trembled as passion licked her, but in a moment he drew back, his silver gaze heavy on her face.

"Why not admit that you long for me?" he whispered. "That you cannot think of another when I am near?"

"'Tis not true."

He watched her from inches away. "Tell me, Shona, are you so foolish that you do not see it, or are you so cold that you do not care?"

"It does not matter," she whispered. "'Tis not meant to be."

Reaching slowly up, he brushed his fingertips across her lips. She shivered beneath his touch.

"Your lips say one thing," he murmured, "but your body says another. Beware, lass, for a time will come when your mind and body will be in accord. Then you shall be in my arms, and all else will be forgotten."

She tried to protest, but he kissed her again, and then, silent as the night, he slipped into the hall.

Chapter 16

Shona sat in the silence of the infirmary, her heart still pounding, her mind awhirl. What the devil was wrong with her? Despite her recent demeanor, she wasn't a wanton. Never did she throw herself at men. Never. So why did she act as she did with Dugald?

True, he was attractive, but he'd accused her of fornicating with the king! Still, she longed to feel his . . .

She stood abruptly to pace the room. Mayhap it was this talk of marriage that was confusing her. Her father insisted that she choose someone or he would choose for her. But how was she supposed to choose?

Hadwin was funny. Stanford was sincere. William was noble in a fatherly sort of way.

She would not think about Dugald. He had nothing for her. Nothing. He was insulting and rude and insane.

But the muscles in his chest felt like polished steel beneath her fingers. His very nearness made her . . .

The door creaked open. Startled from her thoughts, Shona swung around.

"Daughter." Roderic stood in the doorway. "I thought I heard something." He stepped smoothly inside. "What are ye doing here?"

"I . . ." Nearly had sex with a man he didn't approve of—lost my mind—forgot all the honor ye ever taught me. None of these seemed like a particularly wise answer, so she fumbled for a likely lie, but guilt and loyalty changed her mind.

"I bandaged Dugald's arm," she said finally, which, in actually, was also a lie, since the bandage still remained on the floor, forsaken and forgotten.

"Dugald?" Her father's expression grew chilly as his gaze skimmed the room. "He was here?"

"Aye." She forced herself not to wring her hands, but the lightning hot energy caused by Dugald's nearness had to be expelled somehow, so she fiddled with the folds of her gown and refused to lower her eyes.

Roderic watched her for a moment. "What are your plans for the lad, Shona?"

"My plans?"

He was silent, then sighed and walked to the pallet to take a seat. "He is not for ye, lass."

Anger welled up inside her, spurred by confusion, fanned by frustration. "For me? Why does everyone keep assuming I would want him?" Truly, it was a foolish question, for her cheeks were still warm and her heart racing. But that was just the physical.

"Then ye dunna?"

"Nay!" she said quickly, before her soul drowned out the good sense of her mind. "Nay, I—"

"Then the tassel ye gave to William was in good faith."

"I . . ." She blinked. It was difficult thinking of William and Dugald with the same mind. They were worlds apart somehow. "Aye," she said slowly. "I . . . like him."

"Like him." Roderic rose to his feet. "That is good. For fondness can grow into much more. He seems a good man. Staid." He paused. "A bit . . . tedious, mayhap, but better that than the wild excitement of . . ." He paused again and scowled. "These flagrant attractions rarely make successful matches, Daughter."

She chewed her lip. "What flagrant attractions?"

"I am not so old that I have forgotten the feelings, lass. But this Kinnaird fellow . . ." He shook his head.

"Ye need someone with substance, not a preening pea-cock who would forget your needs in favor of his own wardrobe."

"Mayhap he is not what he seems, Father." She said the words against her will. After all, she didn't even like the man.

"I know something of his reputation, Shona. There are more than a few women in his past—rich women, women willing to pay for his company. Though . . ." He scowled. "I truly dunna know what they see in him. He is not all that tall, and . . ."

"They paid?" Shona stood very still, feeling suddenly cold. "They paid him?"

Roderic drew a deep breath and watched her. "It may be no more than rumor, but this much is certain, he lived with the duchess of Crondell for more than six months."

"The duchess . . ."

"I have met the duchess," Roderic said. "'Tis not likely she kept this Dugald about as master of her mews. Though she loves her birds, she loves her pleasures better."

Shona could not think of a single thing to say.

"I am sorry," Roderic said. "Despite what ye say, I know ye have feelings for the lad. I wouldna be the one to slander him, if your happiness did not mean as much as my own life to me. But even if I had not heard this news of him, I still wouldna condone a union between the two of ye. Ye are . . ." He paused, searching for the proper words. "Ye are all fire and light, Shona. The last thing ye need is kindling to set ye ablaze. Better far that ye build yourself a peaceful life."

Peaceful! It sounded ominously like boring. "But ye and mother are not peaceful," she said, feeling drained suddenly and very tired.

"Aye." He frowned, but the expression looked forced. "And look how she torments me. Always I have to worry about who is ogling her. Not for a moment does she listen to a word of my council and stay home as a good wife should."

"Ye are inordinately proud of Mother's accomplishments," Shona objected softly.

"Aye, well . . ." For a moment, he ran out of words. "That has naught to do with ye, Shona. Better far for ye to marry a man who does not inflame your wild passions. One who can keep velvet gowns upon your back and gold rings upon your fingers."

But velvet often chafed, and gold rings had a tendency to catch on limbs when she climbed trees.

"Ye have chosen well," Roderic said, rising to his feet. "William will make ye a fine husband."

"But—"

He kissed her cheek and turned away. "Good night, daughter," he said, and stepping into the hall, closed the door behind him.

"But I did not choose," Shona whispered to the empty room.

Shona awoke to a pounding headache. Nightmares had plagued what little sleep she had gotten. Nightmares of a silver-eyed rogue who lay wrapped in the arms of a wealthy duchess.

But even as she dreamt it, she could not believe it was real. True, Dugald could seem shallow sometimes. He was far too concerned about his looks, and he was vain beyond words. But sometimes she felt something more in him, a slash of sharp power, an ocean of depth.

There was more to him than met the eye, of that she was certain. And if she could just draw that forth, see it in the full light of . . .

Shona jerked herself out of bed. What the devil was wrong with her? She didn't want to draw anything out of Dugald Kinnaird. She did not even like him.

She chanted those words like a mantra as she got dressed, then hurried down the steps, eager to find a distraction.

But the noise of the hall only hurt her head more.

Needing time and fresh air, Shona skirted the crowd and hurried outside.

She walked alone all that morning, wandering along the burn's serpentine course and trying to sort out her thoughts. But the effort did little more than relieve a bit of excess energy.

By the time she returned to Dun Ard, the swordsmanship contest had already been played out. William, his tunic decorated with the tassel she had given him, had competed well. But Boden Blackblade had won the sheath that was the award.

The noon meal passed without incident. Shona fiddled with her herbed ptarmigan then tried to sneak off alone, but Kelvin galloped up to her before she reached the stairs.

"Are ye ready for the hunt?" he asked, all but panting with excitement.

"The hunt?"

"Surely ye have not forgotten. The men are saddling the mounts even now. Might Dugald ride with us?"

"Lady Shona," William said, bowing near her elbow. "I took the liberty of saddling your mare for you."

She blinked at him.

"You did not forget that you promised to ride with me, did you?"

She turned guiltily toward Kelvin. "I fear I—"

"I heard you say you had promised the lad, too, but I think myself man enough to manage to share you for the afternoon."

"Hurry," Kelvin called, seeming unconcerned by this turn of events as he danced toward the door. "The day is fleeting."

They rode out as a large company, perhaps two score of men and a dozen women. Beneath her, Lochan Teine pranced and tossed her flaxen mane, eager to be off.

Kelvin glanced up from the back of his mount. His white pony was shaggy-maned and stout, a dependable gelding that stood only a hand or so beneath Shona's refined mare.

"Ramsay told me of wolves spotted in the west woods," Kelvin said.

"Mayhap it was nothing more than Maggie's Dog," Shona countered.

"Twas wolves," Kelvin argued importantly. "Do ye suppose we will come across them?"

"Tis unlikely, since we are heading east," Shona said, as she shifted the quiver of arrows at her back.

"Are ye scared of wolves, Lady Shona?"

She smiled down at him. "Are ye offering to be my protector, Kelvin?" she asked.

He smiled, showing multiple gaps in his teeth. "Aye," he murmured, leaning closer as he eyed the man on the far side of her. "Unless ye would rather have Lord William defend ye."

"A lady can never have too many brave protectors," she said, and they rode on.

The day was warm and still. The new leaves were a green so bright it all but hurt the eyes to look upon them. There should have been bountiful game, yet they saw little.

But once Shona thought she caught a glimpse of a narrow girl flitting through the woods. Only a little farther on, the shadow of a wolf crossed her path. Maggie, she thought suddenly. Could Sara's little lass have come out to scare off the game? But no. Shona quickly set aside that thought, for even Shona herself would be unlikely to do such a foolhardy thing.

Still she could not help but smile, for if the truth be told, Shona did not much care if they found any game or not. Kelvin was at his most charming, entertaining her with stories and riddles as he jabbered on at his jovial best. As for William, he seemed content to merely stay at Shona's side, offering a few words now and then.

But by mid-afternoon, Kelvin's dialogue had slowed down. He sat slumped atop his pony, his narrow shoulders rounded.

"The lad looks tired," William said, leaning toward her so that Kelvin did not hear.

Shona nodded. "Mayhap I should take him back to Dun Ard."

"And hurt his manly pride?" William asked. "What would his friends say?"

She watched him in silence for a moment. "Ye are kind to think of his feelings."

"It may be hard to believe, but I, too, was young once."

"Not difficult at all," she countered. "And from your experience, what would ye suggest for wee Kelvin?"

"When my own sons grew weary I would oft take them to the water's edge and let them rest. There is something about the sound that is soothing. On my way to Dun Ard, I came upon a bonny spot." He glanced about as if looking for that place. "I think it is not far from here if you'd like to break off from the group."

If she was not mistaken, he was speaking of the very spot where Dugald had found her fishing. Something in her shied from going there with William, but she berated herself for those feelings and smiled. "Tis a fine idea," she said, then turned to Kelvin. "I fear I am in need of a rest, lad. Would ye mind terribly if we tarried for a spell by the burn?"

Kelvin looked up at her through half-lidded eyes. "If we must," he said with a yawn.

She smiled. "We must."

In a matter of minutes they had reached the stream. It burbled pleasantly along.

"There is a sheltered place just a ways ahead," William said.

Shona followed him through the trees, and Kelvin followed her, until at last they came to a lovely place only a short distance from where she had found the trout some days before. Shallow water glistened over silvery stones and the sun peeked happily through low-hanging branches, dappling the verdant earth below.

William helped her dismount. Kelvin, awakened by such a magical place, hopped off his gelding on his own.

"Might I wade in the water?" he asked.

"I think mayhap ye should rest," Shona said, and set her bow upon the grass to prop her hands on her hips.

"'Twas ye that needed to stop," he reminded her.

Shona laughed, and finding no likely argument, helped him out of his footwear before sending him off to play in the water's edge. Then she turned Teine loose to graze.

"There is a copse of berries not far downstream, lad, if you are hungry," William said.

Kelvin wandered off, splashing up geysers of water with his bare toes as he went.

William settled onto the grass as he watched. "You are kind beyond words to care for him as you do, Lady Shona."

She watched Kelvin play in the water for a moment, then turned her attention to William. "Tis strange. If he were my own child none would think me kind for giving him care. But since someone else gave him life, I am considered a martyr."

"Tis the way of the world, I suppose. But mayhap ye would understand it if ye had children of your own. My own Deirdra, God rest her, wanted a dozen children. But the good Lord saw fit to take her after the second was born."

"I am sorry."

He nodded. "I too. But she was not very strong. Not like ye. Ye would not . . ." He paused.

"What?" she asked, eager to learn more about this man her parents favored.

"Ye will have no trouble bearing children," he finished, but somehow she was certain that was not what he had meant to say.

The thought bothered her, though she could not put her finger on why. She glanced at Kelvin again. "Truly, I am not certain I could love him more if he were of my own flesh."

"With the Lord's blessing ye will soon find out."

There was a blank silence, which she hurried to fill. "Ye say ye have sons?" she asked, feeling a need to turn the conversation aside.

"Two," William said.

"And where are they today?"

"I hate to remind you of my age, but they are no longer children. They have responsibilities of their own," he said, and proceeded to tell her of his children, of his life.

Shona settled her back against a tree not far from William and watched the water trickle over its stone bed. Memories of her own childhood came to mind, memories of hours spent with her cousins in a spot much like this. Memories of sitting on her father's knee, listening to his outlandish tales, feeling the thrill of the love her parents shared. She had felt that same thrill first hand when Dugald touched her, had felt the earth shiver and her soul ache.

Memories, warm and titillating as wine swept through her, memories of firm muscles and low laughter, of kisses like licking flames.

Time trickled away like the water.

"Am I boring you, Lady?" William asked.

"Oh." Shona shook herself from her reverie, feeling guilty for her wayward thoughts. "No. Not atall. Ye were right about the water. Tis very soothing. And I suppose I am somewhat sleepy myself."

"I canna blame you. After all, you are hardly older than the lad. Mayhap—"

But his words were cut short by a distant scream.

"Kelvin!" Shona snatched her bow from the ground, trying to ascertain his direction, but William was already on his feet and running, racing through the woods, his sword in his hand.

Shona lunged after him, her heart pounding with terror. "Kelvin!" she screamed again, but just then she caught a glimpse of him racing through the woods. For a moment she saw nothing else, but then she heard a snarl. The bracken rustled in a path behind him.

"No!" Jolting to a halt, Shona fitted an arrow to her bow and loosed it.

The whir of its release alerted Kelvin. "Shona!" he shrieked, and seeing her, spun in her direction. The wolf pivoted with him, and the arrow, meant to pierce its heart, sliced its shoulder, leaving a bloody path.

It snarled in rage, but did not stop.

Kelvin sobbed as he glanced behind him, but just in that instant, his toe caught on a vine and he fell.

Shona reached for another arrow just as William lunged forward. Jumping over the child, he slashed at the beast's neck. It leapt clumsily sideways. Blood sprayed everywhere. But William did not delay. Lunging in, he stabbed his sword through its heart.

It died with a whimper of protest.

"Kelvin!" Shona stumbled forward.

The boy rose with a sob and threw himself into her arms. There was blood on his arms and hands, but she couldn't immediately determine the source.

"What happened?" said William approaching quickly.

"I w—was . . ." He hiccuped. "I was picking berries. I didn't . . . see it in the brush at first. Then I thought it was dead; it was so still." He hiccuped again, still trying to peer past William at the wolf. "Was it . . . was it wounded already?"

"Come," William said. "We'd best take him quickly to Dun Ard, before he loses more blood. Shona, fetch our horses. I'll carry the lad."

Shona gently swept Kelvin's hair back from his face and remained kneeling beside his bed. She had been there for more than an hour now, watching him sleep, making certain no nightmares plagued his dreams. But he seemed peaceful and comfortable after Fiona's ministrations. Shona smoothed her knuckles gently across his cheek, letting his presence soothe her soul. His right arm was bandaged just below the elbow, and around his narrow chest another strip of cloth was tied where the wolf had clawed him, but he was well. He was fine, she assured herself. Still, if William hadn't been there . . .

Her thoughts shuddered to a halt. Dear God, Kelvin had nearly been killed. Her hands trembled at the thought. She had failed him. And why? Because her mind had wandered, because even far from the castle, thoughts of Dugald had plagued her, making her forget her responsibilities, her vows to protect Kelvin. She'd been so immersed in memories—the feel of Dugald's skin, the sound of his voice, the taste of his kiss—that everything else had faded to unreality. Even her ultra-sharp senses had failed her. And tragedy had struck. But William had come to the rescue, had risked his life to save a boy he didn't even know. William, whom she found boring and remote. William, whose patient attentions she had ignored for so long.

Her parents were right; she was wild and undisciplined. She must not choose someone who would insult her, then inflame her, who made her forget all but her own selfish desires, who had no concern for her or Kelvin except how they might aid his cause. Indeed, Kinnaird had never denied that his only interest was in finding a rich bride. In fact, he was not even interested in her in *that* regard, but on an even lower level, a level so primitive that Shona had never known she possessed such feelings. He had said, with his usual arrogance, that someday her mind and body would be in accord and she would come to him. But he was wrong. Instead, she would choose someone staid and steady, someone mature, who would quell her unruly spirit, who could improve her nature, for it was not just herself she had to care for now. She had vowed to protect the lad with her life, vowed on her honor, and failed! Had it not been for William's quick wit and selfless courage, Kelvin's life would surely have been forfeited.

Guilt gnawed at Shona like a hungry beast; fatigue wore at her soul. But she had one more thing to do before she found her own bed. Rising to her feet, Shona turned and strode resolutely out of the room and down the winding stone stairs.

The hall grew hushed when she entered it. She clasped her hands together, praying for strength, for forgiveness for her weaknesses. "I would beg your attention for a moment," she called.

The place grew still as faces of family, friends, and strangers turned toward her.

"As ye have all probably heard, Kelvin was attacked by a wolf this day. I failed . . ." Her voice broke, but she cleared her throat, pushing away the horrid images of what might have happened had William been a little slower, had his mind wandered as hers had. "I failed to keep him safe. Were it not for Laird William . . ." She turned toward him, feeling weak and small. "Twas a very brave and selfless thing he did." She paused a moment, steadying her own mind. "For that I would thank ye, William . . . and accept your offer of marriage."

Chapter 17

⌒◯◯⌒

Shona awoke slowly. The hour was yet early, the sun not quite over the horizon. The world was still cast in a predawn pearlescent gray, but she felt no need to sleep longer. Neither did she wish to awaken. Instead, she wanted nothing more than to lie in oblivion, to forget her obligations as well as her shortcomings. But neither would be forgotten.

She had promised to keep Kelvin safe and she had failed in that mission. She had been distracted, careless, drawn away into her disturbing thoughts of Dugald.

Aye, she had failed. But she would not fail again. She would be the epitome of good sense and self-control, and she had already taken the first step: she had become betrothed to William.

Shona closed her eyes for a moment, remembering the reactions to her announcement the previous night. Her parents, regardless of their own recommendations to marry William, had looked shocked. Sara and Rachel had uttered dutiful congratulations, Hadwin had been so-ber, and Stanford had wept openly. She had scanned the hall, but Dugald had been nowhere to be seen. And a good thing, too. For he was surely the last person she needed to muddle her thinking. Not that she was unsure of her decision.

William was a good man. Solid, steady, fatherly. Still, something inside her ached with her decision.

She had gone to bed soon after her announcement, but Dragonheart had hung cold and heavy against her skin, making her rest fitful and frustrating. Finally she had slipped it from her neck and hung it over a peg on the opposite wall. She could see it now, its ruby glowing like a single angry eye. She remembered how warm it had been at other times, how it would almost purr with a strange, sensual joy when Dugald was near. When he touched her, his hands like magic—

No! She would not think of that. She would not! Sitting up quickly, she lunged from her bed.

Twas not too early to begin the day. The festivities were nearly over. There would be guests to whom to bid adieu, and preparations to make for her wedding.

Going to Dragonheart, she slipped it from the peg and around her neck, then turned toward her window. The shutters stood slightly ajar, allowing her a gray-shadowed glimpse of the bailey, the courtyard, the stables beyond. She remembered where Dugald slept as vividly as she recalled her own name. Was he awake? Was he thinking of her? Had he heard of her plans to wed? Did he, even now—

God's wrath! Slamming the shutters closed, she jerked angrily about. Twas thoughts of him that had made her neglect Kelvin before. She would not do so again.

Yanking her door open, she hurried down the hall to check on the lad. His portal opened with only a slight creak. Upon the wide straw-stuffed mattress, a plethora of boys slept, arms and legs spread everywhere. But Kelvin was alone on a small pallet, giving his wounds a chance to heal. He lay on his side with his lips slightly parted and his hair tousled. For a moment she was tempted to cross the floor and smooth the hair from his brow, to make certain he was still breathing. But such would be folly. There was no need to wake the child. Fiona had said that he needed nothing more than sleep and time to help him mend completely.

She retraced her steps to her room and closed the door behind her.

Refusing to take one more glance out the window, she drew her nightrail over her head with a sigh.

"So ye will marry William?"

"Dugald!" Shona gasped as she spun toward the voice and hugged her nightrail to her chest. He stood in the corner, not three feet from her bed. "What are ye doing here?"

"Watching you."

Desire immediately coiled tight and hungry in her gut. She hugged her gown more tightly to her. "How did ye get in?"

He didn't answer, but said instead, "You should keep your door closed, lass. You never know what lowly soul might breech the sanctity of your quarters."

She stepped back a pace, seeing the anger in his eyes. "I realize that now. In fact, I will make certain to bar myself in from this moment forward."

"Tis a bit late to lock the stable door after the stallion has already mingled with the mares."

She raised a brow at him, trying to calm her breathing. "Ye see yourself as a stallion, do ye?"

"Twas just a figure of speech, Shona," he said, approaching her again. "But if that's how you feel, do not be afraid to state your opinion."

"Stay back!" Her voice sounded far more panicked than she had hoped.

He stopped. "Why? I have only come to wish you all the best and to kiss the future bride."

She swallowed. "I dunna think that is such a good idea."

"Whyever not? You did not mind kissing me before."

"Twas different then."

"Different? However so?" he asked, stepping forward again.

"That was before . . ." She crowded back against the wall.

"Before what? Before you decided that one's title and properties were more important than his soul?"

"What do ye mean by that?"

"This William?" He stopped inches from her. She could feel his nearness like a hot, tangible force. "Are you saying you do not care for his wealth? That you marry him because you admire him so? That his ties to the throne hold no appeal for you?"

"'Tis none of your concern why I marry him," she said.

He reached out to touch her. She tried to draw away, but the wall was behind her. His fingers stroked across her cheek. She nearly shivered at the touch, but managed to hold herself unmoving.

"Mayhap he has a magical allure that you cannot resist," Dugald said. "Mayhap when he is near you cannot keep yourself from him."

She bit her lip. Even now, when he baited her, she wanted nothing more than to fly into his arms.

"Mayhap his touch is like heaven, like magic, beyond understanding." His fingers brushed her ear, and now she did shiver, letting the gossamer feelings sweep through her like fine wine. "Mayhap you lie awake at night thinking of naught but him."

Dugald's voice was no more than a whisper, a sliver of sound that pierced her soul as his hand scooped behind her neck, pulling her nearer. Against her better judgment, she was drawn forward, and suddenly his lips were a breath from hers and his hand skimmed down her bare back to her waist.

"Mayhap he has cast a spell upon you. A spell you would not break even if you could. There is no logic to the things he makes you say and do," Dugald murmured, "and yet you long to be near him. To feel his fingers against your skin. To breathe in his scent, to be naked beneath him."

His hand slipped lower, feather soft, over the curve of her bare buttocks.

"Dugald!" She breathed his name, praying he would leave, but hoping he would not.

"Mayhap your dreams are filled with him," he whispered, slipping his hand down her arm and taking her nightrail from her numb fingers. In an instant he had tugged it away and dropped it to the floor.

She had no way to shield herself from him now. No way to hold the raw, aching desire at bay.

He glanced down. She watched him look at her, and though she knew she should cover herself, she had no wish to do so, for the admiration in his eyes was like a bold caress, as potent as a lover's hot kiss.

She watched his nostrils dilate, watched his self-control slip a notch. A muscle flexed in his jaw, but he held himself still as his gaze swept from her shoulders to her thighs and back.

Shona's nipples hardened under his gaze. She knew she should send him away. But his arm was firm around her back, and her will was weak. He lifted his left hand. As light as a breeze, his fingers touched her breast. She shivered beneath his touch, and though a thousand angels told her to draw away, she let her lids fall closed and her body arch toward him.

His palm cupped her breast, and when next he spoke, his tone was throaty.

"Mayhap your every thought is filled with him," Dugald continued. "His laughter, his beauty, his grace. And though you know you are a fool, you do not care what he is, what he is hiding from you, what he has done, for you would risk your very life for a moment in his arms." She felt his breath on her skin, and then his lips touched her brow. "To be in his dreams." He kissed her cheek. "In his bed," he murmured, and kissed her lips.

She could not help herself. She was weak and she knew it, but his allure was too strong. He was speaking every traitorous thought she had of Dugald. He knew every shameful feeling that sparked through her when he was near. And she could no longer deny it. Her kiss answered his with a heat of its own.

He pressed her back onto the bed. She tugged at his tunic, pulling it free of his plaid, so that her hands could find the hard, rounded muscle of his chest. Strength rippled beneath her fingers, but it was not enough. She needed him naked, needed his skin pressed against hers. He made no objections when she sought the buckle of his belt.

His fingers joined hers in their frenzied quest, and in a moment they were pressed together, flesh against flesh. His thigh lay beneath hers as he leaned over her, kissing her throat, her shoulder, her breast.

Shona arched against him as fire spurred through her. He suckled her nipple into his mouth and she twined her fingers through his hair, trying to hold the world steady as fire exploded inside her.

But in a moment he was moving on, blazing a trail of kisses over her ribs, her belly, her hip. She writhed beneath him, still holding his hair as she bent her legs and ached to ease the building inferno within her. His hands slipped over her thighs. His kisses followed, easing down her sensitive flesh until her legs quivered with her suppressed longing.

She jumped at the explosion of feeling, jerking on his hair as she did so. But Dugald failed to notice. Instead, he kissed her again. She jerked beneath his caresses. His tongue touched her sensitive folds.

"Dugald," she gasped.

He kissed her thighs, her belly, then crept upward. His erection, hard and long, brushed between her legs.

"What do ye want?" he rasped.

She tried to answer. But there were no words. Instead, she pulled his head to her and kissed him. Dragonheart glowed hot and heavy between them.

He drew away from her lips, kissing her cheek, her ear. Against her belly, his desire throbbed with the heat of a volcano. She pressed against it with indescribable need.

"Tell me what ye want, Shona."

She did not delay an instant. "I want ye," she whispered. "Now. This instant."

"Me?" he rasped, pressing against her. "Me and none other?"

"Ye." She found his lips again and kissed them. "Please, Dugald."

He skimmed his hand down her hip, shivering as he did so. "So you know, lass. You know the truth. You are not meant for a man who can bring you wealth and position, but does not move your soul."

Shona went still. Memory flooded back. Guilt came with it. She was betrothed. She was promised. What was wrong with her?

"You were meant for me. For passion. For life. Not for politics and intrigue. I will keep you safe. Isle Fois is—"

"Nay!" she gasped and pushed away. Passion made her careless, made her foolish. And she could not afford to be foolish.

Dugald slipped to the mattress, watching her from inches away. The muscles of his chest felt hard as glass against her breast, and the hard length of his arousal throbbed against her side, making it impossible to remember what she was about to say.

"I will protect you, Shona. It does not matter what you've done," he whispered fervently, slipping his hand along her side.

She swallowed, trying to hold back the feelings, but his hand skimmed over her inner thigh and upward. It touched her core. She nearly shrieked with primitive desire, but her long-suffering honor held her at bay. "I canna!" she gasped, and yanked away. Panic roiling within her, and she scrambled to her feet like a hunted hare. But there was nowhere to flee, so she stood on the mattress with her legs spread for flight and her back to the wall.

He rose more slowly, his feet on the floor, the pallet between them as he watched her. His chest expanded and fell with each quick exhalation. His fists were clenched as if he held himself under careful control.

God, he was a masterpiece, a work of art, his shoulders wide, his thighs muscular, and everything in between hard and long and alluring.

What would it hurt to spend this one time in his

arms—this one moment before she was wed for eternity—to know passion as she had never known it before and would never know it again? Surely that would be no great sin, she thought, then reprimanded herself for her weakness. She was a MacGowan, the daughter of the Flame and the Rogue, honorable, strong.

"I must not!" she rasped. "I dunna know why this happens when ye are near. Tis as if I am bewitched. But I canna do this. I must marry William. I *will* marry William."

"Why?" he asked, stepping toward her as frustration roared through him.

"Tis . . . tis the right thing to do," she said.

"The right thing? To marry a man for his position?" God forgive him, but he could not believe she was involved in a plot against the king. She couldn't be! But if she had no designs against the throne, why marry William? The questions tore at him. "The right thing?" he repeated. "To desire me, to long for me, and to marry him?"

"This . . ." She motioned wildly toward him. "This allure I feel for ye, tis nothing but lust. Tis of little regard."

"Little regard?" He reached for her, but she scampered from the bed to the far side of the room. "You think these feelings happen every day?"

She straightened her back, like a princess, so beautiful it made his soul ache with longing. "For ye? Aye, I do. Or at the least, every day ye find a rich widow."

"So you think me a womanizer."

"I know about the duchess of Crondell."

"Do you, now?" It did not matter where she had acquired her knowledge of him, for every face he wore was false. Only a very select few knew the truth.

"Aye. I do," she whispered.

He drew a careful breath, wanting with burning intensity to tell her the truth, to share secrets unrevealed, to feel her acceptance wrapped around him like the warmth of a plaid. "Mayhap twas not the carnal relationship you think it," he said carefully.

"Oh? And what might it be instead?" she asked.

"Mayhap the duchess' son was held for ransom. Mayhap I risked my life to save him, to retrieve him from the men who took him, and mayhap she was so grateful that she begged me to allow her to fuss over me for a time, to shower me with gifts out of her fierce gratitude."

"And mayhap I am the queen of Spain," Shona said.

He watched her, wanting nothing more than to pull her into his arms, to convince her of his goodness, but first he'd have to convince himself.

"Is that . . ." She paused, her words little more than a breath in the silent room, as if she were fighting to hold them back. "Is that what happened?"

She was a laird's haughty daughter. He a foreign bastard, Dugald reminded himself. The truth would not bridge that gap.

"Nay," he said finally. "She was young, rich, and lusty. And always willing."

"Get out!" she rasped.

"So you can marry the sainted William of Atberry?"

"He is a good man," she said.

"You know nothing of him. Nothing but that he's a wealthy duke in line for the throne."

"He saved Kelvin's life," she said.

"But why?" Dugald growled. "That is what I ask myself. Tis not in his character to risk his life for a ragged child he does not even care for."

"Ye know nothing of his character, good or bad."

He was silent for a moment. "I know that with his power and position he could well be king someday, if that were his goal. Is that why you wish to marry him, Shona?"

"Nay!"

"Then why?"

"Because he is a good man."

Dugald ground his teeth in frustration. "A good man?

The miller is a good man. The tanner is a good man." He stepped closer, near enough for her to feel the heat of his body. "Mayhap I am a good man."

"He saved Kelvin's life," she whispered.

"And for that you would give him yours?" He wanted to shake her, to kiss her, to hold her forever in his arms. "I cannot even believe that myself. Never will I convince Tremay . . ." He stopped the word and ground his teeth in frustration.

"What?" she murmured.

"You marry him because you're afraid of me," Dugald whispered, and suddenly he believed it was true. She wasn't a murderess. She was just a woman trying to find her place in the world. A place where she and Kelvin would be safe. "You're afraid of what I make you feel," he said, and reached for her.

"Nay!" she gasped and leapt away. "Get out. Get out, or I'll call my father."

Her voice had risen and her eyes looked wild. Dugald tightened his fists, trying to hold on to his shaky control.

"I swear I'll do it," she said.

"Aye, I will go," Dugald said, forcing out the words. "But know this, Damsel, if you marry him, I will not be able to protect you."

"Protect me? From what?"

From Tremayne. From the politics that threatened her. From everything. "From your own foolishness."

"Get out!" she ordered.

Dugald snatched his tunic over his head and whipped his plaid about his waist. But he paused with his hand on the door latch, finding he could not quite leave her. Not yet. "If you can no longer bear to think of an eternity with a man old enough to have sired you, I assume you will remember where I sleep."

She raised her chin. "I will throw myself from the turrets first."

He raised one brow at her. "And spend eternity in hell for your sins?"

"Twould be hell either way," she said, and he left.

Chapter 18

◟◞◝◜

The festivities continued, but Shona could no longer enjoy them. Though the men were still courteous, all had heard the news of her impending marriage and gave way to William's claim.

As for William, he was gentlemanly, attentive, but not cloying.

Before noon there was a piping competition. Stanford played beautifully, his hound dog eyes watching her the whole while. Twas mayhap his soulful attitude that won him the prize.

The nooning meal was a feast of poached salmon, pork tarts, and an assortment of other delicacies, after which the horsemanship competitions began.

On a rolling sward of grassy hills beyond the Gael Burn, tall posts had been set into the earth. From the top of the posts, wooden arms protruded four feet, and from those arms, lengths of hemp hung to eight feet above the ground.

Shona watched as the horses champed their bits and pranced in place. There were perhaps two dozen mounted men, and the glory of the day made Shona wish that she too were riding, feeling the wind in her face and freedom in her soul. But if she felt the urge, how much more so her mother must. Shona glanced at Flame, who stood next to her.

"I think ye should compete," Shona said softly.

231

"Me?" Her mother looked surprised as if such a thought was unheard of. "I am an old, married woman."

"Ye mean ye have no wish to best the men?"

Flanna laughed. "Actually, I have every wish, but your father made me promise I would not. He agreed to remain neutral if I would do the same."

"Methinks he simply does not want the men staring at ye again."

"Let us hope he *is* jealous," Flanna said, but Shona's attention had been captured elsewhere, for just then Dugald rode into view.

The afternoon sun made his hair gleam like a raven's wing as it flowed about his shoulders. Beneath him his stallion tossed its thick mane and pranced, making them appear to float.

Flanna turned from Dugald to her daughter and felt her heart swell with a fierce pride. But the feelings were painful, for her daughter was not happy. What would happen to this proud child, this diamond, this flame-haired extension of herself? Shona was certainly not too young to be married, and yet . . . why had she betrothed herself to William? True, both she and Roderic had advised it, but Shona never took their advice. It only made her more determined to follow her own course. Flanna had been certain that her words to the contrary would force Shona to bond with the man called Dugald.

Roderic had said the lad was vain and aloof, but . . . Flanna's gaze slipped to Dugald's steed. He was a powerful animal, without a doubt, but he was also the homeliest specimen she had ever seen. Why would a man of Dugald's reputation ride such a beast?

With an effort, Flanna turned to look at William. He sat aboard a glistening bay, laughing with another rider as rings were attached to the ropes on the posts.

William seemed a good enough man. Still . . . Flanna turned to her daughter again. She had not even blinked, so transfixed was she by Dugald. Pain stabbed Flanna's heart.

"He looks quite splendid," Flanna said softly. Shona nodded. "And he rides well."

"Aye." The word was simple.

"Aye," Flanna said with a sigh. "William will make ye a fine husband."

Shona snapped from her reverie. Her face reddened as she realized her mistake.

They stared at each other. Silence echoed between them. "Ye are sure of your decision, Daughter?"

There was a moment of absolute quiet. "I am sure."

But just at that instant, Dugald turned to glance at them. Even Flanna could feel his gaze, so hard and hot was it. Shona turned. The tension between the two was like a cord of steel, stretched tight, pulling them together.

Flanna drew a deep breath. It had been like that with her and Roderic, and never, not in a thousand lifetimes, would she find a man she could love more. She would not wish less for her only daughter. But what could she do?

"Flanna," Roderic said, but she could not quite pull her gaze from the scene before her.

Roderic, warned by her attention, turned toward Dugald, his brows lowered.

"Nay," Flanna whispered. "Dunna do it, my love."

Roderic turned toward her, his expression haunted.

"Had I listened to *my* father's council, I would not have married *ye*." Love sparked between them. She reached for his hand. "I would not have been whole," she said, and they turned together and left their daughter to her own mistake.

Aboard Eagle, Dugald watched them go. It was as if they were offering her to him, begging him to take her, knowing she did not belong with a man like William of Atberry.

"Riders, gather near the north end of the field," called the master of the games.

The announcement shook Dugald back to reality. What the hell was the matter with him? She was not for him. He should have continued riding alone this morning, investigating the woods, instead of returning here, where he knew he would see her. True, on the morning of the archery contest, he had agreed to compete in the horsemanship exercises also, but he had been insane then, determined to prove himself to Shona in any way possible.

Lucidness had returned since then.

Pulling his gaze from her, Dugald turned his attention to the games. As long as he was here, he would learn what he could, keep low, and think.

Sir Godwin was called to compete first. He rode forward and was given a long wooden shaft. Bracing it against his hip, he placed his mount behind the line and waited.

In a matter of seconds the master called the start.

The knight spurred his mount. It lunged forward. The first ring was speared on the lance. The second also, but on the third, Godwin's mount veered sideways and he missed the next three rings.

He returned to his comrades looking a bit chagrined. But none improved on his performance until William of Atberry rode onto the field.

It was he that won the match.

Dugald watched as William made his way to Shona's side, felt his heart constrict as William kissed her hand. Mother of God, she was beautiful beyond words, and yet . . . and yet as Dugald watched her, he could not fail to see the change in her.

She seemed unusually staid, as if her vibrant life had been stilled, and now and then, when her betrothed was not demanding her attention, she would turn her gaze to his. The shock he used to feel at her touch was now present even at the contact of their gazes.

William turned from his conversation with another, stared directly at Dugald, and smiled—almost a pitying smile, as if there had never been any hope that a bastard would win her.

Anger welled up within Dugald. Damn the noble ass

for winning her, damn him for his superiority.

Hoping to cool his ire, Dugald tied Eagle in the shade of a copse of elms and fetched himself a mug of ale. But the spirits did little to calm him, for each time he looked up, it seemed that William was fondling Shona, brushing his knuckles possessively across her cheek, touching her hair. Dugald tried to pull his attention away, but just then William glanced up and grinned, as if he knew the fire that burned in Dugald's soul.

Mother of God, he ached to wipe that smug expression from the duke's face. An official called the start to a half mile horse race, and suddenly Dugald found himself pulled toward his mount as aggressiveness boiled in his system.

There were a hundred ways a man could accidently die in a horse race, Dugald thought, but as he passed Hadwin, he stopped himself.

What the hell was he thinking? He couldn't kill William of Atberry, accidently or otherwise. Indeed, Dugald had been most careful to portray himself as an arrogant womanizer in search of a rich bride. Hardly should he be ruining that image by riding this lop-eared horse in a competition he was likely to win whether he liked it or not.

It was time he went to work in earnest. Time he learned the truth instead of allowing his wick to lead him about like a hound on a leash. He would return Eagle to the stable, then do some digging, he told himself, but just as he turned, his gaze caught Shona. She stood at the edge of the crowd, her lush mouth pursed, her eyes flat, the fire in them gone.

Turning slightly, Dugald saw that William was mounted and beside the others, his horse restive, his demeanor calm, as if he were completely unaffected by the time he had spent with Shona. What kind of man could so easily forget her presence?

A man that needed to be shaken off balance, Dugald decided. And suddenly there was nothing in the world he could do to stop himself. He found himself walking across the green toward Shona, pulled against his better sense until he stood beside her.

The buzz of the crowd around them hushed a little.

"You are not riding?" he asked.

Her eyes grew wide. She shifted her gaze to her betrothed. "Nay, of course not."

"But you owe me a competition," he said. "Another chance to best you."

A tiny spark of fire flashed in her eyes. Mother of God, he was a fool, but he welcomed it like a summer breeze.

"I would gladly beat ye again, Kinnaird, but as ye see, the field waits, and I dunna even have a horse saddled."

Dugald glanced toward the riders, then back at her. Without so much as acknowledging her betrothed, he bowed as he lifted his reins toward her. "Then twould be only honorable to offer my own mount," he said.

Her strawberry lips parted in surprise, then, "I dunna think William would like it."

Anger spurred through him. For the past two years he had lived alone at Isle Fois in search of peace. Why now would he court the chaos her presence brought? But one glance at her told him the truth. Peace without love was a small comfort, and life without her seemed suddenly shallow and hopeless. "Lord William is your master, then?" he asked stiffly.

The spark in her eyes turned to an inferno. "Twould hardly be your chance to best me if ye yourself are not riding."

"But twould be little victory in winning the prize if the best of the lot was not racing."

"Ye know nothing about my ability with a mount."

"On the contrary," he said, holding her gaze. "I have quite fond memories of seeing ye astride."

Her face grew pink. Mayhap she was remembering the first time they met, thinking of how she had taken his horse. But he could not help but hope she was thinking of another time, of her slim thighs straddling him, of her breasts bare and her face glowing.

"My thanks, Sir," she said, "but—"

"Shona." William rode up on his handsome bay. There was a smile on his face, but beneath that smile there was something else. Something not so jovial and no longer so certain. Satisfaction swelled through Dugald. "Your conversation seems to be delaying the race."

She glanced up into her fiancé's face. "This gentleman offered to let me ride his stallion."

"How gallant," William said. "But I'm certain tis not the kind of thing a sweet maid such as yourself would contemplate."

There was a moment of delay before her answer, "In truth," she said softly, "I *was* considering it."

"I'm sure you've no wish to embarrass me, lass," William said, then turned to Dugald. "If ye plan to race that . . . horse, ye'd best get in the line, Kinnaird. Ye've no wish to cause a scene."

"Don't I?" Dugald raised his brows. He had been born to cause a scene—a blue eyed boy amongst a million dark-eyed natives. Why stop now?

"What is it you fear, William?" Dugald asked. "Do ye think she might best you?"

"Nay." There was the slightest grind in his tone. "I but fear she might be hurt.

"Shona, my love, mayhap ye should return to your mother."

"Aye, return to your mother like a good little lass, Shona," Dugald said, turning away. "Prove that you are no longer a MacGowan."

"What?" Her tone was sharp, breathy.

He turned back. Their gazes met like oil and fire. Pulling his away, he took a step toward Eagle and patted the stallion's broad neck. "He's a powerful animal. I do not blame you for being scared."

"Kinnaird." She nabbed his sleeve suddenly.

He tried to ignore the shock of her touch, but there

was little hope of that. Their gazes clashed like steel on steel.

"Aye?" he asked, barely able to force that one word from between his lips.

"This beast is but a mild mannered hound compared to the stallions I rode as an infant."

Mother of God, he loved her like this, with fire in her eyes and triumph in her soul. He would gladly kill any man who crushed that vibrancy from her.

"Truly?" he asked, raising a brow and trying to disavow the rush of hot emotion she caused in him.

"Truly."

He shrugged as he lifted the reins toward her. "Then he is yours."

Eagle nuzzled her ear. For a moment, he thought she would refuse, but something would not let her. Whether it was his taunting, the thrill of the race, or William's own unintentional goading, he could not tell.

She mounted on her own, for William would not help her and Dugald dared not touch her, but neither was he quite able to let her turn away, so he caught Eagle's reins. The stallion irritably laid back his ears and snapped at his hand.

Dugald tightened his grip. "Watch him at the start," he warned softly. "He's not as mild mannered as he seems."

"Rather like his master?"

"He'll lunge to the side," he said, finding his voice, yet evading her questions. "Let him run. In truth, there's little else you can do." He wanted nothing more than to touch her hand, but he did not dare, not now, not when she was her most vibrant, most alive. It was moments like this that held the ultimate danger for him.

She glanced at William for an instant before turning Eagle toward the starting line. The crowd was silent, the other competitors shocked. As for Dugald, twas all he could do to keep his heart from leaping from his chest.

"It seems I owe you," William said.

Dugald smiled. Twas the first crack he had seen in

the man's careful demeanor. "I will look forward to collecting," he said, and turned away.

Behind the starting line, horses pranced as their riders stared at Shona's approach. It seems they were not quite ready to see their object of obsession become their competition. William rode stiffly behind her toward the line.

Moments passed as riders steadied their mounts. Shona was placed in the middle of the pack. The gray next to her trumpeted and struck with a foreleg, but Eagle did no more than glare, for he, like Dugald, had long ago learned to differentiate between true danger and an empty threat.

Right now there was nothing to consider but the finish line. Eagle's tattered ears pricked forward, his neck bent, and upon his back, Shona sat perfectly still.

For the first time, Dugald realized her feet didn't reach the stirrups, but she seemed unconcerned by that disadvantage. Her hands were low and steady and she was bent low over Eagle's heavy crest, her gaze straight ahead and her cheeks flushed.

"All ready?" Bullock shouted.

No one answered. There was a moment of pause, then, "Go!"

Shona's yell was lost in the cries of the other riders, but it made no difference, for Eagle was the type to win no matter the cost. He lunged into the combatant gray on his right, knocking that horse off balance, then sprang forward, his powerful quarters driving him. But the others sprang with him, and while Eagle was driven by Shona's gentle legs, the other's horses were driven by riders who could not bear to be beaten by a woman. Though they were all willing enough to drool and swoon over her, they had no desire to lose to her.

Stanford yelled. Sir Godwin dug his mount's flanks with his spurs, and William, leaning over his horse's neck like a man possessed, slashed a whip against his bay's rump.

Two horses in the middle of the pack collided and went down, spilling their riders. Eagle leapt to the side to avoid them, throwing Shona over his withers.

She scrambled to regain her balance, grappling with the reins and the mane as Dugald held his breath. Horses thundered past, but in an instant Shona dragged herself back in position.

The last horse was now two horse lengths ahead, but Eagle had been down before, and now, with a feather-weight on his back and the smell of a challenge in his nostrils, he leapt forward. Shona leaned lower, her face nearly pressed against his neck as she screamed into the wind.

They ate up the distance, devoured the stragglers, ran down the main pack, and finally raced past William and the others to soar beneath the finish line.

Dugald soared with them, felt the wind in his hair, the glory of victory. Never had he seen anything so beautiful. She was laughing, her right arm raised in victory, her left slowing a still-pounding stallion. Her face was aglow, her hair, loosed by the wild ride, flowed behind her like a river of fire, and in her eyes there was a joy as deep as forever, a joy he had given her, a joy he would never forget, not as long as he lived.

But suddenly a small girl leapt from the crowd. She was carrying a banner. It whipped wildly in the wind, and Eagle, spurred by the exhilaration of his victory, bolted sideways.

Shona grabbed for the pommel, trying to stay aboard, but suddenly the girth split loose and the entire saddle spilled sideways. There was nothing she could do but go with it, slipping with a shriek of dismay as she fell beneath the horse's pounding hooves.

Chapter 19

Dugald ran to her, pushing people aside, shoving himself through the crowd, until he fell to his knees beside her.

"Shona!" He breathed her name, his fingers skimming her face. Her eyes were closed. A laceration slashed across her left cheek. His hand shook as he felt for a pulse in her throat. It was there, erratic but strong. Without thought, without volition, he lifted her into his arms.

Rachel rushed up, her face pale. "She lives?"

"Aye." He forced out the word.

"To the infirmary. Quickly!" she ordered. "Kelvin, fetch Muriel and my mother. Sara, come with me."

William appeared suddenly before them. "Shona. Shona, wake up. Nay!" He fell to his knees. "This is my fault. Please, lass, awaken."

Dugald said nothing, but pressed quickly past him and hurried toward the keep.

"Carefully. Carefully," Rachel said. "Put her on the bed."

He did so. Her head lolled sideways, her eyes remained closed.

Mayhap he had completed his mission after all, he thought, but the irony of the situation turned his stomach and ripped at his soul. "What shall I do?" he asked, but

Rachel was busy dumping a small bag of herbs into a bowl of water.

She stirred it with a wooden ladle, dunked a cloth into it, then handed the rag to him. "Hold this on her wound."

Dugald pressed it carefully to her cheek. In truth, he had seen a hundred people die, many by his own hand. She was only one more, he told himself. But something in him whispered that he lied. If she died the best of him would die, too.

"Tis not this wound that causes her unconsciousness," he said, but Rachel was already examining her further.

"A bump on the back of her head. A scrape on her neck." She cataloged her cousin's wounds as if to herself, then ran her hands down Shona's arms and pushed up her skirt to examine her legs.

"What goes on here?" William asked. His voice was soft, but his posture was stiff when he stepped into the room.

"I am seeing to her wounds," Rachel said, startled by his entrance.

"You will not!" he growled.

The room went as silent as a tomb.

"What?" Rachel asked.

Anger sparked in William's eyes, but in a moment it flashed away. He stumbled across the room and fell to his knees beside the bed "I am sorry. I just . . . I cannot bear to see her like this. Tis my fault." He rocked back and forth. "My fault. I should not have let her ride, just as I should not have got my Deirdra with another child. Now my Shona will die, too."

"Damn you!" Dugald swore, and lunged across the room to grab William by the shirt and drag him to his feet. "She will not die, you filthy . . ."

A knowing spark gleamed in William's eyes.

Dugald tightened his grip, but the door opened behind him.

"What goes on here?" Roderic asked.

"My lord," William moaned as he drooped in Dugald's fist. "Tis my fault. Tis mine."

"I need peace, Uncle Roddy," Rachel murmured. "I need them gone. Please."

"Ye heard her," Roderic said, his voice stony, his eyes blank. "Leave now, or die where ye stand."

The hours following Shona's injury were agonizing. Even after Rachel assured him that her cousin would soon be well and up to her usual mischief, Dugald paced.

But finally he gained the presence of mind at least to see to his horse. He found Eagle in his stall, unscathed and untroubled. After rubbing him down with a twist of straw, Dugald sought out his saddle. Someone had found it on the green and laid it in the aisle next to his mount. He picked it up and absently glanced at the girth. He should have replaced it long ago, should have been more careful, should never have urged her to ride. Many years this leather girth had supported him. It seemed a cruel joke that it would fail now under Shona's slight weight, he thought, as he ran his fingers over the wasted strap.

It had torn near the buckle. The leather was soft and frayed there, but . . . he scowled. At the right edge of the strap, a small portion of the tear was smooth and straight, almost as if it had been cut with a knife.

Dugald froze. Had someone intentionally cut his girth? And if so, why? And who? He'd passed Hadwin on the way to his mount. Had he been up to his practical jokes, hoping Dugald would be the one felled, or was there something more sinister planned here? Could someone have known Shona would ride Eagle? No. Twas not possible. But her life had also been endangered on the hunt. Kelvin had said the wolf had acted strangely. Dugald had thought it was just the boy's fear talking, but now he wondered. Could it be that someone had known Shona would be at that particular place in the woods? Could they have somehow placed the wolf in her path? Could someone be trying to kill her and make it look like an accident—someone besides himself? Mayhap Tremayne did not trust Dugald to do the job. The king's old advisor had often complained that Kinnaird was unpredictable and was likely to become sympathetic to anything from a tattered-eared horse to an orphaned child. Twas a fault Tremayne detested. So mayhap he had sent someone else to do the job.

Dugald shook his head. He must be wrong. Yet the fact remained that danger seemed to be stalking Shona. And now she had been injured. Did someone wish her harm? And if so, who?

Dugald closed his eyes to the irony. Mayhap someone *was* trying to kill Shona. But it certainly wasn't he. Nay, he could not hurt her, had failed miserably in his plan to do so, in fact. So why not go one step further? Why not become her protector?

Shona awoke slowly. She was lying on her side and could feel her pulse beat in the bump at the back of her skull. Her head pounded with it. Still, it was the cut on her cheek that was most noticeable. But Rachel had assured her the scar would only make her face more interesting.

Shona's sojourn to the great hall, however, had proved that "interesting" was just a euphemism for "frightening." Upon seeing her, William had stared at her in blank silence, Hadwin had gone pale, and Stanford had wept like a baby.

So much for interesting. The isolation of her small chamber seemed much preferable to such ridiculous dramatics. After all, it was only a cut . . . a few stitches . . . a rather impressive bump . . . oh, and a black eye. She'd looked worse after her last attempt to save a toad from the well.

Still, it had taken a good deal of cajoling to convince Rachel to allow her to sleep alone in her own borrowed chamber. But a small show of tears had worked. Generally Rachel would have laughed at such histrionics, but surprisingly, she had relented. Still, Shona barred the door behind her, just to guarantee her solitude.

She lay in silence now, letting her thoughts tick away. By the darkness and the lack of noise, she guessed it was some hours yet until dawn. She wasn't certain what had awakened her, but she assumed it was her own nagging worries. True, she was concerned about her face, but a face was a face, pretty much like any other. Her teeth were all still intact, her uncanny eyesight undiminished, and Rachel assured her that all would be well in time.

What worried her far more was the accident itself. She had ridden in Dugald's saddle. True, he was not a huge man, but he was muscular and solid. If the girth hadn't failed under *his* weight, why would it break under *hers*? How had it broken? Could someone have tampered with it? And if so, had it been Dugald? The thought caused a dull ache to begin in her heart.

He hadn't been in the hall at supper. Why? Was he so unconcerned for her well-being that he could not even spare the time to see how she fared? Was he, even now, flirting with Mavis? Or worse? Were they, perhaps . . .

She wouldn't think of that. Twas none of her concern.

The fact was, he made her careless. She should not have let him challenge her. What if she had been seriously wounded? What then would happen to Kelvin? Indeed . . .

Her thoughts came to an abrupt halt as a breath of noise disturbed her thoughts. What was it? A rodent? But no. Five plump cats roamed the castle. The wind? No, for there was not so much as a breeze this night.

She lay perfectly still, listening, concentrating. And then she heard it—someone's breathing, someone close, not three feet from her bed. She lay frozen in fear. Who was it? What did he want? Had someone indeed tried to kill her? Was he determined to finish the job now? She didn't want to die.

But suddenly her mind cleared, and anger boiled up. This was her home, her chamber, and she wasn't about to let some midnight marauder frighten her. She had but to scream to bring the whole castle down upon them.

But by then he might already have escaped through the window. He must have come through there, but she had no intention of allowing him to leave the same way. But how would she apprehend him? She had yet to regain her full strength. But wouldn't the intruder assume that? Thus, surely the element of surprise would be with her.

She had put the knife Hadwin had given her on the trunk beside her bed. Even in the darkness, she could see the dim glow of jewels that encrusted the handle. All she had to do was grab the knife, spin around, jump out of bed, and grab the brigand before he escaped out the window. Simple, really. Elementary. A child could do it. A woman could do it. A Flame's daughter could certainly . . .

She was stalling. Fear was an ugly thing.

One quick prayer, one moment to draw her courage around her, and then she acted. She was spinning about even as her fingers folded over the knife. Her nightrail billowed behind her as she leapt in the direction the breathing had come from. His face flashed across her line of vision.

She grabbed lower, hoping to nab his shirt, but her balance was still slightly off and she slammed into him. He grunted beneath her impact, but already her right hand had come up and poised the blade at his throat.

For a moment there was no noise but the sound of their breathing, the rush of her excitement, before, ''I shall assume then that ye are healing well,'' he said softly.

''Dugald!'' she gasped, startled and breathless.

''Aye.'' His voice was low.

She steadied her thoughts. In truth, she should have known it was he by the speed of her pulse, for surely one midnight intruder would not worry her so. Twas his presence that disoriented her. She backed away a half step, but then all her doubts about him rushed back to the fore, and she pressed the knife more firmly to his throat.

"What are ye doing here?" she asked.

The muscles beneath his shirt felt firm but relaxed beneath her clenched fist.

"I am watching you," he said evenly.

Against every ounce of good sense, she could feel warmth spread through her at his words. But she fought the sensations and pressed the tip of the blade harder against his neck.

"Why?"

"Because I cannot help myself."

She felt her composure slip another notch, but she held onto it with desperate resolve. "Ye lie," she said.

She heard him release a soft breath. "Frequently," he said. "But you can believe me in this, had I been able to stop myself, I would not have come. I but needed to be certain you were well."

With considerable effort, she remembered falling, remembered the ground slamming against her head, remembered Eagle's gargantuan hoof rapping hard as steel against her cranium. Twas because of him.

"Why did ye cut the girth?" she asked, gripping the knife harder still.

He remained silent. "You think twas *my* doing?"

His tone did not shift a whit. Her certainty wavered, though she dared not show it. "Who else?"

"Who indeed?" he asked. "Can you not think of any enemies you have made?"

"Enemies?" She considered lying, but it seemed like too much effort, for her head was pounding louder still and her confidence was slipping away like sand in an hourglass. "I spent a year at court. Enemies abound."

He was silent for a moment, then said, "Any that would do more than spread gossip behind your back?"

She was not so naive as to think that all of the king's advisors appreciated her closeness to the throne. Still, that was no one's business but her own. This interview was not going at all as she had planned. In fact, she was beginning to feel rather silly holding a knife to his throat. But she had begun down this road and had no wish to appear foolish by turning back.

"Quiet!" she snarled, twisting his shirt in her fist. Her knuckles brushed his chest. She could feel the indentation between the hard mounds of his pectorals, and for a moment her entire consciousness riveted on that one narrow piece of flesh. But she marshaled her senses with an Amazonian effort. "I am the one asking the questions."

He was silent for a moment, then, "As you wish. What would you like to know?"

She breathed deeply, trying to collect her thoughts, but instead, her nostrils were filled with the scent of him. "Who are ye?"

"What?"

She closed her eyes, trying to clear her head, but the dichotomy that he was baffled her and needed explanation.

"Who are ye really?" she asked. "The man who worries more for his hair than the safety of Scotland, or the man who would climb a dark tower wall to make certain I am safe?"

"Can I not be both?"

For a moment it seemed a logical answer, but then she shook her head. "Who are ye? Where are ye from? What do ye want here?"

"Why do you ask?"

She was silent for a moment. "Because I cannot help myself."

He remained silent for a moment, but then he spoke, his voice low. "I am called Dugald, after my father, whom I did not meet until I was twelve. I live on Isle Fois, to the north and west of—"

"But where *really?*" The words sounded desperate to her own ears. "Ye are not just some blithe Scottish lad. Are ye?"

He was quiet again, then, "Nay," he said slowly, but his unspoken words intrigued her, perhaps even more than the muscles she could feel flexing beneath her hand.

"What then?" she asked.

"My mother was a great beauty."

That she could believe, but she had no idea what that had to do with the conversation.

"Half Japanese, half Spanish," he said.

A dozen of Roderic's fanciful tales sprang immediately into Shona's mind. "A beautiful princess married to a dashing nobleman?" she asked.

Her näiveté was rewarded with a sliver of a smile. "A pale-eyed peasant girl sold into virtual slavery. They call them geisha. Revered by some. But not by her family. Still, they did not let me die when she gave me to them."

"Die!"

"I represented two generations of sin. My grandmother was raped by a European. My mother was given to one.

"What are your plans for that knife?"

She felt foolish again, for once again she had forgotten its presence. "I plan to get the truth from ye."

"Thus far you've failed to ask anything to which I feel a need to lie."

"Why are ye here?"

"I told you. To watch you—"

"Nay," she interrupted. "I mean, why did ye come to Dun Ard atall?"

He shrugged. "For the same reasons as the others. To gain my fortune through marriage. Tis a time honored western tradition, is it not?"

She watched him carefully. The moon had slipped from behind a fat cloud and shone through her window now, gilding his face in its pearlescent glow.

"I dunna believe ye. Had ye meant to win my hand, ye would have been less irritating and far more charming."

He laughed. "Shall I be insulted?" he asked, "or shall I remind ye . . ."

She could have sworn he never moved, and yet, suddenly, her knife was gone and her hand empty and resting against the oaken strength of his chest. She stared at him in befuddled amazement.

"None of those who fawned over you have held your attention nearly as surely as I. Admit it," he said, and took a half step closer.

It was a small step, an insignificant distance, really, and yet she could feel his closeness with renewed excitement, as if her blood was pumping from her body into his and their lungs shared the same air.

"I am the one in your bedchamber," he added, and moved even closer—so close, in fact, that the hard planes of his chest brushed her nipples.

The feelings shivered from her chest to every sparkling nerve in her body, but she held them at bay and stepped quickly back.

"Ye are only here because ye have forced your way into my room."

"Into your room," he asked, "or into your thoughts? Into your imaginings?"

She licked her lips. Where was her knife? "Into my *room*," she said.

"Truly?" He touched her hale cheek with his fingertips. "And who do you think of when you dream, then, Damsel?"

There was such a dark allure about him that suddenly she could not speak, could not even move.

"Who do you think of?" he whispered, leaning closer. "Tell me tis William you desire and I shall leave."

William! Dear God, she'd forgotten about him again. Shame spurred through her. But she would not betray his trust again. She would send this scoundrel from her life here and now. "Tis W—" she began, but suddenly his mouth covered hers.

Lightning seared her. Thunder rolled through her. She was consumed by the feelings, lost in his touch, but she could not do this. Could not!

Shona jerked away, breathing hard. "I canna!" she rasped. "I must not."

"Why?" He took a step toward her, his hands clenched and empty. "Because you do not wish to, or because you are promised?"

Mayhap she would be wise to lie, to tell him he did not move her, but how could he believe such a thing when every time she saw him she squashed herself against him like honey on a scone?

"It would not be fair to William."

"William!" he snarled. "You worry about being fair to William?"

She raised her chin at his aggressive tone, but stood her ground. "I am vowed to him."

"Then you are vowed to die young."

It took a moment for his words to sink into her consciousness. "What?"

"You were right, lass. My girth was cut. But not by me."

"Ye lie!"

"Do I? Think on it. If I wished you dead, I could have killed you a hundred times by now, and none would be the wiser. But someone cut the girth. Who?"

"I dunna know!" She shook her head, baffled and scared. "What enemies have ye made?"

A muscle twitched in his lean jaw. "In truth, lass, most of *my* enemies are no longer amongst the living. So I wondered, who would gain most from my demise?"

"No one," she said. "At least, no one here at Dun Ard."

He laughed out loud. "Could it be that you do not realize they know?"

"Know what?"

He stepped forward. Electricity flared through her.

"Know that we are drawn to each other, that no matter how we fight it, still we are drawn. Do ye think that would not disconcert your suitors?"

"Ye accuse one of them?"

"Doesn't it seem unusual that you are always present when there is trouble?"

"Not really," she said wryly, and winced. "Tis usually the way of things."

"Did you not think it strange that the wolf was alone?"

"What?"

"The wolf that attacked Kelvin. Twas a female. Generally they run in packs," he said. "Does it not seem strange to you that this one was alone?"

"I've no idea what ye are hinting at."

"The beast was placed there apurpose," he said. "Awaiting your arrival. Who knew you would be riding?"

She stepped back a pace. "Placed there? You're insane. Wolves do not stay put, like puppies on—"

"Nay, not unless they are wounded and baited and ready to kill anything that crosses their path. Not unless they are placed just so at your favorite place beside the water."

She could not speak, could barely think. "And ye think William did this?"

He was silent a moment. "I said *someone* did it," he said softly. "Tis you who accuses William."

She drew a deep breath. "Get out."

"Shona." He took a step toward her, but she shook her head.

"I knew ye were a scoundrel," she said. "But I did not think ye would stoop to accusing an innocent man just because ye want me for yourself."

"Innocent? Go to the water and look at the—"

"Get out!" she said, her voice rising. "Get out, or so help me God, I will tell my father ye were here."

She watched him tense. Watched him take a step back.

"As ye wish," he said and turning toward the window, slipped outside like a shadow that never was.

Chapter 20

"**D**ugald of Kinnaird."

The great hall echoed with Stanford's words. He stood not four feet away, so there seemed little reason for shouting.

"Stanford," Dugald said softly, nodding slightly from his seat at the trestle table and ignoring the many faces that turned from their meals to stare at them.

"You are a coward and a bastard," Stanford said, his tone strained and his reed thin body stiff.

Dugald remained very still. He was not a man easily riled, but the past days had been trying at best, and his nerves were already stretched taut. Still, he had learned young the importance of holding his temper, so he nodded with as much equanimity as he could muster. "I shall keep that in mind for future reference," he said, and turned back to his meal.

Stanford spun him back around with a hand on his shoulder.

"You shall apologize!" he growled.

Anger bubbled slowly upward in Dugald's gut, but he carefully tamped it back down. He nodded again. "My apologies, then."

"Not to me, you craven bastard!" Grabbing the front of Dugald's tunic, Stanford dragged him to his feet. "To Lady Shona."

"To the lady?" Dugald asked. He had found long ago

that if he gave himself a few moments before respond-
ing, people were less likely to die. And such would definitely be a good idea now, for the hall was filled with
more than a hundred men, all of whom would probably
be happy to see him drawn and quartered for his part in
Shona's injury. Dugald could handle twenty or so of
them, but the last eighty were likely to give him some
trouble. "For what would I apologize, Lord Stanford?"

"Twas you who insisted she ride," snarled the other.
"Twas you who caused her ruin." He sounded almost
as if he might cry.

"Her ruin?"

"Scarred!" Stanford choked. "And all because of
you. Scarred. Her vibrant beauty dulled forever."

Dear Mother of God! This poor chap was seriously
melodramatic, and possibly a mite deranged. Definitely
someone to watch. After all, there was no reason to think
he wasn't the one to place the wolf in the woods by the
burn.

"True beauty cannot be dulled," Dugald said. "It can
only be cherished." Long ago, in another world, his
grandfather had oft quoted such words of wisdom. It had
been just this kind of gibberish that used to drive Dugald
to distraction.

"Cherished?" Stanford scowled as if trying to work
out the meaning. The problem was, there was no meaning. Still, Dugald thought, it gave the scrawny lord
something to think about other than Shona's injuries.
But apparently, he didn't feel like pondering such a deep
topic. "What do you know of beauty?" he finally asked,
his tone weepy.

Dugald shrugged, still trying to defuse the situation
with his philosophical manner. "What do any of us
know, Lord Stanford? Mayhap we could sit and discuss
the phenomena of beauty."

Stanford's face turned from red to purple, and then,
in a fit of rage, he spat.

"Tis your fault she is ruined, and tis you who shall
pay," Stanford sobbed.

Dugald wiped his face with his sleeve and counted backward from fifteen. "What exactly are ye saying, Stanford?" Dugald asked. "Are ye accusing me of cutting my own girth?" There was a kind of sick irony here, he knew. Someday he might be able to appreciate it. But not just now. Just now he had to concentrate on keeping everyone alive—himself first, Stanford second.

"I am saying you are a coward and a bastard," Stanford repeated. It was beginning to get monotonous. "And if you have a grain of honor, you will meet me on the green with your sword." He motioned to his own weapon that hung at his side.

"Tis general knowledge that I do not have a grain of honor. Therefore, it seems I'm exempt," he said, and forced himself to turn away.

"Damn you!" Stanford swore.

Dugald knew the moment the knife was drawn, sensed the attack even before it came. Sheer instinct made him turn. Twas training that made him react. His hand flashed out and chopped hard and fast against Stanford's throat.

The tall man staggered back, his eyes popping. His blade skittered noisily across the floor while his bony fingers gripped his throat.

The hall went absolutely quiet.

Stanford stared straight ahead, his face pasty and his lips turning blue. Dugald swore in silence and damned himself for using too much force; if the man died, Dugald's reputation as a coward was likely to be ruined for life.

But in a moment Stanford dragged in a harsh croaking breath, and then another.

Dugald watched him with some relief, but not for long, for it seemed Stanford was a bit more rabid than Dugald had anticipated. Barely able to breathe, the gawky lord snatched his sword from his scabbard and faced Dugald with a snarl of rage.

Dugald scowled back. "I do not mean to find fault, Lord Stanford. But I doubt this is a good idea. What will

your Shona think if you spill blood in her father's hall?''
He was trying to be reasonable, but his words only
seemed to enrage the man further. With a strangled
shriek, he lunged.

As for Dugald, he had seen better attacks from callow
youths and stepped easily aside. Stanford tromped past
like a bull in full charge, then turned to attack again.

''Truly, I am a known coward and a weakling,'' Dugald said. ''If you kill me, twill do naught but wound
your reputation.''

''I do not care for my reputation. But only for the
lady's vengeance for her hideous disfigurement,'' he
snarled, and lunged again.

Dugald leapt aside, but this time the tip of Stanford's
blade caught his sleeve, ripping it lengthwise down his
arm.

Enough was enough. Twisting quickly, Dugald shot
an arm about Stanford's neck and snatched him back
against his chest.

''You care only for the lady's vengeance?'' Dugald
gritted in the other's ear. He tightened his grip while
easily forcing Stanford's left arm between their bodies.
''Or could it be you have a care for your own life?''
Dugald twisted the arm higher. ''If so, my lord, I would
suggest you do cease baiting me.''

Stanford snarled and tried to jerk away, but in that
instant Shona entered the hall.

''Halt!'' Her voice echoed in the stillness.

Stanford twisted to stare at her. Dugald turned with
him.

She looked like a bright avenging angel, her hair billowed behind her like a scarlet typhoon, her eyes sparking emerald flame. There was little wonder the very
thought of bruising such vibrant life made men insane.

''Stop it, both of ye!'' she rasped, then realized the
way of things and frowned. ''Let him go, Dugald.''

He did as he was told, then gave his tormenter a slight
shove to gain him some distance.

Stanford tottered forward, then stumbled to a halt, the

sword going limp in his hand. "Look what you've done to her," he gasped.

"Twill not help to blame the foreigner," William said, his expression benign as he stepped forward.

"Someone must take the blame. Someone must pay. And if you are too much the coward to exact revenge, I shall do so for you!" Stanford vowed, but Shona stepped forward.

"Tis not his fault!" she said.

"Twas Kinnaird who caused your fall. I have proof."

"Proof?" she asked, glaring at Stanford.

"The girth was cut. No one else knew you would ride."

She waited, apparently for something more conclusive.

"And umm . . ." Stanford paused. "Kinnaird has a knife."

"Heaven's wrath!" Shona swore, then turned angrily to Dugald. "And ye? Do ye have proof that someone else is trying to kill me?"

Her right eye was blackened and her left cheek was stitched with something that looked like white horsehair. Dugald found he wanted nothing more than to kiss her purple eyelid, to smooth his fingers over her wounded cheek.

"Dugald?" she said. His name was soft on her lips. Like a caress.

But he brought himself back to reality with a jolt. The last thing he needed was for the culprit to know Dugald was investigating the accident.

"The only thing I know for certain is that this Stanford is an ass," he said.

"And I know you shall die before nightfall!" Stanford growled.

"Stop it!" Shona said, leaping between them. "Stop it now, or I swear the winner will fight me next."

Roderic stepped up, his expression solemn, his tone low. "Were I ye, I would not doubt her words, lads. If she says she will fight the winner, she will fight the winner. And though she may be a fair archer, she is no master of the sword, and so help me, God, whoever harms a hair on her head, will face me.''

''And me!'' His brother, Leith, stepped up beside Roderic.

''And me!'' Boden Blackblade stood beside him.

''And me,'' said Graham.

''And me.'' Kelvin's voice was high-pitched when he spoke, but it was the one that did the most to clear Dugald's head.

''I've no intention of fighting,'' Dugald said, then turned toward Shona to speak softly, for her ears only. ''Tis sorry I am to see you hurt.'' He was a fool and he knew it, but there was nothing he could do to stop himself from touching her cheek, nothing he could do to stop the spark that began at his fingertips and sizzled through every nerve ending at the touch of her flesh against his.

Her lips parted. The world fell away, but she drew herself back to reality in an instant.

''Tis naught,'' she said, and rapidly stepped back to turn her attention to the sea of faces around them. ''Tis naught for anyone to concern themselves with.''

But that evening, in the solitude of the solar, Shona paced.

She had lied. There was a great deal to be concerned about, a very great deal. Even if Dugald's overt allure did not concern her, there were other things.

She was certain Kinnaird had only been trying to make her suspicious of William, but the point was, it had worked. For a time she had doubted her fiancé, had thought that perhaps he had somehow intentionally caused her accident.

There was no place for that kind of doubt in a marriage. No place at all, especially when Kelvin's life, too, would be affected by her choice of a spouse. William deserved more than that.

''Shona?''

She started at the sound of her name and turned to find the duke of Atberry in the doorway.

"I was told you wished to speak to me."

"Aye." She wasn't the kind to wring her hands, but if a situation ever warranted hand wringing, this was surely it. Fatigue, uncertainty, and frustration over her damned attraction to Dugald had driven her to accept William's proposal. She acted impetuously—again. And now she would have to undue the damage she had done. "Please come in and shut the door."

He did so, then faced her, his expression solemn. "What is it, my dear?"

She reviewed her words for the hundredth time, but they sounded no better than before, so she paced the length of the room before turning to watch him again. "This is most difficult, William. In truth, I dunna know where to begin." She paced again, but finally he strode across the room to take her hands between his own.

"I believe I know what this is about, lass," he said softly.

She felt herself tense, for surely no man would appreciate being told his wife-to-be was in love—not love—*lust*, with another man, and therefore felt a need to call off the marriage. "Ye do?"

He nodded. "I do. But ye needn't worry. I've no plans of setting ye aside."

Her jaw dropped as she absorbed his meaning. If he'd told her he was the king of Kalmar, she wouldn't have been more surprised. "Setting me aside?"

"Nay." He stared boldly at her face—the stitches that were beginning to itch, the purpled eye. For some indefinable reason, she felt like squirming beneath his gaze. "I am a man of honor, Shona," he said gallantly. "I will do as I promised."

She supposed it was odd and very vain, but not for a moment had she considered that William would not want to marry *her*.

She had called him here to tell him the truth, that she did not wish to wed *him*. She had fought the decision for a while, had almost convinced herself that she could go through with it even after Dugald had appeared in her bedchamber. But that one final touch, that simple, innocent moment in the hall, had convinced her differently. All he had done was touch her cheek and she had been a fraction of a moment from shamelessly throwing herself at him in front of God and everybody. Surely twould be a horrible sin to marry when she could not quench this undeniable fire for another. Still, she knew telling William would not be easy.

His attitude, however, simplified the matter considerably.

"So ye are saying ye would marry me out of a sense of duty?" she asked.

"I will treasure ye regardless."

"Even though I am hideously disfigured?" She had meant it as a jest to lighten the mood, but he answered with sincerity and gave her a brave smile. Had he always been so patronizing?

"Mayhap this is not all bad," he said. "Remember, my dear, hardships bring humility."

"Are ye saying that I am not humble?"

He laughed, actually laughed, as he patted her hand. "Ye are young and ye were so bonny. How could ye help but be vain. But now . . ." Putting his hand on her chin, he moved her head to the side so as to examine her wounds more carefully, and then she saw a strange, indefinable light in his eyes. "Ye will make me a fine wife."

A strange thing to say. "What do ye mean by that, William?"

"Do not worry yourself, Shona. I will take care of everything."

"Everything?"

"I will take care of ye, make certain no one laughs at your expense. People can be cruel."

He'd make certain no one laughed at her? He made her sound like a half-wit, like a one- eyed beggar. And by the by, she had never laughed at them, either, much less at someone with a couple of bruises on her face. It was a cut, for God's sake. A few stitches. She'd had worse embroidery accidents.

"Aye. We will get on fine," he said, and for the first time, she wondered if it were glee she saw in his eyes—if he was happy she had been hurt. Doubt niggled in her mind. Mayhap her injury was much worse than she thought. Mayhap she would never be pretty again. Mayhap no man would want her. But in a moment, she remembered Dugald's touch. There had been no pity in his eyes, no revulsion, no glee.

"Nay." She said the word softly.

"Your pardon?"

"Nay, I will not make ye a fine wife."

He smiled. "Ye worry too much. I never planned to marry ye for your beauty."

"Why did ye plan to marry me?"

He shrugged as he dropped her chin and turned away. "Your house and mine combined. We will be invincible."

"Who are we trying to vince?"

He laughed at her wit. "I can hardly blame your father for spoiling ye."

Spoiling her! It could very well be that she didn't like this man at all.

"In fact, tis certain I will spoil ye myself."

"I dunna think so."

He smiled sympathetically into her eyes. "Ye are taking the loss of your beauty too hard. Do not worry so. But for now you'd best get to bed, my dear. Rest. I will take care of the wedding arrangements," he said and turned away.

"Nay, William, ye willna."

He turned slowly toward him, his expression unreadable, his posture stiff. "What say ye?"

"Tis sorry I am, but I canna marry ye, William."

He said nothing, but watched her in tense silence for a moment. "Might I ask why?"

"I . . ." She searched for words she thought she'd already planned. "I simply canna."

"We already announced our intentions." The words were terse, though he forced a smile.

"Again I say, I am sorry."

"I would have the truth, Shona. Is it because of another man? Is it because of the foreigner?"

"Dugald?" she said. The name came out breathy with surprise. "Dugald of Kinnaird?"

His gaze was very steady on hers. "I think I have a right to know the truth."

Aye. He had a right to know the truth. But what man wanted to hear that his fiancée longed for another, could not forget his touch, could do naught but yearn for it again? If she knew men, and she did, that was something they would frown upon. Certainly a tender lie would be kinder.

"Is it the foreigner?" he asked again.

"Nay." The denial came out quickly, perhaps too quickly. She bit her lip. "In all honesty, William, I dunna even like him."

He took a step toward her. "I have reason to believe that Stanford was right," he said. "'Twas Kinnaird that caused your disfigurement."

Disfigurement! She was getting tired of that word, but it brought her sharply back to reality.

"That is just the point, William," she said, touching her cheek. "I canna ask any man to marry me now."

"I told ye—"

"But I see pity in your eyes," she interrupted. "I dunna want pity from the man I marry. Surely ye can understand that."

"What do ye want from a husband, Shona?" he growled. "Someone to bow and scrape when ye enter the room?"

She drew back at his sharp words.

"We've made a public announcement," he said, stepping forward and gripping her arm again. "We have pledged our troth."

"I am certain the public will understand," she said. "After all, mayhap everyone knows I am spoiled and vain." She couldn't stop her words, though she knew they were petty. "Ye are lucky to be rid of me."

"Ye made a vow."

"Surely tis far better to break it now than later after the sanctity of marriage."

A light flamed in his eyes. "No woman cheats on—"

"Lady Shona?" A sharp rap echoed on the door.

Shona did not lower her gaze from William's, but held it perfectly steady, trying to read his thoughts. This was a new William, one she did not much like. "What is it, Muriel?"

"The Irishman called Liam has just arrived."

"Liam?" Despite everything, she could not still the joy that spurred through her heart.

"Aye, Lady. Your cousins said ye would wish to see him immediately."

"Who is this Liam, Shona?" William asked, his hand still on her arm.

"He is a friend."

"Ye have many friends."

"Are ye implying something, William?" she asked.

"If ye leave this room now, you'll not have another chance."

"Another chance at what?"

"At marriage."

"With ye?" she asked, "or are ye assuming every other man will be as shallow as yourself?"

His eyes narrowed. "Make your decision," he said.

"Tell my cousins I will be there immediately, Muriel," Shona called, and pulled her arm from William's grasp.

"I dunna care what ye tell your friends," she said softly. "Ye may tell them I was a shrew or that I was too disfigured to look upon. Ye can even tell them that I was not untried, for ye certainly have implied it. But no matter what lies ye spew, I will expect ye to be gone before dusk tomorrow.'' With that, she turned away and left him.

Chapter 21

She would know the Irishman anywhere, Shona thought, even from the back in the middle of a crowded hall.

"Liam!" she cried, and rushed down the stairs to fly toward him.

He turned just in time to catch her in his arms and hug her to him. Close at hand, Sara and Rachel watched them and smiled.

"Ye are so late for the festivities," she said, still holding him close. "What delayed ye?"

"Nothing of consequence, lass," he assured her.

A tiny bit of peace stole into her soul, soothing her. She was united with Liam and her cousins. All would be well.

But in a moment she felt Liam tense.

"Shona, you're shaking. What is amiss?" he asked, and pressed her to arms' length. But once there, his jaw dropped. "God's balls, lass, what the devil happened to your face?"

Blunt. Liam had always been blunt. Maybe his tactlessness should have offended her. Instead, it did the opposite, for in his eyes she saw no horror, no astonished sorrow, and suddenly her wounds did not seem so hideous.

"Have ye been riding the black bull again?"

She shook her head and laughed out loud.

"Using your embroidery needles for darts? Going down the burn in a barrel?"

"Nay."

"Then what the hell have ye done to yourself this time?"

"It wasn't her fault," Kelvin said, stepping up beside her.

Liam looked down into the boy's face. "It never is, lad. But look at ye. Ye're a good stone heavier than when I first met ye. It seems our Shona has at least been seeing to *your* care."

"Who are ye to be judging her?" Kelvin asked, anger in his voice.

Shona caught her breath. "Surely ye remember Liam. Ye met him en route to Stirling, when ye first went to meet the king," she said, catching the boy's gaze.

Kelvin blinked. She saw wariness cross his face before he raised his chin and cocked his head. "Of course I remember. I simply dunna think such a rogue as this Irishman has the right to find fault with a lady like yourself. Especially when ye are wounded."

"Wounded!" Liam said. "It looks as if she has been offering her face for target practice."

"Damn you! I'll not have ye tormenting the lady," Stanford said, striding forward.

"Oh, shut up," Hadwin said, and reaching up from the bench where he sat, pulled the lanky man down beside him. "Have a drink." He pushed his own mug in front of the other. "And for God's sake, relax. The maid has had a hard enough time as it is."

"'Tis not *my* fault," Stanford said, affronted.

"Well . . ." Hadwin took back the mug for another long swig, before pressing it into the other man's hands again. "Not as much as it is m—"

"Hadwin." William approached his cousin from the right. "I just received word from my sheriff. I will have to curtail my stay here. We will need to prepare to leave."

"Tonight?"

"Immediately. Tell Pith to see to the packing."

From the corner of the hall, Dugald watched Hadwin stumble drunkenly to his feet. What had he been about to say? Stanford was not as much to blame for Shona's hardships as who?

And what of Kelvin? Had he not recognized Liam? If not, why? The lad was as clever as a snake, surely he would recognize this loud Irish rogue.

There were a thousand things afoot here—Liam's arrival, Kelvin's slippery memory, Shona's broken vows.

Dugald almost smiled. So she had sent William packing. Oh yes, Dugald knew. Though no one else had yet been informed, he had heard much of the conversation, for he had been perched just outside her shutters.

Aye, William was being forced to leave. Thus if he was the one planning the king's death, at least he would not have the help of the MacGowans.

"Ye should return to your bed, Shona," Rachel said. "Hardly are ye healed."

"Her bed?" Liam laughed. "Far be it from our Shona to need rest. I have just arrived."

"And are as likely as not to make her ill even when she has her full strength," Rachel said. "With ye here, she—"

"Please," Shona said, lifting a hand. "Could we not have peace this day?" Rachel opened her mouth, and Liam looked as if he were sulking. "The four of us are reunited. Surely ye dunna wish to wound Dragonheart by your bickering."

Sara laughed, Rachel smiled, and Liam, looking chagrined, nodded.

"Peace, then," he said. "Might we find somewhere quiet to talk?"

Rachel glanced at Shona, her amethyst eyes unearthly bright. "The solar should be a fine place," she said, "empty but for William's drowned dreams, I suspect."

Dugald watched Shona turn toward her, and though he could not hear much of what she said, he clearly made out the word "eerie."

Rachel laughed, and Dugald prepared for another night of spying.

"Did William accept your change of heart with good grace?" Rachel asked.

The solar was lit with a trio of candles set on an iron candelabrum and the presence of three of the people Shona loved most in the world.

"Change of heart?" Liam asked, just closing the door behind him. "What's this?"

"Our Shona was betrothed," Sara said.

"Betrothed!" Liam looked at her aghast. "To whom?"

"To the same man she just became unbetrothed to," Rachel said. "Your hopes can remain alive, Liam."

"Well, I should think so," Liam said, turning to take Shona's hand in his own. "What's this I hear? Ye were planning to marry another?"

She smiled at him. Long ago, she had vowed to marry Liam. Twas a dream that was not to be. A modicum of maturity had told her that. Even if her parents would allow it, even if he were not entirely too much like herself to be trusted, even if he weren't a rogue and a vagabond and a wandering magician, he was not the sort to marry. He was always slightly discontented, and though he pretended otherwise, he was forever somewhat distracted, at least when he was around her.

Liam the Irishman, most people called him, as quick with his mind as he was with his fingers. He had been a scrawny thief and a prankster in the raucous border town of Firthport when Shona's aunt had first met him. Supposedly he had been rehabilitated when Tara and Roman brought him to the Highlands, but if the truth be known, Shona doubted Liam would ever change. In his heart he was no more tame than the wild hills they called home.

"Ye failed to ask me to marry ye, Liam," she said. "Tis a prerequisite to the wedding vows. William thought to ask."

"William of Atberry?" he asked, his tone surprised.

"Aye, the same."

"Ye were planning to wed William of Atberry?"

Shona straightened her back. "He is of good family."

"Aye," Liam scoffed. "But so is King Henry. It does not mean that I would wed *him*."

Shona scowled. "I had no idea ye were planning to marry a man atall. Besides, Henry is English, and has a rather disturbing habit of being rid of those he dislikes."

"And ye think William would be better?"

All three cousins turned toward him.

"What do ye mean by that?" Rachel asked, her tone utterly somber suddenly.

Liam shrugged. "I dunna know. It just seems that ye are close enough to the royalty already, Shona, what with your friendship to the young king. The MacGowans are not in such need of power that they would marry off their fairest flower to the old king's nephew. After the last attempt on your James's life, Lord Tremayne and the others are intent on pinning the blame on someone. It seems the further ye are from that intrigue, the better."

Shona tried not to show her tension. This entire group was known to be a bit meddlesome, while Rachel was downright spooky.

"I fear my reasons for breaking off the betrothal were less practical than that," Shona said.

"He did not worship ye as he should?" Liam asked.

His question was too similar to William's to give her comfort. She gave Liam a sneer. "He had a big nose."

Liam laughed. "With your face battered like a squashed turnip, he may be glad to be rid of ye."

She would have liked to tell him that he was miles from the truth, but there was little point in lying to this group. "I suppose I would frighten a rock just now."

Liam's eyes opened wide as he stared at her. "Ye are serious?" he asked, laughter in his voice. "He was offended by your wounds?"

She shrugged. "He was quite noble about it. Said he

was an honorable man and would marry me nevertheless."

"He's more of an ass than I suspected."

Rachel stepped forward. Shona turned her gaze to her and noticed with some misgivings that her eyes held that eerie light they sometimes did. It was a bad omen. She was thinking things she shouldn't be thinking, guessing things she shouldn't be guessing, meddling in other people's minds.

"In truth," Rachel said, reaching out to touch Shona's cheek with gentle fingertips, "he was no worse than I expected. I suppose tis time to reduce the swelling and see to your healing now."

The room went silent.

"What?" Shona asked quietly.

Rachel shrugged. Perhaps it was her ladylike demeanor that always made Shona forget her mischievous side. "I did not think it would do any harm if I allowed your wounds to look their most colorfully hideous for a few days."

"Ye mean to say ye purposefully did nothing to heal them?" Shona asked, appalled.

"Not atall," Rachel countered. "I made certain they did not turn septic while I purposefully made them look worse."

"Rachel!" Shona exclaimed. "How could ye?"

"I didna like that William fellow," Rachel said, and flippantly pattered toward the window to let in the night air. For a moment the shutter caught, seemingly on a bit of rust, but soon it swung free. She turned back to her friends with a shrug. "I had a bad feeling about him."

"And it turns out she was right," Sara said. "Any man who would leave ye because of a few wee bruises does not have the fortitude ye need in a mate."

"A few wee bruises!" Shona cried, knowing she had thought much the same thing herself, but certain she had a right to be indignant nevertheless. "Yesterday I scared Maggie's wolf when I but glanced at him."

"He is not a wolf," Sara argued, looking offended.

"I would *not* allow my daughter to wander about with a wolf."

Shona snorted. "Ye are just as bad as Rachel," she said. "The two of ye acting like fine, swooning damsels when underneath it all ye are a pair of conniving rats."

"Rats who saved ye from a frightful marriage," Rachel said.

"Rats who will make it so that my father marries me off to someone as fat as King Henry but lacks the charm."

"Oh, aye," Liam said. "Roderic has always been the sort to torture his only daughter just for sport."

"Whenever he can unwind himself from your little finger."

Shona scowled at them all in turn. Being the youngest in this group had always been trying. Despite her momentous strides at reaching maturity, they would forever see her as a child.

"I'll have ye know that I am not atall the spoiled lass ye once thought me."

"Nay?" Rachel asked.

"Nay. I have a child to look after now."

"Kelvin!" Liam said suddenly. "That reminds me, I have a missive from the Hawk for ye."

"From Hawk?" Shona asked, hurrying toward him. "Liam, how could ye forget? We were just speaking of the king."

Liam lifted his pouch and pulled out a rolled parchment. Shona reached for it, but he pulled it beyond her grasp.

"If the truth be known, I thought it best to wait to give it to ye, for it looked as if ye had worries enough when I first saw ye."

"Liam!" She scowled at him. "This is not a game we play here. This probably concerns the king himself."

"My point exactly," Liam said, scowling back. "I dunna think it wise to get too involved in that intrigue. I tell ye, the people that surround young James are looking for heads to adorn the pikes atop Stirling Castle's turrets. Never is a man more secure than when he captures the king's would-be assassin.''

"Are ye saying they might accuse *me* of trying to murder the king?''

"I am saying ye should watch your back, Shona.

"What say ye, Rachel?'' he asked, turning to the healer. "Is she hale enough to read this missive?''

"Ye think there is some way to keep it from her, now that she knows about it?'' Rachel asked.

"I could turn her into a toad.''

"Ye would be lucky to turn a toad into a toad,'' Rachel countered. "Give her the note, before she decides to beat ye senseless.''

"Ye've always had a way of making a man feel like a man.''

"That would take a man to begin with.''

"Cease!'' Shona demanded. "And give me the letter, Liam.''

He handed it over with a grin.

Shona broke the seal quickly, but suddenly there were three people looking over her shoulder.

"Have ye no shame?'' she asked, rolling the parchment to glare at them. "Tis a private letter to me.''

"What could the Hawk possibly say that he would not want us to know?'' Rachel asked.

"Mayhap tis of a personal nature,'' Sara said. "Mayhap she and the Hawk share something they dunna want us privy to.''

"Shona!'' Liam chided. "He is your mother's half-brother. What are ye thinking? Twill never work. Even now I can hear the Pope crying consanguinity.''

"Oh, shut up, all of ye!'' Shona cried.

They drew back as a unit.

"Testy, isn't she?'' Liam asked.

"Mayhap she thinks herself too good for the likes of us, now that she consorts with kings and such.''

Shona put her fingers to her temples. "You're giving me a sore head.''

Even Rachel laughed, but at the same time she was hustling the others from the room.

"We will leave ye in peace for a spell, then, Shona, but I warn ye, I will return yet this night to treat your wounds." She stopped in the doorway behind the other two. "And I dunna want any whining about the taste."

"I dunna whine," Shona said, but Rachel only laughed as she shut the door.

Shona unrolled the parchment and read quickly.

From his hiding place where he dangled from the stone beside Shona's window, Dugald peeked through the shutter and saw her face go pale.

"Dear Lord," she whispered, setting the parchment to the flame of the nearest candle, "not the queen!"

Chapter 22

The following morning, Shona found Kelvin just past the drawbridge on an escarpment of the Gael Burn, tossing stones in the water in a test of strength with his friends. Old Magnus sat on a tree stump sawed into the shape of a crude chair and watched the boys play.

"Kelvin, I need to speak to ye," she called.

He came at a run, his bare feet muddy and his smile wide.

She knelt in front of him, feeling a rush of love. "I've had news from the Hawk."

The boy's small face became somber, then he glanced at the old man. Magnus's eyes were closed and his head drooped in sleep. "The king. Is he—"

"The king is fine. But James . . ." She paused for a moment, wondering how much to tell him and deciding to give him the littlest possible information for now. "King James has requested our presence."

They stared at each other for a silent moment.

"When do we leave?" Kelvin asked.

Shona smiled at him; then, rising to her feet, she put her arm around his shoulders. "I know how ye love it here in the Highlands. Ye are not too disappointed that we must leave so soon?"

"'Tis our duty," he said solemnly. "He is, after all, our king, even if he is a mite spoiled."

274

"Aye." She laughed a little, relieved to know he was so willing to do what he must. "He is that. Hawk says His Majesty but wishes for us to help him pass the time. We will not leave until the day after tomorrow. Twill take till then to prepare our retinue for travel. For now, ye may return to your play."

He turned back to the stream, but his expression was somber now, a testimony to the life he had led before meeting her, the life that had taught him hardships come to all. Shona's heart lurched, and she longed to see him smile again

"Oh, and Kelvin," she said.

"Aye?"

"The queen will be arriving at Blackburn shortly after we do."

His smile broke out again. "How long will she be staying?"

"Tis difficult to say," she said. "But ye know how she adores her son."

He laughed out loud. The sound was charming and bright and floated over the morning like summer clouds as he turned back to his play.

Shona stood by the rustling burn. There were a hundred details she should see to, but just now watching Kelvin play seemed the most urgent, so she settled herself down on the bank to watch.

After a moment, Magnus awoke with a soft snort. They sat in companionable silence for a spell, watching as the boys raced to catch a small piece of bark as it spiraled downstream.

Soaked and laughing, Kelvin came away with it in his hands.

"He's a clever lad, that one," Magnus said.

"Kelvin?" Shona asked, turning toward the old man.

"Aye. And kindly. Twas he who helped me out to this spot in the shade."

"He has a good heart," Shona said.

"That he does." Silence settled in, serenaded by the

sweet rustle of water. "He reminds me of someone, though I dunna know who."

Shona smiled gently. "I suspect he is like most young lads, though he seems special to me."

"They are all special, each in his own way. He adores ye, ye know."

"The sentiment is returned twofold."

"I heard the lads talking, praising your beauty," Magnus said.

"It must have been before I was tromped by a horse," Shona responded, but when she touched her cheek she could tell the swelling was greatly reduced from the previous day. Whatever horrible concoctions Rachel had smeared on her face and forced her to drink, they must be doing the job.

"True beauty goes far beyond the surface of the skin," Magnus said. "Young Kelvin knows that. The other lads, they said ye are so beautiful because of the magical amulet ye wear around your neck."

She put her hand to her chest, suddenly nervous. Did everyone know of the dragon?

"But your Kelvin said nay, twas the beauty of your soul that shows through on your face." Magnus chuckled, the sound rusty and rumbling. "Still, he said, he wouldna mind having a magical dragon himself."

She dropped her hand away. "Tis a lad's fierce imagination only, I fear," she said. "The pendant is not magical atall, only beautiful."

"Of course," Magnus agreed. "But I have been thinking I might craft one for him out of wood if I could but get a good look at it."

"At Dragonheart?"

The old man appeared surprised, though he seemed to be looking right past her. In the clear morning light she could see that his eyes were as cloudy as watered milk.

"Ye have named the pendant?" he asked.

She laughed, feeling foolish for her fears. He was, after all, a decrepit old man, lame, nearly blind, and wanting nothing more than to give a gift to a lad who had done him a kindness.

"I did not actually name the dragon," she said.

"Someone else, then?"

She scowled as she drew the pendant into her hand. "I dunna know, exactly. It seems as if he had the name long before I knew of him."

"Him?"

She laughed at her own foolishness. "Tis my way, I fear, to imbue mere objects with personalities. I have named my favorite chair 'Miller,' for it has arms like the man who grinds the grain."

The old man chuckled. "Tis little wonder the lad is fascinated by anything ye wear, for ye surely must make everything seem magical."

"Tis not magic," she repeated.

Magnus turned back to gaze toward the boys again, his bent hands placed, one atop another on the head of his staff. "In truth, lass, I dunna believe in magic. When ye have seen as many years as I, ye find ye believe in naught but hard work and good luck."

"And in God Almighty, of course."

He turned to her, his white eyes disconcerting. "Of course," he said. "And in kind wee lads who have a mind to help old men. Might I take a look at the dragon so as to whittle a rough replica for the boy?"

She paused.

"Ye dunna need to fear that I will run off with it, for I believe ye could best me in a footrace."

Shona laughed. "I guess there would be no reason to deny ye." Slipping Dragonheart from her neck, she approached the old man.

"Shona!"

"What?" She jerked around to find Liam only a few feet behind her.

"I've been calling to ye for half an hour. Didn't ye hear me?"

"Nay, I was speaking to Magnus." She turned toward the old man, but the tree stump was suddenly empty.

Lifting her gaze, she saw his bent figure turn into the woods and disappear.

"Who was that?" Liam asked, gazing into the trees.

Shona tightened her fingers over Dragonheart, and felt almost as if she were awakening from a dream. "Just an old man."

"What?"

She drew herself from her reverie with a start. "God's wrath, Liam, ye look as if ye've seen a ghost. What troubles ye?"

He turned his gaze quickly to hers. "Why is Dragonheart out?"

"Magnus wanted to—"

"Magnus?"

"The old man. He wanted to craft a replica of the dragon for Dugald. But ye must have scared him off. Ye'd scare a troll with that scowl. What ails ye?"

"Shona," He relaxed a bit, becoming more himself. "Have I not warned ye to keep the dragon to yourself?"

"He is just a harmless old man," she said, ascending the bank and heading for the bridge.

"Aye, well some might have thought the same of . . ." His voice trailed off.

"Of who?" She stopped to stare at him.

He shifted his eyes sideways, as if expecting a winged demon to come flying from the woods. "Of Warwick," he murmured.

"The dark wizard is dead, Liam. Killed by Boden's blade. Warwick will bother ye no more."

"Shh. Dunna say his name aloud."

"Are ye still losing sleep over him?" she asked, feigning concern as she touched his forehead with her palm. "Mayhap I should ask Rachel to give ye something to ease your nights."

"Aye, Rachel would be happy indeed to fix me one of her witchy remedies—mayhap a spot of hemlock." He darkened his scowl. "Speaking of old horny, here comes the she devil herself," Liam said. He glanced over Shona's shoulder, and Shona followed his gaze.

But she only saw Rachel approach. Like a dark-haired angel she was, as beautiful as the dark waters of Loch Ness.

"I will never understand your feud," she said. But when she glanced at Liam again she saw that his gaze remained fixed on her cousin. "Liam?"

He stood absolutely immobile, every muscle tensed.

"Liam?"

"What?" He came out of his private thoughts with a start.

She blinked at him. "What's wrong with ye?"

"Nothing!"

"Ye were staring at Rachel as if ye were transfixed—"

"There is naught wrong," he said, but his tone was irritable.

"There is naught wrong with what?" Rachel asked, reaching them.

"There is naught wrong with Liam," Shona said, and Rachel laughed.

"That is indeed a welcome change," she said. "I'll tell the heralds to raise the flags."

"There is the reason I lose sleep at night," Liam said. "Thinking up spells to stifle your cousin's barbed tongue."

"Be careful that in your thrashing ye dunna turn yourself into a wart. But wait," Rachel said. "Ye already are—"

"Rachel," Shona interrupted quickly. Twas always best to stop these two before things got out of hand. "Did ye need something?"

"Aye." She drew her attention from Liam with an obvious effort. "I came to administer your herbs."

Shona made a face. "They taste like horse dung."

"Pray tell, Cousin, when was the last time ye tasted horse dung?"

Liam laughed. "Despite Rachel's evil ministrations, ye seem to be healing. Indeed, ye look far better today compared to—"

"Horrible disfigurement," Shona finished in unison with the Irishman.

Rachel took her arm. "Dunna listen to him. Ye are greatly improved. In fact, ye are healing faster than I dared hope."

"Complimenting your own skills, Rachel?" Liam asked.

She turned toward him. "Mayhap ye'd like to credit the amulet?"

"That would be more likely.

"God's balls, Shona!" he snapped, noticing she still held Dragonheart in her hand. "Get that thing hidden away."

Shona slipped Dragonheart's chain around her neck and shoved the amulet into her bodice. Then she scowled at his tone and placed a hand over Rachel's where it rested on her forearm. "Did ye know he still frets about Warwick?"

Rachel raised her brows and beamed a smile at the Irishman. "Really? Afraid of ghosts, Liam?"

"'Tis no laughing matter," he grumbled, but his expression was sheepish.

"On the contrary. It is," Rachel said, and both women laughed as they turned away.

"Lady Rachel."

Shona sucked in her breath. Dugald stood not ten feet away.

"Speaking of dragons," Rachel said. "I have not seen ye for days."

"Dare I hope you missed me?" he asked, reaching for Rachel's hand and kissing her knuckles.

"I'd hate to be the one to stifle hope," Rachel said, then glanced at Shona, her brows slightly raised as if she could reach her cousin's very thoughts. Shona hated that about Rachel. Twas unnatural.

Dugald laughed as he straightened. "Then I shall continue to do so," he said. "But I fear I must be off to Edinburgh soon. I heard you also would be traveling south, and I wondered if we might journey together?

There would be added safety in numbers."

"What horrible circumstances could worry Dugald the Daring?" Shona asked.

He stared at her, his expression solemn. "Any manner of thing might happen. I only hope to dissuade any disaster."

"If you're worried about your girth breaking, I've tested it for ye," Shona said. She knew she was being shrewish, but the sight of him kissing Rachel's hand irked her no end. So what if she had scratched up her face a little? That didn't mean he immediately had to move on to fairer game. "I'd suggest ye buy a new one."

"I would apologize again, lass," he said, stepping closer, "but I believe you asked me to leave you be."

Not a soul spoke, but finally twas Liam who stepped forward to break the silence.

"I dunna believe we have met. I am Liam, a friend of these two cousins."

Dugald nodded. "Dugald of the Kinnairds."

"I fear ye have been misinformed, Dugald," Liam said. "Rachel's home lies to the north of here."

"Oh? Do you know of another party that might be traveling south?"

"Not that I am aware of," Liam began, but Rachel interrupted him.

"Shona has been called to Blackburn. Mayhap ye could accompany her party."

Panic spurred through Shona. The thought of spending days on the road with him, nights confined in a small company, did horrible things to her imagination.

"I willna be leaving for days," she said, her tone more tense than she had intended. "I am certain he will need to leave before then."

His gaze seared hers. "On the contrary," he said. "I can wait." He bowed at the waist. "My thanks for your invitation."

"I didna invite—" she began, but suddenly he

touched her hand. The contact burned the snipe from her mind.

"How interesting," Rachel murmured, watching them. "Mayhap twould be well worth my time to accompany ye."

"Nay!" Liam said. His sharp tone startled Shona from her reverie.

"What say ye?" Rachel asked.

He gritted his teeth. "I am certain Shona can find enough trouble without ye, Rachel."

"Trouble?" Rachel watched him, her brows arched. "Hardly that, Liam. My cousin has been badly wounded. Horribly disfigured I believe ye called it. Tis my duty as a healer to see to her well-being."

"Rachel!" Liam stepped up close to her, his expression utterly serious. "I know we have had our differences in the past. But I'm asking ye now not to do this."

Shona watched as Rachel turned her eerie eyes up to his. "Why?" she asked. "Why are ye asking?"

A muscle clenched in his jaw. "Dunna push me, Rachel."

"If ye dunna wish to be pushed, Liam, ye dunna have a right to ask me not to go."

"I would say that I agree with the Irishman," Dugald said. "With things as they are it might well prove to be a difficult journey."

"And ye dunna think me up to the task?" Rachel asked.

There was clearly laughter in her voice. Dugald grinned. "I confess you seem a delicate thing."

And what was *she* then, Shona wondered? A road mender?

"I assure ye, I am hardier than I seem," Rachel said. "Isn't that so, Liam?"

The muscle flexed again as did his fists. "Dunna go, Rachel. Shona has chosen this course with the king. But ye dunna have to."

"And yet I made a vow on your precious amulet to

come to her aid when aid was needed,'' she said.

"Your aid is not needed now," Liam said. "Return to the safety of Glen Creag with your father." Silence. "I beg ye."

"Liam? Begging?" she said softly. "Tis hard to believe."

"And harder yet to consent to my wishes," he said, his tone flat.

"I believe Shona might well need me before the journey's end."

"Go then, if ye will," he said finally. "But know this." For a moment he seemed to be fighting a losing battle with himself. Finally he continued. "If ye go, I go."

No one spoke, but finally Dugald broke the silence. "We shall be quite a merry party. The day after tomorrow, then," he said, and turning, left them.

But Shona was not lucky enough to return to the castle without more problems. Just as she crossed the drawbridge it caught up with her.

"Daughter."

She turned with a wince at the sound of Roderic's voice.

"Father?"

He strode toward her, his strides quick. Were they angry strides? Twas not the first time she'd tried to read his mood from his posture.

"Good morningtide, my laird," Rachel said. "I was just about to tend to Shona's wounds."

Roderic scowled, not even bothering to look at Rachel. Twas a bad sign. Every man looked at Rachel. Her sweet gentility drew them. Even her uncles were usually not immune to her charm.

"If she could possibly resist a challenge, she would have no wounds," Roderic said.

"Twas not my fault, Father."

His scowl deepened. She winced. Twas not the thing to say.

"Can ye think of another to blame?"

"If given enough time."

He wasn't amused. "Might I have a word alone with my daughter?" he asked.

"Her wounds truly should be—" Rachel began.

But Liam suddenly took her by the arm and pulled her toward the keep. "I doubt he'll scar her too badly, Rachel," he murmured, then, "We shall wait for ye in the hall, Shona. Take your time, my laird."

Treason. Shona scowled after them, then brightened her expression with an effort and chirped. "Ye wished to speak to me, Father?"

The world was quiet.

"I did not wish to scold ye before. After all, I thought ye had, mayhap, learned your lesson about impetuousness. When I saw ye beneath that beast's hooves . . ." His voice trailed off. His gaze turned away. But in a moment he found his voice and his scowl again. "But to break off the betrothal, Shona! What were ye thinking?"

She winced. "I should have spoken to ye first."

"Spoken to me! Ye made a vow, lass, and your mother and I as well. We promised ye to Lord William. Does our good name mean nothing to ye?"

"It does, Father, but—"

"But what?"

"But . . ." Suddenly she could think of no good reason to give him. Surely she could not tell him that she yearned for another, that she could think of nothing but Dugald's hands on her skin. "But he has a big nose."

"A big nose!"

From the drawbridge, Bullock turned to stare at Roderic's outburst. Near the well, Muriel and Bethia looked up.

"A big nose?" Roderic growled, lowering his voice. "Ye broke off your betrothal to the duke of Atberry because of the size of his *nose?*"

She winced. "Well when ye say it like that, it sounds quite petty."

"Petty!" he all but screamed.

"I jest, Father," she whispered, eyeing the additional faces that turned to peer at them from the bridge. Bullock was accustomed to their battles, but she hated to involve strangers. "Tis just that . . ." She searched for words and finding none, finally touched his arm entreatingly. "Tis just that I do not love William."

Roderic's expression softened. "Love is something that grows with time, Daughter."

"So ye did not love Mother on the day of your wedding? So ye did not adore her and long for her, and think her the most wondrous person ye had ever met?"

Silence, deep and long.

"Father?"

He ground his teeth as he drew himself from his reverie. "Ye are not me, Daughter."

"So I dunna deserve to love as ye did? As ye do?"

"Ye use my words against me."

"Nay, I use the truth."

He sighed and ran splayed fingers through his hair. "Still, ye had no right to break the betrothal without so much as talking to me first."

"I was wrong," she said softly.

"Aye, ye were wrong. And what's this I hear about ye traipsing off to Blackburn again?"

He was softening. She could tell it by the shape of his mouth. "I dunna think ye can call a request from the king traipsing," she said.

"Dunna make light of this, Daughter. All of Scotland is in an uproar. Tis not safe for ye to travel so far."

"Liam is coming with me," she said, and saw no reason to mention Dugald.

"Liam!" he said. "Tell me ye dunna think twill just be he and ye on the road."

"I had no wish to deprive ye of men to guard me."

"Deprive me! Ye'll take a dozen armed men and Bullock, or ye'll not go atall."

"A dozen?"

"In addition to Laird William and his men."

Her jaw dropped. "What?"

Roderic drew a deep breath. "He came to me this morning. It seems even he has heard of your journey. He said ye had had words and he apologized for his harshness. In truth, lass, despite his . . . coolness, I think he cares for ye. He asked to be allowed to escort ye to Blackburn."

"But—"

"And I said yes."

She opened her mouth to protest, but he glared her down. "Yes, Father," she said finally.

"And ye will be kind to him."

"Yes, Father."

"And ye will reconsider his offer."

"Yes, Father."

"And if ye say 'yes, Father' so sweetly once more, I shall know for certain that ye are not truly the daughter I raised from a wee lass, but a changeling left by the fairies.

"When are ye leaving?"

"The day after tomorrow."

"Ye will be careful?"

She smiled at his gentle tone. "Aye. I will."

He looked as if he would say more, but finally he turned away.

"Da," she said softly.

He glanced back over his shoulder at her.

"If William were half the man ye are, we would already be wed."

For a moment his eyes looked strangely bright. But Roderic the Rogue was not the type to cry. Surely it was just the sun in his eyes.

Chapter 23

They assembled outside the great hall at dawn, more than three dozen men and two women.

Sara stood with them in the bailey. "I would go with ye, but—"

"Nay." Rachel took her hand in her own. "This journey is not for ye, not with the babe to consider."

"The babe?" Shona asked, glancing up from where she checked Teine's girth. "What babe?"

Sara smiled and placed a gentle hand to her abdomen. "Twill be born before Christmas."

"Ye are with child?" Liam asked, striding up.

"You're expecting?" Shona gasped. "But I did not think ye could. How did it happen?"

Sara laughed. "The usual way, I suspect. Liam, ye will watch over her, won't ye? She's more naive than she seems."

Shona ignored her cousin's jibe and drew her into an embrace. "I am overjoyed for ye, Sunshine," she said, but from where Dugald listened some fifteen feet away, he wondered if he heard just a hint of envy. Shona might be a warrior, but she was also a woman. "Why didn't ye tell me?"

"There's been a good deal of commotion."

"But ye told Rachel."

"In truth, I didna," Sara said, and exchanged a meaningful glance with Shona.

"Oh, will the two of ye quit acting as if I'm snooping in your minds," Rachel said. "'Tis obvious she's with child. Canna ye see the glow?" Stepping around Shona, she, too, hugged Sara. "Take care, Cousin."

"And ye."

"We will. Never fear. I will journey to Cairn Heights for the child's birth."

Sara nodded and stepped back.

They mounted in silence, and turned away with a wave. Dugald let Eagle kick irritably at the horse behind him. It assured him a little room between himself and William's soldiers.

The air was cool and damp, their horses' hoofbeats muffled as they crossed the drawbridge to the green sward on the opposite side. Mists curled over the Gael Burn and the world seemed silent and expectant.

As expectant as Dugald himself. But what *did* he expect? He was a fool on a fool's errand. He had been sent to kill a traitor, but he could not. Now, here he was, protecting that same traitor. But was she? He would know soon enough, for she was traveling to meet the king.

Why? The question burned in his mind. What did she hope to accomplish there? She said the king had asked for her, but the part of the note left unconsumed by the flame had said nothing about that. It had said only that the queen would soon be arriving at Blackburn Castle, and that Shona would know what she must do.

What must she do? Was she planning some evil against the queen? Or against the king himself? The questions nagged at Dugald's soul.

He would learn the truth, he told himself, for he had no intention of turning off this route. Nay, he would accompany them to Blackburn . . . and save Shona from whatever foolishness she was planning.

The day passed slowly. Bullock kept his huge dappled stallion close to the women. His guards rode in front, William's in back, and the others in the middle.

They stopped just after noon and made a meal of dried

fish, bread, and ale. Kelvin sat beside Dugald and shared a joke the miller's son had told him, and for a while they rode together. But soon the fluffy summer clouds slipped away only to be replaced by a darker variety. Thunder rumbled and lightning forked across the sky.

Excusing himself, Kelvin pushed his mount up close to Shona's. Dugald could not help but wish he could do the same, for there was an evil feel about the day, and if there was trouble, his place was beside the damsel.

He cursed himself for that thought. She was not his responsibility. Indeed, she neither wanted nor needed his protection. And yet . . .

He had no choice; he was bewitched. Whether by the dragon amulet or by her, he wasn't certain. But it no longer mattered, for he had ceased fighting the allure.

Thunder rumbled again, and the sky took on a greenish tint.

He was just about to approach Bullock with the suggestion that they stop, when the wind began. It hit them like a solid force, hard as slate, cold, and followed by a sidelong rain.

"To the trees," Bullock yelled above the storm.

The company turned quickly toward the woods, fighting their mounts, who wanted nothing more than to turn their tails to the wind.

Kelvin's pony balked, but Shona managed to grasp the boy's reins and urge the smaller horse along behind her own.

Beneath the bowed and dripping branches of the woods, the wind was not so fierce, and yet the noise was little reduced. Boughs creaked against boughs, and overhead, the leaves whipped wildly.

Setting up camp was not a simple task. But finally, five tents cowered together under the dripping foliage—one for the ladies and four for the men, and though the interior was not entirely dry, it was a vast improvement over the elements.

The light was fading fast and a fire would have been

a welcome sight, but with the swirling wind and the pelting rain, a flame proved impossible.

Kelvin, it was decided, would share the women's tent. He looked, Dugald noticed, none too happy with the decision, but he did not complain, perhaps because he was simply too tired.

Dugald surreptitiously turned his attention to the others. William was watching Shona, but his expression showed neither the anger of a jilted suitor nor the longing of a hopeful one. Why? Shona had just broken off their engagement. Dugald had heard Shona send him away. What kind of man could look so serene after that?

Dugald spent a damp, uncomfortable night surrounded by grumbling soldiers and a vague feeling of unease.

Morning found conditions little improved. The rain, which had ceased temporarily during the night, picked up just before dawn. It came down in a fine but steady spray.

They broke the fast inside their tents with stale bread and hard cheese, dismally broke up camp, and moved on.

By mid-morning anyone who had managed to dry off during the night was soaked to the skin once again, and the wind, which had fallen away, was reborn with a vengeance. It whirled like an evil dervish, driving stinging raindrops at them from all directions.

By noon, tempers were short. A squabble broke out between William's and Dun Ard's guards. Bullock put a stop to it with a few sharp words, but the tension remained.

By mid-afternoon it was obvious they could not go on much farther.

"Bullock," William called.

The square-built leader stopped and turned. William pressed his mount along the column of riders toward the stout man.

"We cannot press the women and child on like this. Tis surely best to stop. If I'm not mistaken there is a woods off to our right less than half a mile. Before the rain worsened, I could see it quite clearly. I believe they might be rowan trees. Twould surely be a good omen in this evil weather.''

Bullock squinted through the rain toward the west, but if he could see the mentioned trees, his eyesight was a damned site keener than Dugald's. Which might be possible, considering Shona's uncanny senses. Mayhap there was something about Dun Ard's water that sharpened their abilities.

''Lady Shona must arrive at Blackburn in less than three days' time,'' Bullock said, seeming to remind himself as well as the others who surrounded him.

''Surely twould be better if she arrives in full health rather than sick with the ague,'' William said. ''Tis bad enough that she has already been wounded.''

And that latter a personal bite for Dugald. He and Shona had not exchanged a single word since the journey had begun.

''What's this?'' Shona asked, pushing her chestnut up to the circle of men.

Eagle pricked his ears at the mare, then turned his head to snap at William's bay on the far side of him. He almost bit William's leg, and Dugald almost smiled.

''Lord William thinks we should spend the night in yonder woods,'' Bullock said. ''What think ye, Shona?''

''The rowans would surely bring us good luck,'' said a soldier close at hand.

Shona pulled her dripping hood farther over her forehead and glanced at Kelvin. He was huddled over his gelding's neck like a wilting sack of wool.

''I too saw the trees,'' she said. ''But what of the ravine between us and the woods?'' she asked.

''I will see you safely across it,'' William said. ''Never fear.''

She glanced at him for a moment, scowled slightly, then finally nodded. ''We'll have to push on all the harder tomorrow, but I think we've done all we can this day.''

Dugald wondered vaguely if he should be surprised

that no one questioned her authority. In actuality, Bullock had been put in charge, but all seemed to be in accord, so they turned their mounts toward the west and hoped for the best.

The land between them and the trees proved to be rougher than anticipated. They had been following a road of sorts, but now, forced off the main trail, their path was sliced through by a series of jagged cuts.

Neither the keening wind nor the muddy slopes made their passage any easier, but finally they reached the first trees.

Eager to be out of the wind, the horses picked up the pace, jostling each other on their way down.

One of Bullock's men, the final guard in the front column, turned as his mount was bumped from behind. "Watch yourself—" he began, but suddenly his horse began to slip on the muddy slope. It scrambled wildly, trying to gain its footing, but there was too little space. It careened into the horse closest to it, knocking that one to its knees. It's rider lost a stirrup and lurched to the side, startling Shona's mount.

"Shona!" Dugald screamed her name even as he spurred Eagle downhill, but already it was too late.

Panicked, her high-strung mare swung sideways, bumping into Bullock's gray.

He reared, but the mud beneath his feet gave way. He pawed wildly for purchase, but there was no hope, and in a moment he fell over backward, crashing to the earth with Bullock pinned beneath him.

Suddenly all was chaos. Horses screamed and men cursed. Kelvin struggled to control his pony just as Dugald reached for Shona, but she spun her mare away to grasp Kelvin's reins.

There was nothing Dugald could do now but guard her as best he could, for if any evil were planned, now would be the perfect time. He whipped out his knife. It hissed out to full length at the ready as Eagle braced himself to protect Shona and the mare from any that might fall into them from above.

But no one tried to harm Shona, and in a few moments it was all over. Glancing about, Dugald surreptitiously slid his blade back into its sheath.

Bullock lay on his side, clutching his knee in both hands and breathing hard through his teeth. Two of his men had fared no better. One was hugging his arm to his chest while the other, no more than five feet from Eagle's prancing hooves, pressed a hand to his temple. Blood oozed between his fingers.

"Dear God!" Rachel gasped, and leapt to the ground. "Liam, help me," she yelled, but he was already beside her. She put her hand on his arm and turned away. "Shona."

She delayed only for a moment, glancing first at Kelvin, then at the chaos around them, before turning to Dugald. The world seemed to draw back. "Can ye guard him?" she asked softly.

It was not a simple question, he knew. For her eyes were filled with an emotion he could not quite name.

"From what?" he asked.

She glanced quickly at his knife then back to his face. So she had seen him draw it, had noticed its length.

"From everything," she said.

He should say no, hold onto his disguise as best he could, but if ever he wanted a woman to know him, it was this woman.

"I can," he murmured.

She nodded once, then, quick as light, she slipped from Teine's back and off to her cousin's side.

Orders were quick, concise and one-sided. In this moment of crisis not a soul argued with the Lady Rachel as she bent over the wounded.

Her current patient was a narrow soldier. Very fair, he seemed even paler now, with his eyes wide and bleached in his gaunt face.

"Stephen," Rachel said, kneeling beside him. "Where do ye hurt the most?"

He grit his teeth as if loath to show weakness, but finally he managed, "My arm, tis my arm."

"Let me feel it. I will do my best not to hurt ye."

It seemed to take all his strength to allow her to touch him, and when she did, he gasped in pain.

She stood up and turned quickly to her cousin. "Shona, I need three branches, yeah long and very smooth. Also a fire, boiling water, a shelter, and long strips of cloth."

Shona only nodded and turned away, giving orders as she did so.

The men were dispatched in a matter of moments, two going after the horses, several searching for wood and the rest erecting the tents or assisting Rachel as Shona directed.

As for Dugald, he lifted Kelvin from his mount, tied their mounts not far away, and hustled the boy to a relatively dry spot beneath a leaning fir.

The lad huddled there looking lost and scared. For a moment Dugald considered leaving him to help the others, but Shona's request had seemed strangely poignant. So he squatted down beside the boy. Kelvin seemed unusually tense beside him.

"Are you well, lad?" Dugald asked.

"Aye." He was quiet for a moment, then, "Ye dunna suppose this is some kind of evil plot against . . . the king, do ye?"

"The king?" Dugald asked. The boy seemed older than his years suddenly, and very nervous.

"Tis widely known that Lady Shona is James's friend. Mayhap someone is trying to prevent her from reaching Blackburn."

"Twas just an accident that brought us these troubles," Dugald said, but he, too, felt tense and uncertain, as if some unknown evil surrounded them. Tonight would not be a time to sleep, but to watch and listen. "Still . . ." he added, looking down into Kelvin's eyes. "I am glad that you are here."

"Why?"

"To protect me. Do not forget," Dugald said, gently rubbing the wound he'd sustained at Kelvin's hand.

"I've evidence of your skill with a sword."

The boy said nothing, but he put his hand on the hilt of his weapon, and seemed to relax a bit.

Dugald looked away. Aye, he thought, tonight he would stay awake, for the boy, and for Shona.

By the time Rachel had the wounded inside their tents, Kelvin was fast asleep against his shoulder.

Dugald sat unmoving, watching everyone. William and his men mostly kept themselves removed from the others. Hadwin was unusually solemn. There seemed to be an uncomfortable silence between the two royal cousins. The Irishman stayed close to Rachel, he noticed, but it was Shona he watched most. Not because he should, but because even now he could not help himself. She fascinated him, her every move, her every word, the way she turned just so, the way she gave orders, like a small sergeant.

The rain had stopped as quickly as it had started, and though the wind still blew, it was much quieter here, peaceful almost. She had removed her hood and looped the muddy hem of her skirt between her legs and beneath her girdle.

Finally she pushed the hair from her face and made her way through the underbrush to his spot beneath the tree. She glanced at Kelvin's sleeping face. Dugald watched a modicum of peace steal over her features. "Thank ye," she said softly.

Dugald nodded. "I will carry him to your tent. How are the wounded?"

"They will mend. Rachel will see to that," she said, stepping back so that he could rise to his feet with Kelvin in his arms.

They walked side by side to her tent, and despite it all the world seemed strangely content. He did not know this woman's intent. He did not know his own fate if he refused his mission, and yet, for this moment, it did not matter.

They stopped outside her tent and stared at each other over the child's sleeping body.

"Who are ye?" she whispered.

"I already told you."

"Where did ye get the sword?"

He was weak, perhaps weak enough to tell her the truth if they had been somewhere else, somewhere private, somewhere safe.

"You should not be surprised to know that a coward keeps a concealed weapon."

Silence stretched between them. Finally she drew a deep breath and scowled as she reached for the boy.

Their arms brushed as she slipped hers under Kelvin's body. Feelings speared through him, fierce as the crash of lightning, sizzling down his nerve endings like wildfire. It was passion and lust and heat. But it was also more, something that made him want to hold her in his arms and keep the world at bay.

A strange feeling to have for a woman he was sent to kill. The memory spurred another shot of fierce emotion through him.

Shona turned away first, her eyes wide as she glanced to the right. Dugald followed her gaze, and there, not ten rods away, stood Hadwin. He watched them for a moment, his expression sober, and then turned away.

Shona drew in a deep breath as she pulled Kelvin into her arms. Without another word she slipped into her tent.

It was a long night. Without the wind and rain it seemed deadly quiet, almost hauntingly calm. Shona lay on her pallet, sleepless, restive, Dragonheart heavy and cold on his chain. She shifted the amulet and tried to get comfortable.

Morning would come all too soon. They would have to travel to Blackburn without a quarter of their company, for Rachel would never allow the wounded to be forced on.

Thus the remainder of the journey would be increasingly dangerous. And thus she needed all the rest she could get. She thrashed about, half hoping Rachel would wake and talk to her. But that was not to be, for her cousin did not even stir, no matter how much noise Shona made. Shona sighed, then, determined to sleep, she closed her eyes tightly and thought of her favorite place on the bank of the Gael Burn where flowers grew in wild profusion in the summer and heather bloomed bright as a promise in the fall.

In her mind she sat near the water's edge, laughing with her cousins as they raced their tiny, self-built watercrafts down the current. But suddenly Shona's vessel tipped and spilled out the figures of mud she had fashioned into people. Barefoot and laughing, she leaped into the water to save them, but when she glanced up into the sun, a shadow blocked the sunlight.

A man took her hand, and suddenly she was no longer a child, but a woman. She smiled as Dugald's fingers closed over hers and said not a word to her cousins as he led her from the water to the woods beside the burn. The maples here grew stout and lovely, with silvery trucks kissed with moss that traveled down their elegant lengths onto the floor of the forest.

On that nature-soft bed they lay down together, and twas there that he kissed her. The caress was sweet and lingering, filled with hope and promise. But in a moment it changed. Passion built like a stoked flame. Desire flared between them, igniting them body and soul until they were straining against each other with unrestrained desire, stroking and . . .

Shona awoke with a start. Breathless and disoriented, she sat up and silently chastised herself. What the devil was wrong with her? She had just broken off an engagement, and now here she was, lusting after another. Had she no shame? No pride? No sense? Dugald was a scoundrel, a womanizer. Maybe. In truth, she no longer knew what he was, but that was because he refused to tell the truth. That couldn't be a good sign. Still, whatever he was, she was not in love with him. She merely desired him—the touch of his hand, the sound of his voice, the—

Heaven's wrath! She was on her feet in an instant.

One glance about told her that Kelvin and Rachel were still fast asleep and undisturbed by dreams of any kind. All was quiet, safe, peaceful.

Outside the tent, not a breath of air stirred. Cloud-soft mists muffled her exit. Every tent was as quiet as darkness. Indeed, all the world seemed to be asleep—all the world except for herself. From the entrance of her tent, she could not even see a guard. It was as if she were the only person in a magical world.

Not far from camp, a burn rumbled along its shallow course. Barefoot and silent, Shona walked to its edge where she dipped her toes into its hustling waves. The water was cold, awakening her even more. Her thoughts strayed.

They would soon reach Blackburn Castle. But she would not stay long. Soon she would leave there and return to her home. But what then?

Obviously she would not marry William. And indeed, she had found none other who held her interest. None except . . .

"Why do you delight so in taking risks?"

Shona pivoted toward the voice, but even in the darkness, she could not help but identify the speaker.

"What are ye doing here?"

Dugald stepped toward her. "I believe twas the contented snoring of the others that kept me from sleep." He fell silent for a moment, and when he next spoke, his tone was deep and quiet. "Either that, or twas thoughts of you that disturbed me."

Shona felt her pulse leap, then silently scolded herself. He was a womanizer, she reminded herself, a scoundrel. She would not let such thoughts scramble her thinking. She would not. "Or thoughts of Mavis," she said.

She could see the flash of his grin even in the darkness.

"Are you jealous, Damsel?"

"Jealous?" It came out as a soft gasp of sound. "Of what?"

"Of me with another."

"Hardly!"

"Of thinking of me kissing another." He stepped closer. "Touching another. Lying with another."

He was directly in front of her now. And yet somehow this seemed no more real than her dreams of only moments before. There was an unearthly quality about the night, a rare, pristine beauty, for even in the darkness, it seemed she could see the splendor of every emerald frond, every dewy droplet.

She shook her head, trying to clear it. "I am not jealous."

"Truly?" The word was little more than a thought, it was so quiet and so close. "Then you have me at a grave disadvantage, lass, for when I think of you with another, tis like my very heart has been torn from my chest."

Shona held her breath and turned her head sharply to catch his gaze, certain she would see laughter in his eyes. But there was none. Even in the darkness, she was certain of that.

"Ye are jealous?" she whispered. "Of me?"

"Believe me, lass, if I could have it another way, I would. Twould be better to have the flesh flailed from my back than to be enamored with you."

She opened her mouth to object, but suddenly his lips touched her neck. Every thought flew from her mind as her eyes fell closed and her head dropped back to appreciate the glory of his caress.

"Mother of God, I cannot think when you are near." His right hand slipped behind her back, drawing her closer. Sparks soared. His eyes fell closed. "And when I touch you . . ." His fingers tightened upon her waist as he fell silent.

But to her shame, she wanted to hear his words. "What?"

"I no longer care what you have done."

"What I have—" she began, but he kissed her lips.

The caress was not gentle, but fierce and possessive and searing.

She tried to think, to tell him this was wrong, that

there were a hundred reasons it was not to be, but for the life of her she could think of none, and suddenly she was kissing him back.

He crushed her to him. Passion ripped free of its bonds.

Beside the burn there was a bed of moss. It was as soft as thistledown and as thick as carpet against her back. The mists rolled around them like a curtain of silver velvet, hiding them away, sheltering them from reality.

All the world was a dream, his hands magic, his voice ecstasy. Their clothes slipped away in that same dreamlike state, and suddenly there were no boundaries. His hands were everywhere, hot and strong as they slid down her arms, warm and tender as they touched her breasts, her abdomen, her thighs. She writhed beneath him, needing his touch and more. Much more—his heart, his love.

The realization terrified her, but still she could not stop.

''I want ye,'' she said softly, and though she knew he did not understand the full meaning of her words, neither would she explain just now.

Instead, she rolled onto her side and kissed him long and hard. Then, aching with a need as primitive as time, she pressed him onto his back. Knees bent and cushioned by the moss, she straddled him.

He lay propped on his elbows, watching her.

Above them the moon found its way through the silvery veil of fog and shone on him. In the magical light of the three quarters moon, he looked like a bronze statue. Or mayhap twas not the light at all.

Silent and awed, Shona slipped her hand across his chest. She could feel his heart beat with a mystical power, and she was drawn to it. Leaning down, she kissed the spot where it pounded the strongest. His eyes fell closed. Muscles taut, he shivered beneath her caress. The gossamer feelings tingled through his body to hers, making them tremble in unison. But the feelings were too fresh, too strong to quit, so she kissed him again, then again, first his throat, then his shoulders, then his nipples.

His breath came hard and fast, but hers ran along in time, and she could not quit. She smoothed her hands downward, absorbing each feeling, memorizing each moment. Her fingers skimmed across his pectorals, then over the undulating plane of his abdomen. He inhaled sharply, the sound a hiss of hot pleasure as he arched into her hands.

She moved downward still more, transfixed by his masculine beauty, overcome by desire. Her fingers brushed his erection. His every muscle leaped at the contact.

Shona snapped her gaze to his face, but his eyes were still closed, his expression rapt. Intense heat flooded her, and suddenly there was nothing she could do but slip her hands around the strength of his desire.

Dugald sucked air through his teeth and went still beneath her. Primitive need consumed her like a well-stoked fire. Between their bodies, Dragonheart swung like a magic pendulum, winking red fire in the moonlight.

Shona slipped one hand lower, over the soft sacks between Dugald's legs.

He rasped out a breath and came to life like a springing beast. Suddenly he was on top, kissing her with a wild passion.

There was no longer any question of stopping. Not if the world came to an end could they be parted.

She cradled him between her legs and welcomed him inside. Twas now her turn to go perfectly still. Feelings, new and hot and frightening, surged through her.

Dugald forced himself to go still, to wait, to let her adjust. He concentrated on her face, on her thoughts, so clear suddenly in her eyes. The moonlight, soft as a velvet robe, shone on her, turning her eyes to emerald and her hair to sparkling rubies. God, she was beautiful, clever, proud, and a thousand other things that made him love her.

He closed his eyes to the thought. But there was no hope of denying the truth. Against all good sense, he loved her, he thought, and slowly, gently, he rocked into her.

Pleasure, sweet as old wine. But he would not drink it too fast, would not take too much at once, lest he could not enjoy it completely. Instead, he would sip slowly, appreciate every piquant flavor, every erotic scent.

He moved again, pressing them together for a moment, and he noticed now that her eyes were closed and her head pressed back into the moss beneath them.

The first glow of euphoria shone on her face. Twas the sight of that that nearly made him lose control. But he held onto it with awful patience, and leaning down, kissed her shoulder, her throat, her lips.

She moaned into his caress and pressed against him. Her taut body contracted around him. He tensed, fighting to retain the discipline he'd been taught since birth. But there were no guidelines here, for he was beyond the boundaries of everything he had experienced in the past.

Pressing his palms into their mossy bed, he arched away, gritting his teeth and grasping the reins of control once again.

She moaned again and pressed against him, beginning a steady rhythm.

He tried to fight it, tried to be gentle with her, to bring her the full cup of pleasure, but suddenly she wrapped her legs around him, drawing him in even deeper.

There was nothing he could do. Pleasure drowned him. Ecstasy called. With a feral growl of feeling, he buried himself to the hilt.

She gasped beneath him, but did not stop the rhythm. Instead, she pressed harder, faster, and suddenly it was a race of pleasure into pleasure. All thought was lost, all logic abandoned. They were one body, one soul, one being, reaching for euphoria.

Dugald felt her tension increase, felt her pleasure

build, heard her gasp of surprise as orgasm took her.

He watched her as she found utopia, watched her eyes fill with wonder, felt her body tighten with consuming pleasure. He could not stop his own release, but neither could he risk her. With a Herculean effort, he drew out and let himself erupt.

Sated and heavy, he rolled onto his side in the moss and cradled her in his arms.

Their breath melded, their hearts beat in unison. Peace stole over him. He stroked her hair, breathing in her scent, memorizing the feel of her skin, the sound of her breath.

Long ago, in another world, Dugald had been told there was no crime so heinous as to fail to appreciate the joy one is given.

He lay in silence and let the moment fill his soul. For this instant perfect peace was his. Soon that peace would be shattered, and he would be forced to fight. Then he would do what he must. But for this night he would hold her.

Yet the night lasted only for a moment.

"Dugald." She broke the silence with nothing more than his name, but even in that moment, he felt her fear.

"What is it?"

"The camp!" She scrambled to her feet, pulling on her nightrail as she did so.

The peace was shattered like a crystal goblet.

He was beside her in an instant, his tunic already snatched over his head. His course was set. Where she went, he went.

"What is it?" he asked.

"There is someone in the camp," she rasped, and lunged in that direction, but suddenly a dark figure appeared beside her.

Shona gasped and stumbled to a halt.

"You are right," said the man, his voice deeper than sin. "And there is someone *here*."

Chapter 24

"**W**illiam!" Shona felt her body grow cold. Night seemed suddenly torn away like a curtain at dawn, and by the light of the rising sun she could see the sword in his hand. "What are ye doing here?"

"I believe the question is, what are *ye* doing here, my love?"

A scream sounded from camp.

Terror ripped a hole in Shona's heart. "Nay!" she shrieked, and lunged off, but in that instant, William grabbed her by the arm and yanked her to a halt.

She struggled wildly, trying to break free. From the corner of her eye, she saw him lift his hand. Still, she was unprepared for the blow across her cheek.

It echoed in her head. She reeled backward, trying to think. From the left, she heard a noise and tried to turn toward it. But suddenly William's arm was crushing the breath from her throat. Her back was pressed against his chest, and she could feel the sharp point of a knife just below her jaw.

She froze, fighting for breath, for thought, but suddenly he swung about, dragging her with him.

"Halt!" William ordered.

Five yards away, Dugald skidded to a stop.

"There's a good lad," William crooned. He turned his head slowly and kissed her ear. "That's right. Stay just where ye are, or your love will not be so bonny.'' Lifting his hand, he scraped his knife slowly along her healing wound and smiled. "But then, perhaps ye like them scarred."

A muscle jumped in Dugald's jaw, but in a heartbeat his expression went blank and he spread his hands peaceably out at his sides.

From camp, Shona heard the sharp sound of steel against steel. Another man screamed.

Instinct made her jerk toward the noise. Her movement dragged William to the left a few inches. In that moment, Dugald lunged toward them.

But William crushed her back to him with a curse and pressed the blade back against her throat.

"Move another inch," he growled, "and I'll slit her throat like a Christmas hog's."

Dugald froze, but his face was not so stoic now. For a moment Shona saw wild lightning flash in his eyes. William laughed.

"So I was right," he murmured. "Ye *do* care for the little bitch. But who does not? Even Hadwin turned against me in the end. He had nothing against a few practical jokes, a cut girth, a bit of a brawl to make the others look like fools. But he would not hurt the lady." He nuzzled her neck with his cheek. "Poor fool. Another who thought ye might actually care for him. But tell me, Shona love, do ye return Kinnaird's feeling, or is it no more than lust?"

She didn't answer. From camp, a cry was cut short. She whimpered in terror. Where was Kelvin? And what of Rachel?

"Are ye worried for your little friends?" he asked. His lips grazed her ear as he spoke. She shivered at the touch. "If so, perhaps you should have stayed with them, instead of creeping out here to meet your lover."

Someone yelled a curse.

"What do you want with her, William?" Dugald asked. His voice was even, rational, the tone calming, somehow.

"What do I want with her?" William laughed. "I want what any man would want with a haughty bitch like her. I want to teach her humility. She could have avoided all this and taken my suit."

Shona gritted her teeth against the acid taste of terror as his knife bit into her throat.

"But she thought herself too good. Too good for *me*!" William growled. "Ye think I did not see how ye two stared at each other. Like animals in rut. But tis not too late for her to pay for her mistakes. And maybe . . ." He ground his crotch against her buttocks. "Maybe if you're good, Dugald the *Dragon*, I'll let ye watch. Unfortunately, there won't be much left of her when I'm through. Some think my amorous techniques a bit rough. My lovely Deirdra, God rest her, thought it better to throw herself from the turrets than to return to my bed once the child was born. But what can ye expect? I have been patient. So patient, I need to expend my frustration somewhere."

Shona gasped at the ugliness of his words. Panic threatened. But that was what he wanted. He wanted her afraid, terrified, blubbering for mercy. That much she knew, and that she would not give him. But mayhap, if she were lucky, if she were smart, if she'd not misjudged Dugald . . . she forced down the fear, jerked her head to the right, and yelled, "Nay, Kelvin!"

William twisted to the right, and in that second Dugald threw his knife. It hissed through the air and sliced into William's shoulder. He staggered back with a rasp of pain.

Shona jerked away. William reached for her. His fingers snapped her sleeve, but she lurched forward.

From behind her, she could hear the sound of running feet.

"Lord William?" someone cried.

"Get her, damn ye!" he roared.

Shona pivoted about to look, but suddenly a hand grabbed hers. She turned to fight, then realized it was Dugald who was dragging her along. Relief washed through her. She spurted after him, running, bent and wild, through the woods away from camp.

Someone approached from their right. Shona felt his evil presence before she saw him. She screamed to Dugald. He dropped her hand, slammed to a halt, and spun toward the intruder.

There was a moment of silence as he leapt, the sharp crack of bone.

In a heartbeat Dugald was up beside her again, grasping her hand and urging her on. She tried to see over her shoulder, to search for others. But branches and bracken blocked her view. Still, no matter how far they ran, she knew they were pursued, could hear men scrambling after them.

"How many are coming?" Dugald asked.

She had no way of knowing, and yet she did. "Three," she gasped. "Maybe four."

He pulled her sharply to the left. She stumbled and fell to her knees in the bracken. In a moment he was down beside her.

"Stay put!" he hissed and rose.

The pursuers were nearly upon them. "Dugald." She tried to rise, but he pushed her back.

"Down!" he growled and sprang away.

Someone shrieked a battle cry, but the noise ended abruptly. From her hiding place, Shona saw William's soldier drop his sword and stumble back, his torso impaled on a seven-foot branch.

The next man leapt forward, but Dugald snatched the dead man's spilled sword and swept it upward. The villain blocked the cut. Dugald's sword broke in two. The brigand shrieked in glee and lunged. But Dugald spun about in a wild circle and slammed the broken blade into the hollow of his throat.

He fell clawing at the bloody hilt.

The rest was a haze of movement and screams. But in a moment all was silent, and Dugald stood alone. He turned and ran toward her. His sleeve was torn and blood stained the fabric, but otherwise he seemed unscathed.

"How did ye do that?" she whispered, her gaze frozen on the gore.

"Come," he said, reaching for her hand.

Light exploded from the camp. Men screamed.

"Nay!" Twas a boy's cry that issued through the morning air.

"Kelvin!" Shona yelled. She scrambled to her feet. Dugald grabbed her, but she fought him off. "Kelvin!" she yelled again, and jerking free, scrambled away.

"Shona!" Dugald yelled. "Nay. Stay here."

But she could not. Heart pounding, lungs aching, she flew through the woods. It seemed like an eternity before she burst into camp.

Bodies lay strewn everywhere. She stumbled past them, searching for the boy.

Rachel jerked from Liam's arms and ran toward her.

"Rachel." Relief flooded through Shona as she pulled her cousin into her arms. They clung together, blocking out reality for a few brief moments. But the reprieve could not be prolonged. The nightmare was real. "Rachel," Shona said, pressing her to arms' length. "Where is Kelvin?"

Rachel's face was streaked with blood and dirt, but beneath the grime, she was as pale as death. "They took him," she whispered.

"Nay!" Shona fell to her knees, still clasping her cousin's hand. "Tis not so."

Rachel knelt down beside her, holding her in her arms as she rocked back and forth.

"Why?" Liam asked. He was gripping his right arm. Blood oozed between his fingers. "Why did they come? What did they want?"

"Tis my fault." Bullock stumbled up. His leg bandage was bloody and there was a slash cut across his temple. "I failed. I slept." His face was somber, his expression tortured. "I slept while I should have guarded."

Shona rose slowly to her feet. There was no time for mourning—not now. "No one heard them come, Bullock. Not until it was too late. And ye were wounded and drugged.''

''Twas as if we were all drugged,'' Liam said, his tone confused, his face twisted in agony. ''Why?''

''It makes no difference why!'' Bullock growled. ''Twas my duty to stand guard. And twill be me who will make the bastards pay!'' He stepped forward, but even as he did so, he faltered on his wounded knee.

Shona caught his arm. ''Nay! Please dunna go,'' Shona pleaded. Bullock had been her friend and protector long before she had known the meaning of the words. Now, it seemed, it was her time to protect him. ''Ye must not go after them. Stay here.''

He turned to her, surprised by her response. ''What of the boy?'' he asked.

''What of Rachel?'' she countered. ''Ye know how she is. She will tend the wounded and forget all her own needs. What if yet another evil should befall her?''

Bullock scowled. ''But the lad is like a son to ye.''

''And Rachel is like a daughter to the Flame,'' she said. ''Your loyalty lies with her.''

Understanding shone in Bullock's face. ''And what are *your* plans?'' he asked, his eyes narrowed.

''Dunna worry over me,'' she said.

A soldier limped up. ''We must return to Dun Ard. Gather troops,'' he said.

But Rachel's gaze never left Shona's face. ''Ye plan to go after them yourself,'' she whispered.

''Dun Ard is too far,'' Shona said, ignoring Rachel's words. ''Blackburn is closer. Go there. Tell Hawk what has happened. He will send a message to Father.''

''Why did we sleep so?'' Liam asked, still mired in his questions. ''Twas like an evil spell.''

''Shona,'' Rachel said. ''Ye must come with us to Blackburn. Hawk will send troops. They'll find Kelvin. They'll bring him back.''

''Damn William to the depths of hell!'' Bullock swore.

''Why did he do it?'' Liam asked. ''Why attack us?

Why take the boy? Surely he can do them no good. He is but a waif.''

''It matters little why he did it,'' Bullock growled, glancing around at his fallen men. ''For he will roast in hell for his sins, no matter what the reason.''

But Liam was of an entirely different mind. Born without Bullock's tremendous bulk, he had survived by his wit and cunning. He turned his gaze on Shona, his eyes narrowed as if he could see through her to her soul. ''Why?'' he repeated. ''What did they want?''

She shook her head, afraid she knew the reason, yet hoping against hope that she was wrong. ''I dunna know,'' she whispered.

''William wanted Shona,'' Dugald said, striding up. ''She was his quarry.''

''What?'' Rachel and Liam spoke in unison.

''William attacked Shona in the woods.''

''What were ye doing in the woods?'' Rachel asked.

''Revenge, then?'' Liam said. ''Revenge for breaking their engagement?''

''A stinted lover?'' Bullock rasped. ''He has slaughtered my men and his own cousin for naught but his bruised pride?''

''What has happened here?'' A soldier wandered up, his eyes round and bewildered, his gait still unsteady with sleep.

All eyes turned to him.

''Stephen!'' Bullock gasped, ''Ye have survived?''

''Survived? I was fast asleep.'' He glanced dazedly about. ''Surely this is but a dream.''

''A dream!'' Bullock rasped, and lunged toward his own man, but Liam stopped him, able, in Bullock's weakened state, to pull him to a halt easily.

''Do ye say ye slept through the entire battle?'' Liam asked.

''I . . .'' Stephen paused, hugging his wounded arm to his side. The bandage from the night before seemed inordinately clean amidst the chaos. ''I did naught but sleep after Lady Rachel tended my wounds.''

Rachel scowled. "The herbs should not have been so strong that . . ."

A shriek cut her words short.

They turned as a unit toward the noise.

A soldier stumbled from a tent, staring wildly about at the carnage around him. "Merciful God, what has happened?"

"Where have ye been?" Bullock growled.

"I . . . I . . ." The soldier stumbled toward them, looking disoriented and hazy.

"'Tis as if we were bewitched," Liam murmured.

"Did this man take your herbs, Lady Rachel?" Dugald asked.

"Nay, he—"

"Warwick." Liam said the name softly, as if he did not mean to say it at all.

Shona turned quickly toward him, her heart thumping wildly against her ribs, her stomach sick. "What are ye saying, Liam?"

"'Tis the work of the Dark Sorcerer. He made it all seem peaceful here beneath the rowans. *He* did this."

"Nay. The wizard is dead. Boden killed him."

"Boden killed him," Liam murmured, "but he is not dead."

"Ye make no sense," Rachel said, but just then someone groaned. She jerked toward the noise as if wrenched from her own terror and hurried to the downed man's side.

Liam went after her.

Shona watched him go, her mind boggled, her fear escalating.

Warwick! Alive! But how? And if so, why would he have come here?

The answer came to her quickly. She reached up and pulled Dragonheart from beneath her nightgown. The amulet glowed warm against her palm.

Could the old wizard have somehow survived Boden's sword? And if so, could he now be haunting her, still trying to obtain Dragonheart? Twas not possible. Why would anyone want the pendant enough to kill for it?

"Bullock," Liam said, returning to the group. "Rachel says for ye to lie down. Stephen and Andrew, she needs your assistance."

The two soldiers hurried off to help tend the wounded, and Bullock, though told to do otherwise, limped off to do the same.

Liam turned toward Shona. Their gazes met.

"Why does the wizard want Dragonheart?" he asked.

"What are ye talking about?" Shona asked.

"What has the pendant done for ye?"

She shook her head in confusion, but Liam stepped forward and grasped her hand in his own.

"What gifts has it given ye, lass?" he asked.

"Ye canna truly believe tis magic."

"Sara held the dragon before ye," he said. "Three days she was in the wilds alone. Three days with a bairn not old enough to crawl. Not a bite did she have to eat, not a drop of milk for the babe. But neither of them sustained so much as a scratch for their trials."

"And ye would give credit to the pendant?" she asked, incredulous, confused, shaken.

He remained silent, then blew out a heavy breath. "In truth, lass, it matters naught what I believe. It only matters what the wizard believes."

"The wizard," Dugald said. "The one called Warwick?"

"Dunna say his name out loud!" Liam warned, then lowered his voice. "No good can come of it."

"Ye think he is after Shona's pendant because of its powers?"

"Dragonheart is not Shona's," Liam said. "She is only keeping it for a time."

"Keeping it for whom?"

Liam shrugged, impatient and angry. "I dunna know. I only know that she has it now, and as long as she does, the wizard will hound her."

"The wizard is dead," Shona whispered.

"Did ye see his body?" Liam asked. "Nay. And neither did I. I should have searched for him harder. I should not have given up."

"If the pendant endangers her, then she should be rid of it," Dugald said.

"Nay!" Liam's tone was sharp, but softened in a moment. "Nay, it has come to her for a reason."

"Come to me?" The whole thing seemed unreal, and yet, somehow, Shona was not surprised at Liam's words, for there was something about the dragon that was not quite normal, not quite earthly.

"What powers does it give that the wizard would wish to possess?" Dugald asked.

"How would I know what is in his twisted mind? I am not like him!" Liam snapped.

Shona stared at him.

Liam ran splayed fingers through his hair and drew a deep breath. "I dunna know," he said more softly. "Mayhap tis all foolishness conjured up in a sick old man's mind."

There was a moment of silence as each person turned to his own thoughts.

"What kind of bird is behind you, Shona?" Dugald asked, his voice quiet.

"What?" Shona turned to him in surprise, certain he had lost his mind.

"There is a bird on a branch behind you. What kind is it?"

"Our men are dead or wounded and ye would ask about a bird?"

He stared at her. "I would know why William of Atberry held a knife to your throat," Dugald said, his voice deadly soft. "I would know why, before I cut his heart from his chest."

She swallowed, remembering the sharp snap of a broken neck and Dugald's stoic expression as he left the man dead.

"Tis a treecreeper behind me," she whispered. "In fact, there are two of them."

Liam started. "How did ye know?"

Scowling, Shona shrugged. "I dunna know. I suppose I heard their calls."

"In the midst of battle, with your mind boggled by the loss of a boy ye love like a son?" Liam said. "Amidst all that, ye heard the high-pitched call of a tiny bird?"

Shona tightened her fingers over Dragonheart. "He has enhanced my senses?" she asked, awestruck and quiet. "Is that what ye think?"

"I canna explain it, lass. Your senses have always been uncanny. Mayhap it but enhances one's own gifts. I dunna know its mysteries, and for that I am sorry. I only know that the Dark Sorcerer thinks it precious beyond all else."

She straightened. "It matters naught if it is magical or nay," she said. "Nor does it matter why the wizard wants it. All that matters is Kelvin's life."

"We will get him back," Dugald said. "They came for *you*, of that much I am certain. They only took the lad to lure you to them."

Shona's stomach turned over. "They would use him as bait?"

"Aye," Dugald said. "And therefore they dare not kill him."

"Kill him!" She could hear the terror in her own voice, could taste the bile in her throat. "I must go!"

"Go?" Dugald caught her arm. "You are not thinking, Shona. They have two dozen men, all trained and well armed. We have little more than a handful of warriors, and most of them wounded."

"Shona," Rachel called. "Come here."

Shona hurried through the camp to where her cousin knelt beside a fallen man.

"Hadwin." Shona whispered his name as she crouched beside Rachel. "What happened?"

"William!" Hadwin croaked. His eyes were wide and staring, his skin waxy. "I did not know."

Shona grasped his hand between her own. It felt unearthly cold. "He took Kelvin, Hadwin. Why? Where did they go?"

"I swear . . . I was not privy to his plans," he whispered again. "He wanted you, but . . ." His body spasmed. "Forgive me," he rasped, and went limp.

She rose slowly to her feet. Rage coursed through her. She turned away.

"Shona," Liam said, "tis too dangerous. Ye canna go."

"Twill be safer alone."

"Alone?" Dugald's tone was as deep as the earth as he watched her from a few inches away.

"Aye. They are not nearly so likely to see one coming as a whole troop. And too," she said, pressing the pendant's warmth against her chest. "If Dragonheart is powerful, surely he will aid me. For this much I know, the amulet is not evil. Mayhap this is the very purpose for which he came to me, to give me the strength to see Kelvin safely returned."

From the corner of her eye, she saw Liam glance at Rachel. She saw her cousin nod and turned toward the magician.

She knew he would try to stop her. But she would not let him. "Ye needn't worry, Liam," she said. "I am stronger than ye think—"

But suddenly, reality dipped, the earth tilted beneath her feet. And though she fell like a bobbing apple into dark waves, she knew it was Dugald who had betrayed her.

Chapter 25

S hona awoke slowly. She lay on her back inside a
tent. Outside, the world was dim, darkened by either clouds or nightfall. She remained still a moment,
trying to ascertain which. Twas clouds, she decided, then
remained motionless a while longer as she marshaled her
senses. She did not know exactly how much time had
passed since Dugald had spilled her into oblivion, but it
had been less than half an hour, of that she was certain.
Someone had carried her inside her tent, hoping to keep
her safe. Their intentions were good, she knew, but that
knowledge did nothing to improve her mood. After all,
Kelvin's life lay in the balance.

The memory of him brought her fully awake. William
had taken Kelvin. William, who had pretended to care
about her. Anger burned through her, but she stilled it,
forcing herself to think, to plan. She did not know why
the duke had taken the boy. But just now it made no
difference, for it would not change her actions.

Rising to her knees, she swayed, then steadied herself.
The tender dell below her left ear throbbed, but she ignored it.

Now she must gather what she needed and leave before the others realized she was awake, for they would
try to stop her. Glancing about, Shona recognized the
canvas bag that contained her clothing. Dropping to her
hands and knees, she crawled silently to it, pulled out

her leather breeches and a simple tunic, slipped off her nightgown, and dressed in the men's garments. She left her feet bare, plaited her hair into one thick braid, and retrieved her knife from the floor.

Rising silently, she stood motionless and listened. Through the canvas walls of the tent, it seemed she could hear every word spoken—Rachel's quiet orders as she continued to tend the wounded; Liam as he joked with the same. Where was Dugald? She concentrated a moment longer, then placed him some hundred rods away, speaking quietly with Bullock.

Apparently she had awakened before they'd expected her to. Therefore she must leave now, while she still had the chance.

Turning toward the back of the tent, Shona made one quick slice through the canvas. It parted in cooperative silence. She slipped through, glanced warily about, and hurried into the woods.

This would be a mission of stealth and cunning. An arsenal of weapons would do her little good against William's might. All she would need was a horse and a bow . . . and more luck than any one person was likely to have in a lifetime.

The trail was not difficult to see, for William wanted nothing more than to be followed. Dugald urged Eagle on. He could not be more than an hour behind Shona.

But what would happen when she found Kelvin? Dugald's gut tightened with dread. He forced his thoughts aside; he would not think of that now. He would not think of her life in danger, or how her skin felt beneath his hands. Those thoughts only boggled his mind.

He would not even think of how he would kill William, though surely that time would come. For now, he would concentrate on the matter at hand.

They were heading south by west. Why? Where were they going? Unbidden questions burned in his mind, blurring his thinking. He steeled himself, blocking away the fear. Instead, he would plan.

Of one thing he was certain: the element of surprise would be on Shona's side. Never would a coward like William expect a maid to challenge him unaided. Nay, he would be certain she would bring her soldiers, soldiers who had been wounded, soldiers who would slow her progress.

They had fought like true warriors. That much had been obvious in the pale light of morning. Though five of Dun Ard's men had been killed, William had lost nearly twice that many. Where they had come from, Dugald didn't know. Mayhap the Irishman was correct. Maybe there was a wizard who had brought more men and cast an ungodly spell over the camp. If that was the truth, what other kind of dark illusions could he cause to overtake people's minds?

Whatever the case, Shona had not slept. Could the amulet be magical? Could it have called her away from camp? And what about himself? Was the amulet responsible for his own survival, or was it Shona's own bright allure that had kept him awake, had drawn him to her?

No answers came, only more questions, so Dugald rode on, urging the miles to rush away beneath the galloping hooves of his horse.

The trail ended just before dawn of the second day.

Dugald hunkered down in the shadow of the woods and stared through his glass at the distant fortress.

Kirkwood Castle. It was a small estate, but it would be easily fortified. For more than half a league in every direction, the land was devoid of trees, offering no cover to any who might hope to breech the stronghold. Beith Burn flowed deep and fast past the feet of the castle and beneath its huge bridge. Around the entire fortress the land had been dug away so that the water of the Beith swelled about the towering brownstone.

Lowering his leatherbound glass, Dugald settled back on his heels. Where was Shona? Surely she had not already gone to Kirkwood, he thought, and though he believed he must be correct, the idea made him feel sick. He could not be too late.

Dugald calmed his breathing with an effort and turned to logic. She had ridden through one day and one night without sleep. She would rest for a spell before attempting to rescue the boy—alone, herself against an army who held a child for a purpose she did not know.

Dugald gritted his teeth in dire frustration. There was no logic in any of this. How could he plan? How could he think, when none of it made sense?

Why did they want Shona, and why would she go after them alone? True, she was no wilting maid, but surely she did not think she could challenge the might of a fortress alone. Unless, mayhap, she believed Liam's words, that the dragon aided her. Could she think herself invincible?

But no. She had been shocked at the Irishman's words. She would not depend on some pendant of metal and stone to see her through this challenge. Therefore, she must have some other plan in mind, some plan that did not depend on brute force.

So what could she be thinking? What kind of . . .

Dugald's mind froze.

She was not planning to try to breach Kirkwood Castle atall. She was planning to give herself up—an even exchange, her own life for the child's.

The thought struck him like a rock to the back of the head, and he trembled, for suddenly he knew it was true.

He rose with a start, his heart pounding. He must find her now, before it was too late to tell her all the things he had neglected to say. To admit why he had been sent. To beg forgiveness, for he knew the truth now. She was all that was good. No woman who could care so for another's child would ever plan the death of the young king.

Dugald pivoted toward his horse, then stopped abruptly, for there, not two rods in front of him, stood Shona.

"Lass!" he rasped. Was she real, or an illusion conjured up by fatigue—or perhaps by the wizard Liam had spoken of? "Shona?" he said dubiously. Still she did not disappear. He took a tentative step forward. "You are well?"

Her expression was absolutely solemn, strained by worry. "What are ye doing here?" she asked.

She was real. She was hale.

"I've come to find you."

"Why?" She stood with her leather-clad legs spread slightly, her auburn hair plaited and tossed against her back. "To assist me, or to knock me on the head again?"

It was the peeved tone of her voice that made him relax a mite. No illusion could sound so irritated that he had come to save her.

"I did not knock you on the head," he said.

"Then what did ye do?"

"I . . . discouraged you from coming here and risking your life."

"Discouraged me? Warning me of danger is discouraging. Telling me I am a fool to go is discouraging," she said. "Rendering me unconscious with a touch of your hand is something else all together." She was silent for a moment, then, "Who are ye?"

"You know who I am."

"Aye. Ye are a man who says he has come to woo me, yet who insults me at every turn. Ye are a man who proclaims himself a coward, yet who can kill without weapons, without sound, without effort. I would know now who that man is."

He stared at her for a moment, feeding his weakness, letting himself drink in the sight of her. She was well. She was whole, and he must think. "I am someone who knows you cannot do what you hope to do, Shona. Despite your courage, despite your love for the lad, you cannot win this battle. Go back to your friends," he said, and stepped toward her.

She retreated a step and yanked her knife from its sheath. "Stay away."

He raised his brows at her. "Or what, lass? Or you'll kill me?"

She narrowed her eyes. "Dunna laugh at me. I am not so gullible as ye think. I see now that ye have been humoring me all along, that ye have been playing with my emotions. That ye are not at all what ye have portrayed yourself to be. But I am in no mood to be made a fool any longer. If ye will not help me, then go away and leave me to do what I must."

"What you must?" He took another step toward her. Acid terror burned a path to his soul. "Does that mean you will become a martyr? Saint Shona, who sacrificed herself for the life of a lowly waif?"

"It means I will see him freed."

"How?" he asked, still advancing.

She shifted her knife slightly. "'Tis none of your concern," she said. "All I need is for ye to see Kelvin safely back to Blackburn. I ask no more."

He snorted derisively. "And what of you, Damsel? Will ye ride back alone?"

He watched her tense. "Aye," she said. "I will leave Teine in the woods until I need her, then return as soon as ever I can."

"And when do you think that might be, lass? When do you think William will be finished with you? A day, a week, a month? Do you think you will still be able to ride? Do you think you will still be alive?"

She stared at him, her eyes wide, her lips slightly parted, as though she searched for words that would not come.

"I have no choice," she said.

"You have injured the pride of William of Atberry. In his twisted mind 'tis an unforgivable sin. Go to him now and you shall pay with your life."

"Nay!"

"You know I am right, yet you plan to go anyway. Why not admit it?"

Her expression was tense. "Will ye help me or nay?"

He took another two steps toward her. "'Tis a funny

thing about me,'' he said. ''But I have no wish to help kill the woman I love.''

Her knife dropped a smidgen of an inch. ''Ye love me?'' she whispered, and in that moment, he leapt.

He should have known better, should have remembered her reactions were just a mite quicker than a cat's. His fingers brushed her arm, but she twisted wildly away and bolted for cover.

He tore after her, forgetting everything but his need to stop her, to force her to safety. But suddenly she loosed a bent branch. It sprang into place, smacking his forehead with enough force to send him to his knees.

The sound echoed through his cranium like a war drum, but he staggered to his feet. Even through the fog, he saw she was getting away. His legs moved without the benefit of his brain, propelling him forward as fast as he could go. His fingers scraped her tunic, but he could not snatch her back. Up ahead, he saw her mare, ears pricked as she pranced warily toward them. If Shona reached her horse, he would never catch her.

It was that thought that made him leap again. This time he caught her shoulder. She faltered, tried to right herself, but finally fell to her knees. He fell with her, his scrambled mind spinning. But he had no time for disorientation, for she was already lurching away.

Dugald grabbed her leg. She fell again, losing her knife as she went down, but kicking even as she did so. Her heel rapped hard against his right ear. His head snapped to the side, but he held on. He would not let her die. He would not.

Still holding her leg, he tried to capture her arms, but she twisted about. Like a whirling windlass, her knee knocked him on the side of the head. He grunted in agony, but held onto her opposite leg, dragging her closer.

Something smacked against his ear. He was just lucid enough to realize it was her fist, not lucid enough to avoid the next blow. There was nothing he could do but drag himself over her in a limp attempt to crush her into submission.

But she was hardly done fighting. Squirming madly for breath and freedom, she wrenched her knees up, planted her feet on his chest, and kicked him off her. He landed some two feet away, breathing hard and trying to see through the haze in his brain. But the only thought he could muster was that he could not let her escape. He scrambled to his knees, ready for another try just as she did the same.

But just then Shona jerked to attention, her eyes wild as she held her breath.

"What is it?" he hissed.

"Horses!"

"Where?"

She didn't bother to answer, but scrambled wildly toward cover at the edge of the hill. Grabbing her knife from the ground, he followed her until they lay on their bellies, covered in bracken and staring out over a trail a quarter of a mile away.

They waited in absolute silence, watching the road in breathless concentration until the first rider appeared.

Even from above, they could see that the leader was a big man, riding rigid and arrogant on his white stallion. But it was not his confidence that jarred them, it was the fact that behind him rode a hundred men just like him, all dressed in identical plaid, with conical steel helmets on their heads. They rode dark horses and there was an unearthly silence about them, as if they had been sent from hell itself.

Shona watched them with breathless dread. Fear settled into her soul, but she could not let it affect her, for Kelvin's life depended on her courage.

Still crouched, she slunk backward through the bracken, but Dugald caught her arm.

"Where are ye going?"

She tried to wrench away, but dared not make any conspicuous movements. "I go to save Kelvin."

He pulled her back toward him. "And just how do you plan to do that?"

"'Tis none of your affair."

"Mayhap you will simply ask the Munro if you might accompany him into Kirkwood."

"Munro?" She felt her face go pale.

"I heard he was mustering his warriors. But he's arrived now. I'm certain he will have time to oblige you."

"That's the Munro and his infamous clansmen?"

"It looks like that to me, but I could be wrong. Of course, by the time you got your answer, your head would be on his pike. Or mayhap even he would find better use for you."

"Dear God!" She watched them go. "Why? Why has he come here?"

"Because William has something so precious in that castle that he dares try to leash the power of the Munros to keep it for himself."

She stared at him, terrified, immobilized.

"What is it, Shona?"

The last of the Munros rode from sight. She shook her head, trying to clear her thoughts.

He shook her. "Why did William take the boy?"

"How would I know?' she gasped. "Did ye think, mayhap, that I was in league with him?"

Dugald stared at her, his silver eyes level.

The world was as silent as a tomb.

"Ye did," she whispered. "Ye thought that I planned some evil with William."

He didn't deny her words, didn't turn away.

"Is that why ye came?" she asked. "Were ye sent?"

He didn't answer.

"Who are ye?" she murmured.

"It does not matter who I am. If you wish to get the lad back alive, all that matters is what I can do."

"Ye?" She jerked her arm away. "Let me go!"

"To do what? Get yourself killed? Or do you mayhap think yourself so invincible that you can challenge the might of the Munro alone?"

Dear God, not in all her life had she been so afraid.

"And that is not even counting the troops already stationed inside Kirkwood."

Her courage wavered, but she forced it back up. "It changes nothing. I will see Kelvin free."

"And sacrifice your own life?" he asked softly. She could find no words to answer him. He lowered his voice, holding her gaze with his own. "When your father learns that you have been attacked, all of Scotland will come to arms, Shona. Why not await their arrival?"

"Because every minute we delay Kelvin's life hangs in the balance."

"Why would they harm him?" he asked. "What sense would that make?"

She tightened her hands and longed to escape. "When has evil made sense?"

"You cannot do this alone, Shona. And it does not seem right that the boy would die for your impetuousness."

Her gut knotted like a sailor's line. "Dunna think me such a fool that I will fall for your ploys to keep me safe," she said. "Mayhap ye are right. Mayhap he will die, but it willna be because I did nothing." Tears filled her eyes. "Twill not be because I am a coward."

"A coward?" He touched her face. The feelings burned softly through her, like the heat of the sun. "You? Nay. You are nothing but brave, lass. But evil can be clever, so you must be more clever still."

"I canna wait for troops," she whispered. "I canna. For if I wait . . ." She paused and shook her head. "Please believe me, twould be terrible consequences."

"What consequences?"

She paused a moment. "They will kill him," she said. "I know it."

"How do ye know?"

"I feel it. I am certain. I must act and I must act quickly."

"In the broad light of day? Twould be no better than suicide," Dugald hissed.

"And leaving him would be no better than murder!"

"Tis not true."

She jerked away, but he pulled her gently back. "Had they wanted to kill him, they could have done so outright."

"Nay!"

"Tis true," he crooned. "Think on it. They want him alive. Therefore he is safe, unless tis you who endangers his life."

"What shall I do?" she whispered.

"Trust me," he said. "Wait until darkness and trust me."

Chapter 26

Dugald hid their horses behind a thicket of black-thorn bushes where the grass was thick and lush. Then they found a spot in the depths of a small grove of fir trees. Beneath the sheltering boughs, needles lay five inches deep and soft as moss under their feet.

Fatigue lay on Shona like a sack of meal, but worry and frustration kept her from resting.

"But what if ye are wrong, Dugald?" she asked. "What if—"

He strode quickly up to her. Taking her hand, he led her deeper into the trees until they had to crouch to walk beneath the branches. Once there, he urged her onto the bed of needles.

"I am not wrong," he said, and ever so gently touched her face.

"But what if he tries to escape?"

"He will not." Dugald stroked her cheek with ultimate tenderness. "Kelvin is no fool, lass, and he surely knows you will come for him. He will sit tight and wait."

"He can be haughty at times. What if they find out . . . ." She paused. "What if he angers them?"

"How long has he been under your wing, Shona?"

She fidgeted as a thousand memories smote her. "A few months. No more."

"No one could have lived that long with you and not

learned to charm the masses." He smiled and she found she could not look away. "He will be safe until the morrow at least."

"Are ye certain?"

Ever so softly, he kissed her. "I am, lass. Now sleep."

"But—"

"Sleep," he repeated, and kissed her brow.

"But how can ye be so sure?"

His gaze was steady and level. "Tis my job to be certain, lass."

"What?"

"I have dealt with more brigands than I can count. You can trust me to know something of them."

"Who are ye?" she rasped.

For a moment she thought he might tell her. But instead he kissed her lips, softly, tenderly. In a moment he drew away.

"I am Dugald the Dragon," he murmured, but the words no longer seemed haughty. Instead, they seemed almost sad.

"Why do they call ye that?" she whispered.

A corner of his mouth lifted. "Need you ask, even after last night?"

She stared into his eyes, trying to decipher the truth, but there was little hope of that.

"Ye are not what ye seem. That I know," she whispered. "Tell me who ye really are."

The world was silent.

"I am the man who will keep you safe this day," he said. "Now sleep, for surely you will need all your strength when the sun sets."

Dugald lurched into wakefulness. Beside him, Shona sat stiff and silent.

"What is it?" he asked.

She remained silent, her eyes wide and staring.

"Shona?" he whispered.

"Someone is coming."

He sat perfectly still, listening, but he could hear nothing except the usual sounds of the evening woods, the soft call of a dove, the distant rustle of a field mouse in the leaves. Still, he had learned long ago to trust instinct, his as well as others.

"Which way are they headed?"

"Away from Kirkwood."

"How many?" His question was surely too soft for her to hear, and yet she held up a single finger, then pointed off toward the trail to the west.

He rose carefully to his feet, but she grabbed his wrist.

"Where are ye going?"

"I go to make certain I see him before he sees us," he said, and slipped into the woods.

It took nearly a full minute before Dugald could hear the hoofbeats, a minute during which he doubted Shona's hearing and told himself a dozen times that she must have been mistaken. No one could hear that far away. No one could . . .

But suddenly he heard the distant clop of hooves and stiffened. Dear God, she was uncanny. But he had no time to think of that just now.

Crouching lower still, he crept through the woods to the trail. Once there, he found a stout branch that grew over the path. Jumping to reach it, he lifted himself effortlessly over the limb and slipped silently into the leaves. Hidden in the thickest foliage, he waited until finally he caught a glimpse of a horse beneath him.

Dugald held his breath and listened, making certain there was indeed only one person. But all his senses told him that Shona was right again. Twas a lone rider who traversed the trail. Tensed and ready, Dugald waited in silent immobility.

The horse stepped forward, finally bearing his rider into the open. Dugald strained to identify his face, but it did little good, for the person was dressed in a deep green cloak that covered him from head to foot, going so far as to conceal his face with a hood.

Who would hide his face in the midst of the woods

on a warm day? Who would be here now, riding alone
and obviously with confidence, except one of William's
own men? And who better from whom to obtain information?

Holding perfectly still, Dugald waited, one second
more, then two, until finally the horse was nearly below
him.

With a lift and a swoop he swung down from the
branches. The rider twisted wildly about, trying to fight
free, but Dugald gripped the horse's barrel with his legs
and clasped his arm across the man's throat. Quick as
thought, he slipped his knife from its sheath and pressed
it to the rider's jugular.

"One word, one move, and you will die this very
instant," Dugald warned softly.

The horse jolted to a halt. The woods were inordinately quiet.

"I'll have some answers," Dugald said softly. "And
I'll have them now."

"As ye wish. But I thought ye had come to rescue
the boy," Liam said. "Not to kill your friends."

"Liam!" Shona gasped.

Shifting his eyes to the left, Dugald watched Shona
rise from the bracken, bow in hand and eyes wide.
Mother of God! Would she ever learn to stay put?

"Dugald, let him go.

"Liam, what are ye doing here?" she asked.

"The same thing ye are doing here, I would suspect,"
he said. His tone was glib, but his body remained tense
and unmoving in front of Dugald.

"Riding down the middle of the road as bold and
uncaring as ye please?" Dugald asked, his blade still
poised at the other's throat. "Riding *away* from the enemies' stronghold? Tis a strange way to rescue a child,
is it not?"

"Let him go, Dugald," Shona ordered.

"If the truth be told, this is my first child rescue,"
Liam said. "I was not quite certain how to go about it.
And what of ye, Kinnaird? Is this an everyday occur-

rence for ye, or do ye rescue children only when there is a wealthy maid involved?''

"Since I am the one with the knife, I think I should be the one asking questions," Dugald said. "Where were you going? What are you doing here?"

"I am being held at knifepoint by a man who apparently has so many allies, he does not need one more."

Dugald tightened his grip on Liam's throat. "Now might be the time to give me some satisfactory answers."

"And now might not be the time to cut the throat of the only friend ye have in these woods."

"Liam," Shona said, hurrying forward. "Why have ye come here?"

"I followed the brigands' trail here, hoping I would find ye before ye found William. But when I rode to the edge of the woods, I did not feel that ye were in the castle. Something warned me that ye were behind me. So I turned back. And look how well it has turned out," he said, wryly shifting his gaze to Dugald's face.

"But what of Rachel?" Shona murmured. "Ye should have stayed with her."

Liam sighed. "Indeed, I should have," he said. "After all, twas obviously the safest place to be. Even though Bullock is wounded, he is not likely to allow himself to be attacked again."

"Then why did ye come?"

"Do ye think ye might tell Dugald the Daft here to get this sticker out of my neck?"

"Dugald, Liam is amongst my oldest friends," Shona explained.

But he was not Dugald's, and Dugald trusted no one. "If it was safer in camp, why did you come?"

Liam paused for an instant. "I figured Laird Leith would be a mite·unhappy if he knew I let Rachel follow ye alone."

"She threatened to follow me?" Shona asked.

"And ye know she's foolish enough to do it."

From his vantage point behind Liam, Dugald could

see Shona smile, but he himself was not so trusting.

"Or mayhap you have come to warn William of our arrival," he said.

Liam sat very still. "If ye think so little of my Shona, ye dunna deserve to protect her," he murmured.

"What are you talking about?"

"I knew the lass long before she had the face of an angel and the allure of a siren, while she was but a gap-toothed child who was always underfoot and never out of trouble. Do ye think her charm so lacking that after all these years I could do aught to harm her?"

"I have little knowledge of what you're capable of," Dugald said.

"Aye, well ye'd best be certain what *ye're* capable of, then," Liam said. "Because by mine own calculations, William has all of two hundred men stationed inside that fortress."

"Two hundred!" Dugald and Shona spoke in unison.

"How do you know?" Dugald continued. "You said you but went to the edge of the woods."

"Aye, well, I'm a damned good guesser," Liam said. "And this much I know, the two of ye are bigger fools than I think if ye believe ye have a chance against all of William's army."

"Then mayhap you can talk some sense into the maid and convince her to return to her father," Dugald said.

Liam snorted. "Long ago I learned that Shona will do what Shona will do. There is little chance of either of us changing that."

"Then there is no purpose for your being here."

"Aye, if each of ye can overcome a hundred men, ye have no need for me atall."

"Tell, me, Irishman, if there are two hundred men there, what good will you be to us?"

"It seems to me I will improve the odds greater."

"Aye, there will be less than seventy for each of us."

"Just so."

Dugald snorted. "And do you have a plan?"

"Aye. It begins by ye putting down the knife. And it ends with happily ever after."

"For God's sake, put the knife away, Dugald!" Shona scolded. "Surely seventy men to fight should be enough of a challenge even for two dragons."

"I must tell you, Damsel, there is little difference between seventy and one hundred," Dugald said. "And I do not trust this man who can ride so casually through an enemy's woods."

"Then ye had best have a plan that is better than mine," Liam said.

"I do," Dugald said. "I but wonder if I can trust you to see Shona safely back to Dun Ard."

Despite everything, Liam laughed out loud.

Dugald tensed at the noise.

Liam's mirth finally died down. "Do ye mean to tell me that after everything, ye still hope to send her into safety?"

"Shut up!" warned Dugald. He shifted his gaze toward Shona, and saw that her eyes were narrowed and her knuckles white where she held her bow.

"I'll not leave here without the boy," she said. "On that ye can depend."

"And I'll not have you risk your life. I told you once, I am accustomed to this sort of thing. Trained for this sort of thing."

"Then what do ye plan to do?" Liam asked.

"I will storm the castle," Dugald asked.

"Alone?" Shona scoffed.

"I've done it before."

"I'm quite impressed," she said, her tone implying the opposite.

"I say I will not let you go there," Dugald repeated.

"And I say, ye have no say over what I do, Kinnaird. What is your plan, Liam?"

"Liam?" Dugald stormed. "'Tis all I need, to have another innocent life on my hands."

"I fear I am hardly innocent," Liam said.

"And neither are you a warrior."

"Ye are right there," Liam agreed. "I am no warrior, but I am the king of mayhem."

"What are you saying?" Dugald asked.

"I am saying I hope ye are as magnificent as your name implies, for although I can get us into the castle, I may have a hell of a time getting us out."

Chapter 27

The night was as black as sin. The moon was hidden behind a ragged mass of black clouds, and mists rolled like homeless spirits above the rushing burn. Rain fell in a half-hearted drizzle.

Liam felt for the knife at his side. God's nuts, what was he doing here? It was true, he was hardly a warrior. He was an unwanted bastard from a misbegotten border town, a fair juggler, a middling magician, and a damned fine pickpocket, none of which qualified him to endeavor suddenly to become a hero.

Damn Rachel and her weepy eyes.

The damp wood of the drawbridge muffled his footfalls. Behind the portcullis, he could see the haloed glare of a lantern.

Now would certainly be the time to turn tail and run if he were ever going to be wise enough to do so.

But again he saw Rachel's desperate eyes.

God's balls!

"Gatekeeper!" His voice echoed in the surrounding fog, loud and demanding with false bravado. He liked the abrasive sound of it. "Gatekeeper!"

"Who goes there?" The lantern was lifted from a peg as a man, half the size of a mountain, stepped up to the iron-wrought gate. He wore a metal helmet with a nosepiece that made him look somehow more sinister than even this horrid night warranted. His tunic was simple, saffron, and nearly covered by a dark plaid.

"I've come to see the duke of Atberry," Liam said, stepping into the light.

"And who might you be?" The guard's voice was guttural. Another guard, the same in build and attire, stepped up. Damn, these Munros were brawny lads. Twas to be hoped they were also as fiercely independent as rumor said so that he could prick their pride.

"I am Liam the Irishman. Your lord and master, the duke of Atberry, will wish to see me."

The guard snorted. "I have no master. But I've a wish to see you gone, so if you hope to live until daybreak, leave this place now."

"I dunna think ye understand me, lad," Liam said. He straightened, warming to his part. "The duke is wanting to see me, and he does not take kindly to underlings who anger him."

The guard stepped closer to the metal lattice of the gate, his chest pushed out and his mouth sneering. "And I do not take kindly to little men with big mouths who disturb my peace in the middle of the night. Now, be gone, afore—"

"What goes on here?" Another man stepped toward the portcullis. He was a commanding figure dressed identically to the first two, but with a silver brooch pinned to his plaid. The short chain that connected the pin to the brooch flashed in the torchlight when he moved. Interesting workmanship, Liam thought. He'd never filched anything quite like it.

"This offal wishes to see Lord William," said the first guard.

The commander stepped closer to the gate and squinted between the metal bars. "What's your business here?"

Liam smiled. His heart rate picked up a pace, and his breathing escalated. The thing about being a thief was, it was exciting, and once the mood took him there was no turning back.

"Ye look to be a reasonable man," he said, moving

close enough to place a hand on the iron grid of the portcullis. "The truth is, I have information your master will want to hear. But your oversized hound here willna let me in."

"What information do you have to give?"

Liam chuckled. "I fear I can share it with none but your lord and master. Let me in and I'll give him a good word about your performance."

The nearest guard drew his sword. "The Munro has no master!"

"Indeed? I must have misunderstood, then, for I thought the duke hired the lot of ye to do his dirty work."

"Where do you get your news, friend?" the commander asked.

"From the MacCullocks." Their sworn enemies. "In truth," Liam said, gazing at the silver chain that dangled from the Munro's plaid, "I heard ye stole this brooch from them."

He lifted his hand, and quick as light, the brooch came away in his fingers. He snatched it through the portcullis with a grin.

The commander stood perfectly still on the far side of the gate. "Have ye such a wish to die this night, Irishman?"

Liam laughed out loud. "Nay. Indeed, I dunna. I merely have a need to speak to your master."

A muscle jumped in the commander's jaw. "And if I allow the audience, ye will return my brooch?"

"Indeed. As soon as ye let me in."

"Raise the portcullis," Munro ordered.

"But—"

"Raise the portcullis," he repeated. "And let him see how a Munro responds to his badgering."

The guard smiled ghoulishly. "Gladly."

The gate creaked upward. Liam tensed. His knees were shaking like wind chimes, but he must not bolt. The plan had been carefully set, and if he failed his part, Shona would surely die.

The big man ducked beneath the rising iron grid, then straightened. "I have always wanted to kill an Irishman," he said, and snatching his sword from its sheath, lunged.

But in that moment, Liam jumped to the side and reached out at the same time.

The guard's dark plaid came away in his hand. It swept through the air like a tumultuous, flaring cloud.

The guard's jaw dropped in surprise, but in an instant he swore and lunged again. Liam swished the woolen up over the man's head. The guard stumbled to a halt as the plaid settled over him. There was a moment of bewildered silence before Liam snapped the plaid away.

Nothing but thin air lay where the guard had once been.

"What the devil!" swore the second guard, and whipped his sword from its sheath.

But Liam stopped him with a raised hand. "Do ye want your fellow returned?" he asked. "No need to fret." Sweeping the plaid up again, he swung it in the air and whipped the woolen away.

A helmeted man reappeared like black magic, but without his sword this time.

"Devil's work!" gasped the commander, and wrenching out his sword, rushed onto the bridge.

Liam stepped back, every instinct telling him to run.

But in that moment the reappeared man lunged toward the Munro. Quick as lightning, he reached out. There was a crack as he twisted the commander's head backward.

The second guard raised his sword, but a dart whizzed through the darkness and sank into the exposed flesh of his neck. His eyes went wide, his body stiff, and then he sank lifelessly to the bridge.

Dugald removed his confiscated helmet and the dart gun from his mouth.

"Dugald the Dragon," Liam said in some awe.

"Take their plaids and helmets, then get rid of them," Dugald ordered.

"Where's the other guard?" Liam asked, as they both reached for a dead body.

"In the water."

"Too bad," Liam grunted. "There was a bulge beneath his tunic. It looked like coins."

"There are a couple hundred men waiting to use your guts for garters. Mayhap you could concentrate on more important things."

"More important than coins?" Liam asked, quickly stripping off the first man's plaid and grimacing at the sight of his staring eyes.

"Listen, Irish," Dugald said. "If you let Shona get hurt because of your own greed, I swear I will—"

"Hey!" someone yelled. But just at that moment an arrow whirred from the blackness to bury itself in the intruder's throat. The guard fell in silence, but now four others lurched onto the bridge.

Too many of them, Liam thought, and reached for his knife. Another arrow whirred, then another. Dugald lunged, darted, struck. His hands were empty, and yet when he stepped back, there was not a guard standing.

The night went silent. Liam blinked, turning his attention to Dugald.

"If I have said anything to offend ye, tell me now. I feel a sharp need to apologize."

Shona rushed up, bow in hand. "I killed them," she whispered.

"Shona!"

Liam watched Dugald reach for her, watched him pull her into his arms.

"I killed them," she whispered again.

"Shh," he crooned. "Shh. Tis what you had to do, lass. Tis what was right. Do not think on it now." He kissed her forehead with ultimate tenderness. So even the dragon turned to a pup when Shona was near. "Quickly now," Dugald whispered. "Take a plaid and a helmet."

Shona turned from him, her eyes wide in the darkness. "But—"

"Think of the child," Dugald murmured.

She nodded and stepped away.

In a moment the three were dressed in Munro garb and the bodies were gone, tossed into the roiling water below.

Stepping inside, they closed the portcullis as quietly as possible and stood huddled together as they stared into the bailey.

"You must not let them know that the guards are gone," Dugald said.

"Call me the Munro," Liam said, and pinned the chained brooch to his plaid.

"Be careful," Shona told him.

"Rest assured."

"I will check the towers," she said. "Dugald, ye search for a dungeon."

His eyes were steady and hard in the glow of the lantern. "I go with you."

"We have no time to waste on arguments."

"Nay, we do not," he said. "I go with you."

She ground her teeth, but she could delay no longer. "God be with ye, Liam," she whispered, and turned away.

Their luck held as they strode through the bailey, for the rain had driven the soldiers to cover. In the encroaching darkness, it was nearly impossible to see, but they searched blindly for a door.

"There," Shona said, keeping her voice low as she pointed.

Dugald nodded, stepped to the door, and listened for a moment. When no sound came from the opposite side, he pulled it open. It creaked crankily on rusty hinges. Shona held her breath, but not a soul stood in their way.

While waiting for darkness, they had planned carefully, hunkered in the bracken as they guessed where Kelvin might be held. It had been decided then that they would check the dungeon first. But where would the dungeon be?

Finding a flight of stairs, they made their best guess

and followed a stone passageway along the north side of the castle.

The silence was enough to make Shona want to scream, the darkness so intense that she could not see the floor beneath her feet. But they kept going. If Kirkwood had a dungeon, it would probably be near the front of the castle. Searching in the dark seemed futile beyond hope. Still, what else could they do?

A door appeared before them. Dugald opened it. Light streamed out, seeming unearthly bright after the darkness. On the floor, a trio of soldiers lay on pallets. The nearest one sat up with a curse.

"What the devil do ye think ye're doing?"

Dugald staggered in the doorway, his helmet slightly askew. "Got to take a piss."

"Well, don't go leaking on me. The garderobe's down the way."

"My thanks," Dugald mumbled, and closed the door behind him.

Shona's heart hammered in her chest as they hurried silently away. The halls here were lit by flickering wall sconces, making their search easier, but their danger greater.

Where could Kelvin be? she wondered. But suddenly her thoughts were interrupted.

"Guards!" she hissed, and pulled Dugald into an alcove.

They waited there, pressed together, holding their breath and each other. Footfalls approached, echoed closer, and thumped on by.

Shona shuddered as she exhaled, but she did not loosen her grip on Dugald's sleeve. Beneath his stolen helmet, only his eyes looked familiar.

"If I dunna live—" she began, but he hushed her with his fingers on her lips.

"You will."

She grasped his wrist, and kissing his fingers, pulled his hand away. "If I dunna, take the child back to Blackburn. Promise me ye will."

"You will," he repeated, his tone raspy.

"And if I dunna?"

"Then I will be beside you."

"Nay!" Terror and desperation tore at her. "Dunna say that. Ye must not. Ye must promise to take Kelvin back to Blackburn. Ye must vow."

"Shona—"

"*Promise*."

A muscle jumped in his jaw, but despite himself, he could not refuse her. "I promise," he said.

She let her eyes fall closed, but opened them in a moment. "I would have ye know one thing," she whispered. "I love ye. Never in all my years have I loved another so."

She felt the muscles in his arm tighten and tremble.

"You will survive," he said. "If every man here must die to make it so, you will survive. That I vow."

Tilting her head back, she kissed him gently. Soft fire burned her lips, making her forget everything except the strength of his arms, but in a moment he drew away.

"Stay here and remain hidden."

She tried to form a question, but he shushed her.

"You must stay here now. Do not move from this spot. I will return shortly," he said, and stepped away.

She clutched his sleeve harder. "Where are ye going?"

"I am going to ask where I might find the lad."

"Dugald!" she said desperately. He pulled her fingers from his sleeve. Gone was the lover with the gentle touch.

"They will be happy to tell me," he added, and stepped into the hall.

"Nay," she gasped, trying to snatch him back, but he turned and quickly pushed her back into hiding.

"Do you not want to find the child?"

"Aye, but—"

"Then stay put," he ordered, and pivoting away, disappeared down the hall.

Shona stood alone, her heart hammering in her chest, her fingers grasping nothing.

He was going to take a prisoner, to ask questions, to risk his life.

And he was going in the wrong directions. Somehow, though she didn't know how, she suddenly knew she was right, as if an extra sense had just awakened. It seemed to dull all else.

"Dugald," she whispered, and lurched into the hallway to find him. But already he was out of sight. She could hear footfalls up ahead and turned the corner, desperate to stop him.

She struck the soldier head on and bounced off, hitting the floor with considerable force.

"Hey!" Munro's clansman was bearded and gruff. "Watch where you're putting your feet there, laddie," he said, and reached to help her up. But suddenly he stopped and his eyes went wide.

"You're not a laddie," he exclaimed, and with horrible clarity, Shona suddenly realized she had lost her helmet.

Chapter 28

"Who the devil are ye?" growled the soldier. His fingers closed like a vise over her wrist and she was yanked from the floor. His gaze, hot and lurid, skimmed over her. "Who are ye, and where were ye off to in such a rush?" he asked. "Tis a Munro plaid. Who was the lucky lad who lost it to ye?"

Shona tried to find her voice. But it would not come, for already he was tugging her down the hall.

"A bonny wee bit of fluff ye be. I dunna know how ye came here, but neither am I the type to ask questions when my willie is up." He chuckled.

She yanked at her arm, trying to break free. But he turned on her suddenly.

"Hey, now, lass, ye dunna want to make me angry. I can be gentle as a lambkin when I want to, but if ye make me mad, I'll have to get rough. And ye wouldn't like that. That I guarantee."

Panic welled up like a dark tide. "Let me go!"

"Go?" He chuckled. "Go where?"

"I have . . . I must go to Ian."

"Ian? Ian of Woodsward?"

Shona felt a rush of relief. She knew no Ian, twas just a common name, a shot in the dark.

"Aye," she said, trying to think, to hold onto her sanity. "Twas he who sent for me."

"Well, then, for certain ye will want a real man, for

344

Ian's pecker is no bigger than my thumb. Come—''

''Wait!'' She hauled backward, trying to quell her panic, to find her sense. ''Wait!''

He turned again to stare at her. She slowed her breathing and forced herself to look up through her lashes at him. ''I'm a thinking a braw lad like ye will want more than just me. I'm a thinking ye'll want the others.''

His jaw fell slightly. ''There be more like ye?''

She chuckled, hoping the noise sounded seductive instead of mindlessly panicked. ''Oh, aye,'' she said. ''They be but waiting for my word. Just up ahead in the spare room they are.''

He turned to stare down the hall, then glanced back at her with a lascivious grin.

''Well, I wouldna wish to disappoint them.''

''Indeed not,'' she managed, and tugging on his hand, pulled him in the direction she hoped Dugald had taken. But the hall was empty.

''Which room are they in then?'' asked the soldier. He sounded suspicious.

''Just in here,'' she said, and turning to her right, pulled the door open and urged him inside.

''Tis dark,'' he said, but just then, she slammed her knee into his groin.

He grunted like a wounded boar and clutched his crotch. Shona lurched for the door. He came at her with a roar, one hand outstretched.

She lunged away, clawing her knife from its sheath, but he snatched her arm.

The blade snapped from her hand and spun into the darkness as she was yanked forward. But even as she careened toward him, she groped with her free hand. Her fingers brushed across something. Without thought, she grasped it and swung.

A wooden keg toppled to the floor, but its cover came free. She whacked it across the soldier's head. He crashed against the wall.

Shona's every instinct screamed for her to run, but he

would surely overtake her, so she sprang at him like a tigress and swung the lid again.

His head slammed against the wall. Then he slid to the floor in oblivion.

Panting, her chest tight with fear, Shona spun from the room.

"Hey!" Meaty arms enfolded her. "What's going on here, Missy?"

She swallowed a scream and struggled against this newcomer, but he only chuckled.

"Where ye going in such a rush?"

"Who's this, then?" A second soldier appeared in the dimly lit hall.

"She's mine, is who she is," said the first. "Munro property, if ye can't tell from the plaid."

"Seems to me we're all in this together, and since I'm Lord William's man, she should be mine."

Still holding her by the wrist, her captor stepped in front of her and pushed out his chest in an age old sign of male aggression. "The hell she should."

"The hell she shouldn't!"

"To hell with both of ye!" snarled Dugald. Stepping from the shadows, he clasped each of them by the hair and thumped their heads together. They smacked forehead to forehead, bounced back in stunned silence, and sank to the floor.

"Can't I leave you alone for one moment?" rasped Dugald, and grasping her hand, pulled her along the hall.

But Shona skidded to a halt, dragging her heels. "It wasn't my fault, and you're going the wrong way."

"What?" he asked, pivoting toward her. "Did they tell ye where the lad is?"

"Nay. I just know."

"How?"

"Never mind," she whispered, and yanking her arm from his grasp, spun away.

Her footfalls were silent, the stone floor cool beneath her bare feet.

A door appeared in front of her. She put her hand to

the latch, dredged up her nerve, and yanked it open. Stairs ran upward. She lurched toward them, but Dugald was beside her now, his hand on her wrist.

"Where the devil are ye going?"

"To Kelvin."

"Where is he?"

She rushed up the stairs, not thinking, only feeling. "Up," she gasped.

"Up? The tower."

Her breath came in pants now as she ran up the stone steps. "Nay. I dunna think so. A chamber . . . with a trunk."

"That narrows it down to a hundred or so rooms."

"And I see a bed."

"Would you think me a coward if I admitted you're scaring me?"

"He's by a window."

She had reached the top of the stairs and stood panting as she glanced right and left.

"That way," she whispered, and took off again.

The passageways were dark here, but the floor was smooth, the going easy. Up ahead, the faint glow of a lantern could be seen.

Dugald grabbed her hand. She slowed to a walk and moved closer to the wall. Her heart hammered a hard tattoo against her ribs, and her breath came in a rush.

Kelvin was here. He was close. She knew it, could feel it in her soul, in the warm weight of Dragonheart. But the boy would be guarded. That she knew, too.

She slowed her steps even more, until, silent as a cat, she crept along the wall toward the corner. Dugald pulled her to a halt, and she obliged, leaning her head against the wall for a moment as she steadied her breathing.

Dugald dropped her hand and lifted a finger to his lips for silence, then spread his hand in a sign for her to wait.

But she could not. Taking a single step forward, she leaned to the side and peeked around the corner.

Two men were stationed beside an arched wooden door. One was tall and gangly. He leaned against the stone wall while the other sat slumped on the floor. His eyes were closed, his face bearded, his spear beside him. Neither wore a Munro plaid. They were obviously William's personal soldiers, but none Shona had met.

Pulling silently back into the passageway, she glanced at Dugald. He glared back, then pulled his knife from its sheath.

Terror roiled in Shona's stomach. Twas two to one. Surely twould be safer to take them on one at a time.

Without another thought she unwound the plaid from her hips and stepped around the corner.

The standing guard snapped to attention as his gaze caught hers. She smiled. His jaw dropped, his gaze skimmed her body, the tunic that exposed one ivory shoulder, the shocking amount of leg that showed beneath its hem.

"Who are ye?" he rasped.

"Me name is Cara."

The second guard awoke with a snort and a jerk. "Who the hell is she?"

The first guard grinned. "Her name is Cara."

The men glanced at each other and grinned.

"And what might ye be doing here, maid?"

She pulled up her tunic slightly and looked them boldly in the eye, first one, and then the other. "I just come from Laird William. He says the two of ye have had a long shift and I'm to relieve your boredom for a wee spell."

They blinked at each other.

"We're to leave the door unguarded?"

"God, yes!" said the bearded man.

She chuckled. The sound was low and suggestive. She hoped they could not hear the panic in it.

"In me vast experience, men are na usually so loyal to their posts when I am around." She shrugged, exposing a bit more shoulder. "But Willie said ye were to come with me one at a time."

The tall one nodded. "Me first."

"I've been here longer," argued the other.

She laughed again. Dear God, she had no time for this. If they did not fall for her ploy, Dugald would grow impatient and attack them on his own.

"A Munro is coming to relieve ye in a bit," she said. "Till then I'll save plenty for ye," she assured the bearded man. "Come, Longshanks."

She stepped away. The tall guard hurried after her and turned the corner. Dugald stepped forward. The guard's eyes widened, but he had no time to scream as Dugald grasped his head in both hands.

The tall man was dead before he hit the floor.

Shona stepped back, horrified by her own deeds. But Dugald caught her gaze with his own steely eyes.

"I'm here then," he said, quickly understanding her ploy, his voice loud enough to carry to the other guard.

Shona struggled with her senses, trying to do what she must. But her gaze slipped away to the man on the floor again.

"What room do I guard?" Dugald asked and reached out to shake her by the arm.

She came out of her trance. "Just to the left," she said. "Tell the bearded one to join me soon."

Dugald nodded at her, then stepped forward to disappear around the corner.

"Bout time," said the guard.

"Yah," grunted Dugald.

There was a moment's pause, a shuffle of feet, and then all was quiet.

Shona closed her eyes and forced down the bile in her throat as she turned the corner to the guarded door.

"Is he dead?" she asked, staring at the body on the floor.

"Else I'm losing my touch," Dugald said and stepped toward the door.

He put his ear to the timbers, listened for a moment, then lifted the bar and swung the door quickly open. Light streamed into the otherwise dark room.

"Who . . . who is it?" rasped a small voice.

"Kelvin!" Shona rushed inside. He was sitting on a small cot, his eyes wide and his hair tousled. In a second he was in her arms.

"Ye came for me!" he rasped.

"Of course, lad. Of course we did," she crooned. Relief rushed through her.

"But how did you get through? How'll we get out?"

"Not to worry," she soothed, and pulled him tighter against her as Dugald dragged one of the guards into the room.

"Lord William took me. And the wizard!" Kelvin shuddered. "He looked right through me, but I did not tell them, Shona. I did not say. It's so dark. But when they left me . . ." He paused, his arms tight about her. "I laid down and dreamt of ye."

"And your dreams called me to ye," she whispered.

Dugald reappeared with the tall guard. Lifting him onto the bed, he turned him over on his back, and whipped the covers over him so that only a bit of hair showed.

"What is he doing?" Kelvin asked.

"Shh." She hushed him as she stroked his hair. "Shush now."

"Are we ready?" Dugald straightened.

"Aye."

In a moment they were out the door. Dugald closed it behind them.

"How will we get out of the castle?" Kelvin asked again.

"Shh." Shona hustled him along.

"The front gate will surely be guarded," Kelvin said. They hurried down a flight of steps.

"We've a friend there," Dugald said.

"Someone's coming!" Shona gasped, but it was already too late.

Five soldiers stepped around a corner less than rod away. "Who goes there?" one of them called.

"'Tis just me," Shona said, her heart in her throat. "A simple maid and my son."

There was a moment of heart-rending silence, and then the soldier stepped toward them. "What the hell are ye doing up and about at this hour?"

"Lord William said to fetch him some ale."

"The hell ye say. I was just with the duke." He drew his sword out with a metallic twang.

"Run!" Dugald shouted.

Shona delayed a moment, but already Dugald was lunging toward the soldiers. There was nothing she could do but spin away and drag Kelvin with her.

They galloped down the hall.

Grunts and moans and curses followed them, but it was the sound of running feet that made Shona twist about to look behind.

Dear God! A soldier! Not a hundred paces behind them, and Kelvin was already slowing.

They careened around a corner. Which way to the gate? She was all turned around.

But there. They'd come that way before; she remembered the odd shape of the garderobe door. But that meant they had a long stretch ahead of them, and soldiers behind.

"Here!" She grasped Kelvin's hand harder, dragged him toward the latrine, and shoved him inside. "Down the shaft!"

"What?"

"Down the shaft," she whispered. "It'll take ye to the burn."

"Nay! Not without ye."

"Kelvin!" She shook him by the shoulders. "I have sworn to protect ye. Now ye must do as I say. Down the shaft." Dragonheart felt heavy as a log about her neck. "Here . . ." Whipping Dragonheart from her neck, she slipped it over his head. "'Tis magical, lad. It brought me to ye. Twill surely bring ye to freedom. When ye reach the water, follow the flow. I will find ye. I swear I will."

His eyes were wide with terror, his fingers like claws on her hands. "Ye will come for me?"

"I will come," she vowed.

He leapt atop the latrine. Dragonheart glowed like a beacon in the darkness, but she had no more time to watch.

"Run!" she shouted, as if he were ahead of her, and lunged away.

She heard the soldier sprint around the corner after her. And though twas terrifying to hear him come, still twas a relief, for he had not stopped at the garderobe. She could only pray that Dugald was safe, for there was nothing she could do now but save herself. On and on she ran with the soldier drawing nearer. Another corner. In a moment she would be out of sight. She'd find a place to hide.

Shona leapt around the corner.

Three men stood in quiet conversation.

She skidded to a halt. The men turned toward her.

"William!" she gasped.

"What the devil!"

The soldier careened around the corner behind her. She heard him jolt to a halt, but didn't turn toward him, for William held all her attention.

"So, ye have come," William smiled. He took a slow step toward her, and she saw now that his left arm was bandaged.

"Where's the boy?" the soldier gasped, still out of breath.

"What boy?" William snapped.

"The one that was with her."

William turned slowly toward Shona and smiled. "So ye managed to free the lad, did you. I fear I underestimated ye, my dear. But the boy doesn't matter now that I have you."

She backed away, but there was very little room.

"Did I not tell you the lad would draw her, William? They have a bond."

Shona turned toward the speaker. "Magnus," she whispered.

The old man pushed back his hood. "Some call me Warwick, lass."

Terror speared through her. Mayhap against William and his thugs she would have a chance, but not now, for already she could feel the oppressive terror of the wizard's presence. He had been the evil she felt by her door at Dun Ard. She was certain of it suddenly. And now she remembered every moment of her struggle against him in Dugald's room, as if he had somehow clouded her memory.

"So what is the boy to you?" William asked.

She shook her head, trying to clear it.

"Your bastard, I think, though Warwick disagrees. Twould be kind of ye to settle this dispute for us."

She swallowed, trying to calm her nerves, to think.

"Mine? Ye think Kelvin is mine?"

He stepped closer still as did his solders. She moved against the wall. They were closing in.

"In truth, lass, I dunna care if ye have lain with every man in Christendom. I only want one thing from you."

"What?" She shook her head. "What do ye want?"

Warwick stepped forward, his opaque eyes eerie in the flickering light. "Give me the amulet."

"Dragonheart?"

"Ye could have saved yourself a good deal of trouble if ye had handed him over when I asked," William said. "Greed is a terrible thing. Still, tis a sin I can understand."

"Tis just a pendant," she gasped, still backing away. She was fast running out of room. "Why do ye want it?"

"Why?" William laughed. "In truth, tis the wizard who desires it so. I would suggest ye do as he asked, for I fear he will go to great lengths to get it. Indeed, it seems he intended to crawl up the tower to your room, but your brave Dugald distracted him."

"The dragon is meant to be mine," Warwick murmured. "I have waited an eternity for it. It calls to me. I can feel its power even now."

Her throat felt tight with fear. "So twas ye who placed the wolf in the woods?" Shona asked, trying to stall, to give herself a few more moments. "Did ye hope that it would kill me?"

William chuckled. "Ye wound me with your low opinion of me, Shona. I planned that scene exactly as it happened. I knew how attached ye were to the lad, so when I learned he would be riding with ye, I realized how ye would idolize me when I saved him—enough to marry me, surely, thus granting me full access to the amulet, not to mention your family's power."

Warwick was close now, nearly within reach.

She shrank back against the wall.

"Ye should have gone through with the wedding plans, Shona," William said. "Certainly I would not have let Warwick harm my bride. But now . . . I fear he holds a bit of a grudge against your kinsmen. It seems one of your own damaged his arm rather badly when last he tried to take the amulet."

"Give me the dragon," Warwick said. His voice was soft, but his eyes were not, and pulled her in like a cold current.

"I dunna have it," she rasped.

Warwick stopped.

But William only tsked. "I know better. Ye never remove the amulet."

"I dunna have it," she repeated, and wrenching her gaze from Warwick's, pulled her tunic aside.

No chain hung about her neck.

Warwick recoiled as if struck. "Where is it?"

"I gave it away."

"Ye lie!" William snarled. Yanking out his sword, he leapt at her. She pivoted away, but too late. He grabbed her by the tunic and pulled her back. Spinning her about, he ripped at her shirt. It tore down the shoulder seam, baring part of one breast.

She tried to cover herself, but William jerked her arms away.

"Damn ye! Where is it?" he roared. "Who has it?"

Not Kelvin! Not Kelvin! But who? "Liam!" she lied. "I gave it to Liam."

"The Irishman?" snarled William.

"Liam!" rasped Warwick. "'Tis Liam's presence I feel." He stumbled backward as if struck, then lurched away.

"Where are ye going, old man?" bellowed William.

"Liam is at the gate!"

"What the hell are ye talking about?" William roared, but Warwick was already gone.

The castle went quiet but for the harsh sound of Shona's raspy breathing.

"So my bonny maid, ye gave it away did ye?" William asked, turning his attention back to her.

She nodded, barely able to achieve that simple motion for the terror that seared her.

"You gave it to another after refusing me?" he asked, and ran the edge of his sword down her cheek.

She shuddered and shut her eyes.

"That wasn't very nice. But ye know what I think?"

She dared not look at him.

"I think ye lie, Shona, my love. But I believe a bit of steel applied to the right place will help ye tell the truth."

He drew back his sword. She bit her lip and tried not to scream.

Chapter 29

"**W**illiam!" someone yelled.

William yanked his sword up. Dugald threw his knife, but a soldier had already lunged toward him and now caught the blade in his shoulder. He screamed in agony and staggered back.

Another soldier lurched forward. Dugald spun about and kicked him, sending him sprawling into William's sword.

Shona leapt to her feet and hurtled past them.

Dugald gave the dying soldier another shove. He went down in a heap, dragging William with him.

Dugald spun away, grabbed Shona's hand, and leapt around the corner.

"Get them!" screamed William.

The sound of scrambling feet echoed in Dugald's brain. He had to get her out, find a way to safety. A door appeared ahead. They raced away and swung it open.

A troop of soldiers, alerted by the yells, scrambled in the narrow passage, fighting to wrench their swords out.

Shona shrieked. Dugald slammed the door shut. They leapt away, but William was already in sight, tearing down the hall after them. They lunged to the right.

Which way to the gate? It didn't matter now. Nothing mattered but to stay alive, to get her free.

"Surround them!" William screamed.

And suddenly, as if by command, more soldiers appeared up ahead.

Dugald skidded to a halt.

"Dear God!" Shona gasped, and turning wildly about, yanked open a door on their left.

They flew inside. Shona slammed the door shut. By the light from an iron candelabrum, Dugald searched for a bar to lock them in, but there was none. Racing across the room, he snatched a shield from the wall, propped it beneath the door latch, and jammed it against an uneven floor board. Then he grabbed the handle of a nearby trunk and dragged it across the floor to hold the shield in place.

Something shattered behind him. He swung toward the noise. Shona was beating at the window with a stool, but the panes were thick and reinforced with iron. He ran to help her, but even as he did so, the door rattled as someone threw his weight on the far side.

Shona swung the stool harder. Shards of glass sprayed away. Metal twisted but held.

Snatching up a wooden chest by its handle, Dugald slammed it like a mace against the window.

One pane creaked as a small portion twisted outward.

"Break it down!" William screamed.

Bodies slammed against the far side of the door.

Shona swung her stool with renewed vigor. Dugald wielded the iron-bound chest. More window broke away. Nearly enough. Nearly. He swung again.

The trunk scraped inward as the door was forced open. Men streamed in.

Dugald heaved the chest with all his might. It shattered the window, broke away the iron, and fell outside.

But there was no time to follow it. He swung toward the intruders. Snatching up the candelabrum, he wielded it like a sword. It struck the first man full in the face. He screamed as he stumbled sideways. Flames flared like fiery snakes in his hair.

The next man lunged forward. Dugald swung again. A candle soared through the air, leaving its metal prong empty and deadly. The sharp end slashed across the soldier's throat. He stumbled back into his companions, grasping at his throat.

"Through the window!" Dugald yelled. But even now men were swarming past their fallen comrades into the room.

"Back! Get back!" William yelled. The men moved to the side, letting their lord pass. In his hand he held a sword, and in his eyes there was a killing rage. "It seems only right that I slay the dragon. Get the woman," he said, and lunged.

"To the window!" Dugald shouted, but already it was too late and Shona knew it.

Darting forward, she snatched up a fallen sword and swung with all her might.

The closest man leapt back with a scream, holding his arm. The next came on, not knowing he dealt with a desperate woman trained to fight. He dashed toward her, then stumbled back, a diagonal slash across his chest.

"Jump!" Dugald yelled, turning just in time to see she had a respite.

Pain seared through his arm, slamming him back to the reality of his own battle.

William laughed, the sound high-pitched. "So ye think ye can stop me, Kinnaird." He advanced. Dugald retreated, still holding his impromptu weapon. From the corner of his eye, he saw that the bed drapery had caught fire.

Shona stood with a sword held in both hands, her legs spread wide as soldiers fanned out before her.

"Aye," Dugald said, a thousand thoughts racing through his mind. "I will stop you. You shall never be king."

William raised his brows. "How did you know?" he asked, advancing slowly.

Behind him a tapestry caught fire.

"Twas the way you wooed Shona. You were too patient. Twas obvious you had more important things on your mind. And once I met the maid, I wondered what you could think more important. Mayhap the life of a king, I thought. So twas *you* who tried to have him killed.''

William circled, his arms spread wide. ''Young James is inordinately lucky, I fear. But that was before I found the wizard. His gifts are astounding. Ye would be impressed,'' he said, and lunged.

Dugald danced backward, and William smiled. ''I'm in no hurry to kill ye, Kinnaird. As ye said, I'm a patient man. All these years I have waited, amassing my armies, training my sons. Once the king is dead, nothing will stand between me and the throne, and no one will have the power to change that, not with the wizard at my beck and call.''

''So twas your plan to steal Dragonheart from the maid . . . then give the pendant to the sorcerer so that he would have the power to dispense of the boy king?''

''Tis still my plan,'' William snarled, and swung as he leapt.

The blade swept across Dugald's chest. Blood sprayed into the air. William sprang forward, but Dugald wrenched up his weapon, blocking the next swipe before stumbling weakly back.

Pain as hot as the flame that licked the walls swept through him. But he gasped for breath and strength as he held the iron in front of him. He could not fail her. He could not.

''Tis still my plan,'' William repeated. ''I will be king.''

He struck again. Dugald blocked the first stroke, but his weapon was heavy and cumbersome, his arms weakening from loss of blood.

The next swipe came from the side, cutting across his biceps.

The candelabrum fell from his numb fingers.

William lunged forward and Dugald leapt back. But his strength was draining with his blood, and his feet caught in the rug that bunched beneath his feet.

He fell. William leapt forward. Dugald rolled to the

side, and William, unable to stop, stabbed his sword into the wooden floor. It held there for only an instant, but in that moment, Dugald grasped a candle from the floor. Flame soared as he swept it through the air and slammed it into William's face.

The duke screamed and stumbled back. His sword clattered to the floor, but he snatched out his knife and lunged forward.

Death screamed in Dugald's ear, but if he died, so would Shona.

He wrenched the candelabrum from the floor, but had enough strength only to point it upward.

Filled with wild blood lust, William threw himself forward. Too late, he saw the deadly prongs waiting for him.

They sliced into him, impaling him just below the sternum.

His eyes went wide with shock and horror. Bloody froth foamed at the corners of his mouth. He stumbled weakly back, the candlestick protruding from his torso.

"I will . . ." He stumbled again, then caught himself on the wall. Flames licked at his feet, though he did not seem to notice. "I will be king!" he rasped, and toppled backward onto the floor.

"He's dead!" a soldier hissed.

"Jesus God!" another murmured. "He meant to kill the king."

"Heads will roll for this."

"Not mine!" someone rasped, and lunged away.

Panic boiled up like hot tar. Men rushed from the flaming room.

"Dugald!" Shona stumbled toward him and fell at his side. "Dugald, are ye all right?"

He grasped her hand. Something smeared warm and sticky between his fingers. He turned his head and realized with stunning relief that the blood was his own.

He turned his eyes to hers. They looked unearthly bright by the light of the fires that blazed around them.

"Go, Shona."

She laughed. The sound was wild. "Surely ye jest."

"Leave now, before tis too late."

"Never. I will never leave ye."

His back felt wet. He realized vaguely that it was his own blood he felt, seeping like a warm pool into the floor boards.

"And what of Kelvin?" he asked.

"Get up!" she ordered, pulling his arm.

"Where's the boy?" he asked.

"Shut up!" she yelled. "I willna go without ye. If ye stay, I stay!"

Dugald remained as he was for a moment, but if he knew anything, he knew she was stubborn enough to do as she said. Closing his eyes against the numbness, he tried to sit up.

"Give me the amulet."

Dugald snapped his gaze to the doorway. Amidst the flame and smoke, a black robed man stood.

"Warwick," Shona whispered.

"Give it to me," he ordered, his voice low, his opaque eyes eerie.

She pulled at Dugald again, still trying to drag him from the floor. He could not die; she would not let him. "I dunna have it."

Warwick stepped forward, seeming to walk on fire. Flames licked at his robe, but his milky eyes never flickered from her face.

"Ye do," he countered. "The farther I got from you, the weaker I felt the power of the dragon. You still have it. But where?"

Beside her, Dugald forced himself to sit up.

Shona nearly sobbed with relief, but Warwick came on. "Stay back," she ordered, and swept a knife from the floor. "Stay back or I swear ye will die this day."

The old wizard stopped, but then he chuckled. The sound was low and evil. "Such bravery. Tis almost a shame to see it die."

"And if I die . . . then what? Ye shall never have Dragonheart."

"Maybe not," Warwick murmured. "But what if I kill him first?" he asked, nodding toward Dugald. "What then, lass?"

With a strength caused by sheer primal terror, she pulled Dugald to his feet. He felt as limp as a kitten by her side, no more substantial than a doll of rags. "Ye cannot kill him," Shona sobbed. "Ye canna; he is the greatest warrior that ever lived. Dugald the Dragon, they call him."

Warwick laughed. The sound quivered through the crackling air like a banshee's howl. "So you have two dragons! But I only need one!" he shrieked and raised his clawed hand.

Dugald stiffened and staggered backward.

"What's wrong!" Shona cried, struggling to hold him up. "What is it?"

"He is dying!" Warwick screamed. His voice screeched above the roar of the fire that crackled all around them. "Suffocating because of you."

"Nay!"

"Give me the amulet."

"I dunna have it!" she cried.

Dugald staggered sideways. She went with him. Heat seared her legs. Terror scoured her soul.

"Tell me or he dies!" roared Warwick.

Dugald stumbled. She tried to hold him up, but in a moment, he fell to his knees. Shona collapsed to the floor, still encircling him in her arms.

"Let him go! Let him go!" she screamed.

"Give me the amulet!"

"I canna!" she sobbed.

Warwick roared with rage and lunged toward them, arms outstretched.

Death screamed her name. She dropped over Dugald's body, covering him, holding him for one last moment.

"Warwick!"

The name shrieked through the room. The wizard shuddered to a halt and turned.

Barely daring to breathe, Shona raised her head, but the flames obliterated the doorway.

"Who is there?" shrieked Warwick.

"Let them go!"

It was Liam's voice. Shona clasped Dugald's tunic in tight fingers, silently begging him to breathe, to live.

"Who are you?" Warwick asked, stepping forward.

"Let them go," Liam repeated, "or by all that is mighty, ye will pay."

"Liam," Warwick hissed. "Come to me."

"'Tis not likely, old man."

"Come to me now, or I will kill them both."

No one spoke. The flames crackled higher. Terror rode Shona like a spurred horseman.

"Very well then," rasped the old man, and spun toward them.

"Nay!" Liam screamed, and sprang through the doorway.

Flames billowed around him. For a moment he looked like the devil incarnate. But the sparks died in his hair.

"You have come," Warwick crooned, "after all these years. Twill be you and I, now. We will be invincible . . ." He turned slowly toward Shona. "Once we have the dragon."

The breath stopped cold in Shona's throat. She shuddered and squeezed her eyes closed, unable to meet his gaze. But even then she could feel him coming, knew he would kill her.

"I've got the amulet!" Liam's words echoed in the room.

The wizard turned slowly toward him.

Liam held up his fist. A short length of chain dangled from between his fingers.

The dark wizard stepped toward him. "The powers of the dragon!" he hissed. "We will learn them and leash them. Nothing will withstand our might."

"Nay, old man," Liam said. "I have the power." He raised his fist. "So much power that I dare throw it away. Ye want it . . . go get it," he said and twisting about, tossed it into the inferno behind him.

"No!" screamed Warwick. The cry wailed through the castle, and then, like a craven hound, he sprang after it into the flames.

Liam leapt across the floor. Grabbing Shona by the arm, he yanked her to her feet.

"Get out!" he yelled. "Get out!"

She fought wildly against him. "Not without Dugald."

"He's dead."

"Nay!" She jerked her arm free and fell down beside him. "He is not dead!" she cried, and just then she heard him gasp for breath. "He's not dead," she gasped, stunned by the truth. "Liam, help me."

"God's balls," Liam swore. A beam of wood crackled and collapsed from above the doorway. "We'll not get him out that way."

"The window!" Shona cried.

Liam rushed to the shattered pane and glanced below. "Twould be kinder to kill him here."

"When have I ever been kind?" she rasped. "Dugald, get up. We'll have to jump."

His eyes opened. "Jump?" he whispered.

Tears welled in her eyes. She smiled and wiped them away. "Tis no great feat for ye. Not for Dugald the Dragon."

"Tis about time you got my name right."

She sobbed a laugh. "I'll not forget again if ye promise to live."

He raised a hand gently to her cheek. "I fear the choice is not mine, lass," he said, and let his eyes fall closed.

"Nay!" She jerked at his tunic with both hands. "If ye die now, ye will forever be remembered as Dugald the Dastardly."

"I do not think I could live with that," he said.

"Then come," she whispered, and dragged him to his feet.

He grimaced in agony but shuffled slowly to the window. They crawled onto the sill together and glanced down. Fifty feet below them, the river roiled black and cold.

Shona grasped his hand. Fear coiled in her stomach, but there was a stronger emotion.

''I love ye,'' she whispered.

Dugald turned to her, his face streaked with soot and blood. ''And I you, lass. For ever and always, no matter the outcome.''

''God's balls, will ye two hurry up?'' yelled Liam. ''The Irishman is frying in here.''

''Forever and always,'' Shona said, and they leapt together.

Chapter 30

~~~~~~~~∽⟲∞⟳∽~~~~~~~~

"Are ye awake?" Shona whispered into the darkness of Blackburn's infirmary.

Dugald sat up and turned toward the door. "Who's there?"

"Tis no one," she said. "Merely a wild figment of your imagination."

"Ahh." The moon, bright as a silver coin, shone through the open window and gleamed on his smile, on the mounded muscle of his bandaged chest as he pressed it out to push a pillow between the wall and his back. They had arrived at Blackburn five days ago, and thanks to Rachel's talents, Dugald was healing well. "So tell me, Damsel Figment, what brings you here in the wee hours of the morning?"

"Me?" Her nerves were stretched taut. In truth, she had tossed and turned all night, wondering how she would bring him this news. Finally, abandoning the hope of sleep, she had snuck from her bed to come here. "I could not wait any longer," she whispered.

"Oh." The word was breathless.

"I didna mean it like—" she began, but suddenly his hand touched hers. Fire sparked between them.

"I could not wait, either," he murmured, stroking her fingers. "I think you have bewitched me. Or mayhap twas the amulet that ensorceled me."

"Mayhap Dragonheart knew ye were too stubborn to adore me as ye should."

Dugald chuckled. "Mayhap it thought my life too peaceful without you." His fingers skimmed higher over the sensitive crease at her elbow. "Come here," he whispered, and pulled her to the mattress beside him. Her buttocks settled against his hip. Her breast, covered by nothing more substantial than her nightrail, caressed his chest. "Ye look very much like Shona MacGowan, Maid Figment," he murmured, and leaning forward, kissed the side of her mouth.

She sighed. "I missed ye. Rachel has been a tyrant, not letting me spend more than a few minutes at a time with ye."

"Mayhap she thinks I should build up my strength before I see ye," he suggested, and slipped his finger over the swell of her lips.

She closed her eyes to the dreamlike feel of his fingers on her skin.

"Mayhap she thought you would be too much of a temptation for me." He kissed her throat. She moaned and leaned her head away, allowing him greater access. "Mayhap she thought you would tax my strength."

She turned toward him. Already lost to the temptation, she kissed his lips. But in a moment she jerked away.

"Dugald!" she exclaimed, realizing she was once again being distracting and that the truth could wait no longer. "I must tell ye something."

He sighed and leaned back against his pillow. His fingers found hers in the darkness. "In truth, lass, there is something I must tell you, too."

"There is?"

"Aye." His tone was solemn. "I have been lying awake, trying to figure out a way to say it."

"Ye have?"

"Aye." He smoothed his fingers across her cheek. "Lass, I am not who you think I am."

She could not help but smile. "Ye mean to say ye are not a jaded wastrel come to find a wealthy bride?"

"Nay."

"The spoiled son of an Asian princess?"

He cleared his throat. "She was Asian. In my more romantic bents I tell myself my mother cherished my father and thus could not bear to rid herself of his child before it was born. But whatever the case, she gave me life and sent me to live with her family. Mountain people, they were, peasants. . . . masters of ninjutsu."

She repeated the word softly.

"Trained killers," he said. "Spies, assassins. Whatever you wish to call them."

Her jaw dropped.

"There is a long, twisting story to my life," he said. "But suffice it to say, I learned certain skills from my grandfather. Skills I finally brought here to the land of my father's mother. She was of the clan Kinnaird."

"What skills?" she whispered.

"Skills that won me a place amongst men who saw me as nothing more than an expendable foreigner. They did not like me, but they learned they could use me, and that kept me alive, gave me a place in this country. Tis in battle that I first won the name 'Dugald the Dragon.' Twas in battle that I excelled. In truth, I did save the duchess of Crondell from ruin. She kept me with her while I healed. And Lady Fontagne—twas much the same situation. I am no great lover, lass. I am a great killer."

The room went absolutely still. Night slipped along on silent feet.

"I beg to differ," she said quietly.

He smiled a little, but his thoughts were dark. She could tell by his expression as he turned toward the window. She watched the cords in his neck stand out in sharp relief.

"Why do ye kill, Dugald?"

He was silent for a moment. "You want me to say I do it to protect the weak, Shona. That I do it for the good of Scotland, but I do not know if that is true. Mayhap killing is simply in my nature."

"So mayhap ye are an evil man? So evil that ye would risk your life for a young boy from the streets? A boy who meant nothing to ye?"

"I—"

She raised her fingers to his lips, silencing him. "So evil that ye would risk your life for me, a woman who has bedeviled ye since the very first?"

"I did not come to win a wealthy bride, Shona. I came to kill a wealthy bride."

"What?" She breathed the word.

"I was hired by Lord Tremayne to murder you."

"Lord Tremayne?" Her fingers fell from his lips. "Why?"

"He said he had learned through secret means that it was you who planned the king's assassination, that you and your kinsmen had devised a plot to put another on the throne. He can be very convincing." A muscle tightened in his jaw.

"But why would he believe that?" Shona asked. "I am naught but a simple maid from the Highlands. No threat to anyone."

He was silent for a moment, and then he smiled gently. "On the contrary, Damsel, you pose a grave threat, for tis you whom the young king adores, tis you whom he listens to. Think on it. He is surrounded by the wealthy and powerful, old men with shriveled hearts who care for naught but more wealth and more power. Were it not for you and yours, young James might well forget there are others in this land, others who need his good judgment, who need his help.

"I think he feared your influence over the king. Tis a well known fact Tremayne hopes to align Scotland with Spain through James's marriage, mayhap he even thought you might agree to wed the king yourself and spoil his plans." A muscle flexed in his jaw again. "Whatever the case, I shall learn the truth."

She drew a deep breath. "And then what, Dugald? What if ye learn his motives were less than pure?"

"Then I will kill him."

She shook her head. "Nay, ye will not."

His fingers tightened on hers. "And how do you know that?"

"Because ye love me," she whispered. "And I will not have ye risking your life, for I could not bear to lose ye."

"Shona," he rasped, but she would not let him speak. Instead, she kissed him with trembling softness.

He drew her into his arms and moaned against her lips. There was nothing they could do but make love. No way they could resist. Their clothes sighed away. Their bodies slid, warm and sensuous, against each other's, legs entwined, fingers caressing, flesh pressed against flesh as they strove to prove their love to each other.

The night slipped softly away, until finally, sated and at peace, they slept in each other's arms.

"Dugald!" Shona sat up with a start, suddenly chilled and wary. "Someone's coming."

He sat up beside her, snapped his gaze to the burgeoning light in the window, then back to her face.

She wrestled wildly with the covers, then finally managed to scramble out of bed.

"My nightrail! Where's my nightrail?" she gasped, digging madly under the blankets. But although she saw some interesting things, her gown was not among them.

The footfalls grew louder. She searched more frantically, and finally found her gown heaped in a forgotten pile on the floor. She snatched it up and yanked it over her head just as someone knocked at the door.

Panicked, she spun about for a way to escape, found none, and plopped onto a stool beside the bed.

The knock came again.

Dugald's gaze met Shona's. She nodded nervously.

"Who is it?" he asked.

"'Tis me," came Kelvin's voice.

"Come in, lad," Dugald called.

There was relief in his tone, relief that Shona wished

she could share. She managed a smile as she wrung her hands, and realized in that moment that her nightrail was inside out.

The door opened, and Kelvin stepped in.

"Lady Shona!" exclaimed the boy.

She nodded nervously.

"I did not expect to find ye here."

"Well, I . . ." She cleared her throat and tried to smooth her hair. It was hopeless. "I wished to speak to Dugald afore ye came."

"Oh. Tis good," Kelvin said.

"But I didna get a chance to tell—"

"And what brings you by lad?" Dugald interrupted.

The boy approached the bed. "I have come to thank ye, Sir," he said. "For coming to my rescue. For coming to Shona's rescue. Ye are brave beyond words. Scotland will forget neither your courage nor your loyalty."

"Scotland?" Dugald said, his tone uncertain.

"I must go now, but I feared I would not have time to speak to ye later. Twill be a busy day for me."

"Busy?" Dugald asked. "How so?"

But just then another boy stepped through the door. He was approximately the same age and size as Kelvin, with the same red hair and the same mischievous eyes, but he was dressed much more richly, with a large bloodstone brooch pinned to his plaid.

"Your Majesty!" Dugald straightened in his bed. Shona winced.

Absolutely silence held the room. And then the king bowed slightly toward Kelvin. "I thought I might find ye here, James."

Dugald glanced from one to the other. "James?" he said.

"Hawk says I am to fetch ye," said the richly garbed boy. "You've yet to bathe and change into decent clothing. Although I think ye do look good in my rags, your mother might take offense when she arrives."

"Your mother?" Dugald asked.

"The queen, of course," Kelvin said, then laughed.

"I must away, for she would indeed take offence." He turned toward the door, but in a moment he pivoted back around. "Again I apologize for losing your amulet in the burn, Lady Shona," he said softly. "It slipped away as if by magic." He shrugged as he turned, but in a moment, he peered over his shoulder, a very adult gleam in his eye. "I will expect the two of ye to wed soon."

In a moment, he was gone, with the door closed behind him.

Not a soul spoke.

Shona cleared her throat. "He is growing up so fast."

"Who?" Dugald's tone was sharp. "Who is growing up so fast?"

She winced. "Tis a long story, Dugald, and ye should rest." She jerked to her feet, but he yanked her back down.

"Who is growing up so fast, Shona?" he growled.

She tried to look away, but she could not quite break contact with his eyes. "The king?" she said.

"That boy in the rags? That was the king?" His voice was too quiet. It boded ill.

She cleared her throat. "I think it would do ye no good to get all riled now."

"That boy you had all this while at Dun Ard? That boy that you . . ." He stopped suddenly, as if shocked. "You tossed the *king* in the river?"

"He was acting quite arrogant."

"He's the king! And you let him run wild, like some Highland stag?"

"Twas part of his disguise, to keep him safe, until the assassin was apprehended."

"All the time traveling back here? All the intimacies we have shared together, and never once did you tell me he was the king masquerading as . . ." He flipped a hand toward the door. "As a beggar boy?"

"I resent being referred to as a beggar boy," said the lad dressed in opulent riches and so many rings they seemed to weigh down his small hands. "I much prefer to be called a waif."

"Aye," Shona said, jerking from Dugald's grasp. "He prefers to be called a waif."

"Mother of God, Shona, you have been lying to me all this time?"

"I . . . I . . ." She winced. "I never said he *wasn't* the king."

"You knew the king's life was in danger," he said, obviously figuring things out as he spoke. "You knew he was in danger, so you substituted this lad to take his place. You disregarded this boy's life as if he were of no more consequence than a rag doll? I know how that feels, Shona. For I was once just such a lad who—"

The boy laughed suddenly, interrupting his soliloquy. "Ye think playing at being king was some great hardship, do ye?"

"Your life was in danger all the while," Dugald said.

"And what do ye think tis like on the street?" asked the real Kelvin. "Where every drunk may be the one to slit your throat. When I first laid me eyes on Lady Shona, I was debating whether to eat the rotted cabbage the butcher's wife had thrown out, or venture on to the milkmaid's slop heap."

Dugald scowled, then turned his eyes to Shona. "You lied to me," he repeated, his voice softer.

"And . . . and ye to me," she sputtered.

"I could hardly tell you I'd come to kill you. It'd ruin the element of surprise."

"Well, I could hardly tell ye I had the king by my side. It would ruin . . . everything."

"Everything?"

"Someone was trying to murder him, so we moved him to Blackburn and gave him servants that did not recognize him. Only Hawk knew him there. So we closeted him away with Kelvin. They learned each other's idiosyncrasies, each other's lives. He was happy in the Highlands, safe—"

"Safe?" He laughed. "With you? You are the most dangerous woman in all of Christendom. In all the world!"

"Then mayhap ye dunna have the balls to marry me!" she yelled.

"Oh, I have the balls," he growled, and leaping from the bed, he snatched her to his naked body. "Do you need more proof?"

She tried to think of a rejoinder, but no words came immediately to mind.

"Marry me, Shona," Dugald whispered, and kissed her lips. "Live with me at Isle Fois. It may never be peaceful again, but I am willing to risk that."

She glanced up at him mischievously. "Are ye certain ye have the—"

"For God's sake, there's a boy in the room!" Kelvin sputtered.

Shona gasped and spun toward the lad, but he was already leaving.

"The king is right," he said, sounding disgruntled. "The two of ye had best wed, and soon."

The portal slammed behind him.

"Marry me," Dugald said again, pulling her gently back into his arms.

"My father may not approve."

"Your father would let you marry the king of the toads if you so desired."

"Well, as ye wish, then, but if I get ye killed, it willna be my fault," she said, and kissed him.

**Lois Greiman's
unforgettable mini-series
HIGHLAND BRIDES
continues in Spring 1999**

Sara and Shona are both married, but their cousin, Rachel, has yet to discover true love. Rachel is beautiful, refined, and is beloved by her family, but her heart was broken years ago by the careless, carefree Liam. Now Liam is back in her life, but will *this* highland lass ever become his highland bride?

Don't miss the next book in the series **Ro mantic Times** *has called "pure magic!"*

Dear Reader,

Next month, there are so many exciting books coming from Avon romance that I wish I had two or three pages to talk about them all! But I only get one page, so I'll get right to it.

October's Avon Romantic Treasure is *A Rake's Vow*, the next in Stephanie Laurens' scintillating series about the wickedly handsome Cynster family. Vane Cynster has vowed to never marry, no matter that his cousin Devil has just tied the knot. But once he meets the very tempting, delectable Patience Debbington he decides that some vows are meant to be broken.

Kathleen Harrington's *Enchanted by You* is for anyone—like me—who loves a sexy Scottish hero! When dashing Lyon MacLyon is saved by Julie Elkheart he can't help but tell her how much he wants her—in Gaelic. But pretty Julie understands every scandalous word of love that this sexy lord says...

What if you could shed your past and take another's identity? In Linda O'Brien's *Promised to a Stranger* Maddie Beecher does just that, and discovers she's "engaged" to a man she's never met. Trouble is, she falls hard...for her "fiancé's" brother—enigmatic Blaine Knight. And when Maddie's past catches up with her, she must decide if she should tell Blaine the whole truth.

And if you're looking for a sexy hero to sweep you off your feet—and fix your life—then don't miss Elizabeth Bevarly's delicious Contemporary romance *My Man Pendleton*. When a madcap heiress runs off to Florida, her rich father sends Pendleton after her...but he never thinks his wayward daughter will fall in love.

Until next month, enjoy!

Lucia Macro

Lucia Macro

Senior Editor

AEL 0998